THE BOOK OF
Doppelgängers

THE BOOK OF
Doppelgängers

edited by
Robert Sterling

*Featuring stories
from famous authors of the weird, including:*

J. Sheridan LeFanu
E.T.A. Hoffmann
Algernon Blackwood
Guy de Maupassant
Honore de Balzac
Hans Christian Andersen
Henry James
Charlotte Perkins Gilman

BETANCOURT
& COMPANY
Doylestown, Pennsylvania

The Book of Doppelgängers
A publication of
Betancourt & Company, Publishers
P.O. Box 301
Holicong, PA 18928-0301
www.wildsidepress.com

Table of Contents

Introduction

THE HIDDEN FACE

"*E*veryone is a moon," Mark Twain wrote in *Pudd'nhead Wilson,* "and has a dark side which he never shows to anybody."

Alter-egos. Doubles. Evil twins. Doppelgängers. Or, "Jekyll and Hyde," the most famous double-personality of all. Stevenson's 1887 masterpiece is the most famous of a long literary line of men, and even a few women, haunted by themselves.

The idea of a dual nature is found in many religions, from Taoism to Zoroastrianism. Perhaps even God and the Devil can be seen as opposite sides of the same nature; Gnosticism and the Kabbaleh espouse such beliefs.

The idea that a man, not God, could contain entirely separate personalities, one good, and one "evil," or at least — one devoted to life, and the other to death — is the source of the literary fascination with the alter-ego. With the advent of the age of science, the idea that man could control, or perhaps even separate himself from his worst nature, gave rise to tales of creeping unease, where the face in the mirror belongs to a hideous, menacing stranger.

Of all of the stories of the weird ever written, those that deal with the double, or dark twin, are perhaps the most disturbing. While "The Strange Case of Dr. Jekyll and Mr. Hyde" is the most famous tale of literary dualism, Edgar Allan Poe's 1839 story "William Wilson" may be the more frightening of the two tales. "William Wilson" influenced Stevenson, and those who read the final scene cannot help but recall another tale of a hidden nature — "The Picture of Dorian Gray."

Published in the same year as "Jekyll and Hyde," Guy de Maupassant's relentless tale of madness, "The Horla," makes its secret double invisible, and all the more terrifying. But even before Poe, unique and timeless German writer E.T.A. Hoffmann wrote "The Sandman," featuring the hideous Dr. Coppelius/Coppola, driving its poor hero from sanity into other-worldly madness.

Hans Christian Andersen wrote the story of "The Shadow," who reverses his position with his master to a shocking end. Brothers may be linked together as doubles, or sons may sin for their father and son at once, as in Balzac's bitter masterpiece, "The Elixir of Life."

Dark twins may be identical in all respects, as William Wilson's was, or they may be beastly creatures such as the one who haunts the Rev. Mr. Jennings in Le Fanu's "Green Tea." Or, they may be physical manifestations of misery rising in fungoid growths between the printed patterns of "The Yellow Wallpaper." Or perhaps, they are men who have lived our lives while we've been away, like the man who lives in Brydon's boyhood home in Henry James' "The Jolly Corner."

Much has been written about the source of this obsession with dual nature. Critics have cited industrialization, the rise of science and the death of God, and the increasing complexity of urban life.

But the real source lies in the reflection in our own mirrors. As Mark Twain said, each of us is a moon. Each of us has a dark side. It is part of who we are; it is what we fear will destroy us. It is ourselves.

Robert Sterling
July, 2002
Southern California

The Horla
Guy de Maupassant

The narrator of de Maupassant's classic "The Horla" cannot see his tormentor, but the Horla is in all other ways real. He sees "the stalk of one of the roses bend close to me, as if an invisible hand had bent it, and then break, as if that hand had picked it!" Often cited as a story of madness, the terror of the Horla seems all too real . . .

MAY 8. What a lovely day! I have spent all the morning lying on the grass in front of my house, under the enormous plantain tree which covers and shades and shelters the whole of it. I like this part of the country; I am fond of living here because I am attached to it by deep roots, the profound and delicate roots which attach a man to the soil on which his ancestors were born and died, to their traditions, their usages, their food, the local expressions, the peculiar language of the peasants, the smell of the soil, the hamlets, and to the atmosphere itself.

I love the house in which I grew up. From my windows I can see the Seine, which flows by the side of my garden, on the other side of the road, almost through my grounds, the great and wide Seine, which goes to Rouen and Havre, and which is covered with boats passing to and fro.

On the left, down yonder, lies Rouen, populous Rouen with its blue roofs massing under pointed, Gothic towers. Innumerable are they, delicate or broad, dominated by the spire of the cathedral, full of bells which sound through the blue air on fine mornings, sending their sweet and distant iron clang to me, their metallic sounds, now stronger and now weaker, according as the wind is strong or light.

What a delicious morning it was! About eleven o'clock, a long line of boats drawn by a steam-tug, as big a fly, and which scarcely puffed while emitting its thick smoke, passed my gate.

After two English schooners, whose red flags fluttered toward the sky, there came a magnificent Brazilian three-master; it was perfectly white and wonderfully clean and shining. I saluted it, I hardly know why, except that the sight of the vessel gave me great pleasure.

May 12. I have had a slight feverish attack for the last few days, and I feel ill, or rather I feel low-spirited.

Whence come those mysterious influences which change our happiness into discouragement, and our self-confidence into diffidence? One might almost say that the air, the invisible air, is full of unknowable Forces, whose mysterious presence we have to endure. I wake up in the best of spirits, with an inclination to sing in my heart. Why? I go down by the side of the water, and suddenly, after walking a short distance, I return home wretched, as if some misfortune were awaiting me there. Why? Is it a cold shiver which, passing over my skin, has upset my nerves and given me a fit of low spirits? Is it the form of the clouds, or the tints of the sky, or the colors of the surrounding objects which are so changeable, which have troubled my thoughts as they passed before my eyes? Who can tell? Everything that surrounds us, everything that we see without looking at it, everything that we touch without knowing it, everything that we handle without feeling it, everything that we meet without clearly distinguishing it, has a rapid, surprising, and inexplicable effect upon us and upon our organs, and through them on our ideas and on our being itself.

How profound that mystery of the Invisible is! We cannot fathom it with our miserable senses: our eyes are unable to perceive what is either too small or too great, too near to or too far from us; we can see neither the inhabitants of a star nor of a drop of water; our ears deceive us, for they transmit to us the vibrations of the air in sonorous notes. Our senses are fairies who work the miracle of changing that movement into noise, and by that metamorphosis give birth to music, which makes the mute agitation of nature a harmony. So with our sense of smell, which is weaker than that of a dog, and so with our sense of taste, which can scarcely distinguish the age of a wine!

Oh! If we only had other organs which could work other miracles in our favor, what a number of fresh things we might discover around us!

May 16. I am ill, decidedly! I was so well last month! I am feverish, horribly feverish, or rather I am in a state of feverish enervation, which makes my mind suffer as much as my body. I have without ceasing the horrible sensation of some danger threatening me, the apprehension of some coming misfortune or of approaching death, a presentiment which is no doubt, an attack of some illness still unnamed, which germinates in the flesh and in the blood.

May 18. I have just come from consulting my medical man, for I can no longer get any sleep. He found that my pulse was high, my eyes dilated, my nerves highly strung, but no alarming symptoms. I must have a course of shower baths and of bromide of potassium.

May 25. No change! My state is really very peculiar. As the evening comes on, an incomprehensible feeling of disquietude seizes me, just as if night concealed some terrible menace toward me. I dine quickly, and then try to read, but I do not understand the words, and can scarcely distinguish the letters. Then I walk up and down my drawing room, oppressed by a feeling of confused and irresistible fear, a fear of sleep and a fear of my bed.

About ten o'clock I go up to my room. As soon as I have entered I lock and bolt the door. I am frightened — of what? Up till the present time I have been frightened of nothing. I open my cupboards, and look under my bed; I listen — I listen — to what? How strange it is that a simple feeling of discomfort, of impeded or heightened circulation, perhaps the irritation of a nervous center, a slight congestion, a small disturbance in the imperfect and delicate functions of our living machinery, can turn the most light-hearted of men into a melancholy one, and make a coward of the bravest? Then, I go to bed, and I wait for sleep as a man might wait for the executioner. I wait for its coming with dread, and my heart beats and my legs tremble, while my whole body shivers beneath the warmth of the bedclothes, until the moment when I suddenly fall asleep, as a man throws himself into a pool of stagnant water in order to drown. I do not feel this perfidious sleep coming over me as I used to, but a sleep which is close to me and watching me, which is going to seize me by the head, to close my eyes and annihilate me.

I sleep — a long time — two or three hours perhaps — then a dream — no — a nightmare lays hold on me. I feel that I am in bed and asleep — I feel it and I know it — and I feel also that somebody is coming close to me, is looking at me, touching me, is getting on to my bed, is kneeling on my chest, is taking my neck between his hands and squeezing it — squeezing it with all his might in order to strangle me.

I struggle, bound by that terrible powerlessness which paralyzes us in our dreams; I try to cry out — but I cannot; I want to move — I cannot; I try, with the most violent efforts and out of breath, to turn over and throw off this being which is crushing and suffocating me — I cannot!

And then suddenly I wake up, shaken and bathed in perspiration; I light a candle and find that I am alone, and after that crisis, which occurs every night, I at length fall asleep and slumber tranquilly till morning.

June 2. My state has grown worse. What is the matter with me? The bromide does me no good, and the shower baths have no effect whatever. Sometimes, in order to tire myself out, though I am fatigued enough already, I go for a walk in the forest of Roumare. I used to think at first that the fresh light and soft air, impregnated with the odor of herbs and leaves, would instill new life into my veins and impart fresh energy to my heart. One day I turned into a broad ride in the wood, and then I diverged toward La Bouille, through a narrow path, between two rows of exceedingly tall trees, which placed a thick, green, almost black roof between the sky and me.

A sudden shiver ran through me, not a cold shiver, but a shiver of agony, and so I hastened my steps, uneasy at being alone in the wood, frightened stupidly and without reason, at the profound solitude. Suddenly it seemed as if I were being followed, that somebody was walking at my heels, close, quite close to me, near enough to touch me.

I turned round suddenly, but I was alone. I saw nothing behind me except the straight, broad ride, empty and bordered by high trees, horribly empty; on the other side also it extended until it was lost in the distance, and looked just the same — terrible.

I closed my eyes. Why? And then I began to turn round on one heel very quickly, just like a top. I nearly fell down, and opened my eyes; the trees were dancing round me and the earth heaved; I was obliged to sit down. Then, ah! I no longer remembered how I had come! What a strange idea! What a strange, strange idea! I did not the least know. I started off to the right, and got back into the avenue which had led me into the middle of the forest.

June 3. I have had a terrible night. I shall go away for a few weeks, for no doubt a journey will set me up again.

July 2. I have come back, quite cured, and have had a most delightful trip into the bargain. I have been to Mont Saint-Michel, which I had not seen before.

What a sight, when one arrives as I did, at Avranches toward the end of the day! The town stands on a hill, and I was taken into the public garden at the extremity of the town. I uttered a cry of astonishment. An extraordinarily large bay lay extended before me, as far as my eyes could reach, between two hills which were lost to sight in the mist; and in the middle of this immense yellow bay, under a clear, golden sky, a peculiar hill rose up, somber and pointed in the midst of the sand. The sun had just disappeared, and under the still flaming sky stood out the outline of that fantastic rock which bears on its summit a picturesque monument.

At daybreak I went to it. The tide was low, as it had been the night before, and I saw that wonderful abbey rise up before me as I approached it. After several hours' walking, I reached the enormous mass of rock which supports the little town, dominated by the great church. Having climbed the steep and narrow street, I entered the most wonderful Gothic building that has ever been erected to God on earth, large as a town, and full of low rooms which seem buried beneath vaulted roofs, and of lofty galleries supported by delicate columns.

I entered this gigantic granite jewel, which is as light in its effect as a bit of lace and is covered with towers, with slender belfries to which spiral staircases ascend. The flying buttresses raise strange heads that bristle with chimeras, with devils, with fantastic animals, with monstrous flowers, are joined together by finely carved arches, to the blue sky by day, and to the black sky by night.

When I had reached the summit. I said to the monk who accompanied me: "Father, how happy you must be here!" And he replied: "It is very windy, Monsieur"; and so we began to talk while watching the rising tide, which ran over the sand and covered it with a steel cuirass.

And then the monk told me stories, all the old stories belonging to the place — legends, nothing but legends.

One of them struck me forcibly. The country people, those belonging to the Mornet, declare that at night one can hear talking going on in the sand, and also that two goats bleat, one with a strong, the other with a weak voice. Incredulous people declare that it is nothing but the screaming of the sea birds, which occasionally resembles bleatings, and occasionally human lamentations; but belated fishermen swear that they have met an old shepherd, whose cloak covered head they can never see, wandering on the sand, between two tides, round the little town placed so far out of the world. They declare he is guiding and walking before a he-goat with a man's face and a she-goat with a woman's face, both with white hair, who talk incessantly, quarreling in a strange language, and then suddenly cease talking in order to bleat with all their might.

"Do you believe it?" I asked the monk. "I scarcely know," he replied; and I continued: "If there are other beings besides ourselves on this earth, how comes it that we have not known it for so long a time, or why have you not seen them? How is it that I have not seen them?"

He replied: "Do we see the hundred-thousandth part of what exists? Look here; there is the wind, which is the strongest force in nature. It knocks down men, and blows down buildings, uproots trees, raises the sea into mountains of water, destroys cliffs and casts great ships on to the breakers; it kills, it whistles, it sighs, it roars. But have you ever seen it, and can you see it? Yet it exists for all that."

I was silent before this simple reasoning. That man was a philosopher, or perhaps a fool; I could not say which exactly, so I held my tongue. What he had said had often been in my own thoughts.

July 3. I have slept badly; certainly there is some feverish influence here, for my coachman is suffering in the same way as I am. When I went back home yesterday, I noticed his singular paleness, and I asked him: "What is the matter with you, Jean?"

"The matter is that I never get any rest, and my nights devour my days. Since your departure, Monsieur, there has been a spell over me."

However, the other servants are all well, but I am very frightened of having another attack, myself.

July 4. I am decidedly taken again; for my old nightmares have returned. Last night I felt somebody leaning on me who was sucking my life from between my lips with his mouth. Yes, he was sucking it out of my neck like a leech would have done. Then he got up, satiated, and I woke up, so beaten, crushed, and annihilated that I could not move. If this continues for a few days, I shall certainly go away again.

July 5. Have I lost my reason? What has happened? What I saw last night is so strange that my head wanders when I think of it!

As I do now every evening, I had locked my door; then, being thirsty, I drank half a glass of water, and I accidentally noticed that the water bottle was full up to the cut-glass stopper.

Then I went to bed and fell into one of my terrible sleeps, from which I was aroused in about two hours by a still more terrible shock.

Picture to yourself a sleeping man who is being murdered, who wakes up with a knife in his chest, a gurgling in his throat, is covered with blood, can no longer breathe, is going to die and does not understand anything at all about it — there you have it.

Having recovered my senses, I was thirsty again, so I lighted a candle and went to the table on which my water bottle was. I lifted it up and tilted it over my glass, but nothing came out. It was empty!

It was completely empty! At first I could not understand it at all; then suddenly I was seized by such a terrible feeling that I had to sit down, or rather fall into a chair! Then I sprang up with a bound to look about me; then I sat down again, overcome by astonishment and fear, in front of the transparent crystal bottle! I looked at it with fixed eyes, trying to solve the puzzle, and my hands trembled! Some body had drunk the water, but who? I? I without any doubt. It could surely only be I? In that case I was a somnambulist — was living, without knowing it, that double, mysterious life which makes us doubt whether there are not two beings in us — whether a strange, unknowable, and invisible being does not, during our moments of mental and physical torpor, animate the inert body, forcing it to a more willing obedience than it yields to ourselves.

Oh! Who will understand my horrible agony? Who will understand the emotion of a man sound in mind, wide-awake, full of sense, who looks in horror at the disappearance of a little water while he was asleep, through the glass of a water bottle! And I remained sitting until it was daylight, without venturing to go to bed again.

July 6. I am going mad. Again all the contents of my water bottle have been drunk during the night; or rather I have drunk it!

But is it I? Is it I? Who could it be? Who? Oh! God! Am I going mad? Who will save me?

July 10. I have just been through some surprising ordeals. Undoubtedly I must be mad! And yet!

On July 6, before going to bed, I put some wine, milk, water, bread, and strawberries on my table. Somebody drank — I drank — all the water and a little of the milk, but neither the wine, nor the bread, nor the strawberries were touched.

On the seventh of July I renewed the same experiment, with the same results, and on July 8 I left out the water and the milk and nothing was touched.

Lastly, on July 9 I put only water and milk on my table, taking care to wrap up the bottles in white muslin and to tie down the stoppers. Then I rubbed my lips, my beard, and my hands with pencil lead, and went to bed.

Deep slumber seized me, soon followed by a terrible awakening. I had not moved, and my sheets were not marked. I rushed to the table. The muslin round the bottles remained intact; I undid the string, trembling with fear. All the water had been drunk, and so had the milk! Ah! Great God! I must start for Paris immediately.

July 12. Paris. I must have lost my head during the last few days! I must be the plaything of my enervated imagination, unless I am really a somnambulist, or I have been brought under the power of one of those influences — hypnotic suggestion, for example — which are known to exist, but have hitherto been inexplicable. In any case, my mental state bordered on madness, and twenty-four hours of Paris sufficed to restore me to my equilibrium.

Yesterday after doing some business and paying some visits, which instilled fresh and invigorating mental air into me, I wound up my evening at the Theater Francais. A drama by Alexander Dumas the Younger was being acted, and his brilliant and powerful play completed my cure. Certainly solitude is dangerous for active minds. We need men who can think and can talk, around us. When we are alone for a long time, we people space with phantoms.

I returned along the boulevards to my hotel in excellent spirits. Amid the jostling of the crowd I thought, not without irony, of my terrors and surmises of the previous week, because I believed, yes, I believed, that an invisible being lived beneath my roof. How weak our mind is; how quickly it is terrified and unbalanced as soon as we are confronted with a small, incomprehensible fact. Instead of dismissing the problem with: "We do not understand because we cannot find the cause," we immediately imagine terrible mysteries and supernatural powers.

July 14. Fete of the Republic. I walked through the streets, and the crackers and flags amused me like a child. Still, it is very foolish to make merry on a set date, by Government decree. People are like a flock of sheep, now steadily patient, now in ferocious revolt. Say to it: "Amuse yourself," and it amuses itself. Say to it: "Go and fight with your neighbor," and it goes and fights. Say to it: "Vote for the Emperor," and it votes for the Emperor; then say to it: "Vote for the Republic," and it votes for the Republic.

Those who direct it are stupid, too; but instead of obeying men they obey principles, a course which can only be foolish, ineffective, and false, for the very reason that principles are ideas which are considered as certain and unchangeable, whereas in this world one is certain of nothing, since light is an illusion and noise is deception.

July 16. I saw some things yesterday that troubled me very much. I was dining at my cousin's, Madame Sable, whose husband is colonel of the Seventy-sixth Chasseurs at Limoges. There were two young women there, one of whom had married a medical man, Dr. Parent, who devotes himself a great deal to nervous diseases and to the extraordinary manifestations which just now experiments in hypnotism and suggestion are producing.

He related to us at some length the enormous results obtained by English scientists and the doctors of the medical school at Nancy, and the facts which he adduced appeared to me so strange, that I

The Book of Doppelgängers   17

declared that I was altogether incredulous.

"We are," he declared, "on the point of discovering one of the most important secrets of nature, I mean to say, one of its most important secrets on this earth, for assuredly there are some up in the stars, yonder, of a different kind of importance. Ever since man has thought, since he has been able to express and write down his thoughts, he has felt himself close to a mystery which is impenetrable to his coarse and imperfect senses, and he endeavors to supplement the feeble penetration of his organs by the efforts of his intellect. As long as that intellect remained in its elementary stage, this inter-course with invisible spirits assumed forms which were common-place though terrifying. Thence sprang the popular belief in the supernatural, the legends of wandering spirits, of fairies, of gnomes, of ghosts, I might even say the conception of God, for our ideas of the Workman-Creator, from whatever religion they may have come down to us, are certainly the most mediocre, the stupidest, and the most unacceptable inventions that ever sprang from the frightened brain of any human creature. Nothing is truer than what Voltaire says: 'If God made man in His own image, man has certainly paid Him back again.'

"But for rather more than a century, men seem to have had a presentiment of something new. Mesmer and some others have put us on an unexpected track, and within the last two or three years especially, we have arrived at results really surprising."

My cousin, who is also very incredulous, smiled, and Dr. Parent said to her: "Would you like me to try and send you to sleep, Madame?"

"Yes, certainly."

She sat down in an easy chair, and he began to look at her fixedly, as if to fascinate her. I suddenly felt myself somewhat discomposed; my heart beat rapidly and I had a choking feeling in my throat. I saw that Madame Sable's eyes were growing heavy, her mouth twitched, and her bosom heaved, and at the end of ten minutes she was asleep.

"Go behind her," the doctor said to me; so I took a seat behind her. He put a visiting card into her hands, and said to her: "This is a looking-glass; what do you see in it?"

She replied: "I see my cousin."

"What is he doing?"

"He is twisting his mustache."

"And now?"

"He is taking a photograph out of his pocket."

"Whose photograph is it?"

"His own."

That was true, for the photograph had been given me that same evening at the hotel.

"What is his attitude in this portrait?"

"He is standing up with his hat in his hand."

She saw these things in that card, in that piece of white pasteboard, as if she had seen them in a looking glass.

The young women were frightened, and exclaimed: "That is quite enough! Quite, quite enough!"

But the doctor said to her authoritatively: "You will get up at eight o'clock tomorrow morning; then you will go and call on your cousin at his hotel and ask him to lend you the five thousand francs which your husband asks of you, and which he will ask for when he sets out on his coming journey."

Then he woke her up.

On returning to my hotel, I thought over this curious seance and I was assailed by doubts, not as to my cousin's absolute and un-doubted good faith, for I had known her as well as if she had been my own sister ever since she was a child, but as to a possible trick on the doctor's part. Had not he, perhaps, kept a glass hidden in his hand, which he showed to the young woman in her sleep at the same time as he did the card? Professional conjurers do things which are just as singular.

However, I went to bed, and this morning, at about half past eight, I was awakened by my footman, who said to me: "Madame Sable has asked to see you immediately, Monsieur." I dressed hastily and went to her.

She sat down in some agitation, with her eyes on the floor, and without raising her veil said to me: "My dear cousin, I am going to ask a great favor of you."

"What is it, cousin?"

"I do not like to tell you, and yet I must. I am in absolute want of five thousand francs."

"What, you?"

"Yes, I, or rather my husband, who has asked me to procure them for him."

I was so stupefied that I hesitated to answer. I asked myself whether she had not really been making fun of me with Dr. Parent, if it were not merely a very well-acted farce which had been got up beforehand. On looking at her attentively, however, my doubts disappeared. She was trembling with grief, so painful was this step to her, and I was sure that her throat was full of sobs.

I knew that she was very rich and so I continued: "What! Has not your husband five thousand francs at his disposal? Come, think. Are you sure that he commissioned you to ask me for them?"

She hesitated for a few seconds, as if she were making a great effort to search her memory, and then she replied: "Yes — yes, I am quite sure of it."

"He has written to you?"

She hesitated again and reflected, and I guessed the torture of her thoughts. She did not know. She only knew that she was to borrow five thousand francs of me for her husband. So she told a lie.

"Yes, he has written to me."

"When, pray? You did not mention it to me yesterday."

"I received his letter this morning."

"Can you show it to me?"

"No; no — no — it contained private matters, things too personal to ourselves. I burned it."

"So your husband runs into debt?"

She hesitated again, and then murmured: "I do not know."

Thereupon I said bluntly: "I have not five thousand francs at my disposal at this moment, my dear cousin."

She uttered a cry, as if she were in pair; and said: "Oh! oh! I beseech you, I beseech you to get them for me."

She got excited and clasped her hands as if she were praying to me! I heard her voice change its tone; she wept and sobbed, harassed and dominated by the irresistible order that she had received.

"Oh! oh! I beg you to — if you knew what I am suffering — I want them today."

I had pity on her: "You shall have them by and by, I swear to you."

"Oh! thank you! thank you! How kind you are."

I continued: "Do you remember what took place at your house last night?"

"Yes."

"Do you remember that Dr. Parent sent you to sleep?"

"Yes."

"Oh! Very well then; he ordered you to come to me this morning to borrow five thousand francs, and at this moment you are obeying that suggestion."

She considered for a few moments, and then replied: "But as it is my husband who wants them —"

For a whole hour I tried to convince her, but could not succeed, and when she had gone I went to the doctor. He was just going out, and he listened to me with a smile, and said: "Do you believe now?"

"Yes, I cannot help it."

"Let us go to your cousin's."

She was already resting on a couch, overcome with fatigue. The doctor felt her pulse, looked at her for some time with one hand raised toward her eyes, which she closed by degrees under the irresistible power of this magnetic influence. When she was asleep, he said:

"Your husband does not require the five thousand francs any longer! You must, therefore, forget that you asked your cousin to lend them to you, and, if he speaks to you about it, you will not understand him."

Then he woke her up, and I took out a pocketbook and said: "Here is what you asked me for this morning, my dear cousin." But she was so surprised, that I did not venture to persist; nevertheless, I tried to recall the circumstance to her, but she denied it vigorously, thought that I was making fun of her, and in the end, very nearly lost her temper.

There! I have just come back, and I have not been able to eat any lunch, for this experiment has altogether upset me.

July 19. Many people to whom I have told the adventure have laughed at me. I no longer know what to think. The wise man says: Perhaps?

July 21. I dined at Bougival, and then I spent the evening at a boatmen's ball. Decidedly everything depends on place and surroundings. It would be the height of folly to believe in the supernatural on the Ile de la Grenouilliere.* But on the top of Mont Saint-Michel or in India, we are terribly under the influence of our surroundings. I shall return home next week.

July 30. I came back to my own house yesterday. Everything is going on well.

August 2. Nothing fresh; it is splendid weather, and I spend my days in watching the Seine flow past.

August 4. Quarrels among my servants. They declare that the glasses are broken in the cupboards at night. The footman accuses the cook, she accuses the needlewoman, and the latter accuses the other two. Who is the culprit? It would take a clever person to tell.

August 6. This time, I am not mad. I have seen — I have seen — I have seen! — I can doubt no longer — I have seen it!

I was walking at two o'clock among my rose trees, in the full sunlight — in the walk bordered by autumn roses which are beginning to fall. As I stopped to look at a Geant de Bataille, which had three splendid blooms, I distinctly saw the stalk of one of the roses bend close to me, as if an invisible hand had bent it, and then break,

* Frog-island.

as if that hand had picked it! Then the flower raised itself, following the curve which a hand would have described in carrying it toward a mouth, and remained suspended in the transparent air, alone and motionless, a terrible red spot, three yards from my eyes. In desperation I rushed at it to take it! I found nothing; it had disappeared. Then I was seized with furious rage against myself, for it is not wholesome for a reasonable and serious man to have such hallucinations.

But was it a hallucination? I turned to look for the stalk, and I found it immediately under the bush, freshly broken, between the two other roses which remained on the branch. I returned home, then, with a much disturbed mind; for I am certain now, certain as I am of the alternation of day and night, that there exists close to me an invisible being who lives on milk and on water, who can touch objects, take them and change their places; who is, consequently, endowed with a material nature, although imperceptible to sense, and who lives as I do, under my roof —

August 7. I slept tranquilly. He drank the water out of my decanter, but did not disturb my sleep.

I ask myself whether I am mad. As I was walking just now in the sun by the riverside, doubts as to my own sanity arose in me; not vague doubts such as I have had hitherto, but precise and absolute doubts. I have seen mad people, and I have known some who were quite intelligent, lucid, even clear-sighted in every concern of life, except on one point. They could speak clearly, readily, profoundly on everything; till their thoughts were caught in the breakers of their delusions and went to pieces there, were dispersed and swamped in that furious and terrible sea of fogs and squalls which is called *madness*.

I certainly should think that I was mad, absolutely mad, if I were not conscious that I knew my state, if I could not fathom it and analyze it with the most complete lucidity. I should, in fact, be a reasonable man laboring under a hallucination. Some unknown disturbance must have been excited in my brain, one of those disturbances which physiologists of the present day try to note and to fix precisely, and that disturbance must have caused a profound gulf in my mind and in the order and logic of my ideas. Similar phenomena occur in dreams, and lead us through the most unlikely phantasmagoria, without causing us any surprise, because our verifying apparatus and our sense of control have gone to sleep, while our imaginative faculty wakes and works. Was it not possible that one of the imperceptible keys of the cerebral fingerboard had been paralyzed in me? Some men lose the recollection of proper names, or of verbs, or of numbers, or merely of dates, in consequence of an accident. The localization of all the avenues of thought has been accomplished nowadays; what, then, would there be surprising in the fact that my faculty of controlling the unreality of certain hallucinations should be destroyed for the time being?

I thought of all this as I walked by the side of the water. The sun was shining brightly on the river and made earth delightful, while it filled me with love for life, for the swallows, whose swift agility is always delightful in my eyes, for the plants by the riverside, whose rustling is a pleasure to my ears.

By degrees, however, an inexplicable feeling of discomfort seized me. It seemed to me as if some unknown force were numbing and stopping me, were preventing me from going further and were calling me back. I felt that painful wish to return which comes on you when you have left a beloved invalid at home, and are seized by a presentiment that he is worse.

I, therefore, returned despite of myself, feeling certain that I should find some bad news awaiting me, a letter or a telegram. There was nothing, however, and I was surprised and uneasy, more so than if I had had another fantastic vision.

August 8. I spent a terrible evening, yesterday. He does not show himself anymore, but I feel that He is near me, watching me, looking at me, penetrating me, dominating me, and more terrible to me when He hides himself thus than if He were to manifest his constant and invisible presence by supernatural phenomena. However, I slept.

August 9. Nothing, but I am afraid.

August 10. Nothing; but what will happen tomorrow?

August 11. Still nothing. I cannot stop at home with this fear hanging over me and these thoughts in my mind; I shall go away.

August 12. Ten o'clock at night. All day long I have been trying to get away, and have not been able. I contemplated a simple and easy act of liberty, a carriage ride to Rouen — and I have not been able to do it. What is the reason?

August 13. When one is attacked by certain maladies, the springs of our physical being seem broken, our energies destroyed, our muscles relaxed, our bones to be as soft as our flesh, and our blood as liquid as water. I am experiencing the same in my moral being, in a strange and distressing manner. I have no longer any strength, any courage, any self-control, nor even any power to set my own will in motion. I have no power left to *will* anything, but some one does it for me and I obey.

August 14. I am lost! Somebody possesses my soul and governs it! Somebody orders all my acts, all my movements, all my thoughts.

I am no longer master of myself, nothing except an enslaved and terrified spectator of the things which I do. I wish to go out; I cannot. *He* does not wish to; and so I remain, trembling and distracted in the armchair in which he keeps me sitting. I merely wish to get up and to rouse myself, so as to think that I am still master of myself: I cannot! I am riveted to my chair, and my chair adheres to the floor in such a manner that no force of mine can move us.

Then suddenly, I must, I *must* go to the foot of my garden to pick some strawberries and eat them — and I go there. I pick the strawberries and I eat them! Oh! my God! my God! Is there a God? If there be one, deliver me! save me! succor me! Pardon! Pity! Mercy! Save me! Oh! what sufferings! what torture! what horror!

August 15. Certainly this is the way in which my poor cousin was possessed and swayed, when she came to borrow five thousand francs of me. She was under the power of a strange will which had entered into her, like another soul, a parasitic and ruling soul. Is the world coming to an end?

But who is he, this invisible being that rules me, this unknowable being, this rover of a supernatural race?

Invisible beings exist, then! how is it, then, that since the beginning of the world they have never manifested themselves in such a manner as they do to me? I have never read anything that resembles what goes on in my house. Oh! If I could only leave it, if I could only go away and flee, and never return, I should be saved; but I cannot.

August 16. I managed to escape today for two hours, like a prisoner who finds the door of his dungeon accidentally open. I suddenly felt that I was free and that He was far away, and so I gave orders to put the horses in as quickly as possible, and I drove to Rouen. Oh! how delightful to be able to say to my coachman: "Go to Rouen!"

I made him pull up before the library, and I begged them to lend me Dr. Herrmann Herestauss's treatise on the unknown inhabitants of the ancient and modern world.

Then, as I was getting into my carriage, I intended to say: "To the railway station!" but instead of this I shouted — I did not speak; but I shouted — in such a loud voice that all the passers-by turned round: "Home!" and I fell back on to the cushion of my carriage, overcome by mental agony. He had found me out and regained possession of me.

August 17. Oh! What a night! what a night! And yet it seems to me that I ought to rejoice. I read until one o'clock in the morning! Herestauss, Doctor of Philosophy and Theogony, wrote the history and the manifestation of all those invisible beings which hover around man, or of whom he dreams. He describes their origin, their domains, their power; but none of them resembles the one which haunts me. One might say that man, ever since he has thought, has had a foreboding and a fear of a new being, stronger than himself, his successor in this world, and that, feeling him near, and not being able to foretell the nature of the unseen one, he has, in his terror, created the whole race of hidden beings, vague phantoms born of fear.

Having, therefore, read until one o'clock in the morning, I went and sat down at the open window, in order to cool my forehead and my thoughts in the calm night air. It was very pleasant and warm! How I should have enjoyed such a night formerly!

There was no moon, but the stars darted out their rays in the dark heavens. Who inhabits those worlds? What forms, what living beings, what animals are there yonder? Do those who are thinkers in those distant worlds know more than we do? What can they do more than we? What do they see which we do not? Will not one of them, some day or other, traversing space, appear on our earth to conquer it, just as formerly the Norsemen crossed the sea in order to subjugate nations feebler than themselves?

We are so weak, so powerless, so ignorant, so small — we who live on this particle of mud which revolves in liquid air.

I fell asleep, dreaming thus in the cool night air, and then, having slept for about three quarters of an hour, I opened my eyes without moving, awakened by an indescribably confused and strange sensation. At first I saw nothing, and then suddenly it appeared to me as if a page of the book, which had remained open on my table, turned over of its own accord. Not a breath of air had come in at my window, and I was surprised and waited. In about four minutes, I saw, I saw — yes I saw with my own eyes — another page lift itself up and fall down on the others, as if a finger had turned it over. My armchair was empty, appeared empty, but I knew that He was there, He, and sitting in my place, and that He was reading. With a furious bound, the bound of an enraged wild beast that wishes to disembowel its tamer, I crossed my room to seize him, to strangle him, to kill him! But before I could reach it, my chair fell over as if somebody had run away from me. My table rocked, my lamp fell and went out, and my window closed as if some thief had been surprised and had fled out into the night, shutting it behind him.

So He had run away; He had been afraid; He, afraid of me!

So tomorrow, or later — some day or other, I should be able to hold him in my clutches and crush him against the ground! Do not dogs occasionally bite and strangle their masters?

August 18. I have been thinking the whole day long. Oh! yes, I will obey Him, follow His impulses, fulfill all His wishes, show myself humble, submissive, a coward. He is the stronger; but an hour will come.

August 19. I know, I know, I know all! I have just read the following in the "Revue du Monde Scientifique": "A curious piece of news comes to us from Rio de Janeiro. Madness, an epidemic of madness, which may be compared to that contagious madness which attacked the people of Europe in the Middle Ages, is at this moment raging in the Province of San-Paulo. The frightened inhabitants are leaving their houses, deserting their villages, abandoning their land, saying that they are pursued, possessed, governed like human cattle by invisible, though tangible beings, by a species of vampire, which feeds on their life while they are asleep, and which, besides, drinks water and milk without appearing to touch any other nourishment.

"Professor Don Pedro Henriques, accompanied by several medical savants, has gone to the Province of San-Paulo, in order to study the origin and the manifestations of this surprising madness on the spot, and to propose such measures to the Emperor as may appear to him to be most fitted to restore the mad population to reason."

Ah! Ah! I remember now that fine Brazilian three-master which passed in front of my windows as it was going up the Seine, on the eighth of last May! I thought it looked so pretty, so white and bright! That Being was on board of her, coming from there, where its race sprang from. And it saw me! It saw my house, which was also white, and He sprang from the ship on to the land. Oh! Good heavens!

Now I know, I can divine. The reign of man is over, and he has come. He whom disquieted priests exorcised, whom sorcerers evoked on dark nights, without seeing him appear, He to whom the imaginations of the transient masters of the world lent all the monstrous or graceful forms of gnomes, spirits, genii, fairies, and familiar spirits. After the coarse conceptions of primitive fear, men more enlightened gave him a truer form. Mesmer divined him, and ten years ago physicians accurately discovered the nature of his power, even before He exercised it himself. They played with that weapon of their new Lord, the sway of a mysterious will over the human soul, which had become enslaved. They called it mesmerism, hypnotism, suggestion, I know not what? I have seen them diverting themselves like rash children with this horrible power! Woe to us! Woe to man! He has come, the — the — what does He call himself — the — I fancy that he is shouting out his name to me and I do not hear him — the — yes — He is shouting it out — I am listening — I

cannot — repeat — it — Horla — I have heard — the Horla — it is He
— the Horla — He has come! —

Ah! the vulture has eaten the pigeon, the wolf has eaten the lamb;
the lion has devoured the sharp-horned buffalo; man has killed the
lion with an arrow, with a spear, with gunpowder; but the Horla will
make of man what man has made of the horse and of the ox: his
chattel, his slave, and his food, by the mere power of his will. Woe
to us!

But, nevertheless, sometimes the animal rebels and kills the man
who has subjugated it. I should also like — I shall be able to — but
I must know Him, touch Him, see Him! Learned men say that eyes
of animals, as they differ from ours, do not distinguish as ours do.
And my eye cannot distinguish this newcomer who is oppressing
me.

Why? Oh! Now I remember the words of the monk at Mont
Saint-Michel: "Can we see the hundred-thousandth part of what
exists? Listen; there is the wind which is the strongest force in nature;
it knocks men down, blows down buildings, uproots trees, raises the
sea into mountains of water, destroys cliffs, and casts great ships on
to the breakers; it kills, it whistles, it sighs, it roars, — have you ever
seen it, and can you see it? It exists for all that, however!"

And I went on thinking: my eyes are so weak, so imperfect, that
they do not even distinguish hard bodies, if they are as transparent
as glass! If a glass without quicksilver behind it were to bar my way,
I should run into it, just like a bird which has flown into a room
breaks its head against the windowpanes. A thousand things, moreover, deceive a man and lead him astray. How then is it surprising
that he cannot perceive a new body which is penetrated and pervaded
by the light?

A new being! Why not? It was assuredly bound to come! Why
should we be the last? We do not distinguish it, like all the others
created before us? The reason is, that its nature is more delicate, its
body finer and more finished than ours. Our makeup is so weak, so
awkwardly conceived; our body is encumbered with organs that are
always tired, always being strained like locks that are too compli-
cated; it lives like a plant and like an animal nourishing itself with
difficulty on air, herbs, and flesh; it is a brute machine which is a
prey to maladies, to malformations, to decay; it is broken-winded,
badly regulated, simple and eccentric, ingeniously yet badly made,
a coarse and yet a delicate mechanism, in brief, the outline of a being
which might become intelligent and great.

There are only a few — so few — stages of development in this
world, from the oyster up to man. Why should there not be one

more, when once that period is accomplished which separates the successive products one from the other?

Why not one more? Why not, also, other trees with immense, splendid flowers, perfuming whole regions? Why not other elements beside fire, air, earth, and water? There are four, only four, nursing fathers of various beings! What a pity! Why should not there be forty, four hundred, four thousand! How poor everything is, how mean and wretched — grudgingly given, poorly invented, clumsily made! Ah! the elephant and the hippopotamus, what power! And the camel, what suppleness!

But the butterfly, you will say, a flying flower! I dream of one that should be as large as a hundred worlds, with wings whose shape, beauty, colors, and motion I cannot even express. But I see it — it flutters from star to star, refreshing them and perfuming them with the light and harmonious breath of its flight! And the people up there gaze at it as it passes in an ecstasy of delight!

What is the matter with me? It is He, the Horla who haunts me, and who makes me think of these foolish things! He is within me, He is becoming my soul; I shall kill him!

August 20. I shall kill Him. I have seen Him! Yesterday I sat down at my table and pretended to write very assiduously. I knew quite well that He would come prowling round me, quite close to me, so close that I might perhaps be able to touch him, to seize him. And then — then I should have the strength of desperation; I should have my hands, my knees, my chest, my forehead, my teeth to strangle him, to crush him, to bite him, to tear him to pieces. And I watched for him with all my overexcited nerves.

I had lighted my two lamps and the eight wax candles on my mantelpiece, as if, by this light I should discover Him.

My bed, my old oak bed with its columns, was opposite to me; on my right was the fireplace; on my left the door, which was carefully closed, after I had left it open for some time, in order to attract Him; behind me was a very high wardrobe with a looking-glass in it, which served me to dress by every day, and in which I was in the habit of inspecting myself from head to foot every time I passed it.

So I pretended to be writing in order to deceive Him, for He also was watching me, and suddenly I felt, I was certain, that He was reading over my shoulder, that He was there, almost touching my ear.

I got up so quickly, with my hands extended, that I almost fell. Horror! It was as bright as at midday, but I did not see myself in the glass! It was empty, clear, profound, full of light! But my figure was not reflected in it — and I, I was opposite to it! I saw the large, clear glass from top to bottom, and I looked at it with unsteady eyes. I did not dare advance; I did not venture to make a movement; feeling certain, nevertheless, that He was there, but that He would escape me again, He whose imperceptible body had absorbed my reflection.

How frightened I was! And then suddenly I began to see myself through a mist in the depths of the looking-glass, in a mist as it were, or through a veil of water; and it seemed to me as if this water were flowing slowly from left to right, and making my figure clearer every moment. It was like the end of an eclipse. Whatever hid me did not appear to possess any clearly defined outlines, but was a sort of opaque transparency, which gradually grew clearer.

At last I was able to distinguish myself completely, as I do every day when I look at myself.

I had seen Him! And the horror of it remained with me, and makes me shudder even now.

August 21. How could I kill Him, since I could not get hold of Him? Poison? But He would see me mix it with the water; and then, would our poisons have any effect on His impalpable body? No — no — no doubt about the matter. Then? — then?

August 22. I sent for a blacksmith from Rouen and ordered iron shutters of him for my room, such as some private hotels in Paris have on the ground floor, for fear of thieves, and he is going to make me a similar door as well. I have made myself out a coward, but I do not care about that!

September 10. Rouen, Hotel Continental. It is done; it is done — but is He dead? My mind is thoroughly upset by what I have seen.

Well then, yesterday, the locksmith having put on the iron shutters and door, I left everything open until midnight, although it was getting cold.

Suddenly I felt that He was there, and joy, mad joy took possession of me. I got up softly, and I walked to the right and left for some time, so that He might not guess anything; then I took off my boots and put on my slippers carelessly; then I fastened the iron shutters and going back to the door quickly I double-locked it with a padlock, putting the key into my pocket.

Suddenly I noticed that He was moving restlessly round me, that in his turn He was frightened and was ordering me to let Him out. I nearly yielded, though I did not quite, but putting my back to the door, I half opened it, just enough to allow me to go out backward, and as I am very tall, my head touched the lintel. I was sure that He had not been able to escape, and I shut Him up quite alone, quite alone. What happiness! I had Him fast. Then I ran downstairs into the drawing room which was under my bedroom. I took the two lamps and poured all the oil on to the carpet, the furniture, everywhere; then I set fire to it and made my escape, after having carefully double locked the door.

I went and hid myself at the bottom of the garden, in a clump of laurel bushes. How long it was! how long it was! Everything was dark, silent, motionless, not a breath of air and not a star, but heavy banks of clouds which one could not see, but which weighed, oh! so heavily on my soul.

I looked at my house and waited. How long it was! I already began to think that the fire had gone out of its own accord, or that He had extinguished it, when one of the lower windows gave way under the violence of the flames, and a long, soft, caressing sheet of red flame mounted up the white wall, and kissed it as high as the roof. The light fell on to the trees, the branches, and the leaves, and a shiver of fear pervaded them also! The birds awoke; a dog began to howl, and it seemed to me as if the day were breaking! Almost immediately two other windows flew into fragments, and I saw that the whole of the lower part of my house was nothing but a terrible furnace. But a cry, a horrible, shrill, heart-rending cry, a woman's cry, sounded through the night, and two garret windows were opened! I had forgotten the servants! I saw the terror-struck faces, and the frantic waving of their arms!

Then, overwhelmed with horror, I ran off to the village, shouting: "Help! help! fire! fire!" Meeting some people who were already coming on to the scene, I went back with them to see!

By this time the house was nothing but a horrible and magnificent funeral pile, a monstrous pyre which lit up the whole country, a pyre where men were burning, and where He was burning also, He, He, my prisoner, that new Being, the new Master, the Horla!

Suddenly the whole roof fell in between the walls, and a volcano of flames darted up to the sky. Through all the windows which opened on to that furnace, I saw the flames darting, and I reflected that He was there, in that kiln, dead.

Dead? Perhaps? His body? Was not his body, which was transparent, indestructible by such means as would kill ours?

If He were not dead? Perhaps time alone has power over that Invisible and Redoubtable Being. Why this transparent, unrecognizable body, this body belonging to a spirit, if it also had to fear ills, infirmities, and premature destruction?

Premature destruction? All human terror springs from that! After man the Horla. After him who can die every day, at any hour, at any moment, by any accident, He came, He who was only to die at his own proper hour and minute, because He had touched the limits of his existence!

No — no — there is no doubt about it — He is not dead. Then — then — I suppose I must kill *myself!*

The Shadow

Hans Christian Andersen

Not precisely a fairy tale, Hans Christian Andersen's "The Shadow" literalizes dual nature. A shadow turns the table on his owner, exchanging his servitude for mastery. Of course, the "original" is a "learned gentleman" and a writer. By the end, shadow has become man, and man has become . . .

*I*n very hot climates, where the heat of the sun has great power, people are usually as brown as mahogany; and in the hottest countries they are Negroes, with black skins. A learned man once traveled into one of these warm climates, from the cold regions of the north, and thought he would roam about as he did at home; but he soon had to change his opinion. He found that, like all sensible people, he must remain in the house during the whole day, with every window and door closed, so that it looked as if all in the house were asleep or absent. The houses of the narrow street in which he lived were so lofty that the sun shone upon them from morning till evening, and it became quite unbearable. This learned man from the cold regions was young as well as clever; but it seemed to him as if he were sitting in an oven, and he became quite exhausted and weak, and grew so thin that his shadow shriveled up, and became much smaller than it had been at home. The sun took away even what was left of it, and he saw nothing of it till the evening, after sunset. It was really a pleasure, as soon as the lights were brought into the room, to see the shadow stretch itself against the wall, even to the ceiling, so tall was it; and it really wanted a good stretch to recover its strength. The learned man would sometimes go out into the balcony to stretch himself also; and as soon as the stars came forth

in the clear, beautiful sky, he felt revived. People at this hour began
to make their appearance in all the balconies in the street; for in
warm climates every window has a balcony, in which they can
breathe the fresh evening air, which is very necessary, even to those
who are used to a heat that makes them as brown as mahogany; so
that the street presented a very lively appearance. Here were shoe-
makers, and tailors, and all sorts of people sitting. In the street
beneath, they brought out tables and chairs, lighted candles by
hundreds, talked and sang, and were very merry. There were people
walking, carriages driving, and mules trotting along, with their bells
on the harness, "tingle, tingle," as they went. Then the dead were
carried to the grave with the sound of solemn music, and the tolling
of the church bells. It was indeed a scene of varied life in the street.
One house only, which was just opposite to the one in which the
foreign learned man lived, formed a contrast to all this, for it was
quite still; and yet somebody dwelt there, for flowers stood in the
balcony, blooming beautifully in the hot sun; and this could not
have been unless they had been watered carefully. Therefore some
one must be in the house to do this. The doors leading to the balcony
were half opened in the evening; and although in the front room all
was dark, music could be heard from the interior of the house. The
foreign learned man considered this music very delightful; but
perhaps he fancied it; for everything in these warm countries pleased
him, excepting the heat of the sun. The foreign landlord said he did
not know who had taken the opposite house — nobody was to be
seen there; and as to the music, he thought it seemed very tedious,
to him most uncommonly so.

"It is just as if some one was practising a piece that he could not
manage; it is always the same piece. He thinks, I suppose, that he
will be able to manage it at last; but I do not think so, however long
he may play it."

Once the foreigner woke in the night. He slept with the door
open which led to the balcony; the wind had raised the curtain before
it, and there appeared a wonderful brightness over all in the balcony
of the opposite house. The flowers seemed like flames of the most
gorgeous colors, and among the flowers stood a beautiful slender
maiden. It was to him as if light streamed from her, and dazzled his
eyes; but then he had only just opened them, as he awoke from his
sleep. With one spring he was out of bed, and crept softly behind
the curtain. But she was gone — the brightness had disappeared; the
flowers no longer appeared like flames, although still as beautiful as
ever. The door stood ajar, and from an inner room sounded music
so sweet and so lovely, that it produced the most enchanting

thoughts, and acted on the senses with magic power. Who could live there? Where was the real entrance? for, both in the street and in the lane at the side, the whole ground floor was a continuation of shops; and people could not always be passing through them.

One evening the foreigner sat in the balcony. A light was burning in his own room, just behind him. It was quite natural, therefore, that his shadow should fall on the wall of the opposite house; so that, as he sat amongst the flowers on his balcony, when he moved, his shadow moved also.

"I think my shadow is the only living thing to be seen opposite," said the learned man; "see how pleasantly it sits among the flowers. The door is only ajar; the shadow ought to be clever enough to step in and look about him, and then to come back and tell me what he has seen. You could make yourself useful in this way," said he, jokingly; "be so good as to step in now, will you?" and then he nodded to the shadow, and the shadow nodded in return. "Now go, but don't stay away altogether."

Then the foreigner stood up, and the shadow on the opposite balcony stood up also; the foreigner turned round, the shadow turned; and if anyone had observed, they might have seen it go straight into the half-opened door of the opposite balcony, as the learned man reentered his own room, and let the curtain fall. The next morning he went out to take his coffee and read the newspapers.

"How is this?" he exclaimed, as he stood in the sunshine. "I have lost my shadow. So it really did go away yesterday evening, and it has not returned. This is very annoying."

And it certainly did vex him, not so much because the shadow was gone, but because he knew there was a story of a man without a shadow. All the people at home, in his country, knew this story; and when he returned, and related his own adventures, they would say it was only an imitation; and he had no desire for such things to be said of him. So he decided not to speak of it at all, which was a very sensible determination.

In the evening he went out again on his balcony, taking care to place the light behind him; for he knew that a shadow always wants his master for a screen; but he could not entice him out. He made himself little, and he made himself tall; but there was no shadow, and no shadow came. He said, "Hem, a-hem;" but it was all useless. That was very vexatious; but in warm countries everything grows very quickly; and, after a week had passed, he saw, to his great joy, that a new shadow was growing from his feet, when he walked in the sunshine; so that the root must have remained. After three weeks, he had quite a respectable shadow, which, during his return journey to northern lands, continued to grow, and became at last so large that he might very well have spared half of it. When this learned man arrived at home, he wrote books about the true, the good, and the beautiful, which are to be found in this world; and so days and years passed — many, many years.

One evening, as he sat in his study, a very gentle tap was heard at the door. "Come in," said he; but no one came. He opened the door, and there stood before him a man so remarkably thin that he felt seriously troubled at his appearance. He was, however, very well dressed, and looked like a gentleman. "To whom have I the honor of speaking?" said he.

"Ah, I hoped you would recognize me," said the elegant stranger; "I have gained so much that I have a body of flesh, and clothes to wear. You never expected to see me in such a condition. Do you not recognize your old shadow? Ah, you never expected that I should return to you again. All has been prosperous with me since I was with you last; I have become rich in every way, and, were I inclined to purchase my freedom from service, I could easily do so." And as he spoke he rattled between his fingers a number of costly trinkets which hung to a thick gold watch-chain he wore round his neck. Diamond rings sparkled on his fingers, and it was all real.

"I cannot recover from my astonishment," said the learned man. "What does all this mean?"

"Something rather unusual," said the shadow; "but you are yourself an uncommon man, and you know very well that I have followed in your footsteps ever since your childhood. As soon as you found that I have traveled enough to be trusted alone, I went my own way, and I am now in the most brilliant circumstances. But I felt a kind of longing to see you once more before you die, and I wanted to see this place again, for there is always a clinging to the land of one's birth. I know that you have now another shadow; do I owe you anything? If so, have the goodness to say what it is."

"No! Is it really you?" said the learned man. "Well, this is most remarkable; I never supposed it possible that a man's old shadow could become a human being."

"Just tell me what I owe you," said the shadow, "for I do not like to be in debt to any man."

"How can you talk in that manner?" said the learned man. "What question of debt can there be between us? You are as free as anyone. I rejoice exceedingly to hear of your good fortune. Sit down, old friend, and tell me a little of how it happened, and what you saw in the house opposite to me while we were in those hot climates."

"Yes, I will tell you all about it," said the shadow, sitting down;

"but then you must promise me never to tell in this city, wherever you may meet me, that I have been your shadow. I am thinking of being married, for I have more than sufficient to support a family."

"Make yourself quite easy," said the learned man; "I will tell no one who you really are. Here is my hand, — I promise, and a word is sufficient between man and man."

"Between man and a shadow," said the shadow; for he could not help saying so.

It was really most remarkable how very much he had become a man in appearance. He was dressed in a suit of the very finest black cloth, polished boots, and an opera crush hat, which could be folded together so that nothing could be seen but the crown and the rim, besides the trinkets, the gold chain, and the diamond rings already spoken of. The shadow was, in fact, very well dressed, and this made a man of him. "Now I will relate to you what you wish to know," said the shadow, placing his foot with the polished leather boot as firmly as possible on the arm of the new shadow of the learned man, which lay at his feet like a poodle dog. This was done, it might be from pride, or perhaps that the new shadow might cling to him, but the prostrate shadow remained quite quiet and at rest, in order that it might listen, for it wanted to know how a shadow could be sent away by its master, and become a man itself. "Do you know," said the shadow, "that in the house opposite to you lived the most glorious creature in the world? It was poetry. I remained there three weeks, and it was more like three thousand years, for I read all that has ever been written in poetry or prose; and I may say, in truth, that I saw and learnt everything."

"Poetry!" exclaimed the learned man. "Yes, she lives as a hermit in great cities. Poetry! Well, I saw her once for a very short moment, while sleep weighed down my eyelids. She flashed upon me from the balcony like the radiant aurora borealis, surrounded with flowers like flames of fire. Tell me, you were on the balcony that evening; you went through the door, and what did you see?"

"I found myself in an anteroom," said the shadow. "You still sat opposite to me, looking into the room. There was no light, or at least it seemed in partial darkness, for the door of a whole suite of rooms stood open, and they were brilliantly lighted. The blaze of light would have killed me, had I approached too near the maiden myself, but I was cautious, and took time, which is what everyone ought to do."

"And what didst thou see?" asked the learned man.

"I saw everything, as you shall hear. But — it really is not pride on my part, as a free man and possessing the knowledge that I do, besides my position, not to speak of my wealth — I wish you would say you to me instead of thou."

"I beg your pardon," said the learned man; "it is an old habit, which it is difficult to break. You are quite right; I will try to think of it. But now tell me everything that you saw."

"Everything," said the shadow; "for I saw and know everything."

"What was the appearance of the inner rooms?" asked the scholar. "Was it there like a cool grove, or like a holy temple? Were the chambers like a starry sky seen from the top of a high mountain?"

"It was all that you describe," said the shadow; "but I did not go quite in — I remained in the twilight of the anteroom — but I was in a very good position, — I could see and hear all that was going on in the court of poetry."

"But what did you see? Did the gods of ancient times pass through the rooms? Did old heroes fight their battles over again? Were there lovely children at play, who related their dreams?"

"I tell you I have been there, and therefore you may be sure that I saw everything that was to be seen. If you had gone there, you would not have remained a human being, whereas I became one; and at the same moment I became aware of my inner being, my inborn affinity to the nature of poetry. It is true I did not think much about it while I was with you, but you will remember that I was always much larger at sunrise and sunset, and in the moonlight even more visible than yourself, but I did not then understand my inner existence. In the anteroom it was revealed to me. I became a man; I came out in full maturity. But you had left the warm countries. As a man, I felt ashamed to go about without boots or clothes, and that exterior finish by which man is known. So I went my own way; I can tell you, for you will not put it in a book. I hid myself under the cloak of a cake woman, but she little thought who she concealed. It was not till evening that I ventured out. I ran about the streets in the moonlight. I drew myself up to my full height upon the walls, which tickled my back very pleasantly. I ran here and there, looked through the highest windows into the rooms, and over the roofs. I looked in, and saw what nobody else could see, or indeed ought to see; in fact, it is a bad world, and I would not care to be a man, but that men are of some importance. I saw the most miserable things going on between husbands and wives, parents and children, — sweet, incomparable children. I have seen what no human being has the power of knowing, although they would all be very glad to know — the evil conduct of their neighbors. Had I written a newspaper, how eagerly it would have been read! Instead of which, I wrote directly to the persons themselves, and great alarm arose in all the town I visited. They had so much fear of me, and yet how dearly they loved me. The professor made me a professor. The tailor gave me new clothes; I am well provided for in that way. The overseer of the mint struck coins for me. The women declared that I was handsome, and so I became the man you now see me. And now I must say adieu. Here is my card. I live on the sunny side of the street, and always stay at home in rainy weather." And the shadow departed.

"This is all very remarkable," said the learned man.

Years passed, days and years went by, and the shadow came again. "How are you going on now?" he asked.

"Ah!" said the learned man; "I am writing about the true, the beautiful, and the good; but no one cares to hear anything about it. I am quite in despair, for I take it to heart very much."

"That is what I never do," said the shadow; "I am growing quite fat and stout, which everyone ought to be. You do not understand the world; you will make yourself ill about it; you ought to travel; I am going on a journey in the summer, will you go with me? I should like a traveling companion; will you travel with me as my shadow? It would give me great pleasure, and I will pay all expenses."

"Are you going to travel far?" asked the learned man.

"That is a matter of opinion," replied the shadow. "At all events, a journey will do you good, and if you will be my shadow, then all your journey shall be paid."

"It appears to me very absurd," said the learned man.

"But it is the way of the world," replied the shadow, "and always will be." Then he went away.

Everything went wrong with the learned man. Sorrow and trouble pursued him, and what he said about the good, the beautiful, and the true, was of as much value to most people as a nutmeg would be to a cow. At length he fell ill. "You really look like a shadow," people said to him, and then a cold shudder would pass over him, for he had his own thoughts on the subject.

"You really ought to go to some watering-place," said the shadow on his next visit. "There is no other chance for you. I will take you with me, for the sake of old acquaintance. I will pay the expenses of your journey, and you shall write a description of it to amuse us by the way. I should like to go to a watering-place; my beard does not grow as it ought, which is from weakness, and I must have a beard. Now do be sensible and accept my proposal; we shall travel as intimate friends."

And at last they started together. The shadow was master now, and the master became the shadow. They drove together, and rode and walked in company with each other, side by side, or one in front and the other behind, according to the position of the sun. The shadow always knew when to take the place of honor, but the learned man took no notice of it, for he had a good heart, and was exceedingly mild and friendly.

One day the master said to the shadow, "We have grown up together from our childhood, and now that we have become traveling companions, shall we not drink to our good fellowship, and say thee and thou to each other?"

"What you say is very straightforward and kindly meant," said the shadow, who was now really master. "I will be equally kind and straightforward. You are a learned man, and know how wonderful human nature is. There are some men who cannot endure the smell of brown paper; it makes them ill. Others will feel a shuddering sensation to their very marrow, if a nail is scratched on a pane of glass. I myself have a similar kind of feeling when I hear anyone say thou to me. I feel crushed by it, as I used to feel in my former position with you. You will perceive that this is a matter of feeling, not pride. I cannot allow you to say thou to me; I will gladly say it to you, and therefore your wish will be half fulfilled." Then the shadow addressed his former master as thou.

"It is going rather too far," said the latter, "that I am to say you when I speak to him, and he is to say thou to me." However, he was obliged to submit.

They arrived at length at the baths, where there were many strangers, and among them a beautiful princess, whose real disease consisted in being too sharp-sighted, which made everyone very uneasy. She saw at once that the newcomer was very different to everyone else. "They say he is here to make his beard grow," she thought; "but I know the real cause, he is unable to cast a shadow." Then she became very curious on the matter, and one day, while on the promenade, she entered into conversation with the strange gentleman. Being a princess, she was not obliged to stand upon much ceremony, so she said to him without hesitation, "Your illness consists in not being able to cast a shadow."

"Your royal highness must be on the high road to recovery from your illness," said he. "I know your complaint arose from being too sharp-sighted, and in this case it has entirely failed. I happen to have a most unusual shadow. Have you not seen a person who is always at my side? Persons often give their servants finer cloth for their liveries than for their own clothes, and so I have dressed out my shadow like a man; nay, you may observe that I have even given him a shadow of his own; it is rather expensive, but I like to have things about me that are peculiar."

"How is this?" thought the princess; "am I really cured? This must be the best watering-place in existence. Water in our times has certainly wonderful power. But I will not leave this place yet, just as it begins to be amusing. This foreign prince — for he must be a prince — pleases me above all things. I only hope his beard won't grow, or he will leave at once."

In the evening, the princess and the shadow danced together in the large assembly rooms. She was light, but he was lighter still; she had never seen such a dancer before. She told him from what country she had come, and found he knew it and had been there, but not while she was at home. He had looked into the windows of her father's palace, both the upper and the lower windows; he had seen many things, and could therefore answer the princess, and make allusions which quite astonished her. She thought he must be the cleverest man in all the world, and felt the greatest respect for his knowledge. When she danced with him again she fell in love with him, which the shadow quickly discovered, for she had with her eyes looked him through and through. They danced once more, and she was nearly telling him, but she had some discretion; she thought of her country, her kingdom, and the number of people over whom she would one day have to rule. "He is a clever man," she thought to herself, "which is a good thing, and he dances admirably, which is also good. But has he well-grounded knowledge? that is an important question, and I must try him." Then she asked him a most difficult question, she herself could not have answered it, and the shadow made a most unaccountable grimace.

"You cannot answer that," said the princess.

"I learnt something about it in my childhood," he replied; "and believe that even my very shadow, standing over there by the door, could answer it."

"Your shadow," said the princess; "indeed that would be very remarkable."

"I do not say so positively," observed the shadow; "but I am inclined to believe that he can do so. He has followed me for so many years, and has heard so much from me, that I think it is very likely. But your royal highness must allow me to observe, that he is very proud of being considered a man, and to put him in a good humor, so that he may answer correctly, he must be treated as a man."

"I shall be very pleased to do so," said the princess. So she walked up to the learned man, who stood in the doorway, and spoke to him of the sun, and the moon, of the green forests, and of people near home and far off; and the learned man conversed with her pleasantly and sensibly.

"What a wonderful man he must be, to have such a clever shadow!" thought she. "If I were to choose him it would be a real blessing to my country and my subjects, and I will do it." So the princess and the shadow were soon engaged to each other, but no one was to be told a word about it, till she returned to her kingdom.

"No one shall know," said the shadow; "not even my own shadow;" and he had very particular reasons for saying so.

After a time, the princess returned to the land over which she reigned, and the shadow accompanied her.

"Listen my friend," said the shadow to the learned man; "now that I am as fortunate and as powerful as any man can be, I will do something unusually good for you. You shall live in my palace, drive with me in the royal carriage, and have a hundred thousand dollars a year; but you must allow everyone to call you a shadow, and never venture to say that you have been a man. And once a year, when I sit in my balcony in the sunshine, you must lie at my feet as becomes a shadow to do; for I must tell you I am going to marry the princess, and our wedding will take place this evening."

"Now, really, this is too ridiculous," said the learned man. "I cannot, and will not, submit to such folly. It would be cheating the whole country, and the princess also. I will disclose everything, and say that I am the man, and that you are only a shadow dressed up in men's clothes."

"No one would believe you," said the shadow; "be reasonable, now, or I will call the guards."

"I will go straight to the princess," said the learned man.

"But I shall be there first," replied the shadow, "and you will be sent to prison." And so it turned out, for the guards readily obeyed him, as they knew he was going to marry the king's daughter.

"You tremble," said the princess, when the shadow appeared before her. "Has anything happened? You must not be ill today, for this evening our wedding will take place."

"I have gone through the most terrible affair that could possibly happen," said the shadow; "only imagine, my shadow has gone mad; I suppose such a poor, shallow brain, could not bear much; he fancies that he has become a real man, and that I am his shadow."

"How very terrible," cried the princess; "is he locked up?"

"Oh yes, certainly; for I fear he will never recover."

"Poor shadow!" said the princess; "it is very unfortunate for him; it would really be a good deed to free him from his frail existence; and, indeed, when I think how often people take the part of the lower class against the higher, in these days, it would be policy to put him out of the way quietly."

"It is certainly rather hard upon him, for he was a faithful servant," said the shadow; and he pretended to sigh.

"Yours is a noble character," said the princess, and bowed herself before him.

In the evening the whole town was illuminated, and cannons fired "boom," and the soldiers presented arms. It was indeed a grand wedding. The princess and the shadow stepped out on the balcony to show themselves, and to receive one cheer more. But the learned man heard nothing of all these festivities, for he had already been executed.

Green Tea

J. Sheridan LeFanu

In a Glass Darkly was first published in three volumes in 1872;
the several tales having previously appeared in various periodicals.
LeFanu's doctor Hesselius came too late to help the Rev. Mr.
Jennings with his peculiar obsession. A perfect gentleman most of
the time, the good Reverend is haunted by something wild and
strange, perhaps his alter-ego, and perhaps something brought on
by drinking too much . . .

PROLOGUE

MARTIN HESSELIUS, THE GERMAN PHYSICIAN

*Though carefully educated in medicine and surgery, I have never practiced
either. The study of each continues, nevertheless, to interest me profoundly.
Neither idleness nor caprice caused my secession from the honorable calling
which I had just entered. The cause was a very trifling scratch inflicted by a
dissecting knife. This trifle cost me the loss of two fingers, amputated promptly,
and the more painful loss of my health, for I have never been quite well since,
and have seldom been twelve months together in the same place.*

*In my wanderings I became acquainted with Dr. Martin Hesselius, a
wanderer like myself, like me a physician, and like me an enthusiast in his
profession. Unlike me in this, that his wanderings were voluntary, and he
a man, if not of fortune, as we estimate fortune in England, at least in what
our forefathers used to term "easy circumstances." He was an old man when
I first saw him; nearly five-and-thirty years my senior.*

In Dr. . Martin Hesselius I found my master. His knowledge was immense, his grasp of a case was an intuition. He was the very man to inspire a young enthusiast like me with awe and delight. My admiration has stood the test of time and survived the separation of death. I am sure it was well-founded.

For nearly twenty years I acted as his medical secretary. His immense collection of papers he has left in my care, to be arranged, indexed and bound. His treatment of some of these cases is curious. He writes in two distinct characters. He describes what he saw and heard as an intelligent layman might; and when in this style of narrative he had seen the patient either through his own hall-door to the light of day, or through the gates of darkness to the caverns of the dead, he returns upon the narrative, and in the terms of his art, and with all the force and originality of genius, proceeds to the work of analysis, diagnosis and illustration.

Here and there a case strikes me as of a kind to amuse or horrify a lay reader with an interest quite different from the peculiar one which it may possess for an expert. With slight modifications, chiefly of language, and of course a change of names, I copy the following. The narrator is Dr. Martin Hesselius. I find it among the voluminous notes of cases which me made during a tour in England about sixty-four years ago.

It is related to a series of letters to his friend Professor Van Loo of Leyden. The professor was not a physician, but a chemist, and a man who read history and metaphysics and medicine, and had, in his day, written a play.

The narrative is therefore, if somewhat less valuable as a medical record, necessarily written in a manner more likely to interest an unlearned reader.

These letters, from a memorandum attached, appear to have been returned, on the death of the professor in 1819, to Dr. Hesselius. They are written, some in English, some in French, but the greater part in German. I am a faithful, though I am conscious by no means a graceful translator, and although here and there I omit some passages, and shorten others, and disguise names, I have interpolated nothing.

CHAPTER I

DR. HESSELIUS RELATES HOW HE MET THE REV. MR. JENNINGS

*T*he Rev. Mr. Jennings is tall and thin. He is middle-aged, and dresses with a natty, old-fashioned high-church precision. He is naturally a little stately, but not at all stiff. His features, without being handsome, are well formed, and their expression extremely kind, but also shy.

I met him one evening at Lady Mary Heyduke's. The modesty and benevolence of his countenance are extremely prepossessing.

We were but a small party, and he joined agreeably enough in the conversation. He seems to enjoy listening very much more than contributing to the talk; but what he says is always to the purpose and well said. He is a great favorite of Lady Mary's, who it seems, consults him upon many things, and thinks him the most happy and blessed person on earth. Little knows she about him.

The Rev. Mr. Jennings is a bachelor, and has, they say, sixty thousand pounds in the funds. He is a charitable man. He is most anxious to be actively employed in his sacred profession, and yet, though always tolerably well elsewhere, when he goes down to his vicarage in Warwickshire, to engage in the actual duties of his sacred calling, his health soon fails him, and in a very strange way. So says Lady Mary.

There is no doubt that Mr. Jennings' health does break down in generally a sudden and mysterious way, sometimes in the very act of officiating in his old and pretty church at Kenlis. It may be his heart, it may be his brain. But so it has happened, three or four times or oftener, that after proceeding a certain way in the service, he has on a sudden stopped short; and after a silence, apparently quite unable to resume, he has fallen into solitary, inaudible prayer, his hands and his eyes uplifted, and then pale as death, and in the agitation of a strange shame and horror, descended trembling, and got into the vestry-room, leaving his congregation, without explanation, to themselves. This occurred when his curate was absent. When he goes down to Kenlis now, he always takes care to provide a clergyman to share his duty, and to supply his place on the instant should he become thus suddenly incapacitated.

When Mr. Jennings breaks down quite, and beats a retreat from the vicarage, and returns to London — where, in a dark street off Piccadilly, he inhabits a very narrow house — Lady Mary says that he is always perfectly well. I have my own opinion about that. There are degrees, of course. We shall see.

Mr. Jennings is a perfectly gentlemanlike man. People, however, remark something odd. There is an impression a little ambiguous. One thing which certainly contributes to it, people I think don't remember or, perhaps, distinctly remark. But I did, almost immediately. Mr. Jennings has a way of looking sidelong upon the carpet, as if his eye followed the movements of something there. This, of

course, is not always. It occurs only now and then. But often enough
to give a certain oddity, as I have said, to his manner, and in this
glance traveling along the floor there is something both shy and
anxious.

A medical philosopher, as you are good enough to call me,
elaborating theories by the aid of cases sought out by himself and
by him watched and scrutinized with more time at command, and
consequently infinitely more minuteness than the ordinary practi-
tioner can afford, falls insensibly into habits of observation, which
accompany him everywhere, and are exercised, as some people would
say, impertinently, upon every subject that presents itself with the
least likelihood of rewarding inquiry.

There was a promise of this kind in the slight, timid, kindly, but
reserved gentleman, whom I met for the first time at this agreeable
little evening gathering. I observed, of course, more than I here set
down; but I reserve all that borders on the technical for a strictly
scientific paper.

I may remark that when I here speak of medical science, I do so,
as I hope some day to see it more generally understood, in a much
more comprehensive sense than its generally material treatment
would warrant. I believe the entire natural world is but the ultimate
expression of that spiritual world from which, and in which alone,
it has its life. I believe that the essential man is a spirit, that the spirit
is an organized substance, but as different in point of material from
what we ordinarily understand by matter, as light or electricity is;
that the material body is, in the most literal sense, a vesture, and
death consequently no interruption of the living man's existence,
but simply his extrication from the natural body — a process which
commences at the moment of what we term death, and the comple-
tion of which, at furthest a few days later, is the resurrection "in
power."

The person who weighs the consequences of these positions will
probably see their practical bearing upon medical science. This is,
however, by no means the proper place for displaying the proofs
and discussing the consequences of this too generally unrecognized
state of facts.

In pursuance of my habit, I was covertly observing Mr. Jennings
with all my caution — I think he perceived it — and I saw plainly
that he was as cautiously observing me. Lady Mary happening to
address me by name, as Dr. Hesselius, I saw that he glanced at me
more sharply, and then became thoughtful for a few minutes.

After this, as I conversed with a gentleman at the other end of
the room, I saw him look at me more steadily, and with an interest

which I thought I understood. I then saw him take an opportunity of chatting with Lady Mary, and was, as one always is, perfectly aware of being the subject of a distant inquiry and answer.

This tall clergyman approached me by-and-by; and in a little time we had got into conversation. When two people who like reading, and know books and places, having traveled, wish to discourse, it is very strange if they can't find topics. It was not accident that brought him near me, and led him into conversation. He knew German, and had read my *Essays on Metaphysical Medicine*, which suggest more than they actually say.

This courteous man, gentle, shy, plainly a man of thought and reading, who, moving and talking among us, was not altogether of us, and whom I already suspected of leading a life whose transactions and alarms were carefully concealed, with an impenetrable reserve from, not only the world, but his best beloved friends — was cautiously weighing in his own mind the idea of taking a certain step with regard to me.

I penetrated his thoughts without his being aware of it, and was careful to say nothing which could betray to his sensitive vigilance my suspicions respecting his position, or my surmises about his plans respecting myself.

We chatted upon different subjects for a time, but at last he said:

"I was very much interested by some papers of yours, Dr. Hesselius, upon what you term Metaphysical Medicine — I read them in German, ten or twelve years ago — have they been translated?"

"No, I'm sure they have not — I should have heard. They would have asked my leave, I think."

"I asked the publishers here, a few months ago, to get the book for me in the original German; but they tell me it is out of print."

"So it is, and has been for some years; but it flatters me as an author to find that you have not forgotten my little book, although," I added laughing, "ten or twelve years is a considerable time to have managed without it; but I suppose you have been turning the subject over again in your mind, or something has happened lately to revive your interest in it."

At this remark, accompanied by a glance of inquiry, a sudden embarrassment disturbed Mr. Jennings, analogous to that which makes a young lady blush and look foolish. He dropped his eyes, and folded his hands together uneasily, and looked oddly, and you would have said guiltily, for a moment.

I helped him out of his awkwardness in the best way, by appearing not to observe it; and going straight on, I said: "Those revivals of interest in a subject happen to me often; one book suggests another, and often sends me back a wild-goose chase over an interval of twenty years. But if you still care to possess a copy, I shall be only too happy to provide you; I have still got two or three by me – and if you allow me to present one I shall be very much honored."

"You are very good indeed," he said, quite at his ease again, in a moment: "I almost despaired – I don't know how to thank you."

"Pray don't say a word; the thing is really so little worth that I am only ashamed of having offered it, and if you thank me anymore I shall throw it into the fire in a fit of modesty."

Mr. Jennings laughed. He inquired where I was staying in London, and after a little more conversation on a variety of subjects he took his departure.

CHAPTER II

THE DOCTOR QUESTIONS LADY MARY, AND SHE ANSWERS

"*I* like you vicar so much, Lady Mary," said I, as soon as he was gone. "He has read, traveled, and thought, and having also suffered, he ought to be an accomplished companion."

"So he is, and, better still, he is a really good man," said she. "His advice is invaluable about my schools, and all my little undertakings at Dawlbridge, and he's so painstaking, he takes so much trouble – you have no idea – wherever he thinks he can be of use; he's so good natured and so sensible."

"It is pleasant to hear so good an account of his neighborly virtues. I can only testify to his being an agreeable and gentle companion, and in addition to what you have told me, I think I can tell you two or three things about him," said I.

"Really!"

"Yes, to begin with, he's unmarried."

"Yes, that's right – go on."

"He has been writing, that is he *was*; but for two or three years, perhaps, he has not gone on with his work; and the book was upon some rather abstract subject – perhaps theology."

"Well, he was writing a book, as you say; I'm not quite sure what it was about, but only that it was nothing that I cared for; very likely you are right, and he certainly did stop – yes."

"And although he only drank a little coffee here tonight, he likes tea, at least did like it, extravagantly."

"Yes, that's *quite* true."

"He drank green tea a good deal, didn't he?" I pursued.

"Well, that's very odd! Green tea was a subject on which we used almost to quarrel."

"But he has quite given that up," said I.

"So he has."

"And, now, one more fact. His mother or his father, did you know them?"

"Yes, both; his father is only ten years dead, and their place is near Dawlbridge. We knew them very well," she answered.

"Well, either his mother or his father — I should rather think his father, saw a ghost," said I.

"Well, you really are a conjurer, Dr. Hesselius."

"Conjurer or no, haven't I said right?" I answered merrily.

"You certainly have, and it *was* his father: he was a silent, whimsical man, and he used to bore my father about his dreams, and at last he told him a story about a ghost he had seen and talked with; and a very odd story it was. I remember it particularly, because I was so afraid of him. This story was long before he died — when I was quite a child — and his ways were so silent and moping, and he used to drop in sometimes, in the dusk, when I was alone in the drawing room, and I used to fancy there were ghosts about him."

I smiled and nodded.

"And now, having established my character as a conjurer, I think I must say good-night," said I.

"But how *did* you find it out?"

"By the planets, of course, as the gypsies do," I answered, and so, gaily, we said good-night.

Next morning I sent the little book he had been inquiring after, and a note, to Mr. Jennings, and on returning late that evening, I found that he had called at my lodgings and left his card. He asked whether I was at home, and asked at what hour he would be most likely to find me.

Does he intend opening his case, and consulting me "professionally," as they say? I hope so. I have already conceived a theory about him. It is supported by Lady Mary's answers to my parting questions. I should like much to ascertain from his own lips. But what can I do consistently with good breeding to invite a confession? Nothing. I rather think he meditates one. At all events, my dear Van L., I shan't make myself difficult of access; I mean to return his visit tomorrow. It will be only civil, in return for his politeness, to ask to see him.

Perhaps something may come of it. Whether much, little, or nothing, my deal Van L., you shall hear.

CHAPTER III

Dr. HESSELIUS PICKS UP SOMETHING IN LATIN BOOKS

*W*ell, I have called at Blank Street.

On inquiring at the door, the servant told me that Mr. Jennings was engaged very particularly with a gentleman, a clergyman from Kenlis, his parish in the country. Intending to reserve my privilege, and to call again, I merely intimated that I should try another time, and had turned to go, when the servant begged my pardon, and asked me, looking at me a little more attentively than well-bred persons of his order usually do, whether I was Dr. Hesselius; and, on learning that I was, he said, "Perhaps then, sir, you would allow me to mention it to Mr. Jennings, for I am sure he wishes to see you."

The servant returned in a moment, with a message from Mr. Jennings asking me to go into his study, which was in effect his back drawing room, promising to be with me in a very few minutes.

This was really a study — almost a library. The room was lofty, with two tall slender windows, and rich dark curtains. It was much larger than I had expected, and stored with books on every side, from the floor to the ceiling. The upper carpet — for to my tread it felt that there were two or three — was a Turkey carpet. My steps fell noiselessly. The bookcases standing out, placed the windows, particularly narrow ones, in deep recesses. The effect of the room was, although extremely comfortable, and even luxurious, decidedly gloomy and, aided by the silence, almost oppressive. Perhaps, however, I ought to have allowed something for association. My mind had connected peculiar ideas with Mr. Jennings. I stepped into this perfectly silent room, of a very silent house, with a peculiar foreboding; and its darkness and solemn clothing of books — for except where two narrow looking-glasses were set in the wall they were everywhere — helped this somber feeling.

While awaiting Mr. Jennings' arrival, I amused myself by looking into some of the books with which his shelves were laden. Not among these, but immediately under them, with their backs upward, on the floor, I lighted upon a complete set of Swedenborg's *Arcana Caelestia*, in the original Latin, a very fine folio set, bound in the natty livery which theology affects, pure vellum namely, gold letters, and carmine edges. There were paper markers in several of these volumes; I raised and placed them, one after another, upon the table, and opening where these papers were placed, I read in the solemn Latin phraseology a series of sentences indicated by a penciled line at the margin. Of these I copy here a few, translating them into English:

"When man's interior sight is opened, which is that of his spirit, then there appear the things of another life, which cannot possibly be made visible to the bodily sight. . . ."

"By the internal sight it has been granted to me to see the things that are in the other life, more clearly than I see those that are in the world. From these considerations it is evident that external vision exists from interior vision, and this from a vision still more interior, and so on. . . ."

"There are with every man at least two evil spirits. . . ."

"With wicked genii there is also a fluent speech, but harsh and grating. There is also among them a speech which is not fluent, wherein the dissent of the thoughts is perceived as something secretly creeping along within it. . . ."

"The evil spirits associated with man are, indeed, from the hells, but when with man they are not then in hell, but are taken out thence. The place where they then are is in the midst between heaven and hell, and is called the world of spirits — when the evil spirits who are with man, are in that world, they are not in any infernal torment, but in every thought and affection of the man, and so, in all that the man himself enjoys. But when they are remitted into their hell, they return to their former state. . . ."

"If evil spirits could perceive that they were associated with man, and yet that they were spirits separate from him, and if they could flow in into the things of his body, they would attempt by a thousand means to destroy him; for they hate man with a deadly hatred. . . ."

"Knowing, therefore, that I was a man in the body, they were continually striving to destroy me, not as to the body only, but especially as to the soul; for to destroy any man or spirit is the very delight of life of all who are in hell; but I have been continually protected by the Lord. Hence it appears how dangerous it is for man to be in a living consort with spirits, unless he be in the good of faith. . . ."

"Nothing is more carefully guarded from the knowledge of associate spirits than their being thus conjoint with a man, for if they knew it they would speak to him, with the intention to destroy him. . . ."

"The delight of hell is to do evil to man, and to hasten his eternal ruin. . . ."

A long note, written with a very sharp and fine pencil, in Mr. Jennings' neat hand, at the foot of the page, caught my eye. Expecting his criticism upon the text, I read a word or two, and stopped; for it was something quite different, and began with these words, *Deus misereatur mei* — "May God compassionate me." Thus warned of its private nature, I averted my eyes, and shut the book, replacing all the volumes as I had found them, except one which interested me, and in which, as men studious and solitary in their habits will do, I grew so absorbed as to take no cognizance of the outer world, nor to remember where I was.

I was reading some pages which refer to "representatives" and "correspondents," in the technical language of Swedenborg, and had arrived at a passage, the substance of which is that evil spirits, when seen by other eyes than those of their infernal associates, present themselves, by "correspondence," in the shape of the beast (*fera*) which represents their particular lust and life, in aspect direful and atrocious. This is a long passage, and particularizes a number of those bestial forms.

CHAPTER IV

FOUR EYES WERE READING THE PASSAGE

I was running the head of my pencil-case along the line as I read it, and something caused me to raise my eyes.

Directly before me was one of the mirrors I have mentioned, in which I saw reflected the tall shape of my friend Mr. Jennings, leaning over my shoulder, and reading the page at which I was busy, and with a face so dark and wild that I should hardly have known him.

I turned and rose. He stood erect also, and with an effort laughed a little, saying:

"I came in and asked you how you did, but without succeeding in awaking you from your book; so I could not restrain my curiosity, and very impertinently, I'm afraid, peeped over your shoulder. This is not your first time of looking into those pages. You have looked into Swedenborg, no doubt, long ago?"

"Oh dear, yes! I owe Swedenborg a great deal; you will discover traces of him in the little book on *Metaphysical Medicine*, which you were so good to remember."

Although my friend affected a gaiety of manner, there was a slight flush in his face, and I could perceive that he was inwardly much perturbed.

"I'm scarcely yet qualified, I know so little of Swedenborg. I've only had them a fortnight," he answered, "and I think they are rather likely to make a solitary man nervous — that is, judging from the very little I have read — I don't say that they have made me so," he laughed; "and I'm so very much obliged for the book. I hope you got my note?"

I made all proper acknowledgements and modest disclaimers.

"I never read a book that I go with, so entirely, as that of yours," he continued. "I saw at once there is more in it than is quite unfolded. Do you know Dr. Harley?" he asked, rather abruptly.*

I did, having had letters to him, and had experienced from him great courtesy and considerable assistance during my visit to England.

"I think that man one of the very greatest fools I ever met in my life," said Mr. Jennings.

This was the first time I had ever heard him say a sharp thing of anybody, and such a term applied to so high a name a little startled me.

"Really! and in what way?" I asked.

"In his profession," he answered.

I smiled.

"I mean this," he said: "he seems to me, one half, blind — I mean one half of all he looks at is dark — preternaturally bright and vivid all the rest; and the worst of it is, it seems *willful*. I can't get him — I mean he won't — I've had some experience of him as a physician, but I look on him as, in that sense, no better than a paralytic mind, an intellect half dead. I'll tell you — I know I shall some time — all about it," he said, with a little agitation. "You stay some months longer in England. If I should be out of town during your stay for a little time, would you allow me to trouble you with a letter?"

"I should be only too happy," I assured him.

"Very good of you. I am so utterly dissatisfied with Harley."

---

* In passing, the editor remarks that the physician here named was one of the most eminent who had ever practiced in England.

"A little leaning to the materialistic school," I said.

"A *mere* materialist," he corrected me; "you can't think how that sort of thing worries one who knows better. You won't tell anyone — any of my friends you know — that I am hippish; now, for instance, no one knows — not even Lady Mary — that I have seen Dr. Harley, or any other doctor. So pray don't mention it; and, if I should have any threatening of an attack, you'll kindly let me write, or, should I be in town, have a little talk with you."

I was full of conjecture, and unconsciously I found I had fixed my eyes gravely on him, for he lowered his for a moment, and he said:

"I see you think I might as well tell you now, or else you are forming a conjecture; but you may as well give it up. If you were guessing all the rest of your life, you will never hit on it."

He shook his head smiling, and over that wintry sunshine a black cloud suddenly came down, and he drew his breath in through his teeth, as men do in pain.

"Sorry, of course, to learn that you apprehend occasion to consult any of us; but command me when and how you like, and I need not assure you that your confidence is sacred."

He then talked of quite other things, and in a comparatively cheerful way, and after a little time I took my leave.

CHAPTER V

DR. HESSELIUS IS SUMMONED TO RICHMOND

We parted cheerfully, but he was not cheerful, nor was I. There are certain expressions of that powerful organ of spirit — the human face — which, although I have seen them often, and possess a doctor's nerve, yet disturb me profoundly. One look of Mr. Jennings haunted me. It had seized my imagination with so dismal a power that I changed my plans for the evening, and went to the opera, feeling that I wanted a change of ideas.

I heard nothing of or from him for two or three days, when a note in his hand reached me. It was cheerful, and full of hope. He said that he had been for some little time so much better — quite well, in fact — that he was going to make a little experiment, and run down for a month or so to his parish, to try whether a little work might not quite set him up. There was in it a fervent religious expression of gratitude for his restoration, as he now almost hoped he might call it.

A day or two later I saw Lady Mary, who repeated what his note had announced, and told me that he was actually in Warwickshire, having resumed his clerical duties at Kenlis; and she added, "I begin to think that he is really perfectly well, and that there never was anything the matter, more than nerves and fancy; we are all nervous, but I fancy there is nothing like a little hard work for that kind of weakness, and he has made up his mind to try it. I should not be surprised if he did not come back for a year."

Notwithstanding all this confidence, only two days later I had this note, dated from his house off Piccadilly:

DEAR SIR —

I have returned disappointed. If I should feel at all able to see you, I shall write to ask you kindly to call. At present I am too low and, in fact, simply unable to say all I wish to say. Pray don't mention my name to my friends. I can see no one. By-and-by, please God, you shall hear from me. I mean to take a run into Shropshire, where some of my people are. God bless you! May we, on my return, meet more happily than I can now write.

About a week after this I saw Lady Mary at her own house, the last person, she said, left in town, and just on the wing for Brighton, for the London season was quite over. She told me that she had heard from Mr. Jennings' niece, Martha, in Shropshire. There was nothing to be gathered from her letter, more than that he was low and nervous. In those words, of which health people think so lightly, what a world of suffering is sometimes hidden!

Nearly five weeks had passed without any further news of Mr. Jennings. At the end of that time I received a note from him. He wrote:

"I have been in the country, and have had change of air, change of scene, change of faces, change of everything and in everything — but *myself*. I have made up my mind, so far as the most irresolute creature on earth can do it, to tell my case fully to you. If your engagements will permit, pray come to me today, tomorrow, or the next day; but, pray defer as little as possible. You know not how much I need help. I have a quiet house at Richmond, where I now am. Perhaps you can manage to come to dinner, or to luncheon, or even to tea. You shall have no trouble in finding me out. The servant

at Blank Street, who takes this note, will have a carriage at your door
at any hour you please; and I am always to be found. You will say
that I ought not to be alone. I have tried everything. Come and see."

I called up the servant, and decided on going out the same
evening, which accordingly I did.

He would have been much better in a lodging-house, or hotel, I
thought, as I drove up through a short double row of somber elms
to a very old-fashioned brick house, darkened by the foliage of these
trees, which overtopped and nearly surrounded it. It was a perverse
choice, for nothing could be imagined more triste and silent. The
house, I found, belonged to him. He had stayed for a day or two in
town, and, finding it for some cause insupportable, had come out
here, probably because, being furnished and his own, he was relieved
of the thought and delay of selection, by coming here.

The sun had already set, and the red reflected light of the western
sky illuminated the scene with the peculiar effect with which we are
all familiar. The hall seemed very dark, but, getting to the back
drawing room, whose windows command the west, I was again in
the same dusky light.

I sat down, looking out upon the richly-wooded landscape that
glowed in the grand and melancholy light which was every moment
fading. The corners of the room were already dark; all was growing
dim, and the gloom was insensibly toning my mind, already prepared for what was sinister. I was waiting alone for his arrival, which
soon took place. The door communicating with the front room
opened, and the tall figure of Mr. Jennings, faintly seen in the ruddy
twilight, came, with quiet stealthy steps, into the room.

We shook hands, and, taking a chair to the window, where there
was still light enough to enable us to see each other's faces, he sat
down beside me, and, placing his hand upon my arm, with scarcely
a word of preface began his narrative.

CHAPTER VI

HOW MR. JENNINGS MET HIS COMPANION

*T*he faint glow of the west, the pomp of the then lonely woods
of Richmond, were before us, behind and about us the darkening
room, and on the stony face of the sufferer — for the character of

his face, though still gentle and sweet, was changed — rested that dim, odd glow which seems to descend and produce, where it touches, lights, sudden though faint, which are lost, almost without gradation, in darkness. The silence, too, was utter; not a distant wheel, or bark, or whistle from without; and within the depressing stillness of an invalid bachelor's house.

I guessed well the nature, though not even vaguely the particulars of the revelations I was about to receive, from that fixed face of suffering that, so oddly flushed, stood out, like a portrait of Schalken's, before its background of darkness.

"It began," he said, "on the 15th of October, three years and eleven weeks ago, and two days — I keep very accurate count, for every day is torment. If I leave anywhere a chasm in my narrative tell me.

"About four years ago I began a work which had cost me very much thought and reading. It was upon the religious metaphysics of the ancients."

"I know," said I; "the actual religion of educated and thinking paganism, quite apart from symbolic worship? A wide and very interesting field."

"Yes; but not good for the mind — the Christian mind, I mean. Paganism is all bound together in essential unity, and, with evil sympathy, their religion involves their art, and both their manners, and the subject is a degrading fascination and the Nemesis sure. God forgive me!

"I wrote a great deal; I wrote late at night. I was always thinking on the subject, walking about, wherever I was, everywhere. It thoroughly infected me. You are to remember that all the material ideas connected with it were more or less of the beautiful, the subject itself delightfully interesting, and I, then, without a care."

He sighed heavily.

"I believe that everyone who sets about writing in earnest does his work, as a friend of mine phrased it, *on* something — tea, or coffee, or tobacco. I suppose there is a material waste that must be hourly supplied in such occupations, or that we should grow too abstracted, and the mind, as it were, pass out of the body, unless it were reminded often of the connection by actual sensation. At all events I felt the want, and I supplied it. Tea was my companion — at first the ordinary black tea, made in the usual way, not too strong: but I drank a good deal, and increased its strength as I went on. I never experienced an uncomfortable symptom from it. I began to take a little green tea. I found the effect pleasanter, it cleared and intensified the power of thought so. I had come to take it frequently, but not stronger than one might take it for pleasure. I wrote a great deal out here, it was so quiet, and in this room. I used to sit up very late, and it became a habit with me to sip my tea — green tea — every now and then as my work proceeded. I had a little kettle on my table, that swung over a lamp, and made tea two or three times between eleven o'clock and two or three in the morning, my hours of going to bed. I used to go into town everyday. I was not a monk, and, although I spent an hour or two in a library hunting up authorities and looking out lights upon my theme, I was in no morbid state as far as I can judge. I met my friends pretty much as usual and enjoyed their society, and, on the whole, existence had never been, I think, so pleasant before.

"I had met with a man who had some odd old books, German editions in mediaeval Latin, and I was only too happy to be permitted access to them. This obliging person's books were in the City, a very out-of-the-way part of it. I had rather out-stayed my intended hour, and, on coming out, seeing no cab near, I was tempted to get into the omnibus which used to drive past this house. It was darker than this by the time the 'bus had reached an old house you may have remarked, with four poplars at each side of the door, and there the last passenger but myself got out. We drove along rather faster. It was twilight now. I leaned back in my corner next the door, ruminating pleasantly.

"The interior of the omnibus was nearly dark. I had observed in the corner opposite to me at the other side, and at the end next the horses, two small circular reflections, as it seemed to me of a reddish light. They were about two inches apart, and about the size of those small brass buttons that yachting men used to put upon their jackets. I began to speculate, as listless men will, upon this trifle, as it seemed. From what center did that faint but deep red light come, and from what — glass beads, buttons, toy decorations — was it reflected? We were lumbering along gently, having nearly a mile still to go. I had not solved the puzzle, and it became in another minute more odd, for these two luminous points, with a sudden jerk, descended nearer the floor, keeping still their relative distance and horizontal position, and then, as suddenly, they rose to the level of the seat on which I was sitting, and I saw them no more.

"My curiosity was now really excited, and, before I had time to think, I saw again these two dull lamps, again together near the floor; again they disappeared, and again in their old corner I saw them.

"So, keeping my eyes upon them, I edged quietly up to my own side, towards the end at which I still saw these tiny discs of red.

"There was very little light in the 'bus. It was nearly dark. I leaned forward to aid my endeavor to discover what these little circles really were. They shifted their position a little as I did so. I began now to perceive an outline of something black, and I soon saw, with tolerable distinctness, the outline of a small black monkey, pushing its face forward in mimicry to meet mine; those were its eyes, and I now dimly saw its teeth grinning at me.

"I drew back, not knowing whether it might not meditate a spring. I fancied that one of the passengers had forgot this ugly pet, and wishing to ascertain something of its temper, though not caring to trust my fingers to it, I poked my umbrella softly towards it. It remained unmovable – up to it – *through* it. For through it, and back and forward it passed, without the slightest resistance.

"I can't, in the least, convey to you the kind of horror that I felt. When I had ascertained that the thing was an illusion, as I then supposed, there came a misgiving about myself and a terror that fascinated me in impotence to remove my gaze from the eyes of the brute for some moments. As I looked it made a little skip back, quite into the corner, and I, in a panic, found myself at the door, having put my head out, drawing deep breaths of the outer air, and staring at the lights and trees we were passing, too glad to reassure myself of reality.

"I stopped the 'bus and got out. I perceived the man look oddly at me as I paid him. I daresay there was something unusual in my looks and manner, for I had never felt so strangely before.

CHAPTER VII

THE JOURNEY: FIRST STAGE

"When the omnibus drove on, and I was alone on the road, I looked carefully round to ascertain whether the monkey had followed me. To my indescribable relief I saw it nowhere. I can't describe easily what a shock I had received, and my sense of genuine gratitude on finding myself, as I supposed, quite rid of it.

"I had got out a little before we reached this house, two or three hundred steps. A brick wall runs along the footpath, and inside the wall is a hedge of yew, or some dark evergreen of that kind, and within that again the row of fine trees which you may have remarked as you came.

"This brick wall is about as high as my shoulder, and happening to raise my eyes I saw the monkey, with that stooping gait, on all fours, walking or creeping, close beside me on top of the wall. I stopped, looking at it with a feeling of loathing and horror. As I stopped so did it. It sat up on the wall with its long hands on its knees looking at me. There was not light enough to see it much more than in outline, nor was it dark enough to bring the peculiar light of its eye into strong relief. I still saw, however, that red foggy light plainly enough. It did not show its teeth, nor exhibit any sign of irritation, but seemed jaded and sulky, and was observing me steadily.

"I drew back into the middle of the road. It was an unconscious recoil, and there I stood, still looking at it. It did not move.

"With an instinctive determination to try something — anything, I turned about and walked briskly toward town, with askance look, all the time watching the movements of the beast. It crept swiftly along the wall, at exactly my pace.

"Where the wall ends, near the turn of the road, it came down, and with a wiry spring or two brought itself close to my feet, and continued to keep up with me as I quickened my pace. It was at my left side, so close to my leg that I felt every moment as if I should tread upon it.

"The road was quite deserted and silent, and it was darker every moment. I stopped dismayed and bewildered, turning, as I did so, the other way — I mean towards this house, away from which I had been walking. When I stood still the monkey drew back to a distance of, I suppose, about five or six yards, and remained stationary, watching me.

"I had been more agitated that I have said. I had read, of course, as everyone has, something about 'special illusions,' as you physicians term the phenomena of such cases. I considered my situation, and looked my misfortune in the face.

"These affections, I had read, are sometimes transitory and sometimes obstinate. I had read of cases in which the appearance, at first harmless, had, step by step, degenerated into something direful and insupportable, and ended by wearing its victim out. Still, as I stood there, but for my bestial companion quite alone, I tried to comfort myself by repeating again and again the assurance, 'the thing is purely disease, a well-known physical affection, as distinctly as smallpox or neuralgia. Doctors are all agreed on that, philosophy demonstrates it. I must not be a fool. I've been sitting up too late, and I daresay my digestion is quite wrong, and, with God's help, I shall be all right, and this is but a symptom of nervous dyspepsia.' Did I believe all this? Not one word of it, no more than any other miserable being ever did who is once seized and riveted in this satanic captivity. Against my convictions, I might say my knowledge, I was simply bullying myself into a false courage.

"I now walked homeward. I had only a few hundred yards to go. I had forced myself into a sort of resignation, but I had not got over the sickening shock and the flurry of the first certainty of my misfortune.

"I made up my mind to pass the night at home. The brute moved close beside me, and I fancied there was the sort of anxious drawing toward the house, which one sees in tired horses or dogs, sometimes, as they come toward home.

"I was afraid to go into town, I was afraid of anyone's seeing and recognizing me. I was conscious of an irrepressible agitation to my manner. Also, I was afraid of any violent change in my habits, such as going to a place of amusement, or walking from home in order to fatigue myself. At the hall door it waited till I mounted the steps, and when the door was opened entered with me.

"I drank no tea that night. I got cigars and some brandy and water. My idea was that I should act upon my material system, and by living for a while in sensation apart from thought, send myself forcibly, as it were, into a new groove. I came up here to this drawing room. I sat just here. The monkey then got upon a small table that then stood *there*. It looked dazed and languid. An irrepressible uneasiness as to its movements kept my eyes always upon it. Its eyes were half closed, but I could see them glow. It was looking steadily at me. In all situations, at all hours, it is awake and looking at me. That never changes.

"I shall not continue in detail my narrative of this particular night. I shall describe, rather, the phenomena of the first year, which never varied essentially. I shall describe the monkey as it appeared in daylight. In the dark, as you shall presently hear, there are peculiarities. It is a small monkey, perfectly black. It had only one peculiarity — a character of malignity — unfathomable malignity. During the first year it looked sullen and sick. But this character of intense malice and vigilance was always underlying that surly languor. During all that time it acted as if on a plan of giving me as little trouble as was consistent with watching me. Its eyes were never off me. I have never lost sight of it, except in my sleep, light or dark, day or night, since it came here, excepting when it withdraws for some weeks at a time, unaccountably.

"In total dark it is visible as in daylight. I do not merely its eyes. It is *all* visible distinctly in a halo that resembles a glow of red embers, and which accompanies it in all its movements.

"When it leaves me for a time it is always at night, in the dark, and in the same way. It grows at first uneasy, and then furious, and then advances towards me, grinning and shaking, its paws clenched, and, at the same time, there comes the appearance of fire in the grate. I never have any fire. I can't sleep in the room where there is any — and it draws nearer and nearer to the chimney, quivering, it seems, with rage, and when its fury rises to the highest pitch it springs into the grate, and up the chimney, and I see it no more.

"When first this happened I thought I was released. I was now a new man. A day passed — a night — and no return, and a blessed week — a week — another week. I was always on my knees, Dr. Hesselius, always, thanking God and praying. A whole month passed of liberty; but, on a sudden, it was with me again.

CHAPTER VIII

THE SECOND STAGE

"*I*t was with me, and the malice which before was torpid under a sullen exterior was now active. It was perfectly unchanged in every other respect. This new energy was apparent in its activity and its looks, and soon in other ways.

"For a time, you will understand, the change was shown only in an increased vivacity, and an air of menace, as if it was always brooding over some atrocious plan. Its eyes, as before, were never off me."

"Is it here now?" I asked.

"No," he replied, "it has been absent exactly a fortnight and a day — fifteen days. It has sometimes been away so long as nearly two months, once for three. Its absence always exceeds a fortnight, although it may be but by a single day. Fifteen days having past since I saw it last, it may return now at any moment."

"Is its return," I asked, "accompanied by any peculiar manifestation?"

"Nothing — no," he said. "It is simply with me again. On lifting my eyes from a book, or turning my head, I see it, as usual, looking at me, and then it remains, as before, for its appointed time. I have never told so much and so minutely before to anyone."

I perceived that he was agitated, and looking like death, and he repeatedly applied his handkerchief to his forehead; I suggested that he might be tired, and told him that I would call, with pleasure, in the morning, but he said:

"No, if you don't mind hearing it all now. I have got so far, and I should prefer making one effort of it. When I spoke to Dr. Harley, I had nothing like so much to tell. You are a philosophic physician. You give spirit its proper rank. If this thing is real —"

He paused, looking at me with agitated inquiry.

"We can discuss it by-and-by, and very fully. I will give you all I think," I answered, after an interval.

"Well — very well. If it is anything real, I say, it is prevailing, little by little, and drawing me more interiorly into hell. Optic nerves, he talked of. Ah! well — there are other nerves of communication. May God Almighty help me! You shall hear.

"Its power of action, I tell you, has increased. Its malice became, in a way, aggressive. About two years ago, some questions that were pending between me and the bishop having been settled, I went down to my parish in Warwickshire, anxious to find occupation in my profession. I was not prepared for what happened, although I have since thought I might have apprehended something like it. The reason for my saying so is this —"

He was beginning to speak with a great deal more effort and reluctance, and sighed often, and seemed at times nearly overcome. But at this time his manner was not agitated. It was more like that of a sinking patient, who has given himself up.

"Yes, but I will first tell you about Kenlis, my parish.

"It was with me when I left this place for Dawlbridge. It was my silent traveling companion, and it remained with me at the vicarage. When I entered on the discharge of my duties, another change took place. The thing exhibited an atrocious determination to thwart me. It was with me in the church — in the reading-desk — in the pulpit — within the communion rails. At last it reached this extremity, that while I was reading to the congregation it would spring upon the open book and squat there, so that I was unable to see the page. This happened more than once.

"I left Dawlbridge for a time. I placed myself in Dr. Harley's hands. I did everything he told me. He gave my case a great deal of thought. It interested him, I think. He seemed successful. For nearly three months I was perfectly free from a return. I began to think I was safe. With his full asset I returned to Dawlbridge.

"I traveled in a chaise. I was in good spirits. I was more — I was happy and grateful. I was returning, as I thought, delivered from a dreadful hallucination, to the scene of duties which I longed to enter upon. It was a beautiful sunny evening, everything looked serene and cheerful, and I was delighted. I remember looking out of the window to see the spire of my church at Kenlis among the trees, at the point where one has the earliest view of it. It is exactly where the little stream that bounds the parish passes under the road by a culvert; and where it emerges at the roadside a stone with an old inscription is placed. As we passed this point I drew my head in and sat down, and in the corner of the chaise was the monkey.

"For a moment I felt faint, and then quite wild with despair and horror. I called to the driver, and got out, and sat down at the roadside, and prayed to God silently for mercy. A despairing resignation supervened. My companion was with me as I reentered the vicarage. The same persecution followed. After a short struggle I submitted, and soon I left the place.

"I told you," he said, "that the beast has before this become in certain ways aggressive. I will explain a little. It seemed to be actuated by intense and increasing fury whenever I said my prayers, or even meditated prayer. It amounted at last to a dreadful interruption. You will ask, how could a silent immaterial phantom effect that? It was thus, whenever I meditated praying; it was always before me, and nearer and nearer.

"It used to spring on a table, on the back of a chair, on the chimney piece, and slowly to swing itself from side to side, looking at me all the time. There is in its motion an indefinable power to dissipate thought, and to contract one's attention to that monotony, till the ideas shrink, as it were, to a point, and at last to nothing — and unless I had started up, and shook off the catalepsy, I have felt as if my mind were on the point of losing itself. There are other ways," he sighed heavily; "thus, for instance, while I pray with my eyes closed, it comes closer and closer, and I see it. I know it is not to be accounted for physically, but I do actually see it, though my lids are closed, and so it rocks my mind, as it were, and overpowers me, and I am obliged to rise from my knees. If you had ever yourself known this, you would be acquainted with desperation."

CHAPTER IX

THE THIRD STAGE

"*I* see, Dr. Hesselius, that you don't lose one word of my statement. I need not ask you to listen specially to what I am now going to tell you. They talk of optic nerves, and of spectral illusions, as if the organ of sight was the only point assailable by the influences that have fastened upon me – I know better. For two years in my direful case that limitation prevailed. But as food is taken in softly at the lips, and then brought under the teeth, as the tip of the little finger caught in a mill crank will draw in the hand, and the arm, and the whole body, so the miserable mortal who has been once caught firmly by the end of the finest fiber of his nerve is drawn in and in, by the enormous machinery of hell, until he is as I am. Yes, Doctor, as *I* am, for while I talk to you, and implore relief, I feel that my prayer is for the impossible, and my pleading with the inexorable."

I endeavored to calm his visibly increasing agitation, and told him that he must not despair.

While we talked the night had overtaken us. The filmy moonlight was wide over the scene which the window commanded, and I said:

"Perhaps you would prefer having candles. This light, you know, is odd. I should wish you, as much as possible, under your usual conditions, while I make my diagnosis, shall I call it – otherwise I don't care."

"All lights are the same to me," he said. "Except when I read or write, I care not if night were perpetual. I am going to tell you what happened about a year ago. The thing began to speak to me."

"Speak! How do you mean – speak as a man does, do you mean?"

"Yes; speak in words and consecutive sentences, with perfect coherence and articulation; but there is a peculiarity. It is not like the tone of a human voice. It is not by my ears it reaches me – it comes like a singing through me head.

"This faculty, the power of speaking to me, will be my undoing. It won't let me pray, it interrupts me with dreadful blasphemies. I dare not go on, I could not. Oh! Doctor, can the skill, and thought, and prayers of man avail me nothing!"

"You must promise me, my dear sir, not to trouble yourself with unnecessarily exciting thoughts; confine yourself strictly to the narrative of *facts*; and recollect, above all, that even if the thing that infests you be, as you seem to suppose, a reality with an actual independent life and will, yet it can have no power to hurt you, unless it be given from above: its access to your senses depends mainly upon your physical conditions — this is, under God, your comfort and reliance: we are all alike environed. It is only that in your case, the *'paries,'* the veil of the flesh, the screen, is a little out of repair, and sights and sounds are transmitted. We must enter on a new course, sir — be encouraged. I'll give tonight to the careful consideration of the whole case."

"You are very good, sir; you think it worth trying, you don't give me quite up; but, sir, you don't know, it is gaining such an influence over me: it orders me about, it is such a tyrant, and I'm growing so helpless. May God deliver me!"

"It orders you about — of course you mean by speech?"

"Yes, yes; it is always urging me to crimes, to injure others, or myself. You see, Doctor, the situation is urgent, it is indeed. When I was in Shropshire, a few weeks ago" (Mr. Jennings was speaking rapidly and trembling now, holding my arm with one hand, and looking in my face), "I went out one day with a party of friends for a walk: my persecutor, I tell you, was with me at the time. I lagged behind the rest: the country near the Dee, you know, is beautiful. Our path happened to lie near a coal mine, and at the verge of the wood is a perpendicular shaft, they say, a hundred and fifty feet deep. My niece had remained behind with me — she knows, of course, nothing of the nature of my sufferings. She knew, however, that I had been ill, and was low, and she remained to prevent my being quite alone. As we loitered slowly on together, the brute that accompanied me was urging me to throw myself down the shaft. I tell you now — oh, sir, think of it! — the one consideration that saved me from that hideous death was the fear lest the shock of witnessing the occurrence should be too much for the poor girl. I asked her to go on and take her walk with her friends, saying that I could go no further. She made excuses, and the more I urged her the firmer she became. She looked doubtful and frightened. I suppose there was something in my looks or manner that alarmed her; but she would not go, and that literally saved me. You had no idea, sir, that a living man could be made so abject a slave of Satan," he said, with a ghastly groan and a shudder.

There was a pause here, and I said, "You *were* preserved nevertheless. It was the act of God. You are in His hands and in the power of no other being: be therefore confident for the future."

CHAPTER X

HOME

I made him have candles lighted, and saw the room looking cheery and inhabited before I left him. I told him that he must regard his illness strictly as one dependent on physical, though *subtle* physical causes. I told him that he had evidence of God's care and love in the deliverance which he had just described, and that I had perceived with pain that he seemed to regard its peculiar features as indicating that he had been delivered over to spiritual reprobation. Than such a conclusion nothing could be, I insisted, less warranted; and not only so, but more contrary to facts, as disclosed in his mysterious deliverance from that murderous influence during his Shropshire excursion. First, his niece had been retained by his side without his intending to keep her near him; and, secondly, there had been infused into his mind an irritable repugnance to execute the dreadful suggestion in her presence.

As I reasoned this point with him, Mr. Jennings wept. He seemed comforted. One promise I exacted, which was that should the monkey at any time return, I should be sent for immediately; and, repeating my assurance that I would give neither time nor thought to any other subject until I had thoroughly investigated his case, and that tomorrow he should hear the result, I took my leave.

Before getting into the carriage I told the servant that his master was far from well, and that he should make a point of frequently looking into his room.

My own arrangements I made with a view to being quite secure from interruption.

I merely called at my lodgings, and with a traveling-desk and carpet-bag set off in a hackney carriage for an inn, about two miles out of town, called "The Horns," a very quiet and comfortable house with good thick walls. And there I resolved, without the possibility of intrusion or distraction, to devote some hours of the night, in my comfortable sitting room, to Mr. Jennings' case, and so much of the morning as it might require.*

---

* There occurs here a careful note of Dr. Hesselius' opinion upon the case, and of the habits, dietary, and medicines which he prescribed. It is curious — some persons would say mystical. But, on the whole, I doubt whether it would sufficiently interest a reader of the kind I am likely to meet with, to warrant its being here reprinted. The whole let-

I left town for the inn where I slept last night at half-past nine, and did not arrive at my room in town until one o'clock this afternoon. I found a letter in Mr. Jennings' hand upon my table. It had not come by post, and, on inquiry, I learned that Mr. Jennings' servant had brought it, and, on learning that I was not to return until today and that no one could tell him my address, he seemed very uncomfortable, and said that his orders from his master were that he was not to return without an answer.

I opened the letter and read:

Dear Dr. Hesselius. —
    It is here. You had not been an hour gone when it returned. It is speaking. It knows all that has happened. It knows everything — it knows you, and is frantic and atrocious. It reviles. I send you this. It knows every word I have written — I write. This I promised, and I therefore write, but I fear very confused, very incoherently. I am so interrupted, disturbed.

Ever yours, sincerely yours,
Robert Lynder Jennings

"When did this come?" I asked.

"About eleven last night: the man was here again, and has been here three times today. The last time is about an hour since."

Thus answered, and with the notes I had made upon his case in my pocket, I was in a few minutes driving towards Richmond to see Mr. Jennings.

I by no means, as you perceive, despaired of Mr. Jennings' case. He had himself remembered and applied, though quite in a mistaken way, the principle which I lay down in my *Metaphysical Medicine,* and which governs all such cases. I was about to apply it in earnest. I was profoundly interested, and very anxious to see and examine him while the "enemy" was actually present.

I drove up to the somber house, and ran up the steps and knocked. The door, in a little time, was opened by a tall woman in black silk. She looked ill, and as if she had been crying. She curtseyed, and heard my question, but she did not answer. She turned her face away, extending her hand towards two men who were coming downstairs; and thus having, as it were, tacitly made me over to them, she passed through a side-door hastily and shut it.

The man who was nearest the hall, I at once accosted, but being now close to him I was shocked to see that both his hands were

---

ter was plainly written at the inn where he had hid himself for the occasion. The next letter is dated from his town lodgings.

covered with blood.

I drew back a little, and the man, passing downstairs, merely said in a low tone, "Here's the servant, sir."

The servant had stopped on the stairs, confounded and dumb at seeing me. He was rubbing his hands in a handkerchief, and it was steeped in blood.

"Jones, what is it? What has happened?" I asked, while a sickening suspicion overpowered me.

The man asked me to come up to the lobby. I was beside him in a moment, and, frowning and pallid, with contracted eyes, he told me the horror which I already half guessed.

His master had made away with himself.

I went upstairs with him to the room — what I saw there I won't tell you. He had cut his throat with his razor. It was a frightful gash. The two men had laid him on the bed, and composed his limbs. It had happened, as the immense pool of blood on the floor declared, at some distance between the bed and the window. There was carpet round his bed, and a carpet under his dressing-table, but none on the rest of the floor, for the man said he did not like a carpet in his bedroom. In this somber and now terrible room, one of the great elms that darkened the house was slowly moving the shadow of one of its great boughs upon this dreadful floor.

I beckoned to the servant, and we went downstairs together. I turned off the hall into an old-fashioned panelled room, and there standing, I heard all the servant had to tell. It was not a great deal.

"I concluded, sir, from yours words, and looks, sir, as you left last night, that you thought my master seriously ill. I thought it might be that you were afraid of a fit, or something. So I attended very close to your directions. He sat up late, till past three o'clock. He was not writing or reading. He was talking a great deal to himself, but that was nothing unusual. At about that hour I assisted him to undress, and left him in his slippers and dressing gown. I went back softly in about half-an-hour. He was in his bed, quite undressed, and a pair of candles lighted on the table beside his bed. He was leaning on his elbow, and looking out at the other side of the bed when I came in. I asked him if he wanted anything, and he said 'No.'

"I don't know whether it was what you said to me, sir, or something a little unusual about him, but I was uneasy, uncommon uneasy about him last night.

"In another half hour, or it might be a little more, I went up again. I did not hear him talking as before. I opened the door a little. The candles were both out, which was not usual. I had a bedroom candle, and I let the light in, a little bit, looking softly round. I saw

him sitting in that chair beside the dressing-table with his clothes
on again. He turned round and looked at me. I thought it strange
he should get up and dress, and put out the candles to sit in the
dark, that way. But I only asked him again if I could do anything
for him. He said, 'No,' rather sharp, I thought. I asked if I might
light the candles, and he said, 'Do as you like, Jones.' So I lighted
them, and I lingered about the room, and he said, 'Tell me truth,
Jones; why did you come again — you did not hear anyone cursing?'
'No, sir,' I said, wondering what he could mean.

"'No,' said he, after me, 'of course, no'; and I said to him,
'Wouldn't it be well, sir, you went to bed? It's just five o'clock'; and
he said nothing but, 'Very likely; good-night, Jones.' So I went, sir,
but in less than an hour I came again. The door was fast, and he
heard me, and called as I thought from the bed to know what I
wanted, and he desired me not to disturb him again. I lay down and
slept for a little. It must have been between six and seven when I
went up again. The door was still fast, and he made no answer, so I
did not like to disturb him, and thinking he was asleep I left him
till nine. It was his custom to ring when he wished me to come, and
I had no particular hour for calling him. I tapped very gently, and
getting no answer I stayed away a good while, supposing he was
getting some rest then. It was not till eleven o'clock I grew really
uncomfortable about him — for at the latest he was never, that I
could remember, later than half-past ten. I got no answer. I knocked
and called, and still no answer. So not being able to force the door,
I called Thomas from the stables, and together we forced it, and
found him in the shocking way you saw."

Jones had no more to tell. Poor Mr. Jennings was very gentle and
very kind. All his people were fond of him. I could see that the
servant was very much moved.

So, dejected and agitated, I passed from that terrible house, and
its dark canopy of elms, and I hope I shall never see it more. While
I write to you I feel like a man who has but half waked from a
frightful and monotonous dream. My memory rejects the picture
with incredulity and horror. Yet I know it is true. It is the story of
the process of a poison, a poison which excites the reciprocal action
of spirit and nerve, and paralyzes the tissue that separates those
cognate functions of the senses, the external and the interior. Thus
we find strange bed-fellows, and the mortal and immortal prema-
turely make acquaintance.

CONCLUSION

A WORD FOR THOSE WHO SUFFER

*M*y dear Van L——, you have suffered from an affection similar to that which I have just described. You twice complained of a return of it.

Who, under God, cured you? Your humble servant, Martin Hesselius. Let me rather adopt the more emphasised piety of a certain good old French surgeon of three hundred years ago: "I treated, and God cured you."

Come, my friend, you are not be hippish. Let me tell you a fact.

I have met with, and treated, as my book shows, fifty-seven cases of this kind of vision, which I term indifferently "sublimated," "precocious," and "interior."

There is another class of affections which are truly termed — though commonly confounded with those which I describe — spectral illusions. These latter I look upon as being no less simply curable than a cold in the head or a trifling dyspepsia.

It is those which rank in the first category that test our promptitude of thought. Fifty-seven such cases have I encountered, neither more nor less. And in how many of these have I failed? In no one single instance.

There is one affliction of mortality more easily and certainly reducible, with a little patience and a rational confidence in the physician. With these simple conditions I look upon the cure as absolutely certain.

You are to remember that I had not even commenced to treat Mr. Jennings' case. I have not any doubt that I should have cured him perfectly in eighteen months, or possibly it might have extended to two years. Some cases are very rapidly curable, others extremely tedious. Every intelligent physician who will give thought and diligence to the task will effect a cure.

You know my tract on *The Cardinal Functions of the Brain*. I there, by the evidence of innumerable facts, prove, as I think, the high probability of a circulation, arterial and venous in its mechanism, through the nerves. Of this system, thus considered, the brain is the heart. The fluid, which is propagated hence through one class of nerves, returns in an altered state through another, and the nature of that fluid is spiritual, though not immaterial, anymore than, as

I before remarked, light or electricity are so.

By various abuses, among which the habitual use of such agents as green tea is one, this fluid may be affected as to its quality, but it is more frequently disturbed as to equilibrium. This fluid being that which we have in common with spirits, a congestion found upon the masses of brain or nerve, connected with the interior sense, forms a surface unduly exposed, on which disembodied spirits may operate: communication is thus more or less effectually established. Between this brain circulation and the heart circulation there is an intimate sympathy. The seat, or rather the instrument of exterior vision, is the eye. The seat of interior vision is the nervous tissue and brain, immediately about and above the eyebrow. You remember how effectually I dissipated your pictures by the simple application of iced eau-de-cologne. Few cases, however, can be treated exactly alike with anything like rapid success. Cold acts powerfully as a repellant of the nervous fluid. Long enough continued it will even produce that permanent insensibility which we call numbness, and a little longer, muscular as well as sensational paralysis.

I have not, I repeat, the slightest doubt that I should have first dimmed and ultimately sealed that inner eye which Mr. Jennings has inadvertently opened. The same senses are opened in delirium tremens, and entirely shut up again when the overaction of the cerebral heart, and the prodigious nervous congestions that attend it, are terminated by a decided change in the state of the body. It is by acting steadily upon the body, by a simple process, that this result is produced — and inevitably produced — I have never yet failed.

Poor Mr. Jennings made away with himself. But that catastrophe was the result of a totally different malady, which, as it were, projected itself upon that disease which was established. His case was in the distinctive manner a complication, and the complaint under which he really succumbed was hereditary suicidal mania. Poor Mr. Jennings I cannot call a patient of mine, for Ihad not even begun to treat his case, and he had not yet given me, I am convinced, his full and unreserved confidence. If the patient do not array himself on the side of the disease, his cure is certain.

The Sandman*

E.T.A. Hoffmann

Translated by J.T. Bealby, B.A.

E.T.A. Hoffmann wrote "Die Doppelgänger," as well as many other tales of mysterious doubles. The dreaded Doctor Coppelius is the "Sandman" who haunts Nathanael — and who is he? Coppelius, or Coppola? This is the tale of the mechanical girl, Olimpia. Nothing in Hoffmann's world is as it seems as Nathanael descends into madness — "Spin round, fire-wheel! Spin round, fire-wheel!"

NATHANIEL TO LOTHAIR

I know you are all very uneasy because I have not written for such a long, long time. Mother, to be sure, is angry, and Clara, I dare say, believes I am living here in riot and revelry, and quite forgetting my sweet angel, whose image is so deeply engraved upon my heart and mind. But that is not so; daily and hourly do I think of you all, and my lovely Clara's form comes to gladden me in my dreams, and smiles upon me with her bright eyes, as graciously as she used to do in the days when I went in and out amongst you. Oh! how could I write to you in the distracted state of mind in which I have been,

---

* "The Sandman" forms the first of a series of tales called "The Night Pieces," which were published in 1817.

and which, until now, has quite bewildered me! A terrible thing has happened to me. Dark forebodings of some awful fate threatening me are spreading themselves out over my head like black clouds, impenetrable to every friendly ray of sunlight. I must now tell you what has taken place; I must, that I see well enough, but only to think upon it makes the wild laughter burst from my lips. Oh! my dear, dear Lothair, what shall I say to make you feel, if only in an inadequate way, that that which happened to me a few days ago could thus really exercise such a hostile and disturbing influence upon my life? Oh that you were here to see for yourself! but now you will, I suppose, take me for a superstitious ghost-seer. In a word, the terrible thing which I have experienced, the fatal effect of which I in vain exert every effort to shake off, is simply that some days ago, namely, on the 30th October, at twelve o'clock at noon, a dealer in weather-glasses came into my room and wanted to sell me one of his wares. I bought nothing, and threatened to kick him downstairs, whereupon he went away of his own accord.

You will conclude that it can only be very peculiar relations — relations intimately intertwined with my life — that can give significance to this event, and that it must be the person of this unfortunate hawker which has had such a very inimical effect upon me. And so it really is. I will summon up all my faculties in order to narrate to you calmly and patiently as much of the early days of my youth as will suffice to put matters before you in such a way that your keen sharp intellect may grasp everything clearly and distinctly, in bright and living pictures. Just as I am beginning, I hear you laugh and Clara say, "What's all this childish nonsense about!" Well, laugh at me, laugh heartily at me, pray do. But, good God! my hair is standing on end, and I seem to be entreating you to laugh at me in the same sort of frantic despair in which Franz Moor entreated Daniel to laugh him to scorn.* But to my story.

Except at dinner we, *i.e.,* I and my brothers and sisters, saw but little of our father all day long. His business no doubt took up most of his time. After our evening meal, which, in accordance with an old custom, was served at seven o'clock, we all went, mother with us, into father's room, and took our places around a round table. My father smoked his pipe, drinking a large glass of beer to it. Often he told us many wonderful stories, and got so excited over them that his pipe always went out; I used then to light it for him with a spill,

---

* See Schiller's *Räuber,* Act V., Scene I. Franz Moor, seeing that the failure of all his villainous schemes is inevitable, and that his own ruin is close upon him, is at length overwhelmed with the madness of despair, and unburdens the terrors of his conscience to the old servant Daniel, bidding him laugh him to scorn.

and this formed my chief amusement. Often, again, he would give us picture books to look at, whilst he sat silent and motionless in his easy chair, puffing out such dense clouds of smoke that we were all as it were enveloped in mist. On such evenings mother was very sad; and directly it struck nine she said, "Come, children! off to bed! Come! The 'Sandman' is come I see." And I always did seem to hear something trampling upstairs with slow heavy steps; that must be the Sandman. Once in particular I was very much frightened at this dull trampling and knocking; as mother was leading us out of the room I asked her, "O mamma! but who is this nasty Sandman who always sends us away from papa? What does he look like?" Except at dinner we, i.e., I and my brothers and "There is no Sandman, my dear child," mother answered; "when I say the Sandman is come, I only mean that you are sleepy and can't keep your eyes open, as if somebody had put sand in them." This answer of mother's did not satisfy me; nay, in my childish mind the thought clearly unfolded itself that mother denied there was a Sandman only to prevent us being afraid, — why, I always heard him come upstairs. Full of curiosity to learn something more about this Sandman and what he had to do with us children, I at length asked the old woman who acted as my youngest sister's attendant, what sort of a man he was — the Sandman? "Why, 'thanael, darling, don't you know?" she replied. "Oh! he's a wicked man, who comes to little children when they won't go to bed and throws handfuls of sand in their eyes, so that they jump out of their heads all bloody; and he puts them into a bag and takes them to the half-moon as food for his little ones; and they sit there in the nest and have hooked beaks like owls, and they pick naughty little boys' and girls' eyes out with them." After this I formed in my own mind a horrible picture of the cruel Sandman. When anything came blundering upstairs at night I trembled with fear and dismay; and all that my mother could get out of me were the stammered words "The Sandman! the Sandman!" whilst the tears coursed down my cheeks. Then I ran into my bedroom, and the whole night through tormented myself with the terrible apparition of the Sandman. I was quite old enough to perceive that the old woman's tale about the Sandman and his little ones' nest in the half-moon couldn't be altogether true; nevertheless the Sandman continued to be for me a fearful incubus, and I was always seized with terror — my blood always ran cold, not only when I heard anybody come up the stairs, but when I heard anybody noisily open my father's room door and go in. Often he stayed away for a long season altogether; then he would come several times in close succession.

This went on for years, without my being able to accustom myself to this fearful apparition, without the image of the horrible Sandman growing any fainter in my imagination. His intercourse with my father began to occupy my fancy ever more and more; I was restrained from asking my father about him by an unconquerable shyness; but as the years went on the desire waxed stronger and stronger within me to fathom the mystery myself and to see the fabulous Sandman. He had been the means of disclosing to me the path of the wonderful and the adventurous, which so easily find lodgment in the mind of the child. I liked nothing better than to hear or read horrible stories of goblins, witches, Tom Thumbs, and so on; but always at the head of them all stood the Sandman, whose picture I scribbled in the most extraordinary and repulsive forms with both chalk and coal everywhere, on the tables, and cupboard doors, and walls. When I was ten years old my mother removed me from the nursery into a little chamber off the corridor not far from my father's room. We still had to withdraw hastily whenever, on the stroke of nine, the mysterious unknown was heard in the house. As I lay in my little chamber I could hear him go into father's room, and soon afterwards I fancied there was a fine and peculiar smelling steam spreading itself through the house. As my curiosity waxed stronger, my resolve to make somehow or other the Sandman's acquaintance took deeper root. Often when my mother had gone past, I slipped quickly out of my room into the corridor, but I could never see anything, for always before I could reach the place where I could get sight of him, the Sandman was well inside the door. At last, unable to resist the impulse any longer, I determined to conceal myself in father's room and there wait for the Sandman.

One evening I perceived from my father's silence and mother's sadness that the Sandman would come; accordingly, pleading that I was excessively tired, I left the room before nine o'clock and concealed myself in a hiding place close beside the door. The street door creaked, and slow, heavy, echoing steps crossed the passage towards the stairs. Mother hurried past me with my brothers and sisters. Softly – softly – I opened father's room door. He sat as usual, silent and motionless, with his back towards it; he did not hear me; and in a moment I was in and behind a curtain drawn before my father's open wardrobe, which stood just inside the room. Nearer and nearer and nearer came the echoing footsteps. There was a strange coughing and shuffling and mumbling outside. My heart beat with expectation and fear. A quick step now close, close beside the door, a noisy rattle of the handle, and the door flies open with a bang. Recovering my courage with an effort, I take a cautious peep out. In the middle of the room in front of my father stands the Sandman, the bright light of the lamp falling full upon his face. The Sandman, the terrible Sandman, is the old advocate *Coppelius* who often comes to dine with us.

But the most hideous figure could not have awakened greater trepidation in my heart than this Coppelius did. Picture to yourself a large broad-shouldered man, with an immensely big head, a face the color of yellow-ochre, grey bushy eyebrows, from beneath which two piercing, greenish, catlike eyes glittered, and a prominent Roman nose hanging over his upper lip. His distorted mouth was often screwed up into a malicious smile; then two dark-red spots appeared on his cheeks, and a strange hissing noise proceeded from between his tightly clenched teeth. He always wore an ash-grey coat of an old-fashioned cut, a waistcoat of the same, and nether extremities to match, but black stockings and buckles set with stones on his shoes. His little wig scarcely extended beyond the crown of his head, his hair was curled round high up above his big red ears, and plastered to his temples with cosmetic, and a broad closed hair-bag stood out prominently from his neck, so that you could see the silver buckle that fastened his folded neck-cloth. Altogether he was a most disagreeable and horribly ugly figure; but what we children detested most of all was his big coarse hairy hands; we could never fancy anything that he had once touched. This he had noticed; and so, whenever our good mother quietly placed a piece of cake or sweet fruit on our plates, he delighted to touch it under some pretext or other, until the bright tears stood in our eyes, and from disgust and loathing we lost the enjoyment of the tit-bit that was intended to please us. And he did just the same thing when father gave us a glass of sweet wine on holidays. Then he would quickly pass his hand over it, or even sometimes raise the glass to his blue lips, and he laughed quite sardonically when all we dared do was to express our vexation in stifled sobs. He habitually called us the "little brutes;" and when he was present we might not utter a sound; and we cursed the ugly spiteful man who deliberately and intentionally spoilt all our little pleasures. Mother seemed to dislike this hateful Coppelius as much as we did for as soon as he appeared her cheerfulness and bright and natural manner were transformed into sad, gloomy seriousness. Father treated him as if he were a being of some higher race, whose ill-manners were to be tolerated, whilst no efforts ought to be spared to keep him in good-humor. He had only to give a slight hint, and his favorite dishes were cooked for him and rare wine uncorked.

As soon as I saw this Coppelius, therefore, the fearful and hideous

thought arose in my mind that he, and he alone, must be the
Sandman; but I no longer conceived of the Sandman as the bugbear
in the old nurse's fable, who fetched children's eyes and took them
to the half-moon as food for his little ones — no I but as an ugly
specterlike fiend bringing trouble and misery and ruin, both tem-
poral and everlasting, everywhere wherever he appeared.

I was spellbound on the spot. At the risk of being discovered, and,
as I well enough knew, of being severely punished, I remained as I
was, with my head thrust through the curtains listening. My father
received Coppelius in a ceremonious manner. "Come, to work!"
cried the latter, in a hoarse snarling voice, throwing off his coat.
Gloomily and silently my father took off his dressing gown, and
both put on long black smock-frocks. Where they took them from
I forgot to notice. Father opened the folding-doors of a cupboard
in the wall; but I saw that what I had so long taken to be a cupboard
was really a dark recess, in which was a little hearth. Coppelius
approached it, and a blue flame crackled upwards from it. Round
about were all kinds of strange utensils. Good God! as my old father
bent down over the fire how different he looked! His gentle and
venerable features seemed to be drawn up by some dreadful convulsive pain into an ugly, repulsive Satanic mask. He looked like
Coppelius. Coppelius plied the red-hot tongs and drew bright glowing masses out of the thick smoke and began assiduously to hammer
them. I fancied that there were men's faces visible round about, but
without eyes, having ghastly deep black holes where the eyes should
have been. "Eyes here! Eyes here!" cried Coppelius, in a hollow
sepulchral voice. My blood ran cold with horror; I screamed and
tumbled out of my hiding place into the floor. Coppelius immediately seized upon me. "You little brute! You little brute!" he bleated,
grinding his teeth. Then, snatching me up, he threw me on the
hearth, so that the flames began to singe my hair. "Now we've got
eyes — eyes — a beautiful pair of children's eyes," he whispered, and,
thrusting his hands into the flames he took out some red-hot grains
and was about to strew them into my eyes. Then my father clasped
his hands and entreated him, saying, "Master, master, let my
Nathaniel keep his eyes — oh! do let him keep them." Coppelius
laughed shrilly and replied, "Well then, the boy may keep his eyes
and whine and pule his way through the world; but we will now at
any rate observe the mechanism of the hand and the foot." And
therewith he roughly laid hold upon me, so that my joints cracked,
and twisted my hands and my feet, pulling them now this way, and
now that, "That's not quite right altogether! It's better as it was! —
the old fellow knew what he was about." Thus lisped and hissed

Coppelius; but all around me grew black and dark; a sudden convulsive pain shot through all my nerves and bones I knew nothing more.

I felt a soft warm breath fanning my cheek; I awakened as if out of the sleep of death; my mother was bending over me. "Is the Sandman still there?" I stammered. "No, my dear child; he's been gone a long, long time; he'll not hurt you." Thus spoke my mother, as she kissed her recovered darling and pressed him to her heart. But why should I tire you, my dear Lothair? why do I dwell at such length on these details, when there's so much remains to be said? Enough – I was detected in my eavesdropping, and roughly handled by Coppelius. Fear and terror had brought on a violent fever, of which I lay ill several weeks. "Is the Sandman still there?" these were the first words I uttered on coming to myself again, the first sign of my recovery, of my safety. Thus, you see, I have only to relate to you the most terrible moment of my youth for you to thoroughly understand that it must not be ascribed to the weakness of my eyesight if all that I see is colorless, but to the fact that a mysterious destiny has hung a dark veil of clouds about my life, which I shall perhaps only break through when I die.

Coppelius did not show himself again; it was reported he had left the town.

It was about a year later when, in pursuance of the old unchanged custom, we sat around the round table in the evening. Father was in very good spirits, and was telling us amusing tales about his youthful travels. As it was striking nine we all at once heard the street door creak on its hinges, and slow ponderous steps echoed across the passage and up the stairs. "That is Coppelius," said my mother, turning pale. "Yes, it is Coppelius," replied my father in a faint broken voice. The tears started from my mother's eyes. "But, father, father," she cried, "must it be so?" "This is the last time," he replied; "this is the last time he will come to me, I promise you. Go now, go and take the children. Go, go to bed – good-night."

As for me, I felt as if I were converted into cold, heavy stone; I could not get my breath. As I stood there immovable my mother seized me by the arm. "Come, Nathaniel! do come along!" I suffered myself to be led away; I went into my room. "Be a good boy and keep quiet," mother called after me; "get into bed and go to sleep." But, tortured by indescribable fear and uneasiness, I could not close my eyes. That hateful, hideous Coppelius stood before me with his glittering eyes, smiling maliciously down upon me; in vain did I strive to banish the image. Somewhere about midnight there was a terrific crack, as if a cannon were being fired off. The whole house shook; something went rustling and clattering past my door; the house door was pulled to with a bang. "That is Coppelius," I cried, terror-struck, and leapt out of bed. Then I heard a wild heartrending scream; I rushed into my father's room; the door stood open, and clouds of suffocating smoke came rolling towards me. The servant-maid shouted, "Oh! my master! my master!" On the floor in front of the smoking hearth lay my father, dead, his face burned black and fearfully distorted, my sisters weeping and moaning around him, and my mother lying near them in a swoon. "Coppelius, you atrocious fiend, you've killed my father," I shouted. My senses left me. Two days later, when my father was placed in his coffin; his features were mild and gentle again as they had been when he was alive. I found great consolation in the thought that his association with the diabolical Coppelius could not have ended in his everlasting ruin.

Our neighbors had been awakened by the explosion; the affair got talked about, and came before the magisterial authorities, who wished to cite Coppelius to clear himself. But he had disappeared from the place, leaving no traces behind him.

Now when I tell you, my dear friend, that the weather-glass hawker I spoke of was the villain Coppelius, you will not blame me for seeing impending mischief in his inauspicious reappearance. He was differently dressed; but Coppelius's figure and features are too deeply impressed upon my mind for me to be capable of making a mistake in the matter. Moreover, he has not even changed his name. He proclaims himself here, I learn, to be a Piedmontese mechanician, and styles himself Giuseppe Coppola.

I am resolved to enter the lists against him and revenge my father's death, let the consequences be what they may.

Don't say a word to mother about the reappearance of this odious monster. Give my love to my darling Clara; I will write to her when I am in a somewhat calmer frame of mind. Adieu, &c.

LARA TO NATHANIEL

You are right, you have not written to me for a very long time, but nevertheless I believe that I still retain a place in your mind and thoughts. It is a proof that you were thinking a good deal about me when you were sending off your last letter to brother Lothair, for instead of directing it to him you directed it to me. With joy I tore open the envelope, and did not perceive the mistake until I read the words, "Oh! my dear, dear Lothair." Now I know I ought not to have read anymore of the letter, but ought to have given it to my brother. But as you have so often in innocent raillery made it a sort of reproach against me that I possessed such a calm, and, for a woman, cool-headed temperament that I should be like the woman we read of — if the house was threatening to tumble down, I should, before hastily fleeing, stop to smooth down a crumple in the window-curtains — I need hardly tell you that the beginning of your letter quite upset me. I could scarcely breathe; there was a bright mist before my eyes. Oh! my darling Nathaniel! what could this terrible thing be that had happened? Separation from you — never to see you again, the thought was like a sharp knife in my heart. I read on and on. Your description of that horrid Coppelius made my flesh creep. I now learnt for the first time what a terrible and violent death your good old father died. Brother Lothair, to whom I handed over his property, sought to comfort me, but with little success. That horrid weather-glass hawker Giuseppe Coppola followed me everywhere; and I am almost ashamed to confess it, but he was able to disturb my sound and in general calm sleep with all sorts of wonderful dream-shapes. But soon — the next day — I saw everything in a different light. Oh! do not be angry with me, my best-beloved, if, despite your strange presentiment that Coppelius will do you some mischief, Lothair tells you I am in quite as good spirits, and just the same as ever.

I will frankly confess, it seems to me that all that was fearsome and terrible of which you speak, existed only in your own self, and that the real true outer world had but little to do with it. I can quite admit that old Coppelius may have been highly obnoxious to you children, but your real detestation of him arose from the fact that he hated children.

Naturally enough the gruesome Sandman of the old nurse's story was associated in your childish mind with old Coppelius, who, even though you had not believed in the Sandman, would have been to you a ghostly bugbear, especially dangerous to children. His mysterious labors along with your father at night-time were, I daresay, nothing more than secret experiments in alchemy, with which your mother could not be over well pleased, owing to the large sums of money that most likely were thrown away upon them; and besides, your father, his mind full of the deceptive striving after higher knowledge, may probably have become rather indifferent to his family, as so often happens in the case of such experimentalists. So also it is equally probable that your father brought about his death by his own imprudence, and that Coppelius is not to blame for it. I must tell you that yesterday I asked our experienced neighbor, the chemist, whether in experiments of this kind an explosion could take place which would have a momentarily fatal effect. He said, "Oh, certainly!" and described to me in his prolix and circumstantial way how it could be occasioned, mentioning at the same time so many strange and funny words that I could not remember them at all. Now I know you will be angry at your Clara, and will say, "Of the Mysterious which often clasps man in its invisible arms there's not a ray can find its way into this cold heart. She sees only the varied surface of the things of the world, and, like the little child, is pleased with the golden glittering fruit, at the kernel of which lies the fatal poison."

Oh! my beloved Nathaniel, do you believe then that the intuitive prescience of a dark power working within us to our own ruin cannot exist also in minds which are cheerful, natural, free from care? But please forgive me that I, a simple girl, presume in my way to indicate to you what I really think of such an inward strife. After all, I should not find the proper words, and you would only laugh at me, not because my thoughts were stupid, but because I was so foolish as to attempt to tell them to you.

If there is a dark and hostile power which traitorously fixes a thread in our hearts in order that, laying hold of it and drawing us by means of it along a dangerous road to ruin, which otherwise we should not have trod — if, I say, there is such a power, it must assume within us a form like ourselves, nay, it must be ourselves; for only in that way can we believe in it, and only so understood do we yield to it so far that it is able to accomplish its secret purpose. So long as we have sufficient firmness, fortified by cheerfulness, to always acknowledge foreign hostile influences for what they really are, whilst we quietly pursue the path pointed out to us by both inclination and calling, then this mysterious power perishes in its futile struggles to attain the form which is to be the reflected image of ourselves. It is also certain, Lothair adds, that if we have once voluntarily given ourselves up to this dark physical power, it often reproduces within us the strange forms which the outer world throws in our way, so that thus it is we ourselves who engender within ourselves the spirit which by some remarkable delusion we imagine to speak in that outer form. It is the phantom of our own self whose intimate relationship with, and whose powerful influence upon our soul either plunges us into hell or elevates us.to heaven. Thus you will see, my beloved Nathaniel, that I and brother Lothair have well talked over the subject of dark powers and forces; and now, after I have with some difficulty written down the principal results of our discussion, they seem to me to contain many really profound thoughts. Lothair's last words, however, I don't quite understand altogether; I only dimly guess what he means; and yet I cannot help thinking it is all very true. I beg you, dear, strive to forget the ugly advocate Coppelius as well as the weather-glass hawker Giuseppe Coppola. Try and convince yourself that these foreign influences can have no power over you, that it is only the belief in their hostile power which can in reality make them dangerous to you. If every line of your letter did not betray the violent excitement of your mind, and if I did not sympathize with your condition from the bottom of my heart, I could in truth jest about the advocate Sandman and weather-glass hawker Coppelius. Pluck up your spirits! Be cheerful! I have resolved to appear to you as your guardian-angel if that ugly man Coppola should dare take it into his head to bother you in your dreams, and drive him away with a good hearty laugh. I'm not afraid of him and his nasty hands, not the least little bit; I won't let him either as advocate spoil any dainty tit-bit I've taken, or as Sandman rob me of my eyes.

My darling, darling Nathaniel,
Eternally your, &c. &c.

NATHANIEL TO LOTHAIR

I am very sorry that Clara opened and read my last letter to you; of course the mistake is to be attributed to my own absence of mind. She has written me a very deep philosophical letter, proving conclusively that Coppelius and Coppola only exist in my own mind and are phantoms of my own self, which will at once be dissipated, as soon as I look upon them in that light. In very truth one can hardly believe that the mind which so often sparkles in those bright, beautifully smiling, childlike eyes of hers like a sweet lovely dream could draw such subtle and scholastic distinctions. She also mentions your name. You have been talking about me. I suppose you have been giving her lectures, since she sifts and refines everything so acutely. But enough of this! I must now tell you it is most certain that the weather-glass hawker Giuseppe Coppola is not the advocate Coppelius. I am attending the lectures of our recently appointed Professor of Physics, who, like the distinguished naturalist,* is called Spalanzani, and is of Italian origin. He has known Coppola for

---

* Lazaro Spallanzani, a celebrated anatomist and naturalist
(1729-1799), filled for several years the chair of Natural History at
Pavia, and traveled extensively for scientific purposes in Italy, Turkey,
Sicily, Switzerland, &c.

many years; and it is also easy to tell from his accent that he really is a Piedmontese. Coppelius was a German, though no honest German, I fancy. Nevertheless I am not quite satisfied. You and Clara will perhaps take me for a gloomy dreamer, but nohow can I get rid of the impression which Coppelius's cursed face made upon me. I am glad to learn from Spalanzani that he has left the town. This Professor Spalanzani is a very queer fish. He is a little fat man, with prominent cheekbones, thin nose, projecting lips, and small piercing eyes. You cannot get a better picture of him than by turning over one of the Berlin pocket-almanacs* and looking at Cagliostro's† portrait engraved by Chodowiecki;‡ Spalanzani looks just like him.

Once lately, as I went up the steps to his house, I perceived that beside the curtain which generally covered a glass door there was a small chink. What it was that excited my curiosity I cannot explain; but I looked through. In the room I saw a female, tall, very slender, but of perfect proportions, and splendidly dressed, sitting at a little table, on which she had placed both her arms, her hands being folded together. She sat opposite the door, so that I could easily see her angelically beautiful face. She did not appear to notice me, and there was moreover a strangely fixed look about her eyes, I might almost say they appeared as if they had no power of vision; I thought she was sleeping with her eyes open. I felt quite uncomfortable, and so I slipped away quietly into the Professor's lecture-room, which was close at hand. Afterwards I learnt that the figure which I had seen was Spalanzani's daughter, Olimpia, whom he keeps locked in a most wicked and unaccountable way, and no man is ever allowed to come near her. Perhaps, however, there is after all something peculiar about her; perhaps she's an idiot or something of that sort. But why am I telling you all this? I could have told you it all better and more in detail when I see you. For in a fortnight I shall be amongst you. I must see my dear sweet angel, my Clara, again. Then the little bit

---

* Or Almanacs of the Muses, as they were also sometimes called, were periodical, mostly yearly publications, containing all kinds of literary effusions; mostly, however, lyrical. They originated in the eighteenth century. Schiller, A. W. and F. Schlegel, Tieck, and Chamisso, amongst others, conducted undertakings of this nature.

† Joseph Balsamo, a Sicilian by birth, calling himself Count Cagliostro, one of the greatest impostors of modern times, lived during the latter part of the eighteenth century. See Carlyle's "Miscellanies" for an account of his life and character.

‡ Daniel Nikolas Chodowiecki, painter and engraver, of Polish descent, was born at Dantzic in 1726. For some years he was so popular an artist that few books were published in Prussia without plates or vignettes by him. The catalogue of his works is said to include 3000 items.

of ill-temper, which, I must confess, took possession of me after her fearfully sensible letter, will be blown away. And that is the reason why I am not writing to her as well today. With all best wishes, &c.

*N*othing more strange and extraordinary can be imagined, gracious reader, than what happened to my poor friend, the young student Nathaniel, and which I have undertaken to relate to you. Have you ever lived to experience anything that completely took possession of your heart and mind and thoughts to the utter exclusion of everything else? All was seething and boiling within you; your blood, heated to fever pitch, leapt through your veins and inflamed your cheeks. Your gaze was so peculiar, as if seeking to grasp in empty space forms not seen of any other eye, and all your words ended in sighs betokening some mystery. Then your friends asked you, "What is the matter with you, my dear friend? What do you see?" And, wishing to describe the inner pictures in all their vivid colors, with their lights and their shades, you in vain struggled to find words with which to express yourself. But you felt as if you must gather up all the events that had happened, wonderful, splendid, terrible, jocose, and awful, in the very first word, so that the whole might be revealed by a single electric discharge, so to speak. Yet every word and all that partook of the nature of communication by intelligible sounds seemed to be colorless, cold, and dead. Then you try and try again, and stutter and stammer, whilst your friends' prosy questions strike like icy winds upon your heart's hot fire until they extinguish it. But if, like a bold painter, you had first sketched in a few audacious strokes the outline of the picture you had in your soul, you would then easily have been able to deepen and intensify the colors one after the other, until the varied throng of living figures carried your friends away, and they, like you, saw themselves in the midst of the scene that had proceeded out of your own soul.

Strictly speaking, indulgent reader, I must indeed confess to you, nobody has asked me for the history of young Nathaniel; but you are very well aware that I belong to that remarkable class of authors who, when they are bearing anything about in their minds in the manner I have just described, feel as if everybody who comes near them, and also the whole world to boot, were asking, "Oh! what is it? Oh! do tell us, my good sir?" Hence I was most powerfully impelled to narrate to you Nathaniel's ominous life. My soul was full of the elements of wonder and extraordinary peculiarity in it; but, for this very reason, and because it was necessary in the very beginning to dispose you, indulgent reader, to bear with what is fantastic — and that is not a little thing I racked my brain to find a way of commencing the story in a significant and original manner, calculated to arrest your attention. To begin with "Once upon a time," the best beginning for a story, seemed to me too tame; with "In the small country town S—— lived," rather better, at any rate allowing plenty of room to work up to the climax; or to plunge at once *in medias res,* "'Go to the devil!' cried the student Nathaniel, his eyes blazing wildly with rage and fear, when the weather-glass hawker Giuseppe Coppola" — well, that is what I really had written, when I thought I detected something of the ridiculous in Nathaniel's wild glance; and the history is anything but laughable. I could not find any words which seemed fitted to reflect in even the feeblest degree the brightness of the colors of my mental vision. I determined not to begin at all. So I pray you, gracious reader, accept the three letters which my friend Lothair has been so kind as to communicate to me as the outline of the picture, into which I will endeavor to introduce more and more color as I proceed with my narrative. Perhaps, like a good portrait-painter, I may succeed in depicting more than one figure in such wise that you will recognize it as a good likeness without being acquainted with the original, and feel as if you had very often seen the original with your own bodily eyes. Perhaps, too, you will then believe that nothing is more wonderful, nothing more fantastic than real life, and that all that a writer can do is to present it as a dark reflection from a dim cut mirror.

In order to make the very commencement more intelligible, it is necessary to add to the letters that, soon after the death of Nathaniel's father, Clara and Lothair, the children of a distant relative, who had likewise died, leaving them orphans, were taken by Nathaniel's mother into her own house. Clara and Nathaniel conceived a warm affection for each other, against which not the slightest objection in the world could be urged. When therefore Nathaniel left home to prosecute his studies in G——, they were betrothed. It is from G—— that his last letter is written, where he is attending the lectures of Spalanzani, the distinguished Professor of Physics.

I might now proceed comfortably with my narration, did not at this moment Clara's image rise up so vividly before my eyes that I cannot turn them away from it, just as I never could when she looked upon me and smiled so sweetly. Nowhere would she have passed for beautiful that was the unanimous opinion of all who professed to have any technical knowledge of beauty. But whilst architects praised the pure proportions of her figure and form, painters averred that her neck, shoulders, and bosom were almost too chastely modeled, and yet, on the other hand, one and all were in love with her glorious Magdalene hair, and talked a good deal of nonsense about Battoni-like* coloring. One of them, a veritable romanticist, strangely enough likened her eyes to a lake by Ruisdael,† in which is reflected the pure azure of the cloudless sky, the beauty of woods and flowers, and all the bright and varied life of a living landscape. Poets and musicians went still further and said, "What's all this talk about seas and reflections? How can we look upon the girl without feeling that wonderful heavenly songs and melodies beam upon us from her eyes, penetrating deep down into our hearts, till all becomes awake and throbbing with emotion? And if we cannot sing anything at all passable then, why, we are not worth much; and this we can also plainly read in the rare smile which flits around her lips when we have the hardihood to squeak out something in her presence which we pretend to call singing, in spite of the fact that it is nothing more than a few single notes confusedly linked together." And it really was so. Clara had the powerful fancy of a bright, innocent, unaffected child, a woman's deep and sympathetic heart, and an understanding clear, sharp, and discriminating. Dreamers and visionaries had but a bad time of it with her; for without saying very much — she was not by nature of a talkative disposition — she plainly asked, by her calm steady look, and rare ironical smile, "How can you imagine, my dear friends, that I can take these fleeting shadowy images for true living and breathing forms?" For this reason many found fault with her as being cold, prosaic, and devoid of feeling; others, however, who had reached a clearer and deeper conception of life, were extremely fond of the intelligent, childlike, large-hearted girl. But none had such an affection for her as Nathaniel, who was a zealous and cheerful cultivator of the fields of science and art. Clara clung to her lover with all her heart; the first clouds she encountered in life were when he had to separate from her. With what delight did she fly into his arms when, as he had promised in his last letter to Lothair, he really came back to his native town and entered his mother's room! And as Nathaniel had foreseen, the moment he saw Clara again he no longer thought about either the advocate Coppelius or her sensible letter; his ill-humor had quite disappeared.

Nevertheless Nathaniel was right when he told his friend Lothair

---

* Pompeo Girolamo Batoni, an Italian painter of the eighteenth century, whose works were at one time greatly overestimated.

† Jakob Ruysdael (c. 1625-1682), a painter of Haarlem, in Holland. His favorite subjects were remote farms, lonely stagnant water, deep-shaded woods with marshy paths, the seacoast — subjects of a dark melancholy kind. His sea-pieces are greatly admired.

that the repulsive vendor of weather-glasses, Coppola, had exercised a fatal and disturbing influence upon his life. It was quite patent to all; for even during the first Few days he showed that he was completely and entirely changed. He gave himself up to gloomy reveries, and moreover acted so strangely; they had never observed anything at all like it in him before. Everything, even his own life, was to him but dreams and presentiments. His constant theme was that every man who delusively imagined himself to be free was merely the plaything of the cruel sport of mysterious powers, and it was vain for man to resist them; he must humbly submit to whatever destiny had decreed for him. He went so far as to maintain that it was foolish to believe that a man could do anything in art or science of his own accord; for the inspiration in which alone any true artistic work could be done did not proceed from the spirit within outwards, but was the result of the operation directed inwards of some Higher Principle existing without and beyond ourselves.

This mystic extravagance was in the highest degree repugnant to Clara's clear intelligent mind, but it seemed vain to enter upon any attempt at refutation. Yet when Nathaniel went on to prove that Coppelius was the Evil Principle which had entered into him and taken possession of him at the time he was listening behind the curtain, and that this hateful demon would in some terrible way ruin their happiness, then Clara grew grave and said, "Yes, Nathaniel. You are right; Coppelius is an Evil Principle; he can do dreadful things, as bad as could a Satanic power which should assume a living physical form, but only — only if you do not banish him from your mind and thoughts. So long as you believe in him he exists and is at work; your belief in him is his only power." Whereupon Nathaniel, quite angry because Clara would only grant the existence of the demon in his own mind, began to dilate at large upon the whole mystic doctrine of devils and awful powers, but Clara abruptly broke off the theme by making, to Nathaniel's very great disgust, some quite commonplace remark. Such deep mysteries are sealed books to cold, unsusceptible characters, he thought, without being clearly conscious to himself that he counted Clara amongst these inferior natures, and accordingly he did not remit his efforts to initiate her into these mysteries. In the morning, when she was helping to prepare breakfast, he would take his stand beside her, and read all sorts of mystic books to her, until she begged him — "But, my dear Nathaniel, I shall have to scold you as the Evil Principle which exercises a fatal influence upon my coffee. For if I do as you wish, and let things go their own way, and look into your eyes whilst you read, the coffee will all boil over into the fire, and you will none of you get any breakfast." Then Nathaniel hastily banged the book to and ran away in great displeasure to his own room.

Formerly he had possessed a peculiar talent for writing pleasing, sparkling tales, which Clara took the greatest delight in listening to; but now his productions were gloomy, unintelligible, and wanting in form, so that, although Clara out of forbearance towards him did not say so, he nevertheless felt how very little interest she took in them. There was nothing that Clara disliked so much as what was tedious; at such times her intellectual sleepiness was not to be overcome; it was betrayed both in her glances and in her words. Nathaniel's effusions were, in truth, exceedingly tedious. His ill-humor at Clara's cold prosaic temperament continued to increase; Clara could not conceal her distaste of his dark, gloomy, wearying mysticism; and thus both began to be more and more estranged from each other without exactly being aware of it themselves. The image of the ugly Coppelius had, as Nathaniel was obliged to confess to himself, faded considerably in bis fancy, and it often cost him great pains to present him in vivid colors in his literary efforts, in which he played the part of the ghoul of Destiny. At length it entered into his head to make his dismal presentiment that Coppelius would ruin his happiness the subject of a poem. He made himself and Clara, united by true love, the central figures, but represented a black hand as being from time to time thrust into their life and plucking out a joy that had blossomed for them. At length, as they were standing at the altar, the terrible Coppelius appeared and touched Clara's lovely eyes, which leapt into Nathaniel's own bosom, burning and hissing like bloody sparks. Then Coppelius laid hold upon him, and hurled him into a blazing circle of fire, which spun round with the speed of a whirlwind, and, storming and blustering, dashed away with him. The fearful noise it made was like a furious hurricane lashing the foaming sea-waves until they rise up like black, white-headed giants in the midst of the raging struggle. But through the midst of the savage fury of the tempest he heard Clara's voice calling, "Can you not see me, dear? Coppelius has deceived you; they were not my eyes which burned so in your bosom; they were fiery drops of your own heart's blood. Look at me, I have got my own eyes still." Nathaniel thought, "Yes, that is Clara, and I am hers forever." Then this thought laid a powerful grasp upon the fiery circle so that it stood still, and the riotous turmoil died away rumbling down a dark abyss. Nathaniel looked into Clara's eyes; but it was death whose gaze rested so kindly upon him.

Whilst Nathaniel was writing this work he was very quiet and sober-minded; he filed and polished every line, and as he had chosen to submit himself to the limitations of metre, he did not rest until all was pure and musical. When, however, he had at length finished it and read it aloud to himself he was seized with horror and awful dread, and he screamed, "Whose hideous voice is this?" But he soon came to see in it again nothing beyond a very successful poem, and he confidently believed it would enkindle Clara's cold temperament, though to what end she should be thus aroused was not quite clear to his own mind, nor yet what would be the real purpose served by tormenting her with these dreadful pictures, which prophesied a terrible and ruinous end to her affection.

Nathaniel and Clara sat in his mother's little garden. Clara was bright and cheerful, since for three entire days her lover, who had been busy writing his poem, had not teased her with his dreams or forebodings Nathaniel, too, spoke in a gay and vivacious way of things of merry import, as he formerly used to do, so that Clara said, "Ah! now I have you again. We have driven away that ugly Coppelius, you see." Then it suddenly occurred to him that he had got the poem in his pocket which he wished to read to her. He at once took out the manuscript and began to read. Clara, anticipating something tedious as usual, prepared to submit to the infliction, and calmly resumed her knitting. But as the somber clouds rose up darker and darker she let her knitting fall on her lap and sat with her eyes fixed in a set stare upon Nathaniel's face.

He was quite carried away by his own work, the fire of enthusiasm colored his cheeks a deep red, and tears started from his eyes. At length he concluded, groaning and showing great lassitude; grasping Clara's hand, he sighed as if he were being utterly melted in inconsolable grief, "Oh! Clara! Clara!" She drew him softly to her heart and said in a low but very grave and impressive tone, "Nathaniel, my darling Nathaniel, throw that foolish, senseless, stupid thing into the fire." Then Nathaniel leapt indignantly to his feet, crying, as he pushed Clara from him, "You damned lifeless automaton!" and rushed away. Clara was cut to the heart, and wept bitterly. "Oh! he has never loved me, for he does not understand me," she sobbed.

Lothair entered the arbor. Clara was obliged to tell him all that had taken place. He was passionately fond of his sister; and every word of her complaint fell like a spark upon his heart, so that the displeasure which he had long entertained against his dreamy friend Nathaniel was kindled into furious anger. He hastened to find Nathaniel, and upbraided him in harsh words for his irrational behavior towards his beloved sister. The fiery Nathaniel answered him in the same style. "A fantastic, crack-brained fool," was retaliated with, "A miserable, common, everyday sort of fellow." A meeting was the inevitable consequence. They agreed to meet on the following morning behind the garden-wall, and fight, according to the custom of the students of the place, with sharp rapiers. They went about silent and gloomy; Clara had both heard and seen the violent quarrel, and also observed the fencing master bring the rapiers in the dusk of the evening. She had a presentiment of what was to happen. They both appeared at the appointed place wrapped up in the same gloomy silence, and threw off their coats. Their eyes flaming with the bloodthirsty light of pugnacity, they were about to begin their contest when Clara burst through the garden door. Sobbing, she screamed, "You savage, terrible men! Cut me down before you attack each other; for how can I live when my lover has slain my brother, or my brother slain my lover?" Lothair let his weapon fall and gazed silently upon the ground, whilst Nathaniel's heart was rent with sorrow, and all the affection which he had felt for his lovely Clara in the happiest days of her golden youth was awakened within him. His murderous weapon, too, fell from his hand; he threw himself at Clara's feet. "Oh! can you ever forgive me, my only, my dearly loved Clara? Can you, my dear brother Lothair, also forgive me?" Lothair was touched by his friend's great distress; the three young people embraced each other amidst endless tears, and swore never again to break their bond of love and fidelity.

Nathaniel felt as if a heavy burden that had been weighing him down to the earth was now rolled from off him, nay, as if by offering resistance to the dark power which had possessed him, he had rescued his own self from the ruin which had threatened him. Three happy days he now spent amidst the loved ones, and then returned to G——, where he had still a year to stay before settling down in his native town for life.

Everything having reference to Coppelius had been concealed from the mother, for they knew she could not think of him without horror, since she as well as Nathaniel believed him to be guilty of causing her husband's death.

When Nathaniel came to the house where he lived he was greatly astonished to find it burned down to the ground, so that nothing but the bare outer walls were left standing amidst a heap of ruins. Although the fire had broken out in the laboratory of the chemist who lived on the ground-floor, and had therefore spread upwards, some of Nathaniel's bold, active friends had succeeded in time in forcing a way into his room in the upper storey and saving his books and manuscripts and instruments. They had carried them all uninjured into another house, where they engaged a room for him; this he now at once took possession of. That he lived opposite Professor Spalanzani did not strike him particularly, nor did it occur to him as anything more singular that he could, as he observed, by looking out of his window, see straight into the room where Olimpia often sat alone. Her figure he could plainly distinguish, although her features were uncertain and confused. It did at length occur to him, however, that she remained for hours together in the same position in which he had first discovered her through the glass door, sitting at a little table without any occupation whatever, and it was evident that she was constantly gazing across in his direction. He could not but confess to himself that he had never seen a finer figure. However, with Clara mistress of his heart, he remained perfectly unaffected by Olimpia's stiffness and apathy; and it was only occasionally that he sent a fugitive glance over his compendium across to her — that was all.

He was writing to Clara; a light tap came at the door. At his summons to "Come in," Coppola's repulsive face appeared peeping in. Nathaniel felt his heart beat with trepidation; but, recollecting what Spalanzani had told him about his fellow-countryman Coppola, and what he had himself so faithfully promised his beloved in respect to the Sandman Coppelius, he was ashamed at himself for this childish fear of specters. Accordingly, he controlled himself with an effort, and said, as quietly and as calmly as he possibly could, "I don't want to buy any weather-glasses, my good friend; you had better go elsewhere." Then Coppola came right into the room, and said in a hoarse voice, screwing up his wide mouth into a hideous smile, whilst his little eyes flashed keenly from beneath his long grey eyelashes, "What! Nee weather-gless? Nee weather-gless? 've got foine oyes as well — foine oyes!" Affrighted, Nathaniel cried, "You stupid man, how can you have eyes? — eyes — eyes?" But Coppola, laying aside his weather-glasses, thrust his hands into his big coat-pockets and brought out several spy-glasses and spectacles, and put them on the table. "Theer! Theer! Spect'cles! Spect'cles to put 'n nose! Them's my oyes — foine oyes." And he continued to produce more and more spectacles from his pockets until the table began to gleam and flash all over. Thousands of eyes were looking and blinking convulsively, and staring up at Nathaniel; he could not avert his gaze from the table. Coppola went on heaping up his spectacles, whilst wilder and ever wilder burning flashes crossed through and through each other and darted their blood-red rays into Nathaniel's breast. Quite overcome, and frantic with terror, he shouted, "Stop! stop! you terrible man!" and he seized Coppola by the arm, which he had again thrust into his pocket in order to bring out still more spectacles, although the whole table was covered all over with them. With a harsh disagreeable laugh Coppola gently freed himself; and with the words "So! went none! Well, here foine gless!" he swept all his spectacles together, and put them back into his coat-pockets, whilst from a breast pocket he produced a great number of larger and smaller perspectives. As soon as the spectacles were gone Nathaniel recovered his equanimity again; and, bending his thoughts upon Clara, he clearly discerned that the gruesome incubus had proceeded only from himself, as also that Coppola was a right honest mechanician and optician, and far from being Coppelius's dreaded double and ghost. And then, besides, none of the glasses which Coppola now placed on the table had anything at all singular about them, at least nothing so weird as the spectacles; so, in order to square accounts with himself, Nathaniel now really determined to buy something of the man. He took up a small, very beautifully cut pocket perspective, and by way of proving it looked through the window. Never before in his life had he had a glass in his hands that brought out things so clearly and sharply and distinctly. Involuntarily he directed the glass upon Spalanzani's room; Olimpia sat at the little table as usual, her arms laid upon it and her hands folded. Now he saw for the first time the regular and exquisite beauty of her features. The eyes, however, seemed to him to have a singular look of fixity and lifelessness. But as he continued to look closer and more carefully through the glass he fancied a light like humid moonbeams came into them. It seemed as if their power of vision was now being enkindled; their glances shone with ever-increasing vivacity. Nathaniel remained standing at the window as if glued to the spot by a wizard's spell, his gaze rivetted unchangeably upon the divinely beautiful Olimpia A coughing and shuffling of the feet awakened him out of his enchaining dream, as it were. Coppola stood behind him, "Tre zechini" (three ducats). Nathaniel had completely forgotten the optician; he hastily paid the sum demanded. "Ain't 't? Foine gless? foine gless?" asked Coppola in his harsh unpleasant voice, smiling sardonically. "Yes, yes, yes," rejoined Nathaniel impatiently; "adieu, my good friend." But Coppola did not leave the room without casting many peculiar side-glances upon Nathaniel; and the young student heard him laughing loudly on the stairs. "Ah well!" thought he, "he's laughing at me because I've paid him too much for this little perspective — because I've given him too much money — that's it." As he softly murmured these words he fancied he detected a gasping sigh as of a dying man stealing awfully through the room; his heart stopped beating with fear. But to be sure he had heaved a deep sigh himself; it was quite plain. "Clara is quite right," said he to himself, "in holding me to be an incurable ghost-seer; and yet it's very ridiculous – aye, more than ridiculous, that the stupid thought of having paid Coppola too much for his glass should cause me this strange anxiety; I can't see any reason for it."

Now he sat down to finish his letter to Clara; but a glance through the window showed him Olimpia still in her former posture. Urged by an irresistible impulse he jumped up and seized Coppola's perspective; nor could he tear himself away from the fascinating Olimpia until his friend and brother Sigmund called for him to go to Professor Spalanzani's lecture. The curtains before the door of the all-important room were closely drawn, so that he could not see Olimpia Nor could he even see her from his own room during the two following days, notwithstanding that he scarcely ever left his window, and maintained a scarce interrupted watch through Coppola's perspective upon her room. On the third day curtains even were drawn across the window. Plunged into the depths of despair, – goaded by longing and ardent desire, he hurried outside the walls of the town. Olimpia's image hovered about his path in the air and stepped forth out of the bushes, and peeped up at him with large and lustrous eyes from the bright surface of the brook. Clara's image was completely faded from his mind; he had no thoughts except for Olimpia He uttered his love-plaints aloud and in a lachrymose tone, "Oh! my glorious, noble star of love, have you only risen to vanish again, and leave me in the darkness and hopelessness of night?"

Returning home, he became aware that there was a good deal of noisy bustle going on in Spalanzani's house. All the doors stood wide open; men were taking in all kinds of gear and furniture; the windows of the first floor were all lifted off their hinges; busy maid-servants with immense hair-brooms were driving backwards and forwards dusting and sweeping, whilst within could be heard the knocking and hammering of carpenters and upholsterers. Utterly astonished, Nathaniel stood still in the street; then Sigmund joined him, laughing, and said, "Well, what do you say to our old Spalanzani?" Nathaniel assured him that he could not say anything, since he knew not what it all meant; to his great astonishment, he could hear, however, that they were turning the quiet gloomy house almost inside out with their dusting and cleaning and making of alterations. Then he learned from Sigmund that Spalanzani intended giving a great concert and ball on the following day, and that half the university was invited. It was generally reported that Spalanzani was going to let his daughter Olimpia, whom he had so long so jealously guarded from every eye, make her first appearance.

Nathaniel received an invitation. At the appointed hour, when the carriages were rolling up and the lights were gleaming brightly in the decorated halls, he went across to the Professor's, his heart beating high with expectation. The company was both numerous and brilliant. Olimpia was richly and tastefully dressed. One could not but admire her figure and the regular beauty of her features. The striking inward curve of her back, as well as the wasplike smallness of her waist, appeared to be the result of too-tight lacing. There was something stiff and measured in her gait and bearing that made an unfavorable impression upon many; it was ascribed to the constraint imposed upon her by the company. The concert began. Olimpia played on the piano with great skill; and sang as skillfully an *aria di bravura*, in a voice which was, if anything, almost too sharp, but clear as glass bells. Nathaniel was transported with delight; he stood in the background farthest from her, and owing to the blinding lights could not quite distinguish her features. So, without being observed, he took Coppola's glass out of his pocket, and directed it upon the beautiful Olimpia. Oh! then he perceived how her yearning eyes sought him, how every note only reached its full purity in the loving glance which penetrated to and inflamed his heart. Her artificial *roulades* seemed to him to be the exultant cry towards heaven of the soul refined by love; and when at last, after the *cadenza*, the long trill rang shrilly and loudly through the hall, he felt as if he were suddenly grasped by burning arms and could no longer control himself, — he could not help shouting aloud in his mingled pain and delight, "Olimpia!" All eyes were turned upon him; many people laughed. The face of the cathedral organist wore a still more gloomy look than it had done before, but all he said was, "Very well!"

The concert came to an end, and the ball began. Oh! to dance with her — with her — that was now the aim of all Nathaniel's wishes, of all his desires. But how should he have courage to request her, the queen of the ball, to grant him the honor of a dance? And yet he couldn't tell how it came about, just as the dance began, he found himself standing close beside her, nobody having as yet asked her to be his partner; so, with some difficulty stammering out a few words, he grasped her hand. It was cold as ice; he shook with an awful, frosty shiver. But, fixing his eyes upon her face, he saw that her glance was beaming upon him with love and longing, and at the same moment he thought that the pulse began to beat in her cold hand, and the warm life-blood to course through her veins. And passion burned more intensely in his own heart also, he threw his arm round her beautiful waist and whirled her round the hall. He had always thought that he kept good and accurate time in dancing, but from the perfectly rhythmical evenness with which Olimpia danced, and which frequently put him quite out, he perceived how very faulty his own time really was. Notwithstanding, he would not dance with any other lady; and everybody else who approached Olimpia to call upon her for a dance, he would have liked to kill on the spot. This, however, only happened twice; to his astonishment Olimpia remained after this without a partner, and he failed not on each occasion to take her out again. If Nathaniel had been able to see anything else except the beautiful Olimpia, there would inevitably have been a good deal of unpleasant quarreling and strife; for it was evident that Olimpia was the object of the smothered laughter only with difficulty suppressed, which was heard in various corners amongst the young people; and they followed her with very curious looks, but nobody knew for what reason. Nathaniel, excited by dancing and the plentiful supply of wine he had consumed, had laid aside the shyness which at other times characterized him. He sat beside Olimpia, her hand in his own, and declared his love enthusiastically and passionately in words which neither of them understood, neither he nor Olimpia. And yet she perhaps did, for she sat with her eyes fixed unchangeably upon his, sighing repeatedly, "Ach! Ach! Ach!" Upon this Nathaniel would answer, "Oh, you glorious heavenly lady! You ray from the promised paradise of love! Oh! what a profound soul you have! my whole being is mirrored in it!" and a good deal more in the same strain. But Olimpia only continued to sigh "Ach! Ach!" again and again.

Professor Spalanzani passed by the two happy lovers once or twice, and smiled with a look of peculiar satisfaction. All at once it seemed to Nathaniel, albeit he was far away in a different world, as if it were growing perceptibly darker down below at Professor Spalanzani's. He looked about him, and to his very great alarm became aware that there were only two lights left burning in the hall, and they were on the point of going out. The music and dancing had long ago ceased. "We must part — part!" he cried, wildly and despairingly; he kissed Olimpia's hand; he bent down to her mouth, but ice-cold lips met his burning ones. As he touched her cold hand, he felt his heart thrilled with awe; the legend of "The Dead Bride"* shot

---

* Phlegon, the freedman of Hadrian, relates that a young maiden, Philemium, the daughter of Philostratus and Charitas, became deeply enamored of a young man, named Machates, a guest in the house of her father. This did not meet with the approbation of her parents, and they turned Machates away. The young maiden took this so much to heart that she pined away and died. Some time afterwards Machates returned to his old lodgings, when he was visited at night by his beloved, who came from the grave to see him again. The story

suddenly through his mind. But Olimpia had drawn him closer to her, and the kiss appeared to warm her lips into vitality. Professor Spalanzani strode slowly through the empty apartment, his footsteps giving a hollow echo; and his figure had, as the flickering shadows played about him, a ghostly, awful appearance. "Do you love me? Do you love me, Olimpia? Only one little word — Do you love me?" whispered Nathaniel, but she only sighed, "Ach! Ach!" as she rose to her feet. "Yes, you are my lovely, glorious star of love," said Nathaniel, "and will shine forever, purifying and ennobling my heart." "Ach! Ach!" replied Olimpia, as she moved along. Nathaniel followed her; they stood before the Professor. "You have had an extraordinarily animated conversation with my daughter," said he, smiling; "well, well, my dear Mr. Nathaniel, if you find pleasure in talking to the stupid girl, I am sure I shall be glad for you to come and do so." Nathaniel took his leave, his heart singing and leaping in a perfect delirium of happiness.

During the next few days Spalanzani's ball was the general topic of conversation. Although the Professor had done everything to make the thing a splendid success, yet certain gay spirits related more than one thing that had occurred which was quite irregular and out of order. They were especially keen in pulling Olimpia to pieces for her taciturnity and rigid stiffness; in spite of her beautiful form they alleged that she was hopelessly stupid, and in this fact they discerned the reason why Spalanzani had so long kept her concealed from publicity. Nathaniel heard all this with inward wrath, but nevertheless he held his tongue; for, thought he, would it indeed be worth while to prove to these fellows that it is their own stupidity which prevents them from appreciating Olimpia's profound and brilliant parts? One day Sigmund said to him, "Pray, brother, have the kindness to tell me how you, a sensible fellow, came to lose your head over that Miss Wax-face — that wooden doll across there?" Nathaniel was about to fly into a rage, but he recollected himself and replied, "Tell me, Sigmund, how came it that Olimpia's divine charms could escape your eye, so keenly alive as it always is to beauty, and your acute perception as well? But Heaven be thanked for it, otherwise I should have had you for a rival, and then the blood of one of us would have had to be spilled." Sigmund, perceiving how matters stood with his friend, skillfully interposed and said, after remarking that all argument with one in love about the object of his affections was out of place, "Yet it's very strange that several of

may be read in Heywood's (Thos.) "Hierarchie of Blessed Angels," Book vii, p. 479 (London, 1637). Goethe has made this story the foundation of his beautiful poem *Die Braut von Korinth*, with which form of it Hoffmann was most likely familiar.

us have formed pretty much the same opinion about Olimpia We think she is — you won't take it ill, brother? — that she is singularly statuesque and soulless. Her figure is regular, and so are her features, that can't be gainsaid; and if her eyes were not so utterly devoid of life, I may say, of the power of vision, she might pass for a beauty. She is strangely measured in her movements, they all seem as if they were dependent upon some wound-up clock-work. Her playing and singing has the disagreeably perfect, but insensitive time of a singing machine. and her dancing is the same. We felt quite afraid of this Olimpia, and did not like to have anything to do with her; she seemed to us to be only acting *like* a living creature, and as if there was some secret at the bottom of it all." Nathaniel did not give way to the bitter feelings which threatened to master him at these words of Sigmund's; he fought down and got the better of his displeasure, and merely said, very earnestly, "You cold prosaic fellows may very well be afraid of her. It is only to its like that the poetically organized spirit unfolds itself. Upon me alone did her loving glances fall, and through my mind and thoughts alone did they radiate; and only in her love can I find my own self again. Perhaps, however, she doesn't do quite right not to jabber a lot of nonsense and stupid talk like other shallow people. It is true, she speaks but few words; but the few words she does speak are genuine hieroglyphs of the inner world of Love and of the higher cognition of the intellectual life revealed in the intuition of the Eternal beyond the grave. But you have no understanding for all these things, and I am only wasting words." "God be with you, brother," said Sigmund very gently, almost sadly, "but it seems to me that you are in a very bad way. You may rely upon me, if all — No, I can't say anymore." It all at once dawned upon Nathaniel that his cold prosaic friend Sigmund really and sincerely wished him well, and so he warmly shook his proffered hand.

Nathaniel had completely forgotten that there was a Clara in the world, whom he had once loved — and his mother and Lothair. They had all vanished from his mind; he lived for Olimpia alone. He sat beside her every day for hours together, rhapsodizing about his love and sympathy enkindled into life, and about psychic elective affinity* — all of which Olimpia listened to with great reverence. He fished up from the very bottom of his desk all the things that he had ever written — poems, fancy sketches, visions, romances, tales, and the heap was increased daily with all kinds of aimless sonnets, stanzas, canzonets. All these he read to Olimpia hour after hour

---

* This phrase (*Die Wahlverwandschaft* in German) has been made celebrated as the title of one of Goethe's works.

without growing tired; but then he had never had such an exemplary listener. She neither embroidered, nor knitted; she did not look out of the window, or feed a bird, or play with a little pet dog or a favorite cat, neither did she twist a piece of paper or anything of that kind round her finger; she did not forcibly convert a yawn into a low affected cough — in short, she sat hour after hour with her eyes bent unchangeably upon her lover's face, without moving or altering her position, and her gaze grew more ardent and more ardent still. And it was only when at last Nathaniel rose and kissed her lips or her hand that she said, "Ach! Ach!" and then "Good-night, dear." Arrived in his own room, Nathaniel would break out with, "Oh! what a brilliant — what a profound mind! Only you — you alone understand me." And his heart trembled with rapture when he reflected upon the wondrous harmony which daily revealed itself between his own and his Olimpia's character; for he fancied that she had expressed in respect to his works and his poetic genius the identical sentiments which he himself cherished deep down in his own heart in respect to the same, and even as if it was his own heart's voice speaking to him. And it must indeed have been so; for Olimpia never uttered any other words than those already mentioned. And when Nathaniel himself in his clear and sober moments, as, for instance, directly after waking in a morning, thought about her utter passivity and taciturnity, he only said, "What are words — but words? The glance of her heavenly eyes says more than any tongue of earth And how can, anyway, a child of heaven accustom herself to the narrow circle which the exigencies of a wretched mundane life demand?"

Professor Spalanzani appeared to be greatly pleased at the intimacy that had sprung up between his daughter Olimpia and Nathaniel, and showed the young man many unmistakable proofs of his good feeling towards him; and when Nathaniel ventured at length to hint very delicately at an alliance with Olimpia, the Professor smiled all over his face at once, and said he should allow his daughter to make a perfectly free choice. Encouraged by these words, and with the fire of desire burning in his heart, Nathaniel resolved the very next day to implore Olimpia to tell him frankly, in plain words, what he had long read in her sweet loving glances, — that she would be his forever. He looked for the ring which his mother had given him at parting; he would present it to Olimpia as a symbol of his devotion, and of the happy life he was to lead with her from that time onwards. Whilst looking for it he came across his letters from Clara and Lothair; he threw them carelessly aside, found the ring, put it in his pocket, and ran across to Olimpia

Whilst still on the stairs, in the entrance-passage, he heard an extraordinary hubbub; the noise seemed to proceed from Spalanzani's study. There was a stamping — a rattling — pushing — knocking against the door, with curses and oaths intermingled. "Leave hold — leave hold — you monster — you rascal — slaked your life and honor upon it? — Ha! ha! ha! ha! — That was not our wager — I, I made the eyes — I the clock-work. — Go to the devil with your clock-work — you damned dog of a watch-maker — be off — Satan — stop — you paltry turner — you infernal beast! — stop — begone — let me go." The voices which were thus making all this racket and rumpus were those of Spalanzani and the fearsome Coppelius. Nathaniel rushed in, impelled by some nameless dread. The Professor was grasping a female figure by the shoulders, the Italian Coppola held her by the feet; and they were pulling and dragging each other backwards and forwards, fighting furiously to get possession of her. Nathaniel recoiled with horror on recognizing that the figure was Olimpia Boiling with rage, he was about to tear his beloved from the grasp of the madmen, when Coppola by an extraordinary exertion of strength twisted the figure out of the Professor's hands and gave him such a terrible blow with her, that he reeled backwards and fell over the table all amongst the phials and retorts, the bottles and glass cylinders, which covered it: all these things were smashed into a thousand pieces. But Coppola threw the figure across his shoulder, and, laughing shrilly and horribly, ran hastily down the stairs, the figure's ugly feet hanging down and banging and rattling like wood against the steps. Nathaniel was stupefied, — he had seen only too distinctly that in Olimpia's pallid waxed face there were no eyes, merely black holes in their stead; she was an inanimate puppet. Spalanzani was rolling on the floor; the pieces of glass had cut his head and breast and arm; the blood was escaping from him in streams. But he gathered his strength together by an effort.

"After him — after him! What do you stand staring there for? Coppelius — Coppelius — he's stolen my best automaton — at which I've worked for twenty years — staked my life upon it — the clockwork — speech — movement — mine — your eyes — stolen your eyes — damn him — curse him — after him — fetch me back Olimpia — there are the eyes." And now Nathaniel saw a pair of bloody eyes lying on the floor staring at him; Spalanzani seized them with his uninjured hand and threw them at him, so that they hit his breast. Then madness dug her burning talons into him and swept down into his heart, rending his mind and thoughts to shreds.

"Aha! aha! aha! Fire-wheel — fire-wheel! Spin round, fire-wheel! merrily, merrily! Aha! wooden doll! spin round, pretty wooden doll!"

and he threw himself upon the Professor, clutching him fast by the throat. He would certainly have strangled him had not several people, attracted by the noise, rushed in and torn away the madman; and so they saved the Professor, whose wounds were immediately dressed. Sigmund, with all his strength, was not able to subdue the frantic lunatic, who continued to scream in a dreadful way, "Spin round, wooden doll!" and to strike out right and left with his doubled fists. At length the united strength of several succeeded in overpowering him by throwing him on the floor and binding him. His cries passed into a brutish bellow that was awful to hear; and thus raging with the harrowing violence of madness, he was taken away to the madhouse.

Before continuing my narration of what happened further to the unfortunate Nathaniel, I will tell you, indulgent reader, in case you take any interest in that skillful mechanician and fabricator of automata, Spalanzani, that he recovered completely from his wounds. He had, however, to leave the university, for Nathaniel's fate had created a great sensation; and the opinion vas pretty generally expressed that it was an imposture altogether unpardonable to have smuggled a wooden puppet instead of a living person into intelligent tea-circles, — for Olimpia had been present at several with success Lawyers called it a cunning piece of knavery, and all the harder to punish since it was directed against the public; and it had been so craftily contrived that it had escaped unobserved by all except a few preternaturally acute students, although everybody was very wise how and remembered to have thought of several facts which occurred to them as suspicious. But these latter could not succeed in making out any sort of a consistent tale. For was it, for instance, a thing likely to occur to anyone as suspicious that, according to the declaration of an elegant beau of these tea-parties, Olimpia had, contrary to all good manners, sneezed oftener than she had yawned? The former must have been, in the opinion of this elegant gentleman, the winding up of the concealed clock-work; it had always been accompanied by an observable creaking, and so on. The Professor of Poetry and Eloquence took a pinch of snuff, and, slapping the lid to and clearing his throat, said solemnly, "My most honorable ladies and gentlemen, don't you see then where the rub is? The whole thing is an allegory, a continuous metaphor. You understand me? *Sapienti sat.*" But several most honorable gentlemen did not rest satisfied with this explanation; the history of this automaton had sunk deeply into their souls, and an absurd mistrust of human figures began to prevail. Several lovers, in order to be fully convinced that they were not paying court to a wooden puppet, required that their mistress should sing and dance a little out of time, should embroider or knit or play with her little pug, &c., when being read to, but above all things else that she should do something more than merely listen — that she should frequently speak in such a way as to really show that her words presupposed as a condition some thinking and feeling. The bonds of love were in many cases drawn closer in consequence, and so of course became more engaging; in other instances they gradually relaxed and fell away. "I cannot really be made responsible for it," was the remark of more than one young gallant. At the tea-gatherings everybody, in order to ward off suspicion, yawned to an incredible extent and never sneezed. Spalanzani was obliged, as has been said, to leave the place in order to escape a criminal charge of having fraudulently imposed an automaton upon human society. Coppola, too, had also disappeared.

When Nathaniel awoke he felt as if he had been oppressed by a terrible nightmare; he opened his eyes and experienced an indescribable sensation of mental comfort, whilst a soft and most beautiful sensation of warmth pervaded his body. He lay on his own bed in his own room at home; Clara was bending over him, and at a little distance stood his mother and Lothair. "At last, at last, O my darling Nathaniel; now we have you again; now you are cured of your grievous illness, now you are mine again." And Clara's words came from the depths of her heart; and she clasped him in her arms. The bright scalding tears streamed from his eyes, he was so overcome with mingled feelings of sorrow and delight; and he gasped forth, "My Clara, my Clara!" Sigmund, who had staunchly stood by his friend in his hour of need, now came into the room. Nathaniel gave him his hand — "My faithful brother, you have not deserted me." Every trace of insanity had left him, and in the tender hands of his mother and his beloved, and his friends, he quickly recovered his strength again. Good fortune had in the meantime visited the house; a niggardly old uncle, from whom they had never expected to get anything, had died, and left Nathaniel's mother not only a considerable fortune, but also a small estate, pleasantly situated not far from the town. There they resolved to go and live, Nathaniel and his mother, and Clara, to whom he was now to be married, and Lothair. Nathaniel was become gentler and more childlike than he had ever been before, and now began really to understand Clara's supremely pure and noble character.

None of them ever reminded him, even in the remotest degree, of the past. But when Sigmund took leave of him, he said, "By heaven, brother! I was in a bad way, but an angel came just at the right moment and led me back upon the path of light. Yes, it was

Clara." Sigmund would not let him speak further, fearing lest the painful recollections of the past might arise too vividly and too intensely in his mind.

The time came for the four happy people to move to their little property. At noon they were going through the streets. After making several purchases they found that the lofty tower of the town-house was throwing its giant shadows across the marketplace. "Come," said Clara, "let us go up to the top once more and have a look at the distant hills." No sooner said than done. Both of them, Nathaniel and Clara, went up the tower; their mother, however, went on with the servant-girl to her new home, and Lothair, not feeling inclined to climb up all the many steps, waited below. There the two lovers stood arm-in-arm on the topmost gallery of the tower, and gazed out into the sweet scented wooded landscape, beyond which the blue hills rose up like a giant's city.

"Oh! do look at that strange little grey bush, it looks as if it were actually walking towards us," said Clara. Mechanically he put his hand into his side pocket; he found Coppola's perspective and looked for the bush; Clara stood in front of the glass. Then a convulsive thrill shot through his pulse and veins; pale as a corpse, he fixed his staring eyes upon her; but soon they began to roll, and a fiery current flashed and sparkled in them, and he yelled fearfully, like a hunted animal. Leaping up high in the air and laughing horribly at the same time, he began to shout, in a piercing voice, "Spin round, wooden doll! Spin round, wooden doll!" With the strength of a giant he laid hold upon Clara and tried to hurl her over, but in an agony of despair she clutched fast hold of the railing that went round the gallery. Lothair heard the madman raging and Clara's scream of terror: a fearful presentiment flashed across his mind. He ran up the steps; the door of the second flight was locked Clara's scream for help rang out more loudly. Mad with rage and fear, he threw himself against the door, which at length gave way. Clara's cries were growing fainter and fainter, — "Help! save me! save me!" and her voice died away in the air. "She is killed — murdered by that madman," shouted Lothair. The door to the gallery was also locked. Despair gave him the strength of a giant; he burst the door off its hinges. Good God! there was Clara in the grasp of the madman Nathaniel, hanging over the gallery in the air; she only held to the iron bar with one hand. Quick as lightning, Lothair seized his sister and pulled her back, at the same time dealing the madman a blow in the face with his doubled fist, which sent him reeling backwards, forcing him to let go his victim.

Lothair ran down with his insensible sister in his arms. She was saved. But Nathaniel ran round and round the gallery, leaping up in the air and shouting, "Spin round, fire-wheel! Spin round, fire-wheel!" The people heard the wild shouting, and a crowd began to gather. In the midst of them towered the advocate Coppelius, like a giant; he had only just arrived in the town, and had gone straight to the marketplace. Some were going up to overpower and take charge of the madman, but Coppelius laughed and said, "Ha! ha! wait a bit; he'll come down of his own accord;" and he stood gazing upwards along with the rest. All at once Nathaniel stopped as if spellbound; he bent down over the railing, and perceived Coppelius. With a piercing scream, "Ha! foine oyes! foine oyes!" he leapt over.

When Nathaniel lay on the stone pavement with a broken head, Coppelius had disappeared in the crush and confusion.

Several years afterwards it was reported that, outside the door of a pretty country house in a remote district, Clara had been seen sitting hand in hand with a pleasant gentleman, whilst two bright boys were playing at her feet. From this it may be concluded that she eventually found that quiet domestic happiness which her cheerful, blithesome character required, and which Nathaniel, with his tempest-tossed soul, could never have been able to give her.

The Terror of the Twins

Algernon Blackwood

A father's curse links twins in a terrible embrace of life and death in Algernon Blackwood's brief, chilling story of double lives.

*T*hat the man's hopes had built upon a son to inherit his name and estates — a single son, that is — was to be expected; but no one could have foreseen the depth and bitterness of his disappointment, the cold, implacable fury, when there arrived instead — twins. For, though the elder legally must inherit, that other ran him so deadly close. A daughter would have been a more reasonable defeat. But twins — ! To miss his dream by so feeble a device — !

The complete frustration of a hope deeply cherished for years may easily result in strange fevers of the soul, but the violence of the father's hatred, existing as it did side by side with a love he could not deny, was something to set psychologists thinking. More than unnatural, it was positively uncanny. Being a man of rigid self-control, however, it operated inwardly, and doubtless along some morbid line of weakness little suspected even by those nearest to him, preying upon his thought to such dreadful extent that finally the mind gave way. The suppressed rage and bitterness deprived him, so the family decided, of his reason, and he spent the last years of his life under restraint. He was possessed naturally of immense forces — of will, feeling, desire; his dynamic value truly tremendous, driving through life like a great engine; and the intensity of this concentrated

and buried hatred was guessed by few. The twins themselves, however, knew it. They divined it, at least, for it operated ceaselessly
against them side by side with the genuine soft love that occasionally
sweetened it, to their great perplexity. They spoke of it only to each
other, though.

"At twenty-one," Edward, the elder, would remark sometimes,
unhappily, "we shall know more." "Too much," Ernest would reply,
with a rush of unreasoning terror the thought never failed to evoke
— in him. "Things father said always happened — in life." And they
paled perceptibly. For the hatred, thus compressed into a veritable
bomb of psychic energy, had found at the last a singular expression
in the cry of the father's distraught mind. On the occasion of their
final visit to the asylum, preceding his death by a few hours only,
very calmly, but with an intensity that drove the words into their
hearts like points of burning metal, he had spoken. In the presence
of the attendant, at the door of the dreadful padded cell, he said it:
"You are not two, but one. I still regard you as one. And at the coming
of age, by h——, you shall find it out!"

The lads perhaps had never fully divined that icy hatred which
lay so well concealed against them, but that this final sentence was
a curse, backed by all the man's terrific force, they quite well realized;
and accordingly, almost unknown to each other, they had come to
dread the day inexpressibly. On the morning of that twenty-first
birthday — their father gone these five years into the Unknown, yet
still sometimes so strangely close to them — they shared the same
biting, inner terror, just as they shared all other emotions of their
life — intimately, without speech.

During the daytime they managed to keep it at a distance; but
when the dusk fell about the old house they knew the stealthy
approach of a kind of panic sense. Their self-respect weakened swiftly
. . . and they persuaded their old friend, and once tutor, the vicar,
to sit up with them till midnight . . . He had humored them to that
extent, willing to forgo his sleep, and at the same time more than a
little interested in their singular belief — that before the day was out,
before midnight struck, that is, the curse of that terrible man would
somehow come into operation against them.

Festivities over and the guests departed, they sat up in the library,
the room usually occupied by their father, and little used since. Mr.
Curtice, a robust man of fifty-five, and a firm believer in spiritual
principalities and powers, dark as well as good, affected (for their
own good) to regard the youths' obsession with a kindly cynicism.
"I do not think it likely for one moment," he said gravely, "that
such a thing would be permitted. All spirits are in the hands of God,

and the violent ones more especially." To which Edward made the extraordinary reply: "Even if father does not come himself he will — send!" And Ernest agreed: "All this time he's been making preparations for this very day. We've both known it for a long time — by odd things that have happened, by our dreams, by nasty little dark hints of various kinds, and by these persistent attacks of terror that come from nowhere, especially of late. Haven't we, Edward?" Edward assenting with a shudder. "Father has been at us of late with renewed violence. Tonight it will be a regular assault upon our lives, or minds, or souls!"

"Strong personalities may possibly leave behind them forces that continue to act," observed Mr. Curtice with caution, while the brothers replied almost in the same breath: "That's exactly what we feel so curiously. Though — nothing has actually happened yet, you know, and it's a good many years now since —"

This was the way the twins spoke of it all. And it was their profound conviction that had touched their old friend's sense of duty. The experiment should justify itself — and cure them.

Meanwhile none of the family knew. Everything was planned secretly.

The library was the quietest room in the house. It had shuttered bow-windows, thick carpets, heavy doors. Books lined the walls, and there was a capacious open fireplace of brick in which the wood logs blazed and roared, for the autumn night was chilly. Round this the three of them were grouped, the clergyman reading aloud from the Book of Job in low tones; Edward and Ernest, in dinner-jackets, occupying deep leather armchairs, listening. They looked exactly what they were — Cambridge "undergrads," their faces pale against their dark hair, and alike as two peas. A shaded lamp behind the clergyman threw the rest of the room into shadow. The reading voice was steady, even monotonous, but something in it betrayed an underlying anxiety, and although the eyes rarely left the printed page, they took in every movement of the young men opposite, and noted every change upon their faces. It was his aim to produce an unexciting atmosphere, yet to miss nothing; if anything did occur to see it from the very beginning. Not to be taken by surprise was his main idea. . . . And thus, upon this falsely peaceful scene, the minutes passed the hour of eleven and slipped rapidly along towards midnight.

The novel element in his account of this distressing and dreadful occurrence seems to be that what happened — happened without the slightest warning or preparation. There was no gradual presentiment of any horror; no strange blast of cold air; no dwindling of heat or light; no shaking of windows or mysterious tapping upon furniture. Without preliminaries it fell with its black trappings of terror upon the scene.

The clergyman had been reading aloud for some considerable time, one or other of the twins — Ernest usually — making occasional remarks, which proved that his sense of dread was disappearing. As the time grew short and nothing happened they grew more at their ease.

Edward, indeed, actually nodded, dozed, and finally fell asleep. It was a few minutes before midnight. Ernest, slightly yawning, was stretching himself in the big chair. "Nothing's going to happen," he said aloud, in a pause. "Your good influence has prevented it." He even laughed now.

"What superstitious asses we've been, sir; haven't we — ?"

Curtice, then, dropping his Bible, looked hard at him under the lamp. For in that second, even while the words sounded, there had come about a most abrupt and dreadful change; and so swiftly that the clergyman, in spite of himself, was taken utterly by surprise and had no time to think. There had swooped down upon the quiet library — so he puts it — an immense hushing silence, so profound that the peace already reigning there seemed clamor by comparison; and out of this enveloping stillness there rose through the space about them a living and abominable Invasion — soft, motionless, terrific. It was as though vast engines, working at full speed and pressure, yet too swift and delicate to be appreciable to any definite sense, had suddenly dropped down upon them — from nowhere. "It made me think," the vicar used to say afterwards, "of the Mauretania machinery compressed into a nutshell, yet losing none of its awful power."

". . . haven't we?" repeated Ernest, still laughing. And Curtice, making no audible reply, heard the true answer in his heart: "Because everything has already happened — even as you feared."

Yet, to the vicar's supreme astonishment, Ernest still noticed — nothing!

"Look," the boy added, "Eddy's sound asleep — sleeping like a pig. Doesn't say much for your reading, you know, sir!" And he laughed again — lightly, even foolishly. But that laughter jarred, for the clergyman understood now that the sleep of the elder twin was either feigned — or unnatural.

And while the easy words fell so lightly from his lips, the monstrous engines worked and pulsed against him and against his sleeping brother, all their huge energy concentrated down into points fine as Suggestion, delicate as Thought. The Invasion affected everything. The very objects in the room altered incredibly, revealing suddenly behind their normal exteriors horrid little hearts of darkness. It was truly amazing, this vile metamorphosis. Books, chairs, pictures, all yielded up their pleasant aspect, and betrayed, as with silent mocking laughter, their inner soul of blackness — their decay. This is how Curtice tries to body forth in words what he actually witnessed. . . . And Ernest, yawning, talking lightly, half foolishly — still noticed nothing!

For all this, as described, came about in something like ten seconds; and with it swept into the clergyman's mind, like a blow, the memory of that sinister phrase used more than once by Edward: "If father doesn't come, he will certainly — send." And Curtice understood that he had done both — both sent and come himself. . . . That violent mind, released from its spell of madness in the body, yet still retaining the old implacable hatred, was now directing the terrible, unseen assault. This silent room, so hushed and still, was charged to the brim. The horror of it, as he said later, "seemed to peel the very skin from my back. . . ." And, while Ernest noticed nothing, Edward slept! . . . The soul of the clergyman, strong with the desire to help or save, yet realizing that he was alone against a Legion, poured out in wordless prayer to his Deity. The clock just then, whirring before it struck, made itself audible.

"By Jove! It's all right, you see!" exclaimed Ernest, his voice oddly fainter and lower than before. "There's midnight — and nothing's happened. Bally nonsense, all of it!" His voice had dwindled curiously in volume. "I'll get the whisky and soda from the hall." His relief was great and his manner showed it. But in him somewhere was a singular change. His voice, manner, gestures, his very tread as he moved over the thick carpet toward the door, all showed it. He seemed less real, less alive, reduced somehow to littleness, the voice without timbre or quality, the appearance of him diminished in some fashion quite ghastly. His presence, if not actually shrivelled, was at least impaired. Ernest had suffered a singular and horrible decrease. . . .

The clock was still whirring before the strike. One heard the chain running up softly. Then the hammer fell upon the first stroke of midnight.

"I'm off," he laughed faintly from the door; "it's all been pure funk — on my part, at least. . . !"

He passed out of sight into the hall. The Power that throbbed so mightily about the room followed him out. Almost at the same moment Edward woke up. But he woke with a tearing and indescribable cry of pain and anguish on his lips: "Oh, oh, oh! But it hurts!

It hurts! I can't hold you; leave me. It's breaking me asunder —"

The clergyman had sprung to his feet, but in the same instant everything had become normal once more — the room as it was before, the horror gone. There was nothing he could do or say, for there was no longer anything to put right, to defend, or to attack. Edward was speaking; his voice, deep and full as it never had been before: "By Jove, how that sleep has refreshed me! I feel twice the chap I was before — twice the chap. I feel quite splendid. Your voice, sir, must have hypnotised me to sleep. . . ." He crossed the room with great vigor. "Where's — er — where's — Ernie, by the bye?" he asked casually, hesitating — almost searching — for the name. And a shadow as of a vanished memory crossed his face and was gone. The tone conveyed the most complete indifference where once the least word or movement of his twin had wakened solicitude, love. "Gone away, I suppose — gone to bed, I mean, of course."

Curtice has never been able to describe the dreadful conviction that overwhelmed him as he stood there staring, his heart in his mouth — the conviction, the positive certainty, that Edward had changed interiorly, had suffered an incredible accession to his existing personality. But he knew it as he watched. His mind, spirit, soul had most wonderfully increased. Something that hitherto the lad had known from the outside only, or by the magic of loving sympathy, had now passed, to be incorporated with his own being. And, being himself, it required no expression. Yet this visible increase was somehow terrible. Curtice shrank back from him. The instinct — he has never grasped the profound psychology of that, nor why it turned his soul dizzy with a kind of nausea — the instinct to strike him where he stood, passed, and a plaintive sound from the hall, stealing softly into the room between them, sent all that was left to him of self-possession into his feet. He turned and ran. Edward followed him — very leisurely.

They found Ernest, or what had been Ernest, crouching behind the table in the hail, weeping foolishly to himself. On his face lay blackness. The mouth was open, the jaw dropped; he dribbled hopelessly; and from the face had passed all signs of intelligence — of spirit.

For a few weeks he lingered on, regaining no sign of spiritual or mental life before the poor body, hopelessly disorganized, released what was left of him, from pure inertia — from complete and utter loss of vitality.

And the horrible thing — so the distressed family thought, at least — was that all those weeks Edward showed an indifference that was singularly brutal and complete. He rarely even went to visit him. I believe, too, it is true that he only once spoke of him by name; and that was when he said — "Ernie? Oh, but Ernie is much better and happier where he is — !"

The Jolly Corner

Henry James

I

Spencer Brydon returns to New York after a thirty-year European tour. He intends to convert his former home on its "Jolly Corner" into apartments, and pursue his acquaintance with Miss Alice Staverton. At fifty-three, Spencer is full of more regrets than he cares to admit; most of all, he wonders what his life would have been like had he stayed in the house on its "Jolly Corner." Spencer does find out; for someone did stay in that house. Someone very much like him .

"*E*veryone asks me what I 'think' of everything," said Spencer Brydon; "and I make answer as I can — begging or dodging the question, putting them off with any nonsense. It wouldn't matter to any of them really," he went on, "for, even were it possible to meet in that stand-and-deliver way so silly a demand on so big a subject, my 'thoughts' would still be almost altogether about something that concerns only myself." He was talking to Miss Staverton, with whom for a couple of months now he had availed himself of every possible occasion to talk; this disposition and this resource, this comfort and support, as the situation in fact presented itself, having promptly enough taken the first place in the considerable array of rather unattenuated surprises attending his so strangely belated return to America. Everything was somehow a surprise; and that might be natural when one had so long and so consistently neglected everything, taken pains to give surprises so much margin for play. He had given them more than thirty years — thirty-three, to be exact; and they now seemed to him to have organized their performance quite on the scale of that license. He had been twenty-three on leaving New York — he was fifty-six today: unless indeed he were to reckon as he had sometimes, since his repatriation, found himself feeling; in which case he would have lived longer than is often allotted to man. It would have taken a century, he repeatedly said to himself, and said also to Alice Staverton, it would have taken a longer absence and a more averted mind than those even of which he had been guilty, to pile up the differences, the newnesses, the queernesses, above all the bignesses, for the better or the worse, that at present assaulted his vision wherever he looked.

The great fact all the while however had been the incalculability; since he *had* supposed himself, from decade to decade, to be allowing, and in the most liberal and intelligent manner, for brilliancy of change. He actually saw that he had allowed for nothing; he missed what he would have been sure of finding, he found what he would never have imagined. Proportions and values were upside-down; the ugly things he had expected, the ugly things of his far away youth, when he had too promptly waked up to a sense of the ugly — these uncanny phenomena placed him rather, as it happened, under the charm; whereas the "swagger" things, the modern, the monstrous, the famous things, those he had more particularly, like thousands of ingenuous inquirers every year, come over to see, were exactly his sources of dismay. They were as so many set traps for displeasure, above all for reaction, of which his restless tread was constantly pressing the spring. It was interesting, doubtless, the whole show, but it would have been too disconcerting hadn't a certain finer truth saved the situation. He had distinctly not, in this steadier light, come over *all* for the monstrosities; he had come, not only in the last analysis but quite on the face of the act, under an impulse with which they had nothing to do. He had come — putting the thing pompously — to look at his "property," which he had thus for a third of a century not been within four thousand miles of; or, expressing it less sordidly, he had yielded to the humor of seeing again his house on the jolly corner, as he usually, and quite fondly, described it — the one in which he had first seen the light, in which various members of his family had lived and had died, in which the holidays of his overschooled boyhood had been passed and the few

social flowers of his chilled adolescence gathered, and which, alienated then for so long a period, had, through the successive deaths
of his two brothers and the termination of old arrangements, come
wholly into his hands. He was the owner of another, not quite so
"good" — the jolly corner having been, from far back, superlatively
extended and consecrated; and the value of the pair represented his
main capital, with an income consisting, in these later years, of their
respective rents which (thanks precisely to their original excellent
type) had never been depressingly low. He could live in "Europe,"
as he had been in the habit of living, on the product of these
flourishing New York leases, and all the better since, that of the
second structure, the mere number in its long row, having within a
twelvemonth fallen in, renovation at a high advance had proved
beautifully possible.

These were items of property indeed, but he had found himself
since his arrival distinguishing more than ever between them. The
house within the street, two bristling blocks westward, was already
in course of reconstruction as a tall mass of flats; he had acceded,
some time before, to overtures for this conversion — in which, now
that it was going forward, it had been not the least of his
astonishments to find himself able, on the spot, and though without
a previous ounce of such experience, to participate with a certain
intelligence, almost with a certain authority. He had lived his life
with his back so turned to such concerns and his face addressed to
those of so different an order that he scarce knew what to make of
this lively stir, in a compartment of his mind never yet penetrated,
of a capacity for business and a sense for construction. These virtues,
so common all round him now, had been dormant in his own
organism — where it might be said of them perhaps that they had
slept the sleep of the just. At present, in the splendid autumn weather
— the autumn at least was a pure boon in the terrible place — he
loafed about his "work" undeterred, secretly agitated; not in the least
"minding" that the whole proposition, as they said, was vulgar and
sordid, and ready to climb ladders, to walk the plank, to handle
materials and look wise about them, to ask questions, in fine, and
challenge explanations and really "go into" figures.

It amused, it verily quite charmed him; and, by the same stroke,
it amused, and even more, Alice Staverton, though perhaps charming
her perceptibly less. She wasn't however going to be better off for it,
as *he* was — and so astonishingly much: nothing was now likely, he
knew, ever to make her better off than she found herself, in the
afternoon of life, as the delicately frugal possessor and tenant of the
small house in Irving Place to which she had subtly managed to

cling through her almost unbroken New York career. If he knew the way to it now better than to any other address among the dreadful multiplied numberings which seemed to him to reduce the whole place to some vast ledger-page, overgrown, fantastic, of ruled and crisscrossed lines and figures — if he had formed, for his consolation, that habit, it was really not a little because of the charm of his having encountered and recognized, in the vast wilderness of the wholesale, breaking through the mere gross generalisation of wealth and force and success, a small still scene where items and shades, all delicate things, kept the sharpness of the notes of a high voice perfectly trained, and where economy hung about like the scent of a garden. His old friend lived with one maid and herself dusted her relics and trimmed her lamps and polished her silver; she stood off, in the awful modern crush, when she could, but she sallied forth and did battle when the challenge was really to "spirit," the spirit she after all confessed to, proudly and a little shyly, as to that of the better time, that of their common, their quite far-away and antediluvian social period and order. She made use of the street-cars when need be, the terrible things that people scrambled for as the panic-stricken at sea scramble for the boats; she affronted, inscrutably, under stress, all the public concussions and ordeals; and yet, with that slim mystifying grace of her appearance, which defied you to say if she were a fair young woman who looked older through trouble, or a fine smooth older one who looked young through successful indif- ference; with her precious reference, above all, to memories and histories into which he could enter, she was as exquisite for him as some pale pressed flower (a rarity to begin with), and, failing other sweetnesses, she was a sufficient reward of his effort. They had communities of knowledge, "their" knowledge (this discriminating possessive was always on her lips) of presences of the other age, presences all over laid, in his case, by the experience of a man and the freedom of a wanderer, overlaid by pleasure, by infidelity, by passages of life that were strange and dim to her, just by "Europe" in short, but still unobscured, still exposed and cherished, under that pious visitation of the spirit from which she had never been diverted.

She had come with him one day to see how his "apartment-house" was rising; he had helped her over gaps and explained to her plans, and while they were there had happened to have, before her, a brief but lively discussion with the man in charge, the representative of the building-firm that had undertaken his work. He had found himself quite "standing-up" to this personage over a failure on the latter's part to observe some detail of one of their noted conditions, and had so lucidly urged his case that, besides ever so prettily flushing, at the time, for sympathy in his triumph, she had afterwards said to him (though to a slightly greater effect of irony) that he had clearly for too many years neglected a real gift. If he had but stayed at home he would have anticipated the inventor of the skyscraper. If he had but stayed at home he would have discovered his genius in time really to start some new variety of awful architectural hare and run it till it burrowed in a gold-mine. He was to remember these words, while the weeks elapsed, for the small silver ring they had sounded over the queerest and deepest of his own lately most disguised and most muffled vibrations. It had begun to be present to him after the first fortnight, it had broken out with the oddest abruptness, this particular wanton wonderment: it met him there — and this was the image under which he himself judged the matter, or at least, not a little, thrilled and flushed with it — very much as he might have been met by some strange figure, some unexpected occupant, at a turn of one of the dim passages of an empty house. The quaint analogy quite hauntingly remained with him, when he didn't indeed rather improve it by a still intenser form: that of his opening a door behind which he would have made sure of finding nothing, a door into a room shuttered and void, and yet so coming, with a great suppressed start, on some quite erect confronting presence, something planted in the middle of the place and facing him through the dusk. After that visit to the house in construction he walked with his companion to see the other and always so much the better one, which in the eastward direction formed one of the corners, the "jolly" one precisely, of the street now so generally dishonored and disfigured in its westward reaches, and of the comparatively conservative Avenue. The Avenue still had pretensions, as Miss Staverton said, to decency; the old people had mostly gone, the old names were unknown, and here and there an old association seemed to stray, all vaguely, like some very aged person, out too late, whom you might meet and feel the impulse to watch or follow, in kindness, for safe restoration to shelter.

They went in together, our friends; he admitted himself with his key, as he kept no one there, he explained, preferring, for his reasons, to leave the place empty, under a simple arrangement with a good woman living in the neighborhood and who came for a daily hour to open windows and dust and sweep. Spencer Brydon had his reasons and was growingly aware of them; they seemed to him better each time he was there, though he didn't name them: all to his companion, anymore than he told her as yet how often, how quite absurdly often, he himself came. He only let her see for the present, while they walked through the great blank rooms, that absolute vacancy reigned and that, from top to bottom, there was nothing but Mrs. Muldoon's broomstick, in a corner, to tempt the burglar. Mrs. Muldoon was then on the premises, and she loquaciously attended the visitors, preceding them from room to room and pushing back shutters and throwing up sashes — all to show them, as she remarked, how little there was to see. There was little indeed to see in the great gaunt shell where the main dispositions and the general apportionment of space, the style of an age of ampler allowances, had nevertheless for its master their honest pleading message, affecting him as some good old servant's, some lifelong retainer's appeal for a character, or even for a retiring-pension; yet it was also a remark of Mrs. Muldoon's that, glad as she was to oblige him by her noonday round, there was a request she greatly hoped he would never make of her. If he should wish her for any reason to come in after dark she would just tell him, if he "plased," that he must ask it of somebody else.

The fact that there was nothing to see didn't militate for the worthy woman against what one *might* see, and she put it frankly to Miss Staverton that no lady could be expected to like, could she? "scraping up to thim top storeys in the ayvil hours." The gas and the electric light were off the house, and she fairly evoked a gruesome vision of her march through the great grey rooms — so many of them as there were tool — with her glimmering taper. Miss Staverton met her honest glare with a smile and the profession that she herself certainly would recoil from such an adventure. Spencer Brydon meanwhile held his peace — for the moment; the question of the "evil" hours in his old home had already become too grave for him. He had begun some time since to "crape," and he knew just why a packet of candles addressed to that pursuit had been stowed by his own hand three weeks before, at the back of a drawer of the fine old sideboard that occupied, as a "fixture," the deep recess in the dining room. Just now he laughed at his companions — quickly however changing the subject; for the reason that, in the first place, his laugh struck him even at that moment as starting the odd echo, the conscious human resonance (he scarce knew how to qualify it) that sounds made while he was there alone sent back to his ear or his fancy; and that, in the second, he imagined Alice Staverton for the instant on the point of asking him, with a divination, if he ever so prowled. There were divinations he was unprepared for, and he had at all events averted enquiry by the time Mrs. Muldoon had left them, passing on to other parts.

There was happily enough to say, on so consecrated a spot, that could be said freely and fairly; so that a whole train of declarations was precipitated by his friend's having herself broken out, after a yearning look round: "But I hope you don't mean they want you to pull *this* to pieces!" His answer came, promptly, with his re-awakened wrath: it was of course exactly what they wanted, and what they were "at" him for, daily, with the iteration of people who couldn't for their life understand a man's liability to decent feelings. He had found the place, just as it stood and beyond what he could express, an interest and a joy. There were values other than the beastly rent-values, and in short, in short — ! But it was thus Miss Staverton took him up. "In short you're to make so good a thing of your sky-scraper that, living in luxury on *those* ill-gotten gains, you can afford for a while to be sentimental here!" Her smile had for him, with the words, the particular mild irony with which he found half her talk suffused; an irony without bitterness and that came, exactly, from her having so much imagination — not, like the cheap sarcasms with which one heard most people, about the world of "society," bid for the reputation of cleverness, from nobody's really having any. It was agreeable to him at this very moment to be sure that when he had answered, after a brief demur, "Well yes: so precisely, you may put it!" her imagination would still do him justice. He explained that even if never a dollar were to come to him from the other house he would nevertheless cherish this one; and he dwelt, further, while they lingered and wandered, on the fact of the stupe-faction he was already exciting, the positive mystification he felt himself create.

He spoke of the value of all he read into it, into the mere sight of the walls, mere shapes of the rooms, mere sound of the floors, mere feel, in his hand, of the old silver-plated knobs of the several mahogany doors, which suggested the pressure of the palms of the dead; the seventy years of the past in fine that these things repre-sented, the annals of nearly three generations, counting his grand-father's, the one that had ended there, and the impalpable ashes of his long-extinct youth, afloat in the very air like microscopic motes. She listened to everything; she was a woman who answered inti-mately but who utterly didn't chatter. She scattered abroad therefore no cloud of words; she could assent, she could agree, above all she could encourage, without doing that. Only at the last she went a little further than he had done himself. "And then how do you know? You may still, after all, want to live here." It rather indeed pulled him up, for it wasn't what he had been thinking, at least in her sense of the words. "You mean I may decide to stay on for the sake of it?"

"Well, *with* such a home — !" But, quite beautifully, she had too much tact to dot so monstrous an *i*, and it was precisely an illustration of the way she didn't rattle. How could anyone — of any wit — insist on anyone else's "wanting" to live in New York?

"Oh," he said, "I *might* have lived here (since I had my opportunity early in life); I might have put in here all these years. Then everything would have been different enough — and, I dare say, 'funny' enough. But that's another matter. And then the beauty of it — I mean of my perversity, of my refusal to agree to a 'deal' — is just in the total absence of a reason. Don't you see that if I had a reason about the matter at all it would *have* to be the other way, and would then be inevitably a reason of dollars? There are no reasons here *but* of dollars. Let us therefore have none whatever — not the ghost of one.

They were back in the hall then for departure, but from where they stood the vista was large, through an open door, into the great square main saloon, with its almost antique felicity of brave spaces between windows. Her eyes came back from that reach and met his own a moment. "Are you very sure the 'ghost' of one doesn't, much rather, serve — ?"

"He had a positive sense of turning pale. But it was as near as they were then to come. For he made answer, he believed, between a glare and a grin: 'Oh ghosts — of course the place must swarm with them I should be ashamed of it if it didn't. Poor Mrs. Muldoon's right, and it's why I haven't asked her to do more than look in.'

Miss Staverton's gaze again lost itself, and things she didn't utter, it was clear, came and went in her mind. She might even for the minute, off there in the fine room, have imagined some element dimly gathering. Simplified like the death-mask of a handsome face, it perhaps produced for her just then an effect akin to the stir of an expression in the "set" commemorative plaster. Yet whatever her impression may have been she produced instead a vague platitude. "Well, if it were only furnished and lived in — !"

She appeared to imply that in case of its being still furnished he might have been a little less opposed to the idea of a return. But she passed straight into the vestibule, as if to leave her words behind her, and the next moment he had opened the house-door and was standing with her on the steps. He closed the door and, while he re-pocketed his key, looking up and down, they took in the comparatively harsh actuality of the Avenue, which reminded him of the assault of the outer light of the Desert on the traveler emerging from an Egyptian tomb. But he risked before they stepped into the street his gathered answer to her speech. "For me it is lived in. For me it is furnished." At which it was easy for her to sigh "Ah yes — !"

all vaguely and discreetly; since his parents and his favorite sister, to say nothing of other kin, in numbers, had run their course and met their end there. That represented, within the walls, ineffaceable life.

It was a few days after this that, during an hour passed with her again, he had expressed his impatience of the too flattering curiosity — among the people he met — about his appreciation of New York. He had arrived at none at all that was socially producible, and as for that matter of his "thinking" (thinking the better or the worse of anything there) he was wholly taken up with one subject of thought. It was mere vain egoism, and it was moreover, if she liked, a morbid obsession. He found all things come back to the question of what he personally might have been, how he might have led his life and "turned out," if he had not so, at the outset, given it up. And confessing for the first time to the intensity within him of this absurd speculation — which but proved also, no doubt, the habit of too selfishly thinking — he affirmed the impotence there of any other source of interest, any other native appeal. "What would it have made of me, what would it have made of me? I keep forever wondering, all idiotically; as if I could possibly know! I see what it has made of dozens of others, those I meet, and it positively aches within me, to the point of exasperation, that it would have made something of me as well. Only I can't make out *what,* and the worry of it, the small rage of curiosity never to be satisfied, brings back what I remember to have felt, once or twice, after judging best, for reasons, to burn some important letter unopened. I've been sorry, I've hated it — I've never known what was in the letter. You may of course say it's a trifle — !"

"I don't say it's a trifle," Miss Staverton gravely interrupted.

She was seated by her fire, and before her, on his feet and restless, he turned to and fro between this intensity of his idea and a fitful and unseeing inspection, through his single eye-glass, of the dear little old objects on her chimneypiece. Her interruption made him for an instant look at her harder. "I shouldn't care if you did!" he laughed, however; "and it's only a figure, at any rate, for the way I now feel. *Not* to have followed my perverse young course — and almost in the teeth of my father's curse, as I may say; not to have kept it up, so, 'over there,' from that day to this, without a doubt or a pang; not, above all, to have liked it, to have loved it, so much, loved it, no doubt, with such an abysmal conceit of my own preference: some variation from *that,* I say, must have produced some different effect for my life and for my 'form.' I should have stuck here — if it had been possible; and I was too young, at twenty-three, to judge, *pour deux sous,* whether it were possible. If I had waited I might have seen it was, and then I might have been, by staying here, something nearer to one of these types who have been hammered so hard and made so keen by their conditions. It isn't that I admire them so much — the question of any charm in them, or of any charm, beyond that of the rank money-passion, exerted by their conditions *for* them, has nothing to do with the matter: it's only a question of what fantastic, yet perfectly possible, development of my own nature I mayn't have missed. It comes over me that I had then a strange *alter ego* deep down somewhere within me, as the full-blown flower is in the small tight bud, and that I just took the course, I just transferred him to the climate, that blighted him for once and forever."

"And you wonder about the flower," Miss Staverton said. "So do I, if you want to know; and so I've been wondering these several weeks. I believe in the flower," she continued, "I feel it would have been quite splendid, quite huge and monstrous."

"Monstrous above all!" her visitor echoed; "and I imagine, by the same stroke, quite hideous and offensive."

"You don't believe that," she returned; "if you did you wouldn't wonder. You'd know, and that would be enough for you. What you feel — and what I feel *for* you — is that you'd have had power."

"You'd have liked me that way?" he asked.

She barely hung fire. "How should I not have liked you?"

"I see. You'd have liked me, have preferred me, a billionaire!"

"How should I not have liked you?" she simply again asked.

He stood before her still — her question kept him motionless. He took it in, so much there was of it; and indeed his not otherwise meeting it testified to that. "I know at least what I am," he simply went on; "the other side of the medal's clear enough. I've not been edifying — I believe I'm thought in a hundred quarters to have been barely decent. I've followed strange paths and worshipped strange gods; it must have come to you again and again — in fact you've admitted to me as much — that I was leading, at any time these thirty years, a selfish frivolous scandalous life. And you see what it has made of me."

She just waited, smiling at him. "You see what it has made of me."

"Oh you're a person whom nothing can have altered. You were born to be what you are, anywhere, anyway: you've the perfection nothing else could have blighted. And don't you see how, without my exile, I shouldn't have been waiting till now — ?" But he pulled up for the strange pang.

"The great thing to see," she presently said, "seems to me to be that it has spoiled nothing. It hasn't spoiled your being here at last.

It hasn't spoiled this. It hasn't spoiled your speaking —" She also however faltered.

He wondered at everything her controlled emotion might mean. "Do you believe then — too dreadfully! — that I am as good as I might ever have been?"

"Oh no! Far from it!" With which she got up from her chair and was nearer to him. "But I don't care," she smiled.

"You mean I'm good enough?"

She considered a little. "Will you believe it if I say so? I mean will you let that settle your question for you?" And then as if making out in his face that he drew back from this, that he had some idea which, however absurd, he couldn't yet bargain away: "Oh you don't care either — but very differently: you don't care for anything but yourself."

Spencer Brydon recognized it — it was in fact what he had absolutely professed. Yet he importantly qualified. *"He* isn't myself. He's the just so totally other person. But I do want to see him," he added. "And I can. And I shall."

Their eyes met for a minute while he guessed from something in hers that she divined his strange sense. But neither of them otherwise expressed it, and her apparent understanding, with no protesting shock, no easy derision, touched him more deeply than anything yet, constituting for his stifled perversity, on the spot, an element that was like breathable air. What she said however was unexpected. "Well, *I've* seen him."

"You — ?"

"I've seen him in a dream."

"Oh a 'dream' — !" It let him down.

"But twice over," she continued. "I saw him as I see you now."

"You've dreamed the same dream — ?"

"Twice over," she repeated. "The very same."

This did somehow a little speak to him, as it also gratified him. "You dream about me at that rate?"

"Ah about *him!*" she smiled.

His eyes again sounded her. "Then you know all about him." And as she said nothing more: "What's the wretch like?"

She hesitated, and it was as if he were pressing her so hard that, resisting for reasons of her own, she had to turn away. "I'll tell you some other time!"

II

*I*t was after this that there was most of a virtue for him, most of a cultivated charm, most of a preposterous secret thrill, in the particular form of surrender to his obsession and of address to what he more and more believed to be his privilege. It was what in these weeks he was living for — since he really felt life to begin but after Mrs. Muldoon had retired from the scene and, visiting the ample house from attic to cellar, making sure he was alone, he knew himself in safe of in safe possession and, as he tacitly expressed it, let himself go. He sometimes came twice in the twenty-four hours; the moments he liked best were those of gathering dusk, of the short autumn twilight; this was the time of which, again and again, he found himself hoping most. Then he could, as seemed to him, most intimately wander and wait, linger and listen, feel his fine attention, never in his life before so fine, on the pulse of the great vague place: he preferred the lampless hour and only wished he might have prolonged each day the deep crepuscular spell. Later — rarely much before midnight, but then for a considerable vigil — he watched with his glimmering light; moving slowly, holding it high, playing it far, rejoicing above all, as much as he might, in open vistas, reaches of communication between rooms and by passages; the long straight chance or show, as he would have called it, for the revelation he pretended to invite. It was practice he found he could perfectly "work" without exciting remark; no one was in the least the wiser for it; even Alice Staverton, who was moreover a well of discretion, didn't quite fully imagine.

He let himself in and let himself out with the assurance of calm proprietorship; and accident so far favored him that, if a fat Avenue "officer" had happened on occasion to see him entering at eleven-thirty, he had never yet, to the best of his belief, been noticed as emerging at two. He walked there on the crisp November nights, arrived regularly at the evening's end; it was as easy to do this after dining out as to take his way to a club or to his hotel. When he left his club, if he hadn't been dining out, it was ostensibly to go to his hotel; and when he left his hotel, if he had spent a part of the evening there, it was ostensibly to go to his club. Everything was easy in fine; everything conspired and promoted: there was truly even in the strain of his experience something that glossed over, something that salved and simplified, all the rest of consciousness. He circulated, talked, renewed, loosely and pleasantly, old relations — met indeed, so far as he could, new expectations and seemed to make out on the whole that in spite of the career, of such different contacts, which he had spoken of to Miss Staverton as ministering so little, for those who might have watched it, to edification, he was positively rather liked than not. He was a dim secondary social success — and all with people who had truly not an idea of him. It was all mere surface sound, this murmur of their welcome, this popping of their corks — just as his gestures of response were the extravagant shadows, emphatic in proportion as they meant little, of some game of *ombres chinoises.* He projected himself all day, in thought, straight over the bristling line of hard unconscious heads and into the other, the real, the waiting life; the life that, as soon as he had heard behind him the click of his great house-door, began for him, on the jolly corner, as beguilingly as the slow opening bars of some rich music follows the tap of the conductor's wand.

He always caught the first effect of the steel point of his stick on the old marble of the hall pavement, large black-and-white squares that he remembered as the admiration of his childhood and that had then made in him, as he now saw, for the growth of an early conception of style. This effect was the dim reverberating tinkle as of some far-off bell hung who should say where? — in the depths of the house, of the past, of that mystical other world that might have flourished for him had he not, for weal or woe, abandoned it. On this impression he did ever the same thing; he put his stick noiselessly away in a corner — feeling the place once more in the likeness of some great glass bowl, all precious concave crystal, set delicately humming by the play of a moist finger round its edge. The concave crystal held, as it were, this mystical other world, and the indescribably fine murmur of its rim was the sigh there, the scarce audible pathetic wail to his strained ear, of all the old baffled forsworn possibilities. What he did therefore by this appeal of his hushed presence was to wake them into such measure of ghostly life as they might still enjoy. They were shy, all but unappeasably shy, but they weren't really sinister; at least they weren't as he had hitherto felt them — before they had taken the Form he so yearned to make them take, the Form he at moments saw himself in the light of fairly hunting on tiptoe, the points of his evening shoes, from room to room and from storey to storey.

That was the essence of his vision — which was all rank folly, if one would, while he was out of the house and otherwise occupied, but which took on the last verisimilitude as soon as he was placed and posted. He knew what he meant and what he wanted; it was as clear as the figure on a check presented in demand for cash. His *alter ego* "walked" — that was the note of his image of him, while his image of his motive for his own odd pastime was the desire to waylay him and meet him. He roamed, slowly, warily, but all restlessly, he himself did — Mrs. Muldoon had been right, absolutely, with her figure of their "craping"; and the presence he watched for would roam restlessly too. But it would be as cautious and as shifty; the conviction of its probable, in fact its already quite sensible, quite audible evasion of pursuit grew for him from night to night, laying on him finally a rigor to which nothing in his life had been comparable. It had been the theory of many superficially-judging persons, he knew, that he was wasting that life in a surrender to sensations, but he had tasted of no pleasure so fine as his actual tension, had been introduced to no sport that demanded at once the patience and the nerve of this stalking of a creature more subtle, yet at bay perhaps more formidable, than any beast of the forest. The terms, the comparisons, the very practices of the chase positively came again into play; there were even moments when passages of his occasional experience as a sportsman, stirred memories, from his younger time, of moor and mountain and desert, revived for him — and to the increase of his keenness — by the tremendous force of analogy. He found himself at moments — once he had placed his single light on some mantel-shelf or in some recess — stepping back into shelter or shade, effacing himself behind a door or in an embrasure, as he had sought of old the vantage of rock and tree; he found himself holding his breath and living in the joy of the instant, the supreme suspense created by big game alone.

He wasn't afraid (though putting himself the question as he believed gentlemen on Bengal tiger-shoots or in close quarters with the great bear of the Rockies had been known to confess to having put it); and this indeed — since here at least he might be frank! — because of the impression, so intimate and so strange, that he himself produced as yet a dread, produced certainly a strain, beyond the liveliest he was likely to feel. They fell for him into categories, they fairly became familiar, the signs, for his own perception, of the alarm his presence and his vigilance created; though leaving him always to remark, portentously, on his probably having formed a relation, his probably enjoying a consciousness, unique in the experience of man. People enough, first and last, had been in terror of apparitions, but who had ever before so turned the tables and become himself, in the apparitional world, an incalculable terror? He might have found this sublime had he quite dared to think of it; but he didn't too much insist, truly, on that side of his privilege. With habit and repetition he gained to an extraordinary degree the power to penetrate the dusk of distances and the darkness of corners, to resolve back into their innocence the treacheries of uncertain light, the evil-looking forms taken in the gloom by mere shadows, by accidents of the air, by shifting effects of perspective; putting down his dim luminary he could still wander on without it, pass into other rooms and, only knowing it was there behind him in case of need, see his way about, visually project for his purpose a comparative clearness. It made him feel, this acquired faculty, like some monstrous stealthy cat; he wondered if he would have glared at these moments with large shining yellow eyes, and what it mightn't verily be, for the poor hard-pressed *alter ego,* to be confronted with such a type.

He liked however the open shutters; he opened everywhere those Mrs. Muldoon had closed, closing them as carefully afterwards, so that she shouldn't notice: he liked — oh this he did like, and above all in the upper rooms! — the sense of the hard silver of the autumn stars through the windowpanes, and scarcely less the flare of the street-lamps below, the white electric luster which it would have taken curtains to keep out. This was human actual social; this was of the world he had lived in, and he was more at his ease certainly for the countenance, coldly general and impersonal, that all the while and in spite of his detachment it seemed to give him. He had support of course mostly in the rooms at the wide front and the prolonged side; it failed him considerably in the central shades and the parts at the back. But if he sometimes, on his rounds, was glad of his optical reach, so nonetheless often the rear of the house affected him as the very jungle of his prey. The place was there more subdivided; a large "extension" in particular, where small rooms for servants had been multiplied abounded in nooks and corners, in closets and passages, in the ramifications especially of an ample back staircase over which he leaned, many a time, to look far down — not deterred from his gravity even while aware that he might, for a spectator, have figured some solemn simpleton playing at hide-and-seek. Outside in fact he might himself make that ironic *rapprochement*; but within the walls, and in spite of the clear windows, his consistency was proof against the cynical light of New York.

It had belonged to that idea of the exasperated consciousness of his victim to become a real test for him; since he had quite put it to himself from the first that, oh distinctly! he could "cultivate" his whole perception. He had felt it as above all open to cultivation — which indeed was but another name for his manner of spending his time. He was bringing it on, bringing it to perfection, by practice; in consequence of which it had grown so fine that he was now aware

of impressions, attestations of his general postulate, that couldn't
have broken upon him at once. This was the case more specifically
with a phenomenon at last quite frequent for him in the upper
rooms, the recognition — absolutely unmistakable, and by a turn
dating from a particular hour, his resumption of his campaign after
a diplomatic drop, a calculated absence of three nights — of his being
definitely followed, tracked at a distance carefully taken and to the
express end that he should the less confidently, less arrogantly,
appear to himself merely to pursue. It worried, it finally quite broke
him up, for it proved, of all the conceivable impressions, the one
least suited to his book. He was kept in sight while remaining himself
— as regards the essence of his position — sightless, and his only
recourse then was in abrupt turns, rapid recoveries of ground. He
wheeled about, retracing his steps, as if he might so catch in his face
at least the stirred air of some other quick revolution. It was indeed
true that his fully dislocalised thought of these maneuvers recalled
to him Pantaloon, at the Christmas farce, buffeted and tricked from
behind by ubiquitous Harlequin; but it left intact the influence of
the conditions themselves each time he was re-exposed to them, so
that in fact this association, had he suffered it to become constant,
would on a certain side have but ministered to his intenser gravity.
He had made, as I have said, to create on the premises the baseless
sense of a reprieve, his three absences; and the result of the third was
to confirm the after-effect of the second.

On his return, that night — the night succeeding his last intermis-
sion — he stood in the hall and looked up the staircase with a
certainty more intimate than any he had yet known. "He's *there*, at
the top, and waiting — not, as in general, falling back for disappearance. He's holding his ground, and it's the first time — which is a
proof, isn't it? that something has happened for him." So Brydon
argued with his hand on the banister and his foot on the lowest
stair; in which position he felt as never before the air chilled by his
logic. He himself turned cold in it, for he seemed of a sudden to
know what now was involved. "Harder pressed? — yes, he takes it in,
with its thus making clear to him that I've come, as they say, 'to
stay.' He finally doesn't like and can't bear it, in the sense, I mean,
that his wrath, his menaced interest, now balances with his dread.
I've hunted him till he has 'turned': that, up there, is what has
happened — he's the fanged or the antlered animal brought at last
to bay." There came to him, as I say — but determined by an influence
beyond my notation! — the acuteness of this certainty; under which
however the next moment he had broken into a sweat that he would
as little have consented to attribute to fear as he would have dared

immediately to act upon it for enterprise. it marked nonetheless a prodigious thrill, a thrill that represented sudden dismay, no doubt, but also represented, and with the selfsame throb, the strangest, the most joyous, possibly the next minute almost the proudest, duplication of consciousness.

"He has been dodging, retreating, hiding, but now, worked up to anger, he'll fight!" — this intense impression made a single mouthful, as it were, of terror and applause. But what was wondrous was that the applause, for the felt fact, was so eager, since, if it was his other self he was running to earth, this ineffable identity was thus in the last resort not unworthy of him. It bristled there — somewhere near at hand, however unseen still — as the hunted thing, even as the trodden worm of the adage *must* at last bristle; and Brydon at this instant tasted probably of a sensation more complex than had ever before found itself consistent with sanity. It was as if it would have shamed him that a character so associated with his own should triumphantly succeed in just skulking, should to the end not risk the open, so that the drop of this danger was, on the spot, a great lift of the whole situation. Yet with another rare shift of the same subtlety he was already trying to measure by how much more he himself might now be in peril of fear; so rejoicing that he could, in another form, actively inspire that fear, and simultaneously quaking for the form in which he might passively know it.

The apprehension of knowing it must after a little have grown in him, and the strangest moment of his adventure perhaps, the most memorable or really most interesting, afterwards, of his crisis, was the lapse of certain instants of concentrated conscious *combat,* the sense of a need to hold on to something. even after the manner of a man slipping and slipping on some awful incline; the vivid impulse, above all, to move, to act, to charge, somehow and upon something — to show himself, in a word, that he wasn't afraid. The state of "holding-on" was thus the state to which he was momentarily reduced; if there had been anything, in the great vacancy, to seize, he would presently have been aware of having clutched it as he might under a shock at home have clutched the nearest chair-back. He had been surprised at any rate — of this he was aware — into something unprecedented since his original appropriation of the place; he had closed his eyes, held them tight, for a long minute, as with that instinct of dismay and that terror of vision. When he opened them the room, the other contiguous rooms, extraordinarily, seemed lighter — so light, almost, that at first he took the change for day. He stood firm, however that might be, just where he had paused; his resistance had helped him — it was as if there were something he had tided over. He knew after a little what this was — it had been in the imminent danger of flight. He had stiffened his will against going; without this he would have made for the stairs, and it seemed to him that, still with his eyes closed, he would have descended them, would have known how, straight and swiftly, to the bottom.

Well, as he had held out, here he was — still at the top, among the more intricate upper rooms and with the gauntlet of the others, of all the rest of the house, still to run when it should be his time to go. He would go at his time — only at his time: didn't he go every night very much at the same hour? He took out his watch — there was light for that: it was scarcely a quarter past one, and he had never withdrawn so soon. He reached his lodgings for the most part at two — with his walk of a quarter of an hour. He would wait for the last quarter — he wouldn't stir till then; and he kept his watch there with his eyes on it, reflecting while he held it that this deliberate wait, a wait with an effort, which he recognized, would serve perfectly for the attestation he desired to make. It would prove his courage — unless indeed the latter might most be proved by his budging at last from his place. What he mainly felt now was that, since he hadn't originally scuttled, he had his dignities — which had never in his life seemed so many — all to preserve and to carry aloft. This was before him in truth as a physical image, an image almost worthy of an age of greater romance. That remark indeed glimmered for him only to glow the next instant with a finer light; since what age of romance, after all, could have matched either the state of his mind or, "objectively," as they said, the wonder of his situation? The only difference would have been that, brandishing his dignities over his head as in a parchment scroll, he might then — that is in the heroic time — have proceeded downstairs with a drawn sword in his other grasp.

At present, really, the light he had set down on the mantel of the next room would have to figure his sword; which utensil, in the course of a minute, he had taken the requisite number of steps to possess himself of. The door between the rooms was open, and from the second another door opened to a third. These rooms, as he remembered, gave all three upon a common corridor as well, but there was a fourth, beyond them, without issue save through the preceding. To have moved, to have heard his step again, was appreciably a help; though even in recognizing this he lingered once more a little by the chimneypiece on which his light had rested. When he next moved, just hesitating where to turn, he found himself considering a circumstance that, after his first and comparatively vague apprehension of it, produced in him the start that often attends some pang of recollection, the violent shock of having ceased happily to forget. He had come into sight of the door in which the brief chain of communication ended and which he now surveyed from the nearer threshold, the one not directly facing it. Placed at some distance to the left of this point, it would have admitted him to the last room of the four, the room without other approach or egress, had it not, to his intimate conviction, been closed since his former visitation, the matter probably of a quarter of an hour before. He stared with all his eyes at the wonder of the fact, arrested again where he stood and again holding his breath while he sounded its sense. Surely it had been *subsequently* closed — that is it had been on his previous passage indubitably open!

He took it full in the face that something had happened between — that he couldn't not have noticed before (by which he meant on his original tour of all the rooms that evening) that such a barrier had exceptionally presented itself. He had indeed since that moment undergone an agitation so extraordinary that it might have muddled for him any earlier view; and he tried to convince himself that he might perhaps then have gone into the room and, inadvertently, automatically, on coming out, have drawn the door after him. The difficulty was that this exactly was what he never did; it was against his whole policy, as he might have said, the essence of which was to keep vistas clear. He had them from the first, as he was well aware quite on the brain: the strange apparition, at the far end of one of them, of his baffled "prey" (which had become by so sharp an irony so little the term now to apply!) was the form of success his imagination had most cherished, projecting into it always a refinement of beauty. He had known fifty times the start of perception that had afterwards dropped; had fifty times gasped to himself "There!" under some fond brief hallucination. The house, as the case stood, admirably lent itself; he might wonder at the taste, the native architecture of the particular time, which could rejoice so in the multiplication of doors — the opposite extreme to the modern, the actual almost complete proscription of them; but it had fairly contributed to provoke this obsession of the presence encountered telescopically, as he might say, focussed and studied in diminishing perspective and as by a rest for the elbow.

It was with these considerations that his present attention was charged — they perfectly availed to make what he saw portentous. He *couldn't*, by any lapse, have blocked that aperture; and if he hadn't, if it was unthinkable, why what else was clear but that there had been another agent? Another agent? — he had been catching, as he felt, a moment back, the very breath of him; but when had he been so close as in this simple, this logical, this completely personal

act? It was so logical, that is, that one might have *taken* it for personal;
yet for what did Brydon take it, he asked himself, while, softly
panting, he felt his eyes almost leave their sockets. Ah this time at
last they *were*, the two, the opposed projections of him, in presence;
and this time, as much as one would, the question of danger loomed.
With it rose, as not before, the question of courage — for what he
knew the blank face of the door to say to him was "Show us how
much you have!" It stared, it glared back at him with that challenge;
it put to him the two alternatives: should he just push it open or
not? Oh to have this consciousness was to *think* — and to think,
Brydon knew, as he stood there, was, with the lapsing moments, not
to have acted! Not to have acted — that was the misery and the pang
— was even still not to act; was in fact *all* to feel the thing in another,
in a new and terrible way. How long did he pause and how long did
he debate? There was presently nothing to measure it; for his vibra-
tion had already changed — as just by the effect of its intensity. Shut
up there, at bay, defiant, and with the prodigy of the thing palpably
provably *done*, thus giving notice like some stark signboard — under
that accession of accent the situation itself had turned; and Brydon
at last remarkably made up his mind on what it had turned to.

It had turned altogether to a different admonition; to a supreme
hint, for him, of the value of Discretion! This slowly dawned, no
doubt — for it could take its time; so perfectly, on his threshold, had
he been stayed, so little as yet had he either advanced or retreated.
It was the strangest of all things that now when, by his taking ten
steps and applying his hand to a latch, or even his shoulder and his
knee, if necessary, to a panel, all the hunger of his prime need might
have been met, his high curiosity crowned, his unrest assuaged — it
was amazing, but it was also exquisite and rare, that insistence should
have, at a touch, quite dropped from him. Discretion — he jumped
at that; and yet not, verily, at such a pitch, because it saved his nerves
or his skin, but because, much more valuably, it saved the situation.
When I say he "jumped" at it I feel the consonance of this term with
the fact that — at the end indeed of I know not how long — he did
move again, he crossed straight to the door. He wouldn't touch it —
it seemed now that he might *if* he would: he would only just wait
there a little, to show, to prove, that he wouldn't. He had thus
another station, close to the thin partition by which revelation was
denied him; but with his eyes bent and his hands held off in a mere
intensity of stillness. He listened as if there had been something to
hear, but this attitude, while it lasted, was his own communication.
"If you won't then — good: I spare you and I give up. You affect me
as by the appeal positively for pity: you convince me that for reasons

rigid and sublime — what do I know? — we both of us should have suffered. I respect them then, and, though moved and privileged as I believe, it has never been given to man, I retire, I renounce — never, on my honor, to try again. So rest forever — and let *me!*"

That, for Brydon was the deep sense of this last demonstration — solemn, measured, directed, as he felt it to be He brought it to a close, he turned away; and now verily he knew how deeply he had been stirred. He retraced his steps taking up his candle, burned, he observed, well-nigh to the socket, and marking again, lighten it as he would, the distinctness of his footfall; after which, in a moment, he knew himself at the other side of the house. He did here what he had not yet done at these hours — he opened half a casement, one of those in the front, and let in the air of the night; a thing he would have taken at any time previous for a sharp rupture of his spell. His spell was broken now and it didn't matter — broken by his concession and his surrender, which made it idle henceforth that he should ever come back. The empty street — its other life so marked even by the great lamp lit vacancy — was within call, within touch he stayed there as to be in it again, high above it though he was still perched; he watched as for some comforting common fact, some vulgar human note, the passage of a scavenger or a thief, some night-bird however base. He would have blessed that sign of life; he would have welcomed positively the slow approach of his friend the policeman, whom he had hitherto only sought to avoid, and was not sure that if the patrol had come into sight he mightn't have felt the impulse to get into relation with it, to hail it, on some pretext, from his fourth floor.

The pretext that wouldn't have been too silly or too compromising, the explanation that would have saved his dignity and kept his name, in such a case, out of the papers was not definite to him: he was so occupied with the thought of recording his Discretion — as an effect of the vow he had just uttered to his intimate adversary — that the importance of this loomed large and something had overtaken all ironically his sense of proportion. If there had been a ladder applied to the front of the house, even one of the vertiginous perpendiculars employed by painters and roofers and sometimes left standing overnight, he would have managed somehow, astride of the windowsill, to compass by outstretched leg and arm that mode of descent. If there had been some such uncanny thing as he had found in his room at hotels, a workable fire-escape in the form of notched cable or a canvas shoot, he would have availed himself of it as a proof — well, of his present delicacy. He nursed that sentiment, as the question stood, a little in vain, and even — at the end of he scarce knew, once more, how long — found it, as by the action on his mind of the failure of response of the outer world, sinking back to vague anguish. It seemed to him he had waited an age for some stir of the great grim hush; the life of the town was itself under a spell — so unnaturally, up and down the whole prospect of known and rather ugly objects, the blankness and the silence lasted. Had they ever, he asked himself, the hard-faced houses, which had begun to look livid in the dim dawn, had they ever spoken so little to any need of his spirit? Great builded voids, great crowded stillnesses put on, often, in the heart of cities, for the small hours, a sort of sinister mask, and it was of this large collective negation that Brydon presently became conscious — all the more that the break of day was, almost incredibly, now at hand, proving to him what night he had made of it.

He looked again at his watch, saw what had become of his time-values (he had taken hours for minutes — not, as in other tense situations, minutes for hours) and the strange air of the streets was but the weak, the sullen flush of a dawn in which everything was still locked up. His choked appeal from his own open window had been the sole note of life, and he could but break off at last as for a worse despair. Yet while so deeply demoralized he was capable again of an impulse denoting — at least by his present measure — extraordinary resolution; of retracing his steps to the spot where he had turned cold with the extinction of his last pulse of doubt as to there being in the place another presence than his own. This required an effort strong enough to sicken him; but he had his reason, which overmastered for the moment everything else. There was the whole of the rest of the house to traverse, and how should he screw himself to that if the door he had seen closed were at present open? He could hold to the idea that the closing had practically been for him an act of mercy, a chance offered him to descend, depart, get off the ground and never again profane it. This conception held together, it worked; but what it meant for him depended now clearly on the amount of forbearance his recent action, or rather his recent inaction, had engendered. The image of the "presence," whatever it was, waiting there for him to go — this image had not yet been so concrete for his nerves as when he stopped short of the point at which certainty would have come to him. For, with all his resolution, or more exactly with all his dread, he did stop short — he hung back from really seeing. The risk was too great and his fear too definite: it took at this moment an awful specific form.

He knew — yes, as he had never known anything — that, *should* he see the door open, it would all too abjectly be the end of him. It would mean that the agent of his shame — for his shame was the deep abjection — was once more at large and in general possession; and what glared him thus in the face was the act that this would determine for him. It would send him straight about to the window he had left open, and by that window, be long ladder and dangling rope as absent as they would, he saw himself uncontrollably insanely fatally take his way to the street. The hideous chance of this he at least could avert; but he could only avert it by recoiling in time from assurance. He had the whole house to deal with, this fact was still there; only he now knew that uncertainty alone could start him. He stole back from where he had checked himself — merely to do so was suddenly like safety — and, making blindly for the greater staircase, left gaping rooms and sounding passages behind. Here was the top of the stairs, with a fine large dim descent and three spacious landings to mark off. His instinct was all for mildness, but his feet were harsh on the floors, and, strangely, when he had in a couple of minutes become aware of this, it counted somehow for help. He couldn't have spoken, the tone of his voice would have scared him, and the common conceit or resource of "whistling in the dark" (whether literally or figuratively) have appeared basely vulgar; yet he liked nonetheless to hear himself go, and when he had reached his first landing — taking it all with no rush, but quite steadily — that stage of success drew from him a gasp of relief. The house, withal, seemed immense, the scale of space again inordinate; the open rooms to no one of which his eyes deflected, gloomed in their shuttered state like mouths of caverns; only the high skylight that formed the crown of the deep well created for him a medium in which he could advance, but which might have been, for queerness of color, some watery under-world. He tried to think of something noble, as that his property was really grand, a splendid possession; but this noble-ness took the form too of the clear delight with which he was finally to sacrifice it. They might come in now, the builders, the destroyers — they might come as soon as they would. At the end of two flights he had dropped to another zone, and from the middle of the third, with only one more left, he recognized the influence of the lower windows, of half-drawn blinds, of the occasional gleam of street-lamps, of the glazed spaces of the vestibule. This was the bottom of the sea, which showed an illumination of its own and which he even saw paved — when at a given moment he drew up to sink a long look over the banisters — with the marble squares of his childhood. By that time indubitably he felt, as he might have said in a commoner cause, better; it had allowed him to stop and draw breath, and the ease increased with the sight of the old black-and-white slabs. But what he most felt was that now surely, with the element of impunity pulling him as by hard firm hands, the case was settled for what he might have seen above had he dared that last look. The closed door, blessedly remote now, was still closed — and he had only in short to reach that of the house.

He came down further, he crossed the passage forming the access to the last flight; and if here again he stopped an instant it was almost for the sharpness of the thrill of assured escape. It made him shut his eyes — which opened again to the straight slope of the remainder of the stairs. Here was impunity still, but impunity almost excessive; inasmuch as the sidelights and the high fan-tracery of the entrance were glimmering straight into the hall; an appearance produced, he the next instant saw, by the fact that the vestibule gaped wide, that the hinged halves of the inner door had been thrown far back. Out of that again the question sprang at him, making his eyes, as he felt, half start from his head, as they had done, at the top of the house, before the sign of the other door. If he had left that one open, hadn't he left this one closed, and wasn't he now in most immediate presence of some inconceivable occult activity? It was as sharp, the question, as a knife in his side, but the answer hung fire still and seemed to lose itself in the vague darkness to which the thin admitted dawn, glimmering archwise over the whole outer door made a semicircular margin, a cold silvery nimbus that seemed to play a little as he looked — to shift and expand and contract.

It was as if there had been something within it, protected by indistinctness and corresponding in extent with the opaque surface behind, the painted panels of the last barrier to his escape, of which the key was in his pocket. The indistinctness mocked him even while he stared, affected him as somehow shrouding or challenging certitude, so that after faltering an instant on his step he let himself go with the sense that here *was* at last something to meet, to touch, to take, to know — something all unnatural and dreadful, but to advance upon which was the condition for him either of liberation or of supreme defeat. The penumbra, dense and dark, was the virtual screen of a figure which stood in it as still as some image erect in a niche or as some black-visored sentinel guarding a treasure. Brydon was to know afterwards, was to recall and make out, the particular thing he had believed during the rest of his descent. He saw, in its great grey glimmering margin, the central vagueness diminish, and he felt it to be taking the very form toward which, for so many days, the passion of his curiosity had yearned. It gloomed, it loomed, it was something, it was somebody, the prodigy of a personal presence.

Rigid and conscious, spectral yet human, a man of his own

substance and stature waited there to measure himself with his power to dismay. This only could it be — this only till he recognized, with his advance, that what made the face dim was the pair of raised hands that covered it and in which, so far from being offered in defiance, it was buried as for dark deprecation. So Brydon, before him, took him in; with every fact of him now, in the higher light, hard and acute — his planted stillness, his vivid truth, his grizzled bent head and white masking hands, his queer actuality of evening-dress, of dangling double eye-glass, of gleaming silk lappet and white linen, of pearl button and gold watch guard and polished shoe. No portrait by a great modern master could have presented him with more intensity, thrust him out of his frame with more art, as if there had been "treatment," of the consummate sort, in his every shade and salience. The revulsion, for our friend, had become, before he knew it, immense — this drop, in the act of apprehension, to the sense of his adversary's inscrutable maneuver. That meaning at least, while he gaped, it offered him; for he could but gape at his other self in this other anguish, gape as a proof that he, standing there for the achieved, the enjoyed, the triumphant life, couldn't be faced in his triumph. Wasn't the proof in the splendid covering hands, strong and completely spread? — so spread and so intentional that, in spite of a special verity that surpassed every other, the fact that one of these hands had lost two fingers, which were reduced to stumps, as if accidentally shot away, the face was effectually guarded and saved.

"Saved," though, *would* it be? — Brydon breathed his wonder till the very impunity of his attitude and the very insistence of his eyes produced, as he felt, a sudden stir which showed the next instant as a deeper portent, while the head raised itself, the betrayal of a braver purpose. The hands, as he looked, began to move, to open; then, as if deciding in a flash, dropped from the face and left it uncovered and presented. Horror, with the sight, had leaped into Brydon's throat, gasping there in a sound he couldn't utter; for the bared identity was too hideous as *his*, and his glare was the passion of his protest. The face, *that* face, Spencer Brydon's? — he searched it still, but looking away from it in dismay and denial, falling straight from his height and sublimity. It was unknown, inconceivable, awful, disconnected from any possibility — ! He had been "sold," he inwardly moaned, stalking such game as this: the presence before him was a presence, the horror within him a horror, but the waste of his nights had been only grotesque and the success of his adventure an irony. Such an identity fitted his at no point, made its alternative monstrous. A thousand times yes, as it came upon him nearer now — the face was the face of a stranger. It came upon him nearer now,

quite as one of those expanding fantastic images projected by the
magic lantern of childhood; for the stranger, whoever he might be,
evil, odious, blatant, vulgar, had advanced as for aggression, and he
knew himself give ground. Then harder pressed still, sick with the
force of his shock, and falling back as under the hot breath and the
roused passion of a life larger than his own, a rage of personality
before which his own collapsed, he felt the whole vision turn to
darkness and his very feet give way. His head went round; he was
going; he had gone.

III

What had next brought him back, clearly — though after how
long? — was Mrs. Muldoon's voice, coming to him from quite near,
from so near that he seemed presently to see her as kneeling on the
ground before him while he lay looking up at her; himself not wholly
on the ground, but half-raised and upheld — conscious, yes, of
tenderness of support and, more particularly, of a head pillowed in
extraordinary softness and faintly refreshing fragrance. He considered, he wondered, his wit but half at his service — then another face
intervened, bending more directly over him, and he finally knew
that Alice Staverton had made her lap an ample and perfect cushion
to him, and that she had to this end seated herself on the lowest
degree of the staircase, the rest of his long person remaining stretched
on his old black-and-white slabs. They were cold, these marble
squares of his youth; but *he* somehow was not, in this rich return of
consciousness — the most wonderful hour, little by little, that he had
ever known, leaving him, as it did, so gratefully, so abysmally passive,
and yet as with a treasure of intelligence waiting all round him for
quiet appropriation; dissolved, he might call it, in the air of the place
and producing the golden glow of a late autumn afternoon. He had
come back, yes — come back from further away than any man but
himself had ever traveled; but it was strange how with this sense what
he had come back *to* seemed really the great thing, and as if his
prodigious journey had been all for the sake of it. Slowly but surely
his consciousness grew, his vision of his state thus completing itself:
he had been miraculously *carried* back — lifted and carefully borne
as from where he had been picked up, the uttermost end of an
interminable grey passage. Even with this he was suffered to rest, and

what had now brought him to knowledge was the break in the long mild motion.

It had brought him to knowledge, to knowledge — yes, this was the beauty of his state; which came to resemble more and more that of a man who has gone to sleep on some news of a great inheritance, and then, after dreaming it away, after profaning it with matters strange to it, has waked up again to serenity of certitude and has only to lie and watch it grow. This was the drift of his patience — that he had only to let it shine on him. He must moreover, with intermissions, still have been lifted and borne — since why and how else should he have known himself, later on, with the afternoon glow intenser, no longer at the foot of his stairs — situated as these now seemed at that dark other end of his tunnel — but on a deep window-bench of his high saloon, over which had been spread, couch-fashion, a mantle of soft stuff lined with grey fur that was familiar to his eyes and that one of his hands kept fondly feeling as for its pledge of truth. Mrs. Muldoon's face had gone, but the other, the second he had recognized, hung over him in a way that showed how he was still propped and pillowed. He took it all in, and the more he took it the more it seemed to suffice: he was as much at peace as if he had had food and drink. It was the two women who had found him, on Mrs. Muldoon's having plied, at her usual hour, her latchkey — and on her having above all arrived while Miss Staverton still lingered near the house. She had been turning away, all anxiety, from worrying the vain bell-handle — her calculation having been of the hour of the good woman's visit; but the latter, blessedly, had come up while she was still there, and they had entered together. He had then lain, beyond the vestibule, very much as he was lying now — quite, that is, as he appeared to have fallen, but all so wondrously without bruise or gash; only in a depth of stupor. What he most took in, however, at present, with the steadier clearance, was that Alice Staverton had for a long unspeakable moment not doubted he was dead.

"It must have been that I *was.*" He made it out as she held him. "Yes — I can only have died. You brought me literally to life. Only," he wondered, his eyes rising to her, "only, in the name of all the benedictions, how?"

It took her but an instant to bend her face and kiss him, and something in the manner of it, and in the way her hands clasped and locked his head while he felt the cool charity and virtue of her lips, something in all this beatitude somehow answered everything. "And now I keep you," she said.

"Oh keep me, keep me" he pleaded while her face still hung over

him: in response to which it dropped again and stayed close, cling-
ingly close. It was the seal of their situation — of which he tasted the
impress for a long blissful moment in silence. But he came back.
"Yet how did you know — ?"

"I was uneasy. You were to have come, you remember — and you
had sent no word."

"Yes, I remember — I was to have gone to you at one today." It
caught on to their "old" life and relation — which were so near and
so far. "I was still out there in my strange darkness — where was it,
what was it? I must have stayed there so long." He could but wonder
at the death and the duration of his swoon.

"Since last night?" she asked with a shade of fear for her possible
indiscretion.

"Since this morning — it must have been: the cold dim dawn of
today. Where have I been," he vaguely wailed, "where have I been?"
He felt her hold him close, and it was as if this helped him now to
make in all security his mild moan. "What a long dark day!"

All in her tenderness she had waited a moment. "In the cold dim
dawn?" she quavered.

But he had already gone on piecing together the parts of the whole
prodigy. "As I didn't turn up you came straight — ?"

She barely cast about. "I went first to your hotel — where they
told me of your absence. You had dined out last evening and hadn't
been back since. But they appeared to know you had been at your
club."

"So you had the idea of *this* — ?"

"Of what?" she asked in a moment.

"Well — of what has happened."

"I believed at least you'd have been here. I've known, all along,"
she said, "that you've been coming."

"'Known' it — ?"

"Well, I've believed it. I said nothing to you after that talk we had
a month ago — but I felt sure. I knew you would," she declared.

"That I'd persist, you mean?"

"That you'd see him."

"Ah but I didn't" cried Brydon with his long wail. "There's
somebody — an awful beast; whom I brought, too horribly, to bay.
But it's not me."

At this she bent over him again, and her eyes were in his eyes.
"No — it's not you." And it was as if, while her face hovered, he
might have made out in it, hadn't it been so near, some particular
meaning blurred by a smile. "No, thank heaven," she repeated — "it's
not you! Of course it wasn't to have been."

"Ah but it *was,*" he gently insisted. And he stared before him now as he had been staring for so many weeks. "I was to have known myself."

"You couldn't!" she returned consolingly. And then reverting, and as if to account further for what she had herself done, "But it wasn't only *that,* that you hadn't been at home," she went on. "I waited till the hour at which we had found Mrs. Muldoon that day of my going with you; and she arrived, as I've told you, while, failing to bring anyone to the door, I lingered in my despair on the steps. After a little, if she hadn't come, by such a mercy, I should have found means to hunt her up. But it wasn't," said Alice Staverton, as if once more with her fine intention — "it wasn't only that."

His eyes, as he lay, turned back to her. "What more then?"

She met it, the wonder she had stirred. "In the cold dim dawn, you say? Well, in the cold dim dawn of this morning I too saw you."

"Saw *me* — ?"

"Saw *him,*" said Alice Staverton. "It must have been at the same moment."

He lay an instant taking it in — as if he wished to be quite reasonable. "At the same moment?"

"Yes — in my dream again, the same one I've named to you. He came back to me. Then I knew it for a sign. He had come to you."

At this Brydon raised himself; he had to see her better. She helped him when she understood his movement, and he sat up, steadying himself beside her there on the window-bench and with his right hand grasping her left. "*He* didn't come to me."

"You came to yourself," she beautifully smiled.

"Ah I've come to myself now — thanks to you, dearest. But this brute, with his awful face — this brute's a black stranger. He's none of *me,* even as I *might* have been," Brydon sturdily declared.

But she kept the clearness that was like the breath of infallibility. "Isn't the whole point that you'd have been different?"

He almost scowled for it. "As different as *that* — ?"

Her look again was more beautiful to him than the things of this world. "Haven't you exactly wanted to know *how* different? So this morning," she said, "you appeared to me."

"Like *him?*"

"A black stranger!"

"Then how did you know it was I?"

"Because, as I told you weeks ago, my mind, my imagination, had worked so over what you might, what you mightn't have been — to show you, you see, how I've thought of you. In the midst of that you came to me — that my wonder might be answered. So I knew," she went on; "and believed that, since the question held you too so fast, as you told me that day, you too would see for yourself. And when this morning I again saw I knew it would be because you had — and also then, from the first moment, because you somehow wanted me. *He* seemed to tell me of that. So why," she strangely smiled, "shouldn't I like him?"

It brought Spencer Brydon to his feet. "You 'like' that horror — ?"

"I *could* have liked him. And to me," she said, "he was no horror. I had accepted him."

"'Accepted' — ?" Brydon oddly sounded.

"Before, for the interest of his difference — yes. And as *I* didn't disown him, as *I* knew him — which you at last, confronted with him in his difference, so cruelly didn't, my dear — well, he must have been, you see, less dreadful to me. And it may have pleased him that I pitied him.

"She was beside him on her feet, but still holding his hand — still with her arm supporting him. But though it all brought for him thus a dim light, "You 'pitied' him?" he grudgingly, resentfully asked.

"He has been unhappy; he has been ravaged," she said.

"And haven't I been unhappy? Am not I — you've only to look at me! — ravaged?"

"Ah I don't say I like him *better,*" she granted after a thought. "But he's grim, he's worn — and things have happened to him. He doesn't make shift, for sight, with your charming monocle."

"No" — it struck Brydon: "I couldn't have sported mine 'downtown.' They'd have guyed me there."

"His great convex pince-nez — I saw it, I recognized the kind — is for his poor ruined sight. And his poor right hand — !"

"Ah!" Brydon winced — whether for his proved identity or for his lost fingers. Then, "He has a million a year," he lucidly added. "But he hasn't you."

"And he isn't — no, he isn't — *you!*" she murmured as he drew her to his breast.

The Yellow Wallpaper
Charlotte Perkins Gilman

When Charlotte Perkins Gilman's classic story "The Yellow Wallpaper" first appeared in 1891, a physician commented in an editorial that such a story ought not to be written. "It was enough to drive anyone mad to read it." Another woman just like the narrator appears in her wallpaper. The physician may very well have been right — at least about the story's effect on the reader.

*I*t is very seldom that mere ordinary people like John and myself secure ancestral halls for the summer.

A colonial mansion, a hereditary estate, I would say a haunted house, and reach the height of romantic felicity — but that would be asking too much of fate!

Still I will proudly declare that there is something queer about it.

Else, why should it be let so cheaply? And why have stood so long untenanted?

John laughs at me, of course, but one expects that in marriage.

John is practical in the extreme. He has no patience with faith, an intense horror of superstition, and he scoffs openly at any talk of things not to be felt and seen and put down in figures.

John is a physician, and *perhaps* — (I would not say it to a living soul, of course, but this is dead paper and a great relief to my mind) — *perhaps* that is one reason I do not get well faster.

You see he does not believe I am sick!

And what can one do?

If a physician of high standing, and one's own husband, assures friends and relatives that there is really nothing the matter with one but temporary nervous depression — a slight hysterical tendency — what is one to do?

My brother is also a physician, and also of high standing, and he says the same thing.

So I take phosphates or phosphites — whichever it is, and tonics, and journeys, and air, and exercise, and am absolutely forbidden to "work" until I am well again.

Personally, I disagree with their ideas.

Personally, I believe that congenial work, with excitement and change, would do me good.

But what is one to do?

I did write for a while in spite of them; but it *does* exhaust me a good deal — having to be so sly about it, or else meet with heavy opposition.

I sometimes fancy that my condition if I had less opposition and more society and stimulus — but John says the very worst thing I can do is to think about my condition, and I confess it always makes me feel bad.

So I will let it alone and talk about the house.

The most beautiful place! It is quite alone, standing well back from the road, quite three miles from the village. It makes me think of English places that you read about, for there are hedges and walls and gates that lock, and lots of separate little houses for the gardeners and people.

There is a *delicious* garden! I never saw such a garden — large and shady, full of box-bordered paths, and lined with long grape-covered arbors with seats under them.

There were greenhouses, too, but they are all broken now.

There was some legal trouble, I believe, something about the heirs and coheirs; anyhow, the place has been empty for years.

That spoils my ghostliness, I am afraid, but I don't care — there is something strange about the house — I can feel it.

I even said so to John one moonlight evening, but he said what I felt was a *draught,* and shut the window.

I get unreasonably angry with John sometimes. I'm sure I never used to be so sensitive. I think it is due to this nervous condition.

But John says if I feel so, I shall neglect proper self-control; so I take pains to control myself — before him, at least, and that makes me very tired.

I don't like our room a bit. I wanted one downstairs that opened on the piazza and had roses all over the window, and such pretty old-fashioned chintz hangings! but John would not hear of it.

He said there was only one window and not room for two beds, and no near room for him if he took another.

He is very careful and loving, and hardly lets me stir without special direction.

I have a schedule prescription for each hour in the day; he takes all care from me, and so I feel basely ungrateful not to value it more.

He said we came here solely on my account, that I was to have perfect rest and all the air I could get. "Your exercise depends on your strength, my dear," said he, "and your food somewhat on your appetite; but air you can absorb all the time." So we took the nursery at the top of the house.

It is a big, airy room, the whole floor nearly, with windows that look all ways, and air and sunshine galore. It was nursery first and then playroom and gymnasium, I should judge; for the windows are barred for little children, and there are rings and things in the walls.

The paint and paper look as if a boys' school had used it. It is stripped off — the paper — in great patches all around the head of my bed, about as far as I can reach, and in a great place on the other side of the room low down. I never saw a worse paper in my life.

One of those sprawling flamboyant patterns committing every artistic sin.

It is dull enough to confuse the eye in following, pronounced enough to constantly irritate and provoke study, and when you follow the lame uncertain curves for a little distance they suddenly commit suicide — plunge off at outrageous angles, destroy themselves in unheard of contradictions.

The color is repellent, almost revolting; a smouldering unclean yellow, strangely faded by the slow-turning sunlight.

It is a dull yet lurid orange in some places, a sickly sulphur tint in others.

No wonder the children hated it! I should hate it myself if I had to live in this room long.

There comes John, and I must put this away, — he hates to have me write a word.

W e have been here two weeks, and I haven't felt like writing before, since that first day.

I am sitting by the window now, up in this atrocious nursery, and there is nothing to hinder my writing as much as I please, save lack of strength.

John is away all day, and even some nights when his cases are serious.

I am glad my case is not serious!

But these nervous troubles are dreadfully depressing.

John does not know how much I really suffer. He knows there is no *reason* to suffer, and that satisfies him.

Of course it is only nervousness. It does weigh on me so not to do my duty in any way!

I meant to be such a help to John, such a real rest and comfort, and here I am a comparative burden already!

Nobody would believe what an effort it is to do what little I am able, — to dress and entertain, and other things.

It is fortunate Mary is so good with the baby. Such a dear baby!

And yet I *cannot* be with him, it makes me so nervous.

I suppose John never was nervous in his life. He laughs at me so about this wallpaper!

At first he meant to repaper the room, but afterwards he said that I was letting it get the better of me, and that nothing was worse for a nervous patient than to give way to such fancies.

He said that after the wallpaper was changed it would be the heavy bedstead, and then the barred windows, and then that gate at the head of the stairs, and so on.

"You know the place is doing you good," he said, "and really, dear, I don't care to renovate the house just for a three months' rental."

"Then do let us go downstairs," I said, "there are such pretty rooms there."

Then he took me in his arms and called me a blessed little goose, and said he would go down to the cellar, if I wished, and have it whitewashed into the bargain.

But he is right enough about the beds and windows and things.

It is an airy and comfortable room as anyone need wish, and, of course, I would not be so silly as to make him uncomfortable just for a whim.

I'm really getting quite fond of the big room, all but that horrid paper.

Out of one window I can see the garden, those mysterious deep-shaded arbors, the riotous old-fashioned flowers, and bushes and gnarly trees.

Out of another I get a lovely view of the bay and a little private wharf belonging to the estate. There is a beautiful shaded lane that runs down there from the house. I always fancy I see people walking in these numerous paths and arbors, but John has cautioned me not to give way to fancy in the least. He says that with my imaginative power and habit of story-making, a nervous weakness like mine is sure to lead to all manner of excited fancies, and that I ought to use my will and good sense to check the tendency. So I try.

I think sometimes that if I were only well enough to write a little it would relieve the press of ideas and rest me.

But I find I get pretty tired when I try.

It is so discouraging not to have any advice and companionship about my work. When I get really well, John says we will ask Cousin Henry and Julia down for a long visit; but he says he would as soon put fireworks in my pillowcase as to let me have those stimulating people about now.

I wish I could get well faster.

But I must not think about that. This paper looks to me as if it *knew* what a vicious influence it had!

There is a recurrent spot where the pattern lolls like a broken neck and two bulbous eyes stare at you upside down.

I get positively angry with the impertinence of it and the everlastingness. Up and down and sideways they crawl, and those absurd, unblinking eyes are everywhere. There is one place where two breadths didn't match, and the eyes go all up and down the line, one a little higher than the other.

I never saw so much expression in an inanimate thing before, and we all know how much expression they have! I used to lie awake as a child and get more entertainment and terror out of blank walls and plain furniture than most children could find in a toy store.

I remember what a kindly wink the knobs of our big, old bureau used to have, and there was one chair that always seemed like a strong friend.

I used to feel that if any of the other things looked too fierce I could always hop into that chair and be safe.

The furniture in this room is no worse than inharmonious, however, for we had to bring it all from downstairs. I suppose when this was used as a playroom they had to take the nursery things out, and no wonder! I never saw such ravages as the children have made here.

The wallpaper, as I said before, is torn off in spots, and it sticketh closer than a brother — they must have had perseverance as well as hatred.

Then the floor is scratched and gouged and splintered, the plaster itself is dug out here and there, and this great heavy bed which is all we found in the room, looks as if it had been through the wars.

But I don't mind it a bit — only the paper.

There comes John's sister. Such a dear girl as she is, and so careful of me! I must not let her find me writing.

She is a perfect and enthusiastic housekeeper, and hopes for no better profession. I verily believe she thinks it is the writing which made me sick!

But I can write when she is out, and see her a long way off from these windows.

There is one that commands the road, a lovely shaded winding road, and one that just looks off over the country. A lovely country, too, full of great elms and velvet meadows.

This wallpaper has a kind of sub-pattern in a different shade, a particularly irritating one, for you can only see it in certain lights, and not clearly then.

But in the places where it isn't faded and where the sun is just so — I can see a strange, provoking, formless sort of figure, that seems to skulk about behind that silly and conspicuous front design.

There's sister on the stairs!

*W*ell, the Fourth of July is over! The people are gone and I am tired out. John thought it might do me good to see a little company, so we just had mother and Nellie and the children down for a week.

Of course I didn't do a thing. Jennie sees to everything now.

But it tired me all the same.

John says if I don't pick up faster he shall send me to Weir Mitchell in the fall.

But I don't want to go there at all. I had a friend who was in his hands once, and she says he is just like John and my brother, only more so!

Besides, it is such an undertaking to go so far.

I don't feel as if it was worth while to turn my hand over for anything, and I'm getting dreadfully fretful and querulous.

I cry at nothing, and cry most of the time.

Of course I don't when John is here, or anybody else, but when I am alone.

And I am alone a good deal just now. John is kept in town very often by serious cases, and Jennie is good and lets me alone when I want her to.

So I walk a little in the garden or down that lovely lane, sit on the porch under the roses, and lie down up here a good deal.

I'm getting really fond of the room in spite of the wallpaper. Perhaps *because* of the wallpaper.

It dwells in my mind so!

I lie here on this great immovable bed — it is nailed down, I believe

— and follow that pattern about by the hour. It is as good as gymnastics, I assure you. I start, we'll say, at the bottom, down in the corner over there where it has not been touched, and I determine for the thousandth time that I *will* follow that pointless pattern to some sort of a conclusion.

I know a little of the principle of design, and I know this thing was not arranged on any laws of radiation, or alternation, or repetition, or symmetry, or anything else that I ever heard of.

It is repeated, of course, by the breadths, but not otherwise.

Looked at in one way each breadth stands alone, the bloated curves and flourishes — a kind of "debased Romanesque" with delirium tremens — go waddling up and down in isolated columns of fatuity.

But, on the other hand, they connect diagonally, and the sprawling outlines run off in great slanting waves of optic horror, like a lot of wallowing seaweeds in full chase.

The whole thing goes horizontally, too, at least it seems so, and I exhaust myself in trying to distinguish the order of its going in that direction.

They have used a horizontal breadth for a frieze, and that adds wonderfully to the confusion.

There is one end of the room where it is almost intact, and there, when the crosslights fade and the low sun shines directly upon it, I can almost fancy radiation after all, — the interminable grotesques seem to form around a common center and rush off in headlong plunges of equal distraction.

It makes me tired to follow it. I will take a nap I guess.

I don't know why I should write this.

I don't want to.

I don't feel able.

And I know John would think it absurd. But I *must* say what I feel and think in some way — it is such a relief!

But the effort is getting to be greater than the relief.

Half the time now I am awfully lazy, and lie down ever so much.

John says I musn't lose my strength, and has me take cod liver oil and lots of tonics and things, to say nothing of ale and wine and rare meat.

Dear John! He loves me very dearly, and hates to have me sick. I tried to have a real earnest reasonable talk with him the other day, and tell him how I wish he would let me go and make a visit to Cousin Henry and Julia.

But he said I wasn't able to go, nor able to stand it after I got there; and I did not make out a very good case for myself, for I was crying before I had finished.

It is getting to be a great effort for me to think straight. Just this nervous weakness I suppose.

And dear John gathered me up in his arms, and just carried me upstairs and laid me on the bed, and sat by me and read to me till it tired my head.

He said I was his darling and his comfort and all he had, and that I must take care of myself for his sake, and keep well.

He says no one but myself can help me out of it, that I must use my will and self-control and not let any silly fancies run away with me.

There's one comfort, the baby is well and happy, and does not have to occupy this nursery with the horrid wallpaper.

If we had not used it, that blessed child would have! What a fortunate escape! Why, I wouldn't have a child of mine, an impressionable little thing, live in such a room for worlds.

I never thought of it before, but it is lucky that John kept me here after all, I can stand it so much easier than a baby, you see.

Of course I never mention it to them anymore — I am too wise, — but I keep watch of it all the same.

There are things in that paper that nobody knows but me, or ever will.

Behind that outside pattern the dim shapes get clearer every day.

It is always the same shape, only very numerous.

And it is like a woman stooping down and creeping about behind that pattern. I don't like it a bit. I wonder — I begin to think — I wish John would take me away from here!

It is so hard to talk with John about my case, because he is so wise, and because he loves me so.

But I tried it last night.

It was moonlight. The moon shines in all around just as the sun does.

I hate to see it sometimes, it creeps so slowly, and always comes in by one window or another.

John was asleep and I hated to waken him, so I kept still and watched the moonlight on that undulating wallpaper till I felt creepy.

The faint figure behind seemed to shake the pattern, just as if she wanted to get out.

I got up softly and went to feel and see if the paper *did* move, and when I came back John was awake.

"What is it, little girl?" he said. "Don't go walking about like that — you'll get cold."

I though it was a good time to talk, so I told him that I really was not gaining here, and that I wished he would take me away.

"Why darling!" said he, "our lease will be up in three weeks, and I can't see how to leave before.

"The repairs are not done at home, and I cannot possibly leave town just now. Of course if you were in any danger, I could and would, but you really are better, dear, whether you can see it or not. I am a doctor, dear, and I know. You are gaining flesh and color, your appetite is better, I feel really much easier about you."

"I don't weigh a bit more," said I, "nor as much; and my appetite may be better in the evening when you are here, but it is worse in the morning when you are away!"

"Bless her little heart!" said he with a big hug, "she shall be as sick as she pleases! But now let's improve the shining hours by going to sleep, and talk about it in the morning!"

"And you won't go away?" I asked gloomily.

"Why, how can I, dear? It is only three weeks more and then we will take a nice little trip of a few days while Jennie is getting the house ready. Really dear you are better!"

"Better in body perhaps —" I began, and stopped short, for he sat up straight and looked at me with such a stern, reproachful look that I could not say another word.

"My darling," said he, "I beg of you, for my sake and for our child's sake, as well as for your own, that you will never for one instant let that idea enter your mind! There is nothing so dangerous, so fascinating, to a temperament like yours. It is a false and foolish fancy. Can you not trust me as a physician when I tell you so?"

So of course I said no more on that score, and we went to sleep before long. He thought I was asleep first, but I wasn't, and lay there for hours trying to decide whether that front pattern and the back pattern really did move together or separately.

*O*n a pattern like this, by daylight, there is a lack of sequence, a defiance of law, that is a constant irritant to a normal mind.

The color is hideous enough, and unreliable enough, and infuriating enough, but the pattern is torturing.

You think you have mastered it, but just as you get well underway in following, it turns a back-somersault and there you are. It slaps you in the face, knocks you down, and tramples upon you. It is like a bad dream.

The outside pattern is a florid arabesque, reminding one of a fungus. If you can imagine a toadstool in joints, an interminable string of toadstools, budding and sprouting in endless convolutions — why, that is something like it.

That is, sometimes!

There is one marked peculiarity about this paper, a thing nobody seems to notice but myself, and that is that it changes as the light changes.

When the sun shoots in through the east window — I always watch for that first long, straight ray — it changes so quickly that I never can quite believe it.

That is why I watch it always.

By moonlight — the moon shines in all night when there is a moon — I wouldn't know it was the same paper.

At night in any kind of light, in twilight, candle light, lamplight, and worst of all by moonlight, it becomes bars! The outside pattern I mean, and the woman behind it is as plain as can be.

I didn't realize for a long time what the thing was that showed behind, that dim sub-pattern, but now I am quite sure it is a woman.

By daylight she is subdued, quiet. I fancy it is the pattern that keeps her so still. It is so puzzling. It keeps me quiet by the hour.

I lie down ever so much now. John says it is good for me, and to sleep all I can.

Indeed he started the habit by making me lie down for an hour after each meal.

It is a very bad habit I am convinced, for you see I don't sleep.

And that cultivates deceit, for I don't tell them I'm awake — O no!

The fact is I am getting a little afraid of John.

He seems very queer sometimes, and even Jennie has an inexplicable look.

It strikes me occasionally, just as a scientific hypothesis, — that perhaps it is the paper!

I have watched John when he did not know I was looking, and come into the room suddenly on the most innocent excuses, and I've caught him several times *looking at the paper!* And Jennie too. I caught Jennie with her hand on it once.

She didn't know I was in the room, and when I asked her in a quiet, a very quiet voice, with the most restrained manner possible, what she was doing with the paper — she turned around as if she had been caught stealing, and looked quite angry — asked me why I should frighten her so!

Then she said that the paper stained everything it touched, that she had found yellow smooches on all my clothes and John's, and she wished we would be more careful!

Did not that sound innocent? But I know she was studying that pattern, and I am determined that nobody shall find it out but myself!

*L*ife is very much more exciting now than it used to be. You see I have something more to expect, to look forward to, to watch. I really do eat better, and am more quiet than I was.

John is so pleased to see me improve! He laughed a little the other day, and said I seemed to be flourishing in spite of my wallpaper.

I turned it off with a laugh. I had no intention of telling him it was *because* of the wallpaper — he would make fun of me. He might even want to take me away.

I don't want to leave now until I have found it out. There is a week more, and I think that will be enough.

I'm feeling ever so much better! I don't sleep much at night, for it is so interesting to watch developments; but I sleep a good deal in the daytime.

In the daytime it is tiresome and perplexing.

There are always new shoots on the fungus, and new shades of yellow all over it. I cannot keep count of them, though I have tried conscientiously.

It is the strangest yellow, that wallpaper! It makes me think of all the yellow things I ever saw — not beautiful ones like buttercups, but old foul, bad yellow things.

But there is something else about that paper — the smell! I noticed it the moment we came into the room, but with so much air and sun it was not bad. Now we have had a week of fog and rain, and whether the windows are open or not, the smell is here.

It creeps all over the house.

I find it hovering in the dining room, skulking in the parlor, hiding in the hall, lying in wait for me on the stairs.

It gets into my hair.

Even when I go to ride, if I turn my head suddenly and surprise it — there is that smell!

Such a peculiar odor, too! I have spent hours in trying to analyze it, to find what it smelled like.

It is not bad — at first, and very gentle, but quite the subtlest, most enduring odor I ever met.

In this damp weather it is awful, I wake up in the night and find it hanging over me.

It used to disturb me at first. I thought seriously of burning the house — to reach the smell.

But now I am used to it. The only thing I can think of that it is like is the *color* of the paper! A yellow smell.

There is a very funny mark on this wall, low down, near the mopboard. A streak that runs round the room. It goes behind every piece of furniture, except the bed, a long, straight, even *smooch,* as if it had been rubbed over and over.

I wonder how it was done and who did it, and what they did it for. Round and round and round — round and round and round — it makes me dizzy!

I really have discovered something at last.

Through watching so much at night, when it changes so, I have finally found out.

The front pattern *does* move — and no wonder! The woman behind shakes it!

Sometimes I think there are a great many women behind, and sometimes only one, and she crawls around fast, and her crawling shakes it all over.

Then in the very bright spots she keeps still, and in the very shady spots she just takes hold of the bars and shakes them hard.

And she is all the time trying to climb through. But nobody could climb through that pattern — it strangles so; I think that is why it has so many heads.

They get through, and then the pattern strangles them off and turns them upside down, and makes their eyes white!

If those heads were covered or taken off it would not be half so bad.

I think that woman gets out in the daytime!

And I'll tell you why — privately — I've seen her!

I can see her out of every one of my windows!

It is the same woman, I know, for she is always creeping, and most women do not creep by daylight.

I see her on that long road under the trees, creeping along, and when a carriage comes she hides under the blackberry vines.

I don't blame her a bit. It must be very humiliating to be caught creeping by daylight!

I always lock the door when I creep by daylight. I can't do it at night, for I know John would suspect something at once.

And John is so queer now, that I don't want to irritate him. I wish he would take another room! Besides, I don't want anybody to get that woman out at night but myself.

I often wonder if I could see her out of all the windows at once.

But, turn as fast as I can, I can only see out of one at a time.

And though I always see her, she *may* be able to creep faster than I can turn!

I have watched her sometimes away off in the open country, creeping as fast as a cloud shadow in a high wind.

If only that top pattern could be gotten off from the under one! I mean to try it, little by little.

I have found out another funny thing, but I shan't tell it this time! It does not do to trust people too much.

There are only two more days to get this paper off, and I believe John is beginning to notice. I don't like the look in his eyes.

And I heard him ask Jennie a lot of professional questions about me. She had a very good report to give.

She said I slept a good deal in the daytime.

John knows I don't sleep very well at night, for all I'm so quiet!

He asked me all sorts of questions, too, and pretended to be very loving and kind.

As if I couldn't see through him!

Still, I don't wonder he acts so, sleeping under this paper for three months.

It only interests me, but I feel sure John and Jennie are secretly affected by it.

*H*urrah! This is the last day, but it is enough. John is to stay in town over night, and won't be out until this evening.

Jennie wanted to sleep with me – the sly thing! but I told her I should undoubtedly rest better for a night all alone.

That was clever, for really I wasn't alone a bit! As soon as it was moonlight and that poor thing began to crawl and shake the pattern, I got up and ran to help her.

I pulled and she shook, I shook and she pulled, and before morning we had peeled off yards of that paper.

A strip about as high as my head and half around the room.

And then when the sun came and that awful pattern began to laugh at me, I declared I would finish it today!

We go away tomorrow, and they are moving all my furniture down again to leave things as they were before.

Jennie looked at the wall in amazement, but I told her merrily that I did it out of pure spite at the vicious thing.

She laughed and said she wouldn't mind doing it herself, but I must not get tired.

How she betrayed herself that time!

But I am here, and no person touches this paper but me — not *alive!*

She tried to get me out of the room — it was too patent! But I said it was so quiet and empty and clean now that I believed I would lie down again and sleep all I could; and not to wake me even for dinner — I would call when I woke.

So now she is gone, and the servants are gone, and the things are gone, and there is nothing left but that great bedstead nailed down, with the canvas mattress we found on it.

We shall sleep downstairs tonight, and take the boat home tomorrow.

I quite enjoy the room, now it is bare again.

How those children did tear about here!

This bedstead is fairly gnawed!

But I must get to work.

I have locked the door and thrown the key down into the front path.

I don't want to go out, and I don't want to have anybody come in, till John comes.

I want to astonish him.

I've got a rope up here that even Jennie did not find. If that woman does get out, and tries to get away, I can tie her!

But I forgot I could not reach far without anything to stand on!

This bed will *not* move!

I tried to lift and push it until I was lame, and then I got so angry I bit off a little piece at one corner — but it hurt my teeth.

Then I peeled off all the paper I could reach standing on the floor. It sticks horribly and the pattern just enjoys it! All those strangled heads and bulbous eyes and waddling fungus growths just shriek with derision!

I am getting angry enough to do something desperate. To jump out of the window would be admirable exercise, but the bars are too strong even to try.

Besides I wouldn't do it. Of course not. I know well enough that a step like that is improper and might be misconstrued.

I don't like to *look* out of the windows even — there are so many of those creeping women, and they creep so fast.

I wonder if they all come out of that wallpaper as I did?

But I am securely fastened now by my well-hidden rope — you don't get *me* out in the road there!

I suppose I shall have to get back behind the pattern when it comes night, and that is hard!

It is so pleasant to be out in this great room and creep around as I please!

I don't want to go outside. I won't, even if Jennie asks me to.

For outside you have to creep on the ground, and everything is green instead of yellow.

But here I can creep smoothly on the floor, and my shoulder just fits in that long smooch around the wall, so I cannot lose my way.

Why there's John at the door!

It is no use, young man, you can't open it!

How he does call and pound!

Now he's crying for an axe.

It would be a shame to break down that beautiful door!

"John dear!" said I in the gentlest voice, "the key is down by the front steps, under a plantain leaf!"

That silenced him for a few moments.

Then he said — very quietly indeed, "Open the door, my darling!"

"I can't," said I. "The key is down by the front door under a plantain leaf!"

And then I said it again, several times, very gently and slowly, and said it so often that he had to go and see, and he got it of course, and came in. He stopped short by the door.

"What is the matter?" he cried. "For God's sake, what are you doing!"

I kept on creeping just the same, but I looked at him over my shoulder.

"I've got out at last," said I, "in spite of you and Jane. And I've pulled off most of the paper, so you can't put me back!"

Now why should that man have fainted? But he did, and right across my path by the wall, so that I had to creep over him every time!

Enoch Soames

A Memory of the Eighteen-Nineties

Max Beerbohm

Enoch Soames was a "dim man." Max Beerbohm mixes fact and fable in this satirical, yet creepy tale of a "Catholic diabolist" willing to bargain with the un-Miltonic Devil to find out his contribution to posterity. As the time set for Soames' visit to the future reading room has passed, readers can only wonder who Enoch Soames is, or which Enoch ended up where, and when? By authoritative accounts, Enoch Soames mysteriously vanished after a visit to the British Museum Reading Room on 3 June 1897, although the Museum is exhibiting a retrospective of Soames' work, including his classic, "Fungoids," a rare and precious volume of fin de siecle poetry.

*W*hen a book about the literature of the eighteen-nineties was given by Mr. Holbrook Jackson to the world, I looked eagerly in the index for Soames, Enoch. It was as I feared: he was not there. But everybody else was. Many writers whom I had quite forgotten, or remembered but faintly, lived again for me, they and their work, in Mr. Holbrook Jackson's pages. The book was as thorough as it was brilliantly written. And thus the omission found by me was an all the deadlier record of poor Soames's failure to impress himself on his decade.

I dare say I am the only person who noticed the omission. Soames had failed so piteously as all that! Nor is there a counterpoise in the thought that if he had had some measure of success he might have passed, like those others, out of my mind, to return only at the historian's beck. It is true that had his gifts, such as they were, been acknowledged in his lifetime, he would never have made the bargain I saw him make — that strange bargain whose results have kept him always in the foreground of my memory. But it is from those very results that the full piteousness of him glares out.

Not my compassion, however, impels me to write of him. For his sake, poor fellow, I should be inclined to keep my pen out of the ink. It is ill to deride the dead. And how can I write about Enoch Soames without making him ridiculous? Or, rather, how am I to hush up the horrid fact that he *was* ridiculous? I shall not be able to do that. Yet, sooner or later, write about him I must. You will see in due course that I have no option. And I may as well get the thing done now.

In the summer term of '93 a bolt from the blue flashed down on Oxford. It drove deep; it hurtlingly embedded itself in the soil. Dons and undergraduates stood around, rather pale, discussing nothing but it. Whence came it, this meteorite? From Paris. Its name? Will Rothenstein. Its aim? To do a series of twenty-four portraits in lithograph. These were to be published from the Bodley Head, London. The matter was urgent. Already the warden of A, and the master of B, and the Regius Professor of C had meekly "sat." Dignified and doddering old men who had never consented to sit to anyone could not withstand this dynamic little stranger. He did not sue; he invited: he did not invite; he commanded. He was twenty-one years old. He wore spectacles that flashed more than any other pair ever seen. He was a wit. He was brimful of ideas. He knew Whistler. He knew Daudet and the Goncourts. He knew everyone in Paris. He knew them all by heart. He was Paris in Oxford. It was whispered that, so soon as he had polished off his selection of dons, he was going to include a few undergraduates. It was a proud day for me when I — I was included. I liked Rothenstein not less than I feared him; and there arose between us a friendship that has grown ever warmer, and been more and more valued by me, with every passing year.

At the end of term he settled in, or, rather, meteorically into, London. It was to him I owed my first knowledge of that forever-enchanting little world-in-itself, Chelsea, and my first acquaintance with Walter Sickert and other August elders who dwelt there. It was

Rothenstein that took me to see, in Cambridge Street, Pimlico, a young man whose drawings were already famous among the few — Aubrey Beardsley by name. With Rothenstein I paid my first visit to the Bodley Head. By him I was inducted into another haunt of intellect and daring, the domino-room of the Café Royal.

There, on that October evening — there, in that exuberant vista of gilding and crimson velvet set amidst all those opposing mirrors and upholding caryatids, with fumes of tobacco ever rising to the painted and pagan ceiling, and with the hum of presumably cynical conversation broken into so sharply now and again by the clatter of dominoes shuffled on marble tables, I drew a deep breath and, "This indeed," said I to myself, "is life!" (Forgive me that theory. Remember the waging of even the South African War was not yet.)

It was the hour before dinner. We drank vermouth. Those who knew Rothenstein were pointing him out to those who knew him only by name. Men were constantly coming in through the swing-doors and wandering slowly up and down in search of vacant tables or of tables occupied by friends. One of these rovers interested me because I was sure he wanted to catch Rothenstein's eye. He had twice passed our table, with a hesitating look; but Rothenstein, in the thick of a disquisition on Puvis de Chavannes, had not seen him. He was a stooping, shambling person, rather tall, very pale, with longish and brownish hair. He had a thin, vague beard, or, rather, he had a chin on which a large number of hairs weakly curled and clustered to cover its retreat. He was an odd-looking person; but in the nineties odd apparitions were more frequent, I think, than they are now. The young writers of that era — and I was sure this man was a writer — strove earnestly to be distinct in aspect. This man had striven unsuccessfully. He wore a soft black hat of clerical kind, but of Bohemian intention, and a gray waterproof cape which, perhaps because it was waterproof, failed to be romantic. I decided that "dim" was the mot juste for him. I had already essayed to write, and was immensely keen on the mot juste , that Holy Grail of the period.

The dim man was now again approaching our table, and this time he made up his mind to pause in front of it.

"You don't remember me," he said in a toneless voice.

Rothenstein brightly focused him.

"Yes, I do," he replied after a moment, with pride rather than effusion — pride in a retentive memory. "Edwin Soames."

"Enoch Soames," said Enoch.

"Enoch Soames," repeated Rothenstein in a tone implying that it was enough to have hit on the surname. "We met in Paris a few times when you were living there. We met at the Café Groche."

"And I came to your studio once."

"Oh, yes; I was sorry I was out."

"But you were in. You showed me some of your paintings, you know. I hear you're in Chelsea now."

"Yes."

I almost wondered that Mr. Soames did not, after this monosyllable, pass along. He stood patiently there, rather like a dumb animal, rather like a donkey looking over a gate. A sad figure, his. It occurred to me that "hungry" was perhaps the mot juste for him; but — hungry for what? He looked as if he had little appetite for anything. I was sorry for him; and Rothenstein, though he had not invited him to Chelsea, did ask him to sit down and have something to drink.

Seated, he was more self-assertive. He flung back the wings of his cape with a gesture which, had not those wings been waterproof, might have seemed to hurl defiance at things in general. And he ordered an absinthe. *"Je me tiens toujours fidele,"* he told Rothenstein, *"a la sorciere glauque."*

"It is bad for you," said Rothenstein, dryly.

"Nothing is bad for one," answered Soames. *"Dans ce monde il n'y a ni bien ni mal."*

"Nothing good and nothing bad? How do you mean?"

"I explained it all in the preface to 'Negations.'"

"'Negations'?"

"Yes, I gave you a copy of it."

"Oh, yes, of course. But, did you explain, for instance, that there was no such thing as bad or good grammar?"

"N-no," said Soames. "Of course in art there is the good and the evil. But in life — no." He was rolling a cigarette. He had weak, white hands, not well washed, and with fingertips much stained with nicotine. "In life there are illusions of good and evil, but" — his voice trailed away to a murmur in which the words *"vieux jeu"* and *"rococo"* were faintly audible. I think he felt he was not doing himself justice, and feared that Rothenstein was going to point out fallacies. Anyhow, he cleared his throat and said, *"Parlons d'autre chose."*

It occurs to you that he was a fool? It didn't to me. I was young, and had not the clarity of judgment that Rothenstein already had. Soames was quite five or six years older than either of us. Also — he had written a book. It was wonderful to have written a book.

If Rothenstein had not been there, I should have revered Soames. Even as it was, I respected him. And I was very near indeed to reverence when he said he had another book coming out soon. I asked if I might ask what kind of book it was to be.

"My poems," he answered. Rothenstein asked if this was to be the title of the book. The poet meditated on this suggestion, but said he rather thought of giving the book no title at all. "If a book is good in itself —" he murmured, and waved his cigarette.

Rothenstein objected that absence of title might be bad for the sale of a book.

"If," he urged, "I went into a bookseller's and said simply, 'Have you got?' or, 'Have you a copy of?' how would they know what I wanted?"

"Oh, of course I should have my name on the cover," Soames answered earnestly. "And I rather want," he added, looking hard at Rothenstein, "to have a drawing of myself as frontispiece." Rothenstein admitted that this was a capital idea, and mentioned that he was going into the country and would be there for some time. He then looked at his watch, exclaimed at the hour, paid the waiter, and went away with me to dinner. Soames remained at his post of fidelity to the glaucous witch.

"Why were you so determined not to draw him?" I asked.

"Draw him? Him? How can one draw a man who doesn't exist?"

"He is dim," I admitted. But my mot juste fell flat. Rothenstein repeated that Soames was non-existent.

Still, Soames had written a book. I asked if Rothenstein had read "Negations." He said he had looked into it, "but," he added crisply, "I don't profess to know anything about writing." A reservation very characteristic of the period! Painters would not then allow that anyone outside their own order had a right to any opinion about painting. This law (graven on the tablets brought down by Whistler from the summit of Fujiyama) imposed certain limitations. If other arts than painting were not utterly unintelligible to all but the men who practiced them, the law tottered — the Monroe Doctrine, as it were, did not hold good. Therefore no painter would offer an opinion of a book without warning you at any rate that his opinion was worthless. No one is a better judge of literature than Rothenstein; but it wouldn't have done to tell him so in those days, and I knew that I must form an unaided judgment of "Negations."

Not to buy a book of which I had met the author face to face would have been for me in those days an impossible act of self-denial. When I returned to Oxford for the Christmas term I had duly secured "Negations." I used to keep it lying carelessly on the table in my room, and whenever a friend took it up and asked what it was about, I would say: "Oh, it's rather a remarkable book. It's by a man whom I know." Just "what it was about" I never was able to say.

Head or tail was just what I hadn't made of that slim, green volume.
I found in the preface no clue to the labyrinth of contents, and in
that labyrinth nothing to explain the preface.

> Lean near to life. Lean very near — nearer.
> Life is web and therein nor warp nor woof is, but web only.
> It is for this I am Catholick in church and in thought, yet
> do let swift Mood weave there what the shuttle of Mood wills.

These were the opening phrases of the preface, but those which
followed were less easy to understand. Then came "Stark: A Conte,"
about a midinette who, so far as I could gather, murdered, or was
about to murder, a mannequin. It was rather like a story by Catulle
Mendes in which the translator had either skipped or cut out every
alternate sentence. Next, a dialogue between Pan and St. Ursula,
lacking, I rather thought, in "snap." Next, some aphorisms (entitled
"Απηορισματα"). Throughout, in fact, there was a great variety of
form, and the forms had evidently been wrought with much care. It
was rather the substance that eluded me. Was there, I wondered, any
substance at all? It did not occur to me: suppose Enoch Soames was
a fool! Up cropped a rival hypothesis: suppose *I* was! I inclined to
give Soames the benefit of the doubt. I had read *"L'Apres-midi d'un
faune"* without extracting a glimmer of meaning; yet Mallarme, of
course, was a master. How was I to know that Soames wasn't another?
There was a sort of music in his prose, not indeed, arresting, but
perhaps, I thought, haunting, and laden, perhaps, with meanings as
deep as Mallarme's own. I awaited his poems with an open mind.

And I looked forward to them with positive impatience after I
had had a second meeting with him. This was on an evening in
January. Going into the aforesaid domino-room, I had passed a table
at which sat a pale man with an open book before him. He had
looked from his book to me, and I looked back over my shoulder
with a vague sense that I ought to have recognized him. I returned
to pay my respects. After exchanging a few words, I said with a glance
to the open book, "I see I am interrupting you," and was about to
pass on, but, "I prefer," Soames replied in his toneless voice, "to be
interrupted," and I obeyed his gesture that I should sit down.

I asked him if he often read here.

"Yes; things of this kind I read here," he answered, indicating the
title of his book — "The Poems of Shelley."

"Anything that you really" — and I was going to say "admire?"
But I cautiously left my sentence unfinished, and was glad that I
had done so, for he said with unwonted emphasis, "Anything

second-rate."

I had read little of Shelley, but, "Of course," I murmured, "he's very uneven."

"I should have thought evenness was just what was wrong with him. A deadly evenness. That's why I read him here. The noise of this place breaks the rhythm. He's tolerable here." Soames took up the book and glanced through the pages. He laughed. Soames's laugh was a short, single, and mirthless sound from the throat, unaccompanied by any movement of the face or brightening of the eyes. "What a period!" he uttered, laying the book down. And, "What a country!" he added.

I asked rather nervously if he didn't think Keats had more or less held his own against the drawbacks of time and place. He admitted that there were "passages in Keats," but did not specify them. Of "the older men," as he called them, he seemed to like only Milton. "Milton," he said, "wasn't sentimental." Also, "Milton had a dark insight." And again, "I can always read Milton in the reading-room."

"The reading-room?"

"Of the British Museum. I go there every day."

"You do? I've only been there once. I'm afraid I found it rather a depressing place. It — it seemed to sap one's vitality."

"It does. That's why I go there. The lower one's vitality, the more sensitive one is to great art. I live near the museum. I have rooms in Dyott Street."

"And you go round to the reading-room to read Milton?"

"Usually Milton." He looked at me. "It was Milton," he certificatively added, "who converted me to diabolism."

"Diabolism? Oh, yes? Really?" said I, with that vague discomfort and that intense desire to be polite which one feels when a man speaks of his own religion. "You — worship the devil?"

Soames shook his head.

"It's not exactly worship," he qualified, sipping his absinthe. "It's more a matter of trusting and encouraging."

"I see, yes. I had rather gathered from the preface to 'Negations' that you were a — a Catholic."

"*Je l'etais a cette epoque.* In fact, I still am. I am a Catholic diabolist."

But this profession he made in an almost cursory tone. I could see that what was uppermost in his mind was the fact that I had read "Negations." His pale eyes had for the first time gleamed. I felt as one who is about to be examined viva voce on the very subject in which he is shakiest. I hastily asked him how soon his poems were to be published.

"Next week," he told me.

"And are they to be published without a title?"

"No. I found a title at last. But I shan't tell you what it is," as though I had been so impertinent as to inquire. "I am not sure that it wholly satisfies me. But it is the best I can find. It suggests something of the quality of the poems — strange growths, natural and wild, yet exquisite," he added, "and many-hued, and full of poisons."

I asked him what he thought of Baudelaire. He uttered the snort that was his laugh, and, "Baudelaire," he said, "was a *bourgeois malgre lui.*" France had had only one poet — Villon; "and two thirds of Villon were sheer journalism." Verlaine was "an epic*ier malgre lui.*" Altogether, rather to my surprise, he rated French literature lower than English. There were "passages" in Villiers de l'Isle-Adam. But, "I," he summed up, "owe nothing to France." He nodded at me. "You'll see," he predicted.

I did not, when the time came, quite see that. I thought the author of "Fungoids" did, unconsciously of course, owe something to the young Parisian decadents or to the young English ones who owed something to *them.* I still think so. The little book, bought by me in Oxford, lies before me as I write. Its pale-gray buckram cover and silver lettering have not worn well. Nor have its contents. Through these, with a melancholy interest, I have again been looking. They are not much. But at the time of their publication I had a vague suspicion that they *might* be. I suppose it is my capacity for faith, not poor Soames's work, that is weaker than it once was.

TO A YOUNG WOMAN

Thou art, who hast not been!
Pale tunes irresolute
And traceries of old sounds
Blown from a rotted flute
Mingle with noise of cymbals rouged with rust,
Nor not strange forms and epicene
Lie bleeding in the dust,
Being wounded with wounds.
For this it is
That in thy counterpart
Of age-long mockeries
Thou hast not been nor art!

There seemed to me a certain inconsistency as between the first and last lines of this. I tried, with bent brows, to resolve the discord. But I did not take my failure as wholly incompatible with a meaning in Soames's mind. Might it not rather indicate the depth of his meaning? As for the craftsmanship, "rouged with rust" seemed to me a fine stroke, and "nor not" instead of "and" had a curious felicity. I wondered who the "young woman" was and what she had made of it all. I sadly suspect that Soames could not have made more of it than she. Yet even now, if one doesn't try to make any sense at all of the poem, and reads it just for the sound, there is a certain grace of cadence. Soames was an artist, in so far as he was anything, poor fellow!

It seemed to me, when first I read "Fungoids," that, oddly enough, the diabolistic side of him was the best. Diabolism seemed to be a cheerful, even a wholesome influence in his life.

NOCTURNE

Round and round the shutter'd square
I strolled with the Devil's arm in mine.
No sound but the scrape of his hoofs was there
And the ring of his laughter and mine.
We had drunk black wine.

I scream'd, "I will race you, Master!"
"What matter," he shriek'd, "tonight
Which of us runs the faster?
There is nothing to fear tonight
In the foul moon's light!"

Then I look'd him in the eyes
And I laugh'd full shrill at the lie he told
And the gnawing fear he would fain disguise.
It was true, what I'd time and again been told:
He was old — old.

There was, I felt, quite a swing about that first stanza — a joyous and rollicking note of comradeship. The second was slightly hysterical, perhaps. But I liked the third, it was so bracingly unorthodox, even according to the tenets of Soames's peculiar sect in the faith. Not much "trusting and encouraging" here! Soames triumphantly exposing the devil as a liar, and laughing "full shrill," cut a quite heartening figure, I thought, then! Now, in the light of what befell, none of his other poems depresses me so much as "Nocturne."

I looked out for what the metropolitan reviewers would have to say. They seemed to fall into two classes: those who had little to say and those who had nothing. The second class was the larger, and the words of the first were cold; insomuch that

"Strikes a note of modernity. . . . These tripping numbers."
— *The Preston Telegraph*

was the only lure offered in advertisements by Soames's publisher. I had hoped that when next I met the poet I could congratulate him on having made a stir, for I fancied he was not so sure of his intrinsic greatness as he seemed. I was but able to say, rather coarsely, when next I did see him, that I hoped "Fungoids" was "selling splendidly." He looked at me across his glass of absinthe and asked if I had bought a copy. His publisher had told him that three had been sold. I laughed, as at a jest.

"You don't suppose I *care*, do you?" he said, with something like a snarl. I disclaimed the notion. He added that he was not a tradesman. I said mildly that I wasn't, either, and murmured that an artist who gave truly new and great things to the world had always to wait long for recognition. He said he cared not a sou for recognition. I agreed that the act of creation was its own reward.

His moroseness might have alienated me if I had regarded myself as a nobody. But ah! hadn't both John Lane and Aubrey Beardsley suggested that I should write an essay for the great new venture that was afoot — "The Yellow Book?" And hadn't Henry Harland, as editor, accepted my essay? And wasn't it to be in the very first number? At Oxford I was still in *statu pupillari.* In London I regarded myself as very much indeed a graduate now — one whom no Soames could ruffle. Partly to show off, partly in sheer good-will, I told Soames he ought to contribute to "The Yellow Book." He uttered from the throat a sound of scorn for that publication.

Nevertheless, I did, a day or two later, tentatively ask Harland if he knew anything of the work of a man called Enoch Soames. Harland paused in the midst of his characteristic stride around the room, threw up his hands toward the ceiling, and groaned aloud: he had often met "that absurd creature" in Paris, and this very morning had received some poems in manuscript from him.

"Has he *no* talent?" I asked.

"He has an income. He's all right." Harland was the most joyous of men and most generous of critics, and he hated to talk of anything about which he couldn't be enthusiastic. So I dropped the subject of Soames. The news that Soames had an income did take the edge off solicitude. I learned afterward that he was the son of an unsuccessful and deceased bookseller in Preston, but had inherited an annuity of three hundred pounds from a married aunt, and had no surviving relatives of any kind. Materially, then, he was "all right." But there was still a spiritual pathos about him, sharpened for me now by the possibility that even the praises of "The Preston Telegraph" might not have been forthcoming had he not been the son of a Preston man He had a sort of weak doggedness which I could not but admire. Neither he nor his work received the slightest encouragement; but he persisted in behaving as a personage: always he kept his dingy little flag flying. Wherever congregated the *jeunes feroces* of the arts, in whatever Soho restaurant they had just discovered, in whatever music hall they were most frequently, there was Soames in the midst of them, or, rather, on the fringe of them, a dim, but inevitable, figure. He never sought to propitiate his fellow-writers, never bated a jot of his arrogance about his own work or of his contempt for theirs. To the painters he was respectful, even humble; but for the poets and prosaists of "The Yellow Book" and later of "The Savoy" he had never a word but of scorn. He wasn't resented. It didn't occur to anybody that he or his Catholic diabolism mattered. When, in the autumn of '96, he brought out (at his own expense, this time) a third book, his last book, nobody said a word for or against it. I meant, but forgot, to buy it. I never saw it, and am ashamed to say I don't even remember what it was called. But I did, at the time of its publication, say to Rothenstein that I thought poor old Soames was really a rather tragic figure, and that I believed he would literally die for want of recognition. Rothenstein scoffed. He said I was trying to get credit for a kind heart which I didn't possess; and perhaps this was so. But at the private view of the New English Art Club, a few weeks later, I beheld a pastel portrait of "Enoch Soames, Esq." It was very like him, and very like Rothenstein to have done it. Soames was standing near it, in his soft hat and his waterproof cape, all through the afternoon. Anybody who knew him would have recognized the portrait at a glance, but nobody who didn't know him would have recognized the portrait from its bystander: it "existed" so much more than he; it was bound to. Also, it had not that expression of faint happiness which on that day was discernible, yes, in Soames's countenance. Fame had breathed on him. Twice again in the course of the month I went to the New English, and on both occasions Soames himself was on view there. Looking back, I regard the close of that exhibition as having been virtually the close of his career. He had felt the breath of Fame against his cheek — so late, for such a little while; and at its withdrawal he gave in, gave up, gave out. He, who had never looked strong or well, looked ghastly now — a shadow of the shade he had once been. He still frequented the domino-room, but having lost all wish to excite curiosity, he no longer read books there. "You read only at the museum now?" I asked, with attempted cheerfulness. He said he never went there now. "No absinthe there," he muttered. It was the sort of thing that in old days he would have said for effect; but it carried conviction now. Absinthe, erst but a point in the "personality" he had striven so hard to build up, was solace and necessity now. He no longer called it *"la sorciere glauque."* He had shed away all his French phrases. He had become a plain, unvarnished Preston man.

Failure, if it be a plain, unvarnished, complete failure, and even though it be a squalid failure, has always a certain dignity. I avoided Soames because he made me feel rather vulgar. John Lane had published, by this time, two little books of mine, and they had had a pleasant little success of esteem. I was a — slight, but definite — "personality." Frank Harris had engaged me to kick up my heels in "The Saturday Review," Alfred Harmsworth was letting me do likewise in "The Daily Mail." I was just what Soames wasn't. And he shamed my gloss. Had I known that he really and firmly believed in the greatness of what he as an artist had achieved, I might not have shunned him. No man who hasn't lost his vanity can be held to have altogether failed. Soames's dignity was an illusion of mine. One day, in the first week of June, 1897, that illusion went. But on the evening of that day Soames went, too.

I had been out most of the morning and, as it was too late to reach home in time for luncheon, I sought the Vingtieme. This little place — Restaurant du Vingtieme Siecle, to give it its full title — had been discovered in '96 by the poets and prosaists, but had now been more or less abandoned in favor of some later find. I don't think it lived long enough to justify its name; but at that time there it still was, in Greek Street, a few doors from Soho Square, and almost opposite to that house where, in the first years of the century, a little girl, and with her a boy named De Quincey, made nightly encampment in darkness and hunger among dust and rats and old legal parchments. The Vingtieme was but a small whitewashed room, leading out into the street at one end and into a kitchen at the other. The proprietor and cook was a Frenchman, known to us as Monsieur Vingtieme; the waiters were his two daughters, Rose and Berthe; and the food, according to faith, was good. The tables were so narrow and were set so close together that there was space for twelve of them, six jutting from each wall.

Only the two nearest to the door, as I went in, were occupied. On one side sat a tall, flashy, rather Mephistophelian man whom I had seen from time to time in the domino-room and elsewhere. On the other side sat Soames. They made a queer contrast in that sunlit room, Soames sitting haggard in that hat and cape, which nowhere at any season had I seen him doff, and this other, this keenly vital man, at sight of whom I more than ever wondered whether he were a diamond merchant, a conjurer, or the head of a private detective agency. I was sure Soames didn't want my company; but I asked, as it would have seemed brutal not to, whether I might join him, and took the chair opposite to his. He was smoking a cigarette, with an untasted salmi of something on his plate and a half-empty bottle of Sauterne before him, and he was quite silent. I said that the preparations for the Jubilee made London impossible. (I rather liked them, really.) I professed a wish to go right away till the whole thing was over. In vain did I attune myself to his gloom. He seemed not to hear me or even to see me. I felt that his behavior made me ridiculous in the eyes of the other man. The gangway between the two rows of tables at the Vingtieme was hardly more than two feet wide (Rose and Berthe, in their ministrations, had always to edge past each other, quarreling in whispers as they did so), and anyone at the table abreast of yours was virtually at yours. I thought our neighbor was amused at my failure to interest Soames, and so, as I could not explain to him that my insistence was merely charitable, I became silent. Without turning my head, I had him well within my range of vision. I hoped I looked less vulgar than he in contrast with Soames. I was sure he was not an Englishman, but what *was* his nationality? Though his jet-black hair was *en brosse,* I did not think he was French. To Berthe, who waited on him, he spoke French fluently, but with a hardly native idiom and accent. I gathered that this was his first visit to the Vingtieme; but Berthe was offhand in her manner to him: he had not made a good impression. His eyes were handsome, but, like the Vingtieme's tables, too narrow and set too close together. His nose was predatory, and the points of his mustache, waxed up behind his nostrils, gave a fixity to his smile. Decidedly, he was sinister. And my sense of discomfort in his presence was intensified by the scarlet waistcoat which tightly, and so unseasonably in June, sheathed his ample chest. This waistcoat wasn't wrong merely because of the heat, either. It was somehow all wrong in itself. It wouldn't have done on Christmas morning. It would have struck a jarring note at the first night of "Hernani." I was trying to account for its wrongness when Soames suddenly and strangely broke silence. "A hundred years hence!" he murmured, as in a trance.

"We shall not be here," I briskly, but fatuously, added.

"We shall not be here. No," he droned, "but the museum will still be just where it is. And the reading-room just where it is. And people will be able to go and read there." He inhaled sharply, and a spasm as of actual pain contorted his features.

I wondered what train of thought poor Soames had been following. He did not enlighten me when he said, after a long pause, "You think I haven't minded."

"Minded what, Soames?"

"Neglect. Failure."

"*Failure?*" I said heartily. "Failure?" I repeated vaguely. "Neglect — yes, perhaps; but that's quite another matter. Of course you haven't been — appreciated. But what, then? Any artist who — who gives —" What I wanted to say was, "Any artist who gives truly new and great things to the world has always to wait long for recognition"; but the flattery would not out: in the face of his misery — a misery so genuine and so unmasked — my lips would not say the words.

And then he said them for me. I flushed. "That's what you were going to say, isn't it?" he asked.

"How did you know?"

"It's what you said to me three years ago, when 'Fungoids' was published." I flushed the more. I need not have flushed at all. "It's the only important thing I ever heard you say," he continued. "And I've never forgotten it. It's a true thing. It's a horrible truth. But — d'you remember what I answered? I said, 'I don't care a sou for recognition.' And you believed me. You've gone on believing I'm above that sort of thing. You're shallow. What should *you* know of the feelings of a man like me? You imagine that a great artist's faith in himself and in the verdict of posterity is enough to keep him happy. You've never guessed at the bitterness and loneliness, the" — his voice broke; but presently he resumed, speaking with a force that I had never known in him. "Posterity! What use is it to *me?* A dead man doesn't know that people are visiting his grave, visiting his birthplace, putting up tablets to him, unveiling statues of him. A dead man can't read the books that are written about him. A hundred years hence! Think of it! If I could come back to life *then* — just for a few hours — and go to the reading-room and *read!* Or, better still, if I could be projected now, at this moment, into that future, into that reading-room, just for this one afternoon! I'd sell myself body and soul to the devil for that! Think of the pages and pages in the catalogue: 'Soames, Enoch' endlessly — endless editions, commentaries, prolegomena, biographies" — But here he was interrupted by a sudden loud crack of the chair at the next table. Our neighbor had half risen from his place. He was leaning toward us, apologetically intrusive.

"Excuse — permit me," he said softly. "I have been unable not to hear. Might I take a liberty? In this little *restaurant-sans-façon* — might I, as the phrase is, cut in?"

I could but signify our acquiescence. Berthe had appeared at the kitchen door, thinking the stranger wanted his bill. He waved her away with his cigar, and in another moment had seated himself beside me, commanding a full view of Soames.

"Though not an Englishman," he explained, "I know my London well, Mr. Soames. Your name and fame — Mr. Beerbohm's, too — very known to me. Your point is, who am *I?*" He glanced quickly over his shoulder, and in a lowered voice said, "I am the devil."

I couldn't help it; I laughed. I tried not to, I knew there was nothing to laugh at, my rudeness shamed me; but — I laughed with increasing volume. The devil's quiet dignity, the surprise and disgust of his raised eyebrows, did but the more dissolve me. I rocked to and fro; I lay back aching; I behaved deplorably.

"I am a gentleman, and," he said with intense emphasis, "I thought I was in the company of *gentlemen.*"

"Don't!" I gasped faintly. "Oh, don't!"

"Curious, *nicht wahr?*" I heard him say to Soames. "There is a type of person to whom the very mention of my name is — oh, so awfully — funny! In your theaters the dullest comedien needs only to say 'The devil!' and right away they give him 'the loud laugh what speaks the vacant mind.' Is it not so?"

I had now just breath enough to offer my apologies. He accepted them, but coldly, and re-addressed himself to Soames.

"I am a man of business," he said, "and always I would put things through 'right now,' as they say in the States. You are a poet. *Les affaires* — you detest them. So be it. But with me you will deal, eh? What you have said just now gives me furiously to hope."

Soames had not moved except to light a fresh cigarette. He sat crouched forward, with his elbows squared on the table, and his head just above the level of his hands, staring up at the devil.

"Go on," he nodded. I had no remnant of laughter in me now.

"It will be the more pleasant, our little deal," the devil went on, "because you are — I mistake not? — a diabolist."

"A Catholic diabolist," said Soames.

The devil accepted the reservation genially.

"You wish," he resumed, "to visit now — this afternoon as-ever-is — the reading-room of the British Museum, yes? But of a hundred years hence, yes? *Parfaitement.* Time — an illusion. Past and future — they are as ever present as the present, or at any rate only what you call 'just round the corner.' I switch you on to any date. I project you — pouf! You wish to be in the reading-room just as it will be on the afternoon of June 3, 1997? You wish to find yourself standing in that room, just past the swing-doors, this very minute, yes? And to stay there till closing-time? Am I right?"

Soames nodded.

The devil looked at his watch. "Ten past two," he said. "Closing-time in summer same then as now — seven o'clock. That will give you almost five hours. At seven o'clock — pouf! — you find yourself again here, sitting at this table. I am dining tonight *dans le monde — dans le higlif.* That concludes my present visit to your great city. I come and fetch you here, Mr. Soames, on my way home."

"Home?" I echoed.

"Be it never so humble!" said the devil, lightly.

"All right," said Soames.

"Soames!" I entreated. But my friend moved not a muscle.

The devil had made as though to stretch forth his hand across the table, but he paused in his gesture.

"A hundred years hence, as now," he smiled, "no smoking allowed in the reading-room. You would better therefore —"

Soames removed the cigarette from his mouth and dropped it into his glass of Sauterne.

"Soames!" again I cried. "Can't you" — but the devil had now stretched forth his hand across the table. He brought it slowly down on the tablecloth. Soames's chair was empty. His cigarette floated sodden in his wine-glass. There was no other trace of him.

For a few moments the devil let his hand rest where it lay, gazing at me out of the corners of his eyes, vulgarly triumphant.

A shudder shook me. With an effort I controlled myself and rose from my chair. "Very clever," I said condescendingly. "But — 'The Time Machine' is a delightful book, don't you think? So entirely original!"

"You are pleased to sneer," said the devil, who had also risen, "but it is one thing to write about an impossible machine; it is a quite other thing to be a supernatural power." All the same, I had scored.

Berthe had come forth at the sound of our rising. I explained to her that Mr. Soames had been called away, and that both he and I would be dining here. It was not until I was out in the open air that I began to feel giddy. I have but the haziest recollection of what I did, where I wandered, in the glaring sunshine of that endless afternoon. I remember the sound of carpenters' hammers all along Piccadilly and the bare chaotic look of the half-erected "stands." Was it in the Green Park or in Kensington Gardens or *where* was it that I sat on a chair beneath a tree, trying to read an evening paper? There was a phrase in the leading article that went on repeating itself in my fagged mind: "Little is hidden from this August Lady full of the garnered wisdom of sixty years of Sovereignty." I remember wildly conceiving a letter (to reach Windsor by an express messenger told to await answer): "Madam: Well knowing that your Majesty is full of the garnered wisdom of sixty years of Sovereignty, I venture to ask your advice in the following delicate matter. Mr. Enoch Soames, whose poems you may or may not know —" Was there *no* way of helping him, saving him? A bargain was a bargain, and I was the last man to aid or abet anyone in wriggling out of a reasonable obligation. I wouldn't have lifted a little finger to save Faust. But poor Soames! Doomed to pay without respite an eternal price for nothing but a fruitless search and a bitter disillusioning.

Odd and uncanny it seemed to me that he, Soames, in the flesh, in the waterproof cape, was at this moment living in the last decade of the next century, poring over books not yet written, and seeing and seen by men not yet born. Uncannier and odder still that tonight and evermore he would be in hell. Assuredly, truth was stranger than fiction.

Endless that afternoon was. Almost I wished I had gone with Soames, not, indeed, to stay in the reading-room, but to sally forth for a brisk sight-seeing walk around a new London. I wandered restlessly out of the park I had sat in. Vainly I tried to imagine myself an ardent tourist from the eighteenth century. Intolerable was the strain of the slow-passing and empty minutes. Long before seven o'clock I was back at the Vingtieme.

I sat there just where I had sat for luncheon. Air came in listlessly through the open door behind me. Now and again Rose or Berthe appeared for a moment. I had told them I would not order any dinner till Mr. Soames came. A hurdy-gurdy began to play, abruptly drowning the noise of a quarrel between some Frenchmen farther up the street. Whenever the tune was changed I heard the quarrel still raging. I had bought another evening paper on my way. I unfolded it. My eyes gazed ever away from it to the clock over the kitchen door.

Five minutes now to the hour! I remembered that clocks in restaurants are kept five minutes fast. I concentrated my eyes on the paper. I vowed I would not look away from it again. I held it upright, at its full width, close to my face, so that I had no view of anything but it. Rather a tremulous sheet? Only because of the draft, I told myself.

My arms gradually became stiff; they ached; but I could not drop them — now. I had a suspicion, I had a certainty. Well, what, then?

What else had I come for? Yet I held tight that barrier of newspaper. Only the sound of Berthe's brisk footstep from the kitchen enabled me, forced me, to drop it, and to utter:

"What shall we have to eat, Soames?"

"Il est souffrant, ce pauvre Monsieur Soames?" asked Berthe.

"He's only — tired." I asked her to get some wine — Burgundy — and whatever food might be ready. Soames sat crouched forward against the table exactly as when last I had seen him. It was as though he had never moved — he who had moved so unimaginably far. Once or twice in the afternoon it had for an instant occurred to me that perhaps his journey was not to be fruitless, that perhaps we had all been wrong in our estimate of the works of Enoch Soames. That we had been horribly right was horribly clear from the look of him. But, "Don't be discouraged," I falteringly said. "Perhaps it's only that you — didn't leave enough time. Two, three centuries hence, perhaps —"

"Yes," his voice came; "I've thought of that."

"And now — now for the more immediate future! Where are you going to hide? How would it be if you caught the Paris express from Charing Cross? Almost an hour to spare. Don't go on to Paris. Stop at Calais. Live in Calais. He'd never think of looking for you in Calais."

"It's like my luck," he said, "to spend my last hours on earth with an ass." But I was not offended. "And a treacherous ass," he strangely added, tossing across to me a crumpled bit of paper which he had been holding in his hand. I glanced at the writing on it — some sort of gibberish, apparently. I laid it impatiently aside.

"Come, Soames, pull yourself together! This isn't a mere matter of life or death. It's a question of eternal torment, mind you! You don't mean to say you're going to wait limply here till the devil comes to fetch you."

"I can't do anything else. I've no choice."

"Come! This is 'trusting and encouraging' with a vengeance! This is diabolism run mad!" I filled his glass with wine. "Surely, now that you've *seen* the brute —"

"It's no good abusing him."

"You must admit there's nothing Miltonic about him, Soames."

"I don't say he's not rather different from what I expected."

"He's a vulgarian, he's a swell mobs-man, he's the sort of man who hangs about the corridors of trains going to the Riviera and steals ladies' jewel-cases. Imagine eternal torment presided over by *him!*"

"You don't suppose I look forward to it, do you?"

"Then why not slip quietly out of the way?"

Again and again I filled his glass, and always, mechanically, he emptied it; but the wine kindled no spark of enterprise in him. He did not eat, and I myself ate hardly at all. I did not in my heart believe that any dash for freedom could save him. The chase would be swift, the capture certain. But better anything than this passive, meek, miserable waiting. I told Soames that for the honor of the human race he ought to make some show of resistance. He asked what the human race had ever done for him. "Besides," he said, "can't you understand that I'm in his power? You saw him touch me, didn't you? There's an end of it. I've no will. I'm sealed."

I made a gesture of despair. He went on repeating the word "sealed." I began to realize that the wine had clouded his brain. No wonder! Foodless he had gone into futurity, foodless he still was. I urged him to eat, at any rate, some bread. It was maddening to think that he, who had so much to tell, might tell nothing. "How was it all," I asked, "yonder? Come, tell me your adventures!"

"They'd make first-rate 'copy,' wouldn't they?"

"I'm awfully sorry for you, Soames, and I make all possible allowances; but what earthly right have you to insinuate that I should make 'copy,' as you call it, out of you?"

The poor fellow pressed his hands to his forehead.

"I don't know," he said. "I had some reason, I know. I'll try to remember. He sat plunged in thought.

"That's right. Try to remember everything. Eat a little more bread. What did the reading-room look like?"

"Much as usual," he at length muttered.

"Many people there?"

"Usual sort of number."

"What did they look like?"

Soames tried to visualize them.

"They all," he presently remembered, "looked very like one another."

My mind took a fearsome leap.

"All dressed in sanitary woolen?"

"Yes, I think so. Grayish-yellowish stuff."

"A sort of uniform?" He nodded. "With a number on it perhaps — a number on a large disk of metal strapped round the left arm? D. K. F. 78,910 — that sort of thing?" It was even so. "And all of them, men and women alike, looking very well cared for? Very Utopian, and smelling rather strongly of carbolic, and all of them quite hairless?" I was right every time. Soames was only not sure whether the men and women were hairless or shorn. "I hadn't time to look at them very closely," he explained.

"No, of course not. But —"

"They stared at *me,* I can tell you. I attracted a great deal of attention." At last he had done that! "I think I rather scared them. They moved away whenever I came near. They followed me about, at a distance, wherever I went. The men at the round desk in the middle seemed to have a sort of panic whenever I went to make inquiries."

"What did you do when you arrived?"

Well, he had gone straight to the catalogue, of course, — to the S volumes, — and had stood long before SN-SOF, unable to take this volume out of the shelf because his heart was beating so. At first, he said, he wasn't disappointed; he only thought there was some new arrangement. He went to the middle desk and asked where the catalogue of twentieth-century books was kept. He gathered that there was still only one catalogue. Again he looked up his name, stared at the three little pasted slips he had known so well. Then he went and sat down for a long time.

"And then," he droned, "I looked up the 'Dictionary of National Biography,' and some encyclopedias. I went back to the middle desk and asked what was the best modern book on late nineteenth-century literature. They told me Mr. T. K. Nupton's book was considered the best. I looked it up in the catalogue and filled in a form for it. It was brought to me. My name wasn't in the index, but — yes!" he said with a sudden change of tone, "that's what I'd forgotten. Where's that bit of paper? Give it me back."

I, too, had forgotten that cryptic screed. I found it fallen on the floor, and handed it to him.

He smoothed it out, nodding and smiling at me disagreeably.

"I found myself glancing through Nupton's book," he resumed. "Not very easy reading. Some sort of phonetic spelling. All the modern books I saw were phonetic."

"Then I don't want to hear anymore, Soames, please."

"The proper names seemed all to be spelt in the old way. But for that I mightn't have noticed my own name."

"Your own name? Really? Soames, I'm *very* glad."

"And yours."

"No!"

"I thought I should find you waiting here tonight, so I took the trouble to copy out the passage. Read it."

I snatched the paper. Soames's handwriting was characteristically dim. It and the noisome spelling and my excitement made me all the slower to grasp what T. K. Nupton was driving at.

The document lies before me at this moment. Strange that the words I here copy out for you were copied out for me by poor Soames just eighty-two years hence!

From page 234 of "Inglish Littracher 1890–1900" bi T. K. Nupton, publishd bi th Stait, 1992.

> Fr egzarmpl, a riter ov th time, naimed Max Beerbohm, hoo woz stil alive in th twentith senchri, rote a stauri in wich e pautraid an immajnari karrakter kauld "Enoch Soames" — a thurd-rait poit hoo beleevz imself a grate jeneus an maix a bargin with th Devvl in auder ter no wot posterriti thinx ov im! It iz a sumwot labud sattire, but not without vallu az showing hou seriusli the yung men ov th aiteen-ninetiz took themselvz. Nou that th littreri profeshn haz bin auganized az a departmnt of publik servis, our riters hav found their levvl an hav lernt ter doo their duti without thort ov th morro. "Th laibrer iz werthi ov hiz hire" an that iz aul. Thank hevvn we hav no Enoch Soameses amung us todai!

I found that by murmuring the words aloud (a device which I commend to my reader) I was able to master them little by little. The clearer they became, the greater was my bewilderment, my distress and horror. The whole thing was a nightmare. Afar, the great grisly background of what was in store for the poor dear art of letters; here, at the table, fixing on me a gaze that made me hot all over, the poor fellow whom — whom evidently — but no: whatever down-grade my character might take in coming years, I should never be such a brute as to —

Again I examined the screed. "Immajnari." But here Soames was, no more imaginary, alas! than I. And "labud" — what on earth was that? (To this day I have never made out that word.) "It's all very — baffling," I at length stammered.

Soames said nothing, but cruelly did not cease to look at me.

"Are you sure," I temporized, "quite sure you copied the thing out correctly?"

"Quite."

"Well, then, it's this wretched Nupton who must have made — must be going to make — some idiotic mistake. Look here Soames, you know me better than to suppose that I — After all, the name Max Beerbohm is not at all an uncommon one, and there must be several Enoch Soameses running around, or, rather, Enoch Soames is a name that might occur to anyone writing a story. And I don't write stories; I'm an essayist, an observer, a recorder. I admit that it's an extraordinary coincidence. But you must see —"

"I see the whole thing," said Soames, quietly. And he added, with a touch of his old manner, but with more dignity than I had ever known in him, *"Parlons d'autre chose."*

I accepted that suggestion very promptly. I returned straight to the more immediate future. I spent most of the long evening in renewed appeals to Soames to come away and seek refuge somewhere. I remember saying at last that if indeed I was destined to write about him, the supposed "stauri" had better have at least a happy ending. Soames repeated those last three words in a tone of intense scorn.

"In life and in art," he said, "all that matters is an *inevitable* ending."

"But," I urged more hopefully than I felt, "an ending that can be avoided *isn't* inevitable."

"You aren't an artist," he rasped. "And you're so hopelessly not an artist that, so far from being able to imagine a thing and make it seem true, you're going to make even a true thing seem as if you'd made it up. You're a miserable bungler. And it's like my luck."

I protested that the miserable bungler was not I, was not going to be I, but T. K. Nupton; and we had a rather heated argument, in the thick of which it suddenly seemed to me that Soames saw he was in the wrong: he had quite physically cowered. But I wondered why — and now I guessed with a cold throb just why — he stared so past me. The bringer of that "inevitable ending" filled the doorway.

I managed to turn in my chair and to say, not without a semblance of lightness, "Aha, come in!" Dread was indeed rather blunted in me by his looking so absurdly like a villain in a melodrama. The sheen of his tilted hat and of his shirt-front, the repeated twists he was giving to his mustache, and most of all the magnificence of his sneer, gave token that he was there only to be foiled.

He was at our table in a stride. "I am sorry," he sneered witheringly, "to break up your pleasant party, but —"

"You don't; you complete it," I assured him. "Mr. Soames and I want to have a little talk with you. Won't you sit? Mr. Soames got nothing, frankly nothing, by his journey this afternoon. We don't wish to say that the whole thing was a swindle, a common swindle. On the contrary, we believe you meant well. But of course the bargain, such as it was, is off."

The devil gave no verbal answer. He merely looked at Soames and pointed with rigid forefinger to the door. Soames was wretchedly rising from his chair when, with a desperate, quick gesture, I swept together two dinner-knives that were on the table, and laid their blades across each other. The devil stepped sharp back against the table behind him, averting his face and shuddering.

"You are not superstitious!" he hissed.

"Not at all," I smiled.

"Soames," he said as to an underling, but without turning his face, "put those knives straight!"

With an inhibitive gesture to my friend, "Mr. Soames," I said emphatically to the devil, "is a Catholic diabolist"; but my poor friend did the devil's bidding, not mine; and now, with his master's eyes again fixed on him, he arose, he shuffled past me. I tried to speak. It was he that spoke. "Try," was the prayer he threw back at me as the devil pushed him roughly out through the door — "*Try* to make them know that I did exist!"

In another instant I, too, was through that door. I stood staring all ways, up the street, across it, down it. There was moonlight and lamplight, but there was not Soames nor that other.

Dazed, I stood there. Dazed, I turned back at length into the little room, and I suppose I paid Berthe or Rose for my dinner and luncheon and for Soames's; I hope so, for I never went to the Vingtieme again. Ever since that night I have avoided Greek Street altogether. And for years I did not set foot even in Soho Square, because on that same night it was there that I paced and loitered, long and long, with some such dull sense of hope as a man has in not straying far from the place where he has lost something. "Round and round the shutter'd Square" — that line came back to me on my lonely beat, and with it the whole stanza, ringing in my brain and bearing in on me how tragically different from the happy scene imagined by him was the poet's actual experience of that prince in whom of all princes we should put not our trust!

But strange how the mind of an essayist, be it never so stricken, roves and ranges! I remember pausing before a wide doorstep and wondering if perchance it was on this very one that the young De Quincey lay ill and faint while poor Ann flew as fast as her feet would carry her to Oxford Street, the "stony-hearted stepmother" of them both, and came back bearing that "glass of port wine and spices" but for which he might, so he thought, actually have died. Was this the very doorstep that the old De Quincey used to revisit in homage? I pondered Ann's fate, the cause of her sudden vanishing from the ken of her boy friend; and presently I blamed myself for letting the past override the present. Poor vanished Soames!

And for myself, too, I began to be troubled. What had I better do? Would there be a hue and cry — "Mysterious Disappearance of an Author," and all that? He had last been seen lunching and dining in my company. Hadn't I better get a hansom and drive straight to Scotland Yard? They would think I was a lunatic. After all, I reassured myself, London was a very large place, and one very dim figure might easily drop out of it unobserved, now especially, in the blinding glare of the near Jubilee. Better say nothing at all, I thought.

And I was right. Soames's disappearance made no stir at all. He was utterly forgotten before anyone, so far as I am aware, noticed that he was no longer hanging around. Now and again some poet or prosaist may have said to another, "What has become of that man Soames?" but I never heard any such question asked. As for his landlady in Dyott Street, no doubt he had paid her weekly, and what possessions he may have had in his rooms were enough to save her from fretting. The solicitor through whom he was paid his annuity may be presumed to have made inquiries, but no echo of these resounded. There was something rather ghastly to me in the general unconsciousness that Soames had existed, and more than once I caught myself wondering whether Nupton, that babe unborn, were going to be right in thinking him a figment of my brain.

In that extract from Nupton's repulsive book there is one point which perhaps puzzles you. How is it that the author, though I have here mentioned him by name and have quoted the exact words he is going to write, is not going to grasp the obvious corollary that I have invented nothing? The answer can be only this: Nupton will not have read the later passages of this memoir. Such lack of thoroughness is a serious fault in anyone who undertakes to do scholar's work. And I hope these words will meet the eye of some contemporary rival to Nupton and be the undoing of Nupton.

I like to think that some time between 1992 and 1997 somebody will have looked up this memoir, and will have forced on the world his inevitable and startling conclusions. And I have reason for believing that this will be so. You realize that the reading-room into which Soames was projected by the devil was in all respects precisely as it will be on the afternoon of June 3, 1997. You realize, therefore, that on that afternoon, when it comes round, there the selfsame crowd will be, and there Soames will be, punctually, he and they doing precisely what they did before. Recall now Soames's account of the sensation he made. You may say that the mere difference of his costume was enough to make him sensational in that uniformed crowd. You wouldn't say so if you had ever seen him, and I assure you that in no period would Soames be anything but dim. The fact that people are going to stare at him and follow him around and seem afraid of him, can be explained only on the hypothesis that they will somehow have been prepared for his ghostly visitation. They will have been awfully waiting to see whether he really would come. And when he does come the effect will of course be — awful.

An authentic, guaranteed, proved ghost, but; only a ghost, alas! Only that. In his first visit Soames was a creature of flesh and blood, whereas the creatures among whom he was projected were but ghosts, I take it — solid, palpable, vocal, but unconscious and automatic ghosts, in a building that was itself an illusion. Next time that building and those creatures will be real. It is of Soames that there will be but the semblance. I wish I could think him destined to revisit the world actually, physically, consciously. I wish he had this one brief escape, this one small treat, to look forward to. I never forget him for long. He is where he is and forever. The more rigid moralists among you may say he has only himself to blame. For my part, I think he has been very hardly used. It is well that vanity should be chastened; and Enoch Soames's vanity was, I admit, above the average, and called for special treatment. But there was no need for vindictiveness. You say he contracted to pay the price he is paying. Yes; but I maintain that he was induced to do so by fraud. Well informed in all things, the devil must have known that my friend would gain nothing by his visit to futurity. The whole thing was a very shabby trick. The more I think of it, the more detestable the devil seems to me.

Of him I have caught sight several times, here and there, since that day at the Vingtieme. Only once, however, have I seen him at close quarters. This was a couple of years ago, in Paris. I was walking one afternoon along the rue d'Antin, and I saw him advancing from the opposite direction, overdressed as ever, and swinging an ebony cane and altogether behaving as though the whole pavement belonged to him. At thought of Enoch Soames and the myriads of other sufferers eternally in this brute's dominion, a great cold wrath filled me, and I drew myself up to my full height. But — well, one is so used to nodding and smiling in the street to anybody whom one knows that the action becomes almost independent of oneself; to prevent it requires a very sharp effort and great presence of mind. I was miserably aware, as I passed the devil, that I nodded and smiled to him. And my shame was the deeper and hotter because he, if you please, stared straight at me with the utmost haughtiness.

To be cut, deliberately cut, by *him!* I was, I still am, furious at having had that happen to me.

The Elixir of Life

Honore de Balzac

Translated By
Clara Bell & James Waring

Don Juan's father says that he is God in Balzac's weird and horrific tale. Fathers, sons, God and the Devil mix with three linked generations of fathers and sons in the French master's brilliant "The Elixir of Life."

BALZAC'S NOTE TO THE READER

At the very outset of the writer's literary career, a friend, long since dead, gave him the subject of this Study. Later on he found the same story in a collection published about the beginning of the present century. To the best of his belief, it is some stray fancy of the brain of Hoffmann of Berlin; probably it appeared in some German almanac, and was omitted in the published editions of his collected works. The Comedie Humaine is sufficiently rich in original creations for the author to own to this innocent piece of plagiarism; when, like the worthy La Fontaine, he has told unwittingly, and after his own fashion, a tale already related by another. This is not one of the hoaxes in vogue in the year 1830, when every author wrote his "tale of horror" for the amusement of young ladies. When

you have read the account of Don Juan's decorous parricide,
try to picture to yourself the part which would be played under
very similar circumstances by honest folk who, in this nineteenth century, will take a man's money and undertake to pay
him a life annuity on the faith of a chill, or let a house to an
ancient lady for the term of her natural life! Would they be for
resuscitating their clients? I should dearly like a connoisseur
in consciences to consider how far there is a resemblance
between a Don Juan and fathers who marry their children to
great expectations. Does humanity, which, according to certain
philosophers, is making progress, look on the art of waiting
for dead men's shoes as a step in the right direction? To this
art we owe several honorable professions, which open up ways
of living on death. There are people who rely entirely on an
expected demise; who brood over it, crouching each morning
upon a corpse, that serves again for their pillow at night. To
this class belong bishops' coadjutors, cardinals' supernumerar-
ies, tontiniers, and the like. Add to the list many delicately
scrupulous persons eager to buy landed property beyond their
means, who calculate with dry logic and in cold blood the
probable duration of the life of a father or of a step-mother,
some old man or woman of eighty or ninety, saying to themselves, "I shall be sure to come in for it in three years' time,
and then —" A murderer is less loathsome to us than a spy. The
murderer may have acted on a sudden mad impulse; he may
be penitent and amend; but a spy is always a spy, night and
day, in bed, at table, as he walks abroad; his vileness pervades
every moment of his life. Then what must it be to live when
every moment of your life is tainted with murder? And have
we not just admitted that a host of human creatures in our
midst are led by our laws, customs, and usages to dwell without
ceasing on a fellow-creature's death? There are men who put
the weight of a coffin into their deliberations as they bargain
for Cashmere shawls for their wives, as they go up the staircase
of a theater, or think of going to the Bouffons, or of setting
up a carriage; who are murderers in thought when dear ones,
with the irresistible charm of innocence, hold up childish
foreheads to be kissed with a "Good-night, father!" Hourly they
meet the gaze of eyes that they would fain close forever, eyes
that still open each morning to the light, like Belvidero's in
this Study. God alone knows the number of those who are
parricides in thought. Picture to yourself the state of mind of
a man who must pay a life annuity to some old woman whom

he scarcely knows; both live in the country with a brook between them, both sides are free to hate cordially, without offending against the social conventions that require two brothers to wear a mask if the older will succeed to the entail, and the other to the fortune of a younger son. The whole civilization of Europe turns upon the principle of hereditary succession as upon a pivot; it would be madness to subvert the principle; but could we not, in an age that prides itself upon its mechanical inventions, perfect this essential portion of the social machinery?

If the author has preserved the old-fashioned style of address To the Reader before a work wherein he endeavors to represent all literary forms, it is for the purpose of making a remark that applies to several of the Studies, and very specially to this. Every one of his compositions has been based upon ideas more or less novel, which, as it seemed to him, needed literary expression; he can claim priority for certain forms and for certain ideas which have since passed into the domain of literature, and have there, in some instances, become common property; so that the date of the first publication of each Study cannot be a matter of indifference to those of his readers who would fain do him justice.

Reading brings us unknown friends, and what friend is like a reader? We have friends in our own circle who read nothing of ours. The author hopes to pay his debt, by dedicating this work *Diis ignotis.*

*O*ne winter evening, in a princely palace at Ferrara, Don Juan Belvidero was giving a banquet to a prince of the house of Este. A banquet in those times was a marvelous spectacle which only royal wealth or the power of a mightly* lord could furnish forth. Seated about a table lit up with perfumed tapers, seven laughter-loving women were interchanging sweet talk. The white marble of the noble works of art about them stood out against the red stucco walls, and made strong contrasts with the rich Turkey carpets. Clad in satin, glittering with gold, and covered with gems less brilliant than their eyes, each told a tale of energetic passions as diverse as their styles of beauty. They differed neither in their ideas nor in their language; but the expression of their eyes, their glances, occasional gestures, or the tones of their voices supplied a commentary, dissolute,

* sic

wanton, melancholy, or satirical, to their words.

One seemed to be saying — "The frozen heart of age might kindle at my beauty."

Another — "I love to lounge upon cushions, and think with rapture of my adorers."

A third, a neophyte at these banquets, was inclined to blush. "I feel remorse in the depths of my heart! I am a Catholic, and afraid of hell. But I love you, I love you so that I can sacrifice my hereafter to you."

The fourth drained a cup of Chian wine. "Give me a joyous life!" she cried; "I begin life afresh each day with the dawn. Forgetful of the past, with the intoxication of yesterday's rapture still upon me, I drink deep of life — a whole lifetime of pleasure and of love!"

The woman who sat next to Juan Belvidero looked at him with a feverish glitter in her eyes. She was silent. Then — "I should need no hired bravo to kill my lover if he forsook me!" she cried at last, and laughed, but the marvelously wrought gold comfit box in her fingers was crushed by her convulsive clutch.

"When are you to be Grand Duke?" asked the sixth. There was the frenzy of a Bacchante in her eyes, and her teeth gleamed between the lips parted with a smile of cruel glee.

"Yes, when is that father of yours going to die?" asked the seventh, throwing her bouquet at Don Juan with bewitching playfulness. It was a childish girl who spoke, and the speaker was wont to make sport of sacred things.

"Oh! don't talk about it," cried Don Juan, the young and handsome giver of the banquet. "There is but one eternal father, and, as ill luck will have it, he is mine."

The seven Ferrarese, Don Juan's friends, the Prince himself, gave a cry of horror. Two hundred years later, in the days of Louis XV., people of taste would have laughed at this witticism. Or was it, perhaps, that at the outset of an orgy there is a certain unwonted lucidity of mind? Despite the taper light, the clamor of the senses, the gleam of gold and silver, the fumes of wine, and the exquisite beauty of the women, there may perhaps have been in the depths of the revelers' hearts some struggling glimmer of reverence for things divine and human, until it was drowned in glowing floods of wine! Yet even then the flowers had been crushed, eyes were growing dull, and drunkenness, in Rabelais' phrase, had "taken possession of them down to their sandals."

During that brief pause a door opened; and as once the Divine presence was revealed at Belshazzar's feast, so now it seemed to be manifest in the apparition of an old white-haired servant, who tottered in, and looked sadly from under knitted brows at the revelers. He gave a withering glance at the garlands, the golden cups, the pyramids of fruit, the dazzling lights of the banquet, the flushed scared faces, the hues of the cushions pressed by the white arms of the women.

"My lord, your father is dying!" he said; and at those solemn words, uttered in hollow tones, a veil of crape* seemed to be drawn over the wild mirth.

Don Juan rose to his feet with a gesture to his guests that might be rendered by, "Excuse me; this kind of thing does not happen every day."

Does it so seldom happen that a father's death surprises youth in the full-blown splendor of life, in the midst of the mad riot of an orgy? Death is as unexpected in his caprice as a courtesan in her disdain; but death is truer — Death has never forsaken any man.

Don Juan closed the door of the banqueting-hall; and as he went down the long gallery, through the cold and darkness, he strove to assume an expression in keeping with the part he had to play; he had thrown off his mirthful mood, as he had thrown down his table napkin, at the first thought of this role. The night was dark. The mute servitor, his guide to the chamber where the dying man lay, lighted the way so dimly that Death, aided by cold, silence, and darkness, and it may be by a reaction of drunkenness, could send some sober thoughts through the spendthrift's soul. He examined his life, and became thoughtful, like a man involved in a lawsuit on his way to the Court.

Bartolommeo Belvidero, Don Juan's father, was an old man of ninety, who had devoted the greatest part of his life to business pursuits. He had acquired vast wealth in many a journey to magical Eastern lands, and knowledge, so it was said, more valuable than the gold and diamonds, which had almost ceased to have any value for him.

"I would give more to have a tooth in my head than for a ruby," he would say at times with a smile. The indulgent father loved to hear Don Juan's story of this and that wild freak of youth. "So long as these follies amuse you, dear boy —" he would say laughingly, as he lavished money on his son. Age never took such pleasure in the sight of youth; the fond father did not remember his own decaying powers while he looked on that brilliant young life.

Bartolommeo Belvidero, at the age of sixty, had fallen in love with an angel of peace and beauty. Don Juan had been the sole fruit of this late and short-lived love. For fifteen years the widower had

---

* sic

mourned the loss of his beloved Juana; and to this sorrow of age, his son and his numerous household had attributed the strange habits that he had contracted. He had shut himself up in the least comfortable wing of his palace, and very seldom left his apartments; even Don Juan himself must first ask permission before seeing his father. If this hermit, unbound by vows, came or went in his palace or in the streets of Ferrara, he walked as if he were in a dream, wholly engrossed, like a man at strife with a memory, or a wrestler with some thought.

The young Don Juan might give princely banquets, the palace might echo with clamorous mirth, horses pawed the ground in the courtyards, pages quarreled and flung dice upon the stairs, but Bartolommeo ate his seven ounces of bread daily and drank water. A fowl was occasionally dressed for him, simply that the black poodle, his faithful companion, might have the bones. Bartolommeo never complained of the noise. If the huntsmen's horns and baying dogs disturbed his sleep during his illness, he only said, "Ah! Don Juan has come back again." Never on earth has there been a father so little exacting and so indulgent; and, in consequence, young Belvidero, accustomed to treat his father unceremoniously, had all the faults of a spoiled child. He treated old Bartolommeo as a willful courtesan treats an elderly adorer; buying indemnity for insolence with a smile, selling good-humor, submitting to be loved.

Don Juan, beholding scene after scene of his younger years, saw that it would be a difficult task to find his father's indulgence at fault. Some newborn remorse stirred the depths of his heart; he felt almost ready to forgive this father now about to die for having lived so long. He had an accession of filial piety, like a thief's return in thought to honesty at the prospect of a million adroitly stolen.

Before long Don Juan had crossed the lofty, chilly suite of rooms in which his father lived; the penetrating influences of the damp close air, the mustiness diffused by old tapestries and presses thickly covered with dust had passed into him, and now he stood in the old man's antiquated room, in the repulsive presence of the deathbed, beside a dying fire. A flickering lamp on a Gothic table sent broad uncertain shafts of light, fainter or brighter, across the bed, so that the dying man's face seemed to wear a different look at every moment. The bitter wind whistled through the crannies of the ill-fitting casements; there was a smothered sound of snow lashing the windows. The harsh contrast of these sights and sounds with the scenes which Don Juan had just quitted was so sudden that he could not help shuddering. He turned cold as he came towards the bed; the lamp flared in a sudden vehement gust of wind and lighted up his father's face; the features were wasted and distorted; the skin that cleaved to their bony outlines had taken wan livid hues, all the more ghastly by force of contrast with the white pillows on which he lay. The muscles about the toothless mouth had contracted with pain and drawn apart the lips; the moans that issued between them with appalling energy found an accompaniment in the howling of the storm without.

In spite of every sign of coming dissolution, the most striking thing about the dying face was its incredible power. It was no ordinary spirit that wrestled there with Death. The eyes glared with strange fixity of gaze from the cavernous sockets hollowed by disease. It seemed as if Bartolommeo sought to kill some enemy sitting at the foot of his bed by the intent gaze of dying eyes. That steady remorseless look was the more appalling because the head that lay upon the pillow was passive and motionless as a skull upon a doctor's table. The outlines of the body, revealed by the coverlet, were no less rigid and stiff; he lay there as one dead, save for those eyes. There was something automatic about the moaning sounds that came from the mouth. Don Juan felt something like shame that he must be brought thus to his father's bedside, wearing a courtesan's bouquet, redolent of the fragrance of the banqueting-chamber and the fumes of wine.

"You were enjoying yourself!" the old man cried as he saw his son.

Even as he spoke the pure high notes of a woman's voice, sustained by the sound of the viol on which she accompanied her song, rose above the rattle of the storm against the casements, and floated up to the chamber of death. Don Juan stopped his ears against the barbarous answer to his father's speech.

"I bear you no grudge, my child," Bartolommeo went on.

The words were full of kindness, but they hurt Don Juan; he could not pardon this heart-searching goodness on his father's part.

"What a remorseful memory for me!" he cried, hypocritically.

"Poor Juanino," the dying man went on, in a smothered voice, "I have always been so kind to you, that you could not surely desire my death?"

"Oh, if it were only possible to keep you here by giving up a part of my own life!" cried Don Juan.

("We can always *say* this sort of thing," the spendthrift thought; "it is as if I laid the whole world at my mistress' feet.")

The thought had scarcely crossed his mind when the old poodle barked. Don Juan shivered; the response was so intelligent that he fancied the dog must have understood him.

"I was sure that I could count upon you, my son!" cried the dying man. "I shall live. So be it; you shall be satisfied. I shall live, but without depriving you of a single day of your life."

"He is raving," thought Don Juan. Aloud he added, "Yes, dearest father, yes; you shall live, of course, as long as I live, for your image will be forever in my heart."

"It is not that kind of life that I mean," said the old noble, summoning all his strength to sit up in bed; for a thrill of doubt ran through him, one of those suspicions that come into being under a dying man's pillow. "Listen, my son," he went on, in a voice grown weak with that last effort, "I have no more wish to give up life than you to give up wine and mistresses, horses and hounds, and hawks and gold —"

"I can well believe it," thought the son; and he knelt down by the bed and kissed Bartolommeo's cold hands. "But, father, my dear father," he added aloud, "we must submit to the will of God."

"I am God!" muttered the dying man.

"Do not blaspheme!" cried the other, as he saw the menacing expression on his father's face. "Beware what you say; you have received extreme unction, and I should be inconsolable if you were to die before my eyes in mortal sin."

"Will you listen to me?" cried Bartolommeo, and his mouth twitched.

Don Juan held his peace; an ugly silence prevailed. Yet above the muffled sound of the beating of the snow against the windows rose the sounds of the beautiful voice and the viol in unison, far off and faint as the dawn. The dying man smiled.

"Thank you," he said, "for bringing those singing voices and the music, a banquet, young and lovely women with fair faces and dark tresses, all the pleasure of life! Bid them wait for me; for I am about to begin life anew."

"The delirium is at its height," said Don Juan to himself.

"I have found out a way of coming to life again," the speaker went on. "There, just look in that table drawer, press the spring hidden by the griffin, and it will fly open."

"I have found it, father."

"Well, then, now take out a little phial of rock crystal."

"I have it."

"I have spent twenty years in —" but even as he spoke the old man felt how very near the end had come, and summoned all his dying strength to say, "As soon as the breath is out of me, rub me all over with that liquid, and I shall come to life again."

"There is very little of it," his son remarked.

Though Bartolommeo could no longer speak, he could still hear and see. When those words dropped from Don Juan, his head turned with appalling quickness, his neck was twisted like the throat of some marble statue which the sculptor had condemned to remain stretched out forever, the wide eyes had come to have a ghastly fixity.

He was dead, and in death he lost his last and sole illusion.

He had sought a shelter in his son's heart, and it had proved to be a sepulcher, a pit deeper than men dig for their dead. The hair on his head had risen and stiffened with horror, his agonized glance still spoke. He was a father rising in just anger from his tomb, to demand vengeance at the throne of God.

"There! it is all over with the old man!" cried Don Juan.

He had been so interested in holding the mysterious phial to the lamp, as a drinker holds up the wine-bottle at the end of a meal, that he had not seen his father's eyes fade. The cowering poodle looked from his master to the elixir, just as Don Juan himself glanced again and again from his father to the flask. The lamplight flickered. There was a deep silence; the viol was mute. Juan Belvidero thought that he saw his father stir, and trembled. The changeless gaze of those accusing eyes frightened him; he closed them hastily, as he would have closed a loose shutter swayed by the wind of an autumn night. He stood there motionless, lost in a world of thought.

Suddenly the silence was broken by a shrill sound like the creaking of a rusty spring. It startled Don Juan; he all but dropped the phial. A sweat, colder than the blade of a dagger, issued through every pore. It was only a piece of clockwork, a wooden cock that sprang out and crowed three times, an ingenious contrivance by which the learned of that epoch were wont to be awakened at the appointed hour to begin the labors of the day. Through the windows there came already a flush of dawn. The thing, composed of wood, and cords, and wheels, and pulleys, was more faithful in its service than he in his duty to Bartolommeo — he, a man with that peculiar piece of human mechanism within him that we call a heart.

Don Juan the skeptic shut the flask again in the secret drawer in the Gothic table — he meant to run no more risks of losing the mysterious liquid.

Even at that solemn moment he heard the murmur of a crowd in the gallery, a confused sound of voices, of stifled laughter and light footfalls, and the rustling of silks — the sounds of a band of revelers struggling for gravity. The door opened, and in came the Prince and Don Juan's friends, the seven courtesans, and the singers, disheveled and wild like dancers surprised by the dawn, when the tapers that have burned through the night struggle with the sunlight.

They had come to offer the customary condolence to the young heir.

"Oho! is poor Don Juan really taking this seriously?" said the Prince in Brambilla's ear.

"Well, his father was very good," she returned.

But Don Juan's night-thoughts had left such unmistakable traces on his features, that the crew was awed into silence. The men stood motionless. The women, with wine-parched lips and cheeks marbled with kisses, knelt down and began a prayer. Don Juan could scarce help trembling when he saw splendor and mirth and laughter and song and youth and beauty and power bowed in reverence before Death. But in those times, in that adorable Italy of the sixteenth century, religion and revelry went hand in hand; and religious excess became a sort of debauch, and a debauch a religious rite!

The Prince grasped Don Juan's hand affectionately, then when all faces had simultaneously put on the same grimace — half-gloomy, half-indifferent — the whole masque disappeared, and left the chamber of death empty. It was like an allegory of life.

As they went down the staircase, the Prince spoke to Rivabarella: "Now, who would have taken Don Juan's impiety for a boast? He loves his father."

"Did you see that black dog?" asked La Brambilla.

"He is enormously rich now," sighed Bianca Cavatolino.

"What is that to me?" cried the proud Veronese (she who had crushed the comfit-box).

"What does it matter to you, forsooth?" cried the Duke. "With his money he is as much a prince as I am."

At first Don Juan was swayed hither and thither by countless thoughts, and wavered between two decisions. He took counsel with the gold heaped up by his father, and returned in the evening to the chamber of death, his whole soul brimming over with hideous selfishness. He found all his household busy there. "His lordship" was to lie in state tomorrow; all Ferrara would flock to behold the wonderful spectacle; and the servants were busy decking the room and the couch on which the dead man lay. At a sign from Don Juan all his people stopped, dumfounded and trembling.

"Leave me alone here," he said, and his voice was changed, "and do not return until I leave the room."

When the footsteps of the old servitor, who was the last to go, echoed but faintly along the paved gallery, Don Juan hastily locked the door, and sure that he was quite alone, "Let us try," he said to himself.

Bartolommeo's body was stretched on a long table. The embalmers had laid a sheet over it, to hide from all eyes the dreadful spectacle of a corpse so wasted and shrunken that it seemed like a skeleton, and only the face was uncovered. This mummylike figure lay in the middle of the room. The limp clinging linen lent itself to the outlines it shrouded — so sharp, bony, and thin. Large violet patches had already begun to spread over the face; the embalmers' work had not been finished too soon.

Don Juan, strong as he was in his skepticism, felt a tremor as he opened the magic crystal flask. When he stood over that face, he was trembling so violently, that he was actually obliged to wait for a moment. But Don Juan had acquired an early familiarity with evil; his morals had been corrupted by a licentious court, a reflection worthy of the Duke of Urbino crossed his mind, and it was a keen sense of curiosity that goaded him into boldness. The devil himself might have whispered the words that were echoing through his brain, Moisten one of the eyes with the liquid! He took up a linen cloth, moistened it sparingly with the precious fluid, and passed it lightly over the right eyelid of the corpse. The eye unclosed. . . .

"Aha!" said Don Juan. He gripped the flask tightly, as we clutch in dreams the branch from which we hang suspended over a precipice.

For the eye was full of life. It was a young child's eye set in a death's head; the light quivered in the depths of its youthful liquid brightness. Shaded by the long dark lashes, it sparkled like the strange lights that travelers see in lonely places in winter nights. The eye seemed as if it would fain dart fire at Don Juan; he saw it thinking, upbraiding, condemning, uttering accusations, threatening doom; it cried aloud, and gnashed upon him. All anguish that shakes human souls was gathered there; supplications the most tender, the wrath of kings, the love in a girl's heart pleading with the headsman; then, and after all these, the deeply searching glance a man turns on his fellows as he mounts the last step of the scaffold. Life so dilated in this fragment of life that Don Juan shrank back; he walked up and down the room, he dared not meet that gaze, but he saw nothing else. The ceiling and the hangings, the whole room was sown with living points of fire and intelligence. Everywhere those gleaming eyes haunted him.

"He might very likely have lived another hundred years!" he cried involuntarily. Some diabolical influence had drawn him to his father, and again he gazed at that luminous spark. The eyelid closed and opened again abruptly; it was like a woman's sign of assent. It was an intelligent movement. If a voice had cried "Yes!" Don Juan could not have been more startled.

"What is to be done?" he thought.

He nerved himself to try to close the white eyelid. In vain.

"Kill it? That would perhaps be parricide," he debated with himself.

"Yes," the eye said, with a strange sardonic quiver of the lid.

"Aha!" said Don Juan to himself, "here is witchcraft at work!" And he went closer to crush the thing. A great tear trickled over the hollow cheeks, and fell on Don Juan's hand.

"It is scalding!" he cried. He sat down. The struggle exhausted him; it was as if, like Jacob of old, he was wrestling with an angel.

At last he rose. "So long as there is no blood —" he muttered.

Then, summoning all the courage needed for a coward's crime, he extinguished the eye, pressing it with the linen cloth, turning his head away. A terrible groan startled him. It was the poor poodle, who died with a long-drawn howl.

"Could the brute have been in the secret?" thought Don Juan, looking down at the faithful creature.

Don Juan Belvidero was looked upon as a dutiful son. He reared a white marble monument on his father's tomb, and employed the greatest sculptors of the time upon it. He did not recover perfect ease of mind till the day when his father knelt in marble before Religion, and the heavy weight of the stone had sealed the mouth of the grave in which he had laid the one feeling of remorse that sometimes flitted through his soul in moments of physical weariness.

He had drawn up a list of the wealth heaped up by the old merchant in the East, and he became a miser: had he not to provide for a second lifetime? His views of life were the more profound and penetrating; he grasped its significance, as a whole, the better, because he saw it across a grave. All men, all things, he analyzed once and for all; he summed up the Past, represented by its records; the Present in the law, its crystallized form; the Future, revealed by religion. He took spirit and matter, and flung them into his crucible, and found — Nothing. Thenceforward he became *Don Juan*.

At the outset of his life, in the prime of youth and the beauty of youth, he knew the illusions of life for what they were; he despised the world, and made the utmost of the world. His felicity could not have been of the bourgeois kind, rejoicing in periodically recurrent bouilli, in the comforts of a warming-pan, a lamp of a night, and a new pair of slippers once a quarter. Nay, rather he seized upon existence as a monkey snatches a nut, and after no long toying with it, proceeds deftly to strip off the mere husks to reach the savory kernel within.

Poetry and the sublime transports of passion scarcely reached ankle-depth with him now. He in nowise fell into the error of strong natures who flatter themselves now and again that little souls will believe in a great soul, and are willing to barter their own lofty thoughts of the future for the small change of our life-annuity ideas. He, even as they, had he chosen, might well have walked with his feet on the earth and his head in the skies; but he liked better to sit on earth, to wither the soft, fresh, fragrant lips of a woman with kisses, for like Death, he devoured everything without scruple as he passed; he would have full fruition; he was an Oriental lover, seeking prolonged pleasures easily obtained. He sought nothing but a woman in women, and cultivated cynicism, until it became with him a habit of mind. When his mistress, from the couch on which she lay, soared and was lost in regions of ecstatic bliss, Don Juan followed suit, earnest, expansive, serious as any German student. But he said I, while she, in the transports of intoxication, said We. He understood to admiration the art of abandoning himself to the influence of a woman; he was always clever enough to make her believe that he trembled like some boy fresh from college before his first partner at a dance, when he asks her, "Do you like dancing?" But, no less, he could be terrible at need, could unsheathe a formidable sword and make short work of Commandants. Banter lurked beneath his simplicity, mocking laughter behind his tears — for he had tears at need, like any woman nowadays who says to her husband, "Give me a carriage, or I shall go into a consumption."

For the merchant the world is a bale of goods or a mass of circulating bills; for most young men it is a woman, and for a woman here and there it is a man; for a certain order of mind it is a salon, a coterie, a quarter of the town, or some single city; but Don Juan found his world in himself.

This model of grace and dignity, this captivating wit, moored his bark by every shore; but wherever he was led he was never carried away, and was only steered in a course of his own choosing. The more he saw, the more he doubted. He watched men narrowly, and saw how, beneath the surface, courage was often rashness; and prudence, cowardice; generosity, a clever piece of calculation; justice, a wrong; delicacy, pusillanimity; honesty, a modus vivendi; and by some strange dispensation of fate, he must see that those who at heart were really honest, scrupulous, just, generous, prudent, or brave were held cheaply by their fellow-men.

"What a cold-blooded jest!" said he to himself. "It was not devised by a God."

From that time forth he renounced a better world, and never uncovered himself when a Name was pronounced, and for him the carven saints in the churches became works of art. He understood the mechanism of society too well to clash wantonly with its prejudices; for, after all, he was not as powerful as the executioner, but he evaded social laws with the wit and grace so well rendered in the scene with M. Dimanche. He was, in fact, Moliere's Don Juan, Goethe's Faust, Byron's Manfred, Maturin's Melmoth — great allegorical figures drawn by the greatest men of genius in Europe, to which Mozart's harmonies, perhaps, do no more justice than Rossini's lyre. Terrible allegorical figures that shall endure as long as the principle of evil existing in the heart of man shall produce a few copies from century to century. Sometimes the type becomes half-human when incarnate as a Mirabeau, sometimes it is an inarticulate force in a Bonaparte, sometimes it overwhelms the universe with irony as a Rabelais; or, yet again, it appears when a Marechal de Richelieu elects to laugh at human beings instead of scoffing at things, or when one of the most famous of our ambassadors goes a step further and scoffs at both men and things. But the profound genius of Juan Belvidero anticipated and resumed all these. All things were a jest to him. His was the life of a mocking spirit. All men, all institutions, all realities, all ideas were within its scope. As for eternity, after half an hour of familiar conversation with Pope Julius II. he said, laughing:

"If it is absolutely necessary to make a choice, I would rather believe in God than in the Devil; power combined with goodness always offers more resources than the spirit of Evil can boast."

"Yes; still God requires repentance in this present world —"

"So you always think of your indulgences," returned Don Juan Belvidero. "Well, well, I have another life in reserve in which to repent of the sins of my previous existence."

"Oh, if you regard old age in that light," cried the Pope, "you are in danger on canonization —"

"After your elevation to the Papacy nothing is incredible." And they went to watch the workmen who were building the huge basilica dedicated to Saint Peter.

"Saint Peter, as the man of genius who laid the foundation of our double power," the Pope said to Don Juan, "deserves this monument. Sometimes, though, at night, I think that a deluge will wipe all this out as with a sponge, and it will be all to begin over again."

Don Juan and the Pope began to laugh; they understood each other. A fool would have gone on the morrow to amuse himself with Julius II. in Raphael's studio or at the delicious Villa Madama; not so Belvidero. He went to see the Pope as pontiff, to be convinced of any doubts that he (Don Juan) entertained. Over his cups the Rovere would have been capable of denying his own infallibility and of commenting on the Apocalypse.

*N*evertheless, this legend has not been undertaken to furnish materials for future biographies of Don Juan; it is intended to prove to honest folk that Belvidero did not die in a duel with stone, as some lithographers would have us believe.

When Don Juan Belvidero reached the age of sixty he settled in Spain, and there in his old age he married a young and charming Andalusian wife. But of set purpose he was neither a good husband nor a good father. He had observed that we are never so tenderly loved as by women to whom we scarcely give a thought. Dona Elvira had been devoutly brought up by an old aunt in a castle a few leagues from San-Lucar in a remote part of Andalusia. She was a model of devotion and grace. Don Juan foresaw that this would be a woman who would struggle long against a passion before yielding, and therefore hoped to keep her virtuous until his death. It was a jest undertaken in earnest, a game of chess which he meant to reserve till his old age. Don Juan had learned wisdom from the mistakes made by his father Bartolommeo; he determined that the least details of his life in old age should be subordinated to one object — the success of the drama which was to be played out upon his deathbed.

For the same reason the largest part of his wealth was buried in the cellars of his palace at Ferrara, whither he seldom went. As for the rest of his fortune, it was invested in a life annuity, with a view to give his wife and children an interest in keeping him alive; but this Machiavellian piece of foresight was scarcely necessary. His son, young Felipe Belvidero, grew up as a Spaniard as religiously conscientious as his father was irreligious, in virtue, perhaps, of the old rule, "A miser has a spendthrift son." The Abbot of San-Lucar was chosen by Don Juan to be the director of the consciences of the Duchess of Belvidero and her son Felipe. The ecclesiastic was a holy man, well shaped, and admirably well proportioned. He had fine dark eyes, a head like that of Tiberius, worn with fasting, bleached by an ascetic life, and, like all dwellers in the wilderness, was daily tempted. The noble lord had hopes, it may be, of dispatching yet another monk before his term of life was out.

But whether because the Abbot was every whit as clever as Don Juan himself, or Dona Elvira possessed more discretion or more virtue than Spanish wives are usually credited with, Don Juan was compelled to spend his declining years beneath his own roof, with no more scandal under it than if he had been an ancient country parson. Occasionally he would take wife and son to task for negligence in the duties of religion, peremptorily insisting that they should carry out to the letter the obligations imposed upon the flock by the Court of Rome. Indeed, he was never so well pleased as when he had set the courtly Abbot discussing some case of conscience with Dona Elvira and Felipe.

At length, however, despite the prodigious care that the great magnifico, Don Juan Belvidero, took of himself, the days of decrepitude came upon him, and with those days the constant importunity of physical feebleness, an importunity all the more distressing by contrast with the wealth of memories of his impetuous youth and the sensual pleasures of middle age. The unbeliever who in the height of his cynical humor had been wont to persuade others to believe in laws and principles at which he scoffed, must repose nightly upon a *perhaps.* The great Duke, the pattern of good breeding, the champion of many a carouse, the proud ornament of Courts, the man of genius, the graceful winner of hearts that he had wrung as carelessly as a peasant twists an osier withe, was now the victim of a cough, of a ruthless sciatica, of an unmannerly gout. His teeth gradually deserted him, as at the end of an evening the fairest and best-dressed women take their leave one by one till the room is left empty and desolate. The active hands became palsy-stricken, the shapely legs tottered as he walked. At last, one night, a stroke of apoplexy caught him by the throat in its icy clutch. After that fatal day he grew morose and stern.

He would reproach his wife and son with their devotion, casting it in their teeth that the affecting and thoughtful care that they lavished so tenderly upon him was bestowed because they knew that his money was invested in a life annuity. Then Elvira and Felipe would shed bitter tears and redouble their caresses, and the wicked old man's insinuating voice would take an affectionate tone — "Ah, you will forgive me, will you not, dear friends, dear wife? I am rather a nuisance. Alas, Lord in heaven, how canst Thou use me as the instrument by which Thou provest these two angelic creatures? I who should be the joy of their lives am become their scourge . . ."

In this manner he kept them tethered to his pillow, blotting out the memory of whole months of fretfulness and unkindness in one short hour when he chose to display for them the ever-new treasures of his pinchbeck tenderness and charm of manner — a system of paternity that yielded him an infinitely better return than his own father's indulgence had formerly gained. At length his bodily infirmities reached a point when the task of laying him in bed became as difficult as the navigation of a felucca in the perils of an intricate channel. Then came the day of his death; and this brilliant skeptic, whose mental faculties alone had survived the most dreadful of all destructions, found himself between his two special antipathies — the doctor and the confessor. But he was jovial with them. Did he not see a light gleaming in the future beyond the veil? The pall that is like lead for other men was thin and translucent for him; the light-footed, irresistible delights of youth danced beyond it like shadows.

*I*t was on a beautiful summer evening that Don Juan felt the near approach of death. The sky of Spain was serene and cloudless; the air was full of the scent of orange-blossom; the stars shed clear, pure gleams of light; nature without seemed to give the dying man assurance of resurrection; a dutiful and obedient son sat there watching him with loving and respectful eyes. Towards eleven o'clock he desired to be left alone with this single-hearted being.

"Felipe," said the father, in tones so soft and affectionate that the young man trembled, and tears of gladness came to his eyes; never had that stern father spoken his name in such a tone. "Listen, my son," the dying man went on. "I am a great sinner. All my life long, however, I have thought of my death. I was once the friend of the great Pope Julius II.; and that illustrious Pontiff, fearing lest the excessive excitability of my senses should entangle me in mortal sin between the moment of my death and the time of my anointing with the holy oil, gave me a flask that contains a little of the holy water that once issued from the rock in the wilderness. I have kept the secret of this squandering of a treasure belonging to Holy Church, but I am permitted to reveal the mystery in articulo mortis to my son. You will find the flask in a drawer in that Gothic table that always stands by the head of the bed. . . . The precious little crystal flask may be of use yet again for you, dearest Felipe. Will you swear to me, by your salvation, to carry out my instructions faithfully?"

Felipe looked at his father, and Don Juan was too deeply learned in the lore of the human countenance not to die in peace with that look as his warrant, as his own father had died in despair at meeting the expression in his son's eyes.

"You deserved to have a better father," Don Juan went on. "I dare to confess, my child, that while the reverend Abbot of San-Lucar was administering the Viaticum I was thinking of the incompatibility of the co-existence of two powers so infinite as God and the Devil —"

"Oh, father!"

"And I said to myself, when Satan makes his peace he ought surely to stipulate for the pardon of his followers, or he will be the veriest scoundrel. The thought haunted me; so I shall go to hell, my son, unless you carry out my wishes."

"Oh, quick; tell me quickly, father."

"As soon as I have closed my eyes," Don Juan went on, "and that may be in a few minutes, you must take my body before it grows cold and lay it on a table in this room. Then put out the lamp; the light of the stars should be sufficient. Take off my clothes, reciting Aves and Paters the while, raising your soul to God in prayer, and carefully anoint my lips and eyes with this holy water; begin with the face, and proceed successively to my limbs and the rest of my body; my dear son, the power of God is so great that you must be astonished at nothing."

Don Juan felt death so near, that he added in a terrible voice, "Be careful not to drop the flask."

Then he breathed his last gently in the arms of his son, and his son's tears fell fast over his sardonic, haggard features.

It was almost midnight when Don Felipe Belvidero laid his father's body upon the table. He kissed the sinister brow and the gray hair; then he put out the lamp.

By the soft moonlight that lit strange gleams across the country without, Felipe could dimly see his father's body, a vague white thing among the shadows. The dutiful son moistened a linen cloth with the liquid, and, absorbed in prayer, he anointed the revered face. A deep silence reigned. Felipe heard faint, indescribable rustlings; it was the breeze in the tree-tops, he thought. But when he had moistened the right arm, he felt himself caught by the throat, a young strong hand held him in a tight grip — it was his father's hand! He shrieked aloud; the flask dropped from his hand and broke in pieces. The liquid evaporated; the whole household hurried into the room, holding torches aloft. That shriek had startled them, and filled them with as much terror as if the Trumpet of the Angel sounding on the Last Day had rung through earth and sky. The room was full of people, and a horror-stricken crowd beheld the fainting Felipe upheld by the strong arm of his father, who clutched him by the throat. They saw another thing, an unearthly spectacle — Don Juan's face grown young and beautiful as Antinous, with its dark hair and brilliant eyes and red lips, a head that made horrible efforts, but could not move the dead, wasted body.

An old servitor cried, "A miracle! a miracle!" and all the Spaniards echoed, "A miracle! a miracle!"

Dona Elvira, too pious to attribute this to magic, sent for the

Abbot of San-Lucar; and the Prior beholding the miracle with his own eyes, being a clever man, and withal an Abbot desirous of augmenting his revenues, determined to turn the occasion to profit. He immediately gave out that Don Juan would certainly be canonized; he appointed a day for the celebration of the apotheosis in his convent, which thenceforward, he said, should be called the convent of San Juan of Lucar. At these words a sufficiently facetious grimace passed over the features of the late Duke.

The taste of the Spanish people for ecclesiastical solemnities is so well known, that it should not be difficult to imagine the religious pantomime by which the Convent of San-Lucar celebrated the translation of the blessed Don Juan Belvidero to the abbey-church. The tale of the partial resurrection had spread so quickly from village to village, that a day or two after the death of the illustrious nobleman the report had reached every place within fifty miles of San-Lucar, and it was as good as a play to see the roads covered already with crowds flocking in on all sides, their curiosity whetted still further by the prospect of a *Te Deum* sung by torchlight. The old abbey church of San-Lucar, a marvelous building erected by the Moors, a mosque of Allah, which for three centuries had heard the name of Christ, could not hold the throng that poured in to see the ceremony. Hidalgos in their velvet mantles, with their good swords at their sides, swarmed like ants, and were so tightly packed in among the pillars that they had not room to bend the knees, which never bent save to God. Charming peasant girls, in the *basquina* that defines the luxuriant outlines of their figures, lent an arm to white-haired old men. Young men, with eyes of fire, walked beside aged crones in holiday array. Then came couples tremulous with joy, young lovers led thither by curiosity, newly-wedded folk; children timidly clasping each other by the hand. This throng, so rich in coloring, in vivid contrasts, laden with flowers, enameled like a meadow, sent up a soft murmur through the quiet night. Then the great doors of the church opened.

Late comers who remained without saw afar, through the three great open doorways, a scene of which the theatrical illusions of modern opera can give but a faint idea. The vast church was lighted up by thousands of candles, offered by saints and sinners alike eager to win the favor of this new candidate for canonization, and these self-commending illuminations turned the great building into an enchanted fairyland. The black archways, the shafts and capitals, the recessed chapels with gold and silver gleaming in their depths, the galleries, the Arab traceries, all the most delicate outlines of that delicate sculpture, burned in the excess of light like the fantastic figures in the red heart of a brazier. At the further end of the church, above that blazing sea, rose the high altar like a splendid dawn. All the glories of the golden lamps and silver candlesticks, of banners and tassels, of the shrines of the saints and votive offerings, paled before the gorgeous brightness of the reliquary in which Don Juan lay. The blasphemer's body sparkled with gems, and flowers, and crystal, with diamonds and gold, and plumes white as the wings of seraphim; they had set it up on the altar, where the pictures of Christ had stood. All about him blazed a host of tall candles; the air quivered in the radiant light. The worthy Abbot of San-Lucar, in pontifical robes, with his mitre set with precious stones, his rochet and golden crosier, sat enthroned in imperial state among his clergy in the choir. Rows of impassive aged faces, silver-haired old men clad in fine linen albs, were grouped about him, as the saints who confessed Christ on earth are set by painters, each in his place, about the throne of God in heaven. The precentor and the dignitaries of the chapter, adorned with the gorgeous insignia of ecclesiastical vanity, came and went through the clouds of incense, like stars upon their courses in the firmament.

When the hour of triumph arrived, the bells awoke the echoes far and wide, and the whole vast crowd raised to God the first cry of praise that begins the *Te Deum*. A sublime cry! High, pure notes, the voices of women in ecstasy, mingled in it with the sterner and deeper voices of men; thousands of voices sent up a volume of sound so mighty, that the straining, groaning organ-pipes could not dominate that harmony. But the shrill sound of children's singing among the choristers, the reverberation of deep bass notes, awakened gracious associations, visions of childhood, and of man in his strength, and rose above that entrancing harmony of human voices blended in one sentiment of love.

Te Deum laudamus!

The chant went up from the black masses of men and women kneeling in the cathedral, like a sudden breaking out of light in darkness, and the silence was shattered as by a peal of thunder. The voices floated up with the clouds of incense that had begun to cast thin bluish veils over the fanciful marvels of the architecture, and the aisles were filled with splendor and perfume and light and melody. Even at the moment when that music of love and thanksgiving soared up to the altar, Don Juan, too well bred not to express his acknowledgments, too witty not to understand how to take a jest, bridled up in his reliquary, and responded with an appalling burst of laughter. Then the Devil having put him in mind of the risk he was running of being taken for an ordinary man, a saint, a

Boniface, a Pantaleone, he interrupted the melody of love by a yell, the thousand voices of hell joined in it. Earth blessed, Heaven banned. The church was shaken to its ancient foundations.

Te Deum laudamus! cried the many voices.

"Go to the devil, brute beasts that you are! *Dios! Dios! Garajos demonios!* Idiots! What fools you are with your dotard God!" and a torrent of imprecations poured forth like a stream of red-hot lava from the mouth of Vesuvius.

"Deus Sabaoth. . . ! Sabaoth!" cried the believers.

"You are insulting the majesty of Hell," shouted Don Juan, gnashing his teeth. In another moment the living arm struggled out of the reliquary, and was brandished over the assembly in mockery and despair.

"The saint is blessing us," cried the old women, children, lovers, and the credulous among the crowd.

And note how often we are deceived in the homage we pay; the great man scoffs at those who praise him, and pays compliments now and again to those whom he laughs at in the depths of his heart.

Just as the Abbot, prostrate before the altar, was chanting *"Sancte Johannes, ora pro noblis!"* he heard a voice exclaim sufficiently distinctly: *"O coglione!"*

"What can be going on up there?" cried the Sub-prior, as he saw the reliquary move.

"The saint is playing the devil," replied the Abbot.

Even as he spoke the living head tore itself away from the lifeless body, and dropped upon the sallow cranium of the officiating priest.

"Remember Dona Elvira!" cried the thing, with its teeth set fast in the Abbot's head.

The Abbot's horror-stricken shriek disturbed the ceremony; all the ecclesiastics hurried up and crowded about their chief.

"Idiot, tell us now if there is a God!" the voice cried, as the Abbot, bitten through the brain, drew his last breath.

Paris, October 1830.

William Wilson

Edgar Allan Poe

There are two William Wilsons. Dogged from boyhood by his fearful specter, Poe's narrator can never escape his pale, identical namesake. Or can he?

What say of it? what say of *conscience* grim,
That specter in my path?

Chamberlayne's Pharronida

*L*et me call myself, for the present, William Wilson. The fair page now lying before me need not be sullied with my real appellation. This has been already too much an object for the scorn — for the horror — for the detestation of my race. To the uttermost regions of the globe have not the indignant winds bruited its unparalleled infamy? Oh, outcast of all outcasts most abandoned! — to the earth art thou not forever dead? to its honors, to its flowers, to its golden aspirations? — and a cloud, dense, dismal, and limitless, does it not hang eternally between thy hopes and heaven?

I would not, if I could, here or today, embody a record of my later years of unspeakable misery, and unpardonable crime. This epoch — these later years — took unto themselves a sudden elevation in turpitude, whose origin alone it is my present purpose to assign. Men usually grow base by degrees. From me, in an instant, all virtue dropped bodily as a mantle. From comparatively trivial wickedness

I passed, with the stride of a giant, into more than the enormities
of an Elah-Gabalus. What chance — what one event brought this evil
thing to pass, bear with me while I relate. Death approaches; and
the shadow which foreruns him has thrown a softening influence
over my spirit. I long, in passing through the dim valley, for the
sympathy — I had nearly said for the pity — of my fellow men. I
would fain have them believe that I have been, in some measure, the
slave of circumstances beyond human control. I would wish them
to seek out for me, in the details I am about to give, some little oasis
of fatality amid a wilderness of error. I would have them allow —
what they cannot refrain from allowing — that, although temptation
may have erewhile existed as great, man was never thus, at least,
tempted before — certainly, never thus fell. And is it therefore that
he has never thus suffered? Have I not indeed been living in a dream?
And am I not now dying a victim to the horror and the mystery of
the wildest of all sublunary visions?

I am the descendant of a race whose imaginative and easily
excitable temperament has at all times rendered them remarkable;
and, in my earliest infancy, I gave evidence of having fully inherited
the family character. As I advanced in years it was more strongly
developed; becoming, for many reasons, a cause of serious disquietude to my friends, and of positive injury to myself. I grew self-willed,
addicted to the wildest caprices, and a prey to the most ungovernable
passions. Weak-minded, and beset with constitutional infirmities
akin to my own, my parents could do but little to check the evil
propensities which distinguished me. Some feeble and ill-directed
efforts resulted in complete failure on their part, and, of course, in
total triumph on mine. Thenceforward my voice was a household
law; and at an age when few children have abandoned their leading-
strings, I was left to the guidance of my own will, and became, in
all but name, the master of my own actions.

My earliest recollections of a school-life, are connected with a
large, rambling, Elizabethan house, in a misty-looking village of
England, where were a vast number of gigantic and gnarled trees,
and where all the houses were excessively ancient. In truth, it was a
dreamlike and spirit-soothing place, that venerable old town. At this
moment, in fancy, I feel the refreshing chilliness of its deeply-shad-
owed avenues, inhale the fragrance of its thousand shrubberies, and
thrill anew with undefinable delight, at the deep hollow note of the
church-bell, breaking, each hour, with sullen and sudden roar, upon
the stillness of the dusky atmosphere in which the fretted Gothic
steeple lay imbedded and asleep.

It gives me, perhaps, as much of pleasure as I can now in any manner experience, to dwell upon minute recollections of the school and its concerns. Steeped in misery as I am — misery, alas! only too real — I shall be pardoned for seeking relief, however slight and temporary, in the weakness of a few rambling details. These, moreover, utterly trivial, and even ridiculous in themselves, assume, to my fancy, adventitious importance, as connected with a period and a locality when and where I recognize the first ambiguous monitions of the destiny which afterwards so fully overshadowed me. Let me then remember.

The house, I have said, was old and irregular. The grounds were extensive, and a high and solid brick wall, topped with a bed of mortar and broken glass, encompassed the whole. This prisonlike rampart formed the limit of our domain; beyond it we saw but thrice a week — once every Saturday afternoon, when, attended by two ushers, we were permitted to take brief walks in a body through some of the neighboring fields — and twice during Sunday, when we were paraded in the same formal manner to the morning and evening service in the one church of the village. Of this church the principal of our school was pastor. With how deep a spirit of wonder and perplexity was I wont to regard him from our remote pew in the gallery, as, with step solemn and slow, he ascended the pulpit! This reverend man, with countenance so demurely benign, with robes so glossy and so clerically flowing, with wig so minutely powdered, so rigid and so vast, — -could this be he who, of late, with sour visage, and in snuffy habiliments, administered, ferule in hand, the Draconian laws of the academy? Oh, gigantic paradox, too utterly monstrous for solution!

At an angle of the ponderous wall frowned a more ponderous gate. It was riveted and studded with iron bolts, and surmounted with jagged iron spikes. What impressions of deep awe did it inspire! It was never opened save for the three periodical egressions and ingressions already mentioned; then, in every creak of its mighty hinges, we found a plenitude of mystery — a world of matter for solemn remark, or for more solemn meditation.

The extensive enclosure was irregular in form, having many capacious recesses. Of these, three or four of the largest constituted the play-ground. It was level, and covered with fine hard gravel. I well remember it had no trees, nor benches, nor anything similar within it. Of course it was in the rear of the house. In front lay a small parterre, planted with box and other shrubs; but through this sacred division we passed only upon rare occasions indeed — such as a first advent to school or final departure thence, or perhaps, when a parent or friend having called for us, we joyfully took our way home for the Christmas or Midsummer holy-days.

But the house! — how quaint an old building was this! — to me how veritably a palace of enchantment! There was really no end to its windings — to its incomprehensible subdivisions. It was difficult, at any given time, to say with certainty upon which of its two stories one happened to be. From each room to every other there were sure to be found three or four steps either in ascent or descent. Then the lateral branches were innumerable — inconceivable — and so return-ing in upon themselves, that our most exact ideas in regard to the whole mansion were not very far different from those with which we pondered upon infinity. During the five years of my residence here, I was never able to ascertain with precision, in what remote locality lay the little sleeping apartment assigned to myself and some eighteen or twenty other scholars.

The school-room was the largest in the house — I could not help thinking, in the world. It was very long, narrow, and dismally low, with pointed Gothic windows and a ceiling of oak. In a remote and terror-inspiring angle was a square enclosure of eight or ten feet, comprising the sanctum, "during hours," of our principal, the Reverend Dr. Bransby. It was a solid structure, with massy door, sooner than open which in the absence of the "Dominic," we would all have willingly perished by the *peine forte et dure.* In other angles were two other similar boxes, far less reverenced, indeed, but still greatly matters of awe. One of these was the pulpit of the "classical" usher, one of the "English and mathematical." Interspersed about the room, crossing and recrossing in endless irregularity, were innu-merable benches and desks, black, ancient, and time-worn, piled desperately with much-bethumbed books, and so beseamed with initial letters, names at full length, grotesque figures, and other multiplied efforts of the knife, as to have entirely lost what little of original form might have been their portion in days long departed. A huge bucket with water stood at one extremity of the room, and a clock of stupendous dimensions at the other.

Encompassed by the massy walls of this venerable academy, I passed, yet not in tedium or disgust, the years of the third lustrum of my life. The teeming brain of childhood requires no external world of incident to occupy or amuse it; and the apparently dismal monotony of a school was replete with more intense excitement than my riper youth has derived from luxury, or my full manhood from crime. Yet I must believe that my first mental development had in it much of the uncommon — even much of the outré. Upon mankind at large the events of very early existence rarely leave in mature age any definite impression. All is gray shadow — a weak and irregular remembrance — an indistinct regathering of feeble pleasures and phantasmagoric pains. With me this is not so. In childhood I must have felt with the energy of a man what I now find stamped upon memory in lines as vivid, as deep, and as durable as the exergues of the Carthaginian medals.

Yet in fact — in the fact of the world's view — how little was there to remember! The morning's awakening, the nightly summons to bed; the connings, the recitations; the periodical half-holidays, and perambulations; the play-ground, with its broils, its pastimes, its intrigues; — these, by a mental sorcery long forgotten, were made to involve a wilderness of sensation, a world of rich incident, an universe of varied emotion, of excitement the most passionate and spirit-stirring. *"Oh, le bon temps, que ce siecle de fer!"*

In truth, the ardor, the enthusiasm, and the imperiousness of my disposition, soon rendered me a marked character among my school-mates, and by slow, but natural gradations, gave me an ascendancy over all not greatly older than myself; — over all with a single exception. This exception was found in the person of a scholar, who, although no relation, bore the same Christian and surname as myself; — a circumstance, in fact, little remarkable; for, notwithstanding a noble descent, mine was one of those everyday appellations which seem, by prescriptive right, to have been, time out of mind, the common property of the mob. In this narrative I have therefore designated myself as William Wilson, — a fictitious title not very dissimilar to the real. My namesake alone, of those who in school phraseology constituted "our set," presumed to compete with me in the studies of the class — in the sports and broils of the play-ground — to refuse implicit belief in my assertions, and submission to my will — indeed, to interfere with my arbitrary dictation in any respect whatsoever. If there is on earth a supreme and unqualified despotism, it is the despotism of a mastermind in boyhood over the less energetic spirits of its companions.

Wilson's rebellion was to me a source of the greatest embarrassment; — the more so as, in spite of the bravado with which in public I made a point of treating him and his pretensions, I secretly felt that I feared him, and could not help thinking the equality which he maintained so easily with myself, a proof of his true superiority; since not to be overcome cost me a perpetual struggle. Yet this superiority — even this equality — was in truth acknowledged by no one but myself; our associates, by some unaccountable blindness, seemed not even to suspect it. Indeed, his competition, his resistance, and especially his impertinent and dogged interference with my purposes, were not more pointed than private. He appeared to be destitute alike of the ambition which urged, and of the passionate energy of mind which enabled me to excel. In his rivalry he might have been supposed actuated solely by a whimsical desire to thwart, astonish, or mortify myself; although there were times when I could not help observing, with a feeling made up of wonder, abasement, and pique, that he mingled with his injuries, his insults, or his contradictions, a certain most inappropriate, and assuredly most unwelcome affectionateness of manner. I could only conceive this singular behavior to arise from a consummate self-conceit assuming the vulgar airs of patronage and protection.

Perhaps it was this latter trait in Wilson's conduct, conjoined with our identity of name, and the mere accident of our having entered the school upon the same day, which set afloat the notion that we were brothers, among the senior classes in the academy. These do not usually inquire with much strictness into the affairs of their juniors. I have before said, or should have said, that Wilson was not, in the most remote degree, connected with my family. But assuredly if we had been brothers we must have been twins; for, after leaving Dr. Bransby's, I casually learned that my namesake was born on the nineteenth of January, 1813 — and this is a somewhat remarkable coincidence; for the day is precisely that of my own nativity.

It may seem strange that in spite of the continual anxiety occasioned me by the rivalry of Wilson, and his intolerable spirit of contradiction, I could not bring myself to hate him altogether. We had, to be sure, nearly every day a quarrel in which, yielding me publicly the palm of victory, he, in some manner, contrived to make me feel that it was he who had deserved it; yet a sense of pride on my part, and a veritable dignity on his own, kept us always upon what are called "speaking terms," while there were many points of strong congeniality in our tempers, operating to awake me in a sentiment which our position alone, perhaps, prevented from ripening into friendship. It is difficult, indeed, to define, or even to describe, my real feelings towards him. They formed a motley and heterogeneous admixture; — some petulant animosity, which was not yet hatred, some esteem, more respect, much fear, with a world of uneasy curiosity. To the moralist it will be unnecessary to say, in addition, that Wilson and myself were the most inseparable of companions.

It was no doubt the anomalous state of affairs existing between us, which turned all my attacks upon him, (and they were many, either open or covert) into the channel of banter or practical joke (giving pain while assuming the aspect of mere fun) rather than into a more serious and determined hostility. But my endeavors on this head were by no means uniformly successful, even when my plans were the most wittily concocted; for my namesake had much about him, in character, of that unassuming and quiet austerity which, while enjoying the poignancy of its own jokes, has no heel of Achilles in itself, and absolutely refuses to be laughed at. I could find, indeed, but one vulnerable point, and that, lying in a personal peculiarity, arising, perhaps, from constitutional disease, would have been spared by any antagonist less at his wit's end than myself; — my rival had a weakness in the faucial or guttural organs, which precluded him from raising his voice at any time above a very low whisper. Of this defect I did not fall to take what poor advantage lay in my power.

Wilson's retaliations in kind were many; and there was one form of his practical wit that disturbed me beyond measure. How his sagacity first discovered at all that so petty a thing would vex me, is a question I never could solve; but, having discovered, he habitually practiced the annoyance. I had always felt aversion to my uncourtly patronymic, and its very common, if not plebeian praenomen. The words were venom in my ears; and when, upon the day of my arrival, a second William Wilson came also to the academy, I felt angry with him for bearing the name, and doubly disgusted with the name because a stranger bore it, who would be the cause of its twofold repetition, who would be constantly in my presence, and whose concerns, in the ordinary routine of the school business, must inevitably, on account of the detestable coincidence, be often confounded with my own.

The feeling of vexation thus engendered grew stronger with every circumstance tending to show resemblance, moral or physical, between my rival and myself. I had not then discovered the remarkable fact that we were of the same age; but I saw that we were of the same height, and I perceived that we were even singularly alike in general contour of person and outline of feature. I was galled, too, by the rumor touching a relationship, which had grown current in the upper forms. In a word, nothing could more seriously disturb me, although I scrupulously concealed such disturbance,) than any allusion to a similarity of mind, person, or condition existing between us. But, in truth, I had no reason to believe that (with the exception of the matter of relationship, and in the case of Wilson himself,) this similarity had ever been made a subject of comment, or even observed at all by our schoolfellows. That he observed it in all its bearings, and as fixedly as I, was apparent; but that he could discover in such circumstances so fruitful a field of annoyance, can only be attributed, as I said before, to his more than ordinary penetration.

His cue, which was to perfect an imitation of myself, lay both in words and in actions; and most admirably did he play his part. My dress it was an easy matter to copy; my gait and general manner were, without difficulty, appropriated; in spite of his constitutional defect, even my voice did not escape him. My louder tones were, of course, unattempted, but then the key, it was identical; and his singular whisper, it grew the very echo of my own.

How greatly this most exquisite portraiture harassed me, (for it could not justly be termed a caricature,) I will not now venture to describe. I had but one consolation — in the fact that the imitation, apparently, was noticed by myself alone, and that I had to endure only the knowing and strangely sarcastic smiles of my namesake himself. Satisfied with having produced in my bosom the intended effect, he seemed to chuckle in secret over the sting he had inflicted, and was characteristically disregardful of the public applause which the success of his witty endeavors might have so easily elicited. That the school, indeed, did not feel his design, perceive its accomplishment, and participate in his sneer, was, for many anxious months, a riddle I could not resolve. Perhaps the gradation of his copy rendered it not so readily perceptible; or, more possibly, I owed my security to the master air of the copyist, who, disdaining the letter, (which in a painting is all the obtuse can see,) gave but the full spirit of his original for my individual contemplation and chagrin.

I have already more than once spoken of the disgusting air of patronage which he assumed toward me, and of his frequent officious interference withy my will. This interference often took the ungracious character of advice; advice not openly given, but hinted or insinuated. I received it with a repugnance which gained strength as I grew in years. Yet, at this distant day, let me do him the simple justice to acknowledge that I can recall no occasion when the suggestions of my rival were on the side of those errors or follies so usual to his immature age and seeming inexperience; that his moral sense, at least, if not his general talents and worldly wisdom, was far keener than my own; and that I might, today, have been a better, and thus a happier man, had I less frequently rejected the counsels embodied in those meaning whispers which I then but too cordially hated and too bitterly despised.

As it was, I at length grew restive in the extreme under his distasteful supervision, and daily resented more and more openly what I considered his intolerable arrogance. I have said that, in the first years of our connection as schoolmates, my feelings in regard to him might have been easily ripened into friendship: but, in the latter months of my residence at the academy, although the intrusion of his ordinary manner had, beyond doubt, in some measure, abated, my sentiments, in nearly similar proportion, partook very much of positive hatred. Upon one occasion he saw this, I think, and afterwards avoided, or made a show of avoiding me.

It was about the same period, if I remember aright, that, in an altercation of violence with him, in which he was more than usually thrown off his guard, and spoke and acted with an openness of demeanor rather foreign to his nature, I discovered, or fancied I discovered, in his accent, his air, and general appearance, a something which first startled, and then deeply interested me, by bringing to mind dim visions of my earliest infancy — wild, confused and thronging memories of a time when memory herself was yet unborn. I cannot better describe the sensation which oppressed me than by saying that I could with difficulty shake off the belief of my having been acquainted with the being who stood before me, at some epoch very long ago — some point of the past even infinitely remote. The delusion, however, faded rapidly as it came; and I mention it at all but to define the day of the last conversation I there held with my singular namesake.

The huge old house, with its countless subdivisions, had several large chambers communicating with each other, where slept the greater number of the students. There were, however, (as must necessarily happen in a building so awkwardly planned,) many little nooks or recesses, the odds and ends of the structure; and these the economic ingenuity of Dr. Bransby had also fitted up as dormitories; although, being the merest closets, they were capable of accommodating but a single individual. One of these small apartments was occupied by Wilson.

One night, about the close of my fifth year at the school, and immediately after the altercation just mentioned, finding everyone wrapped in sleep, I arose from bed, and, lamp in hand, stole through a wilderness of narrow passages from my own bedroom to that of my rival. I had long been plotting one of those ill-natured pieces of practical wit at his expense in which I had hitherto been so uniformly unsuccessful. It was my intention, now, to put my scheme in operation, and I resolved to make him feel the whole extent of the malice with which I was imbued. Having reached his closet, I noiselessly entered, leaving the lamp, with a shade over it, on the outside. I advanced a step, and listened to the sound of his tranquil breathing. Assured of his being asleep, I returned, took the light, and with it again approached the bed. Close curtains were around it, which, in the prosecution of my plan, I slowly and quietly withdrew, when the bright rays fell vividly upon the sleeper, and my eyes, at the same moment, upon his countenance. I looked; — and a numbness, an iciness of feeling instantly pervaded my frame. My breast heaved, my knees tottered, my whole spirit became possessed with an objectless yet intolerable horror. Gasping for breath, I lowered the lamp in still nearer proximity to the face. Were these — these the lineaments of William Wilson? I saw, indeed, that they were his, but I shook as if with a fit of the ague in fancying they were not. What was there about them to confound me in this manner? I gazed; — while my brain reeled with a multitude of incoherent thoughts. Not thus he appeared — assuredly not thus — in the vivacity of his waking hours. The same name! the same contour of person! the same day of arrival at the academy! And then his dogged and meaningless imitation of my gait, my voice, my habits, and my manner! Was it, in truth, within the bounds of human possibility, that what I now saw was the result, merely, of the habitual practice of this sarcastic imitation? Awe-stricken, and with a creeping shudder, I extinguished the lamp, passed silently from the chamber, and left, at once, the halls of that old academy, never to enter them again.

After a lapse of some months, spent at home in mere idleness, I found myself a student at Eton. The brief interval had been sufficient to enfeeble my remembrance of the events at Dr. Bransby's, or at least to effect a material change in the nature of the feelings with which I remembered them. The truth — the tragedy — of the drama was no more. I could now find room to doubt the evidence of my senses; and seldom called up the subject at all but with wonder at extent of human credulity, and a smile at the vivid force of the imagination which I hereditarily possessed. Neither was this species of skepticism likely to be diminished by the character of the life I led at Eton. The vortex of thoughtless folly into which I there so immediately and so recklessly plunged, washed away all but the froth of my past hours, engulfed at once every solid or serious impression, and left to memory only the veriest levities of a former existence.

I do not wish, however, to trace the course of my miserable profligacy here — a profligacy which set at defiance the laws, while it eluded the vigilance of the institution. Three years of folly, passed without profit, had but given me rooted habits of vice, and added, in a somewhat unusual degree, to my bodily stature, when, after a week of soulless dissipation, I invited a small party of the most dissolute students to a secret carousal in my chambers. We met at a late hour of the night; for our debaucheries were to be faithfully protracted until morning. The wine flowed freely, and there were not wanting other and perhaps more dangerous seductions; so that the gray dawn had already faintly appeared in the east, while our delirious extravagance was at its height. Madly flushed with cards and intoxication, I was in the act of insisting upon a toast of more than wonted profanity, when my attention was suddenly diverted by the violent, although partial unclosing of the door of the apartment, and by the eager voice of a servant from without. He said that some person, apparently in great haste, demanded to speak with me in the hall.

Wildly excited with wine, the unexpected interruption rather delighted than surprised me. I staggered forward at once, and a few steps brought me to the vestibule of the building. In this low and small room there hung no lamp; and now no light at all was admitted, save that of the exceedingly feeble dawn which made its way through the semi-circular window. As I put my foot over the threshold, I became aware of the figure of a youth about my own height, and habited in a white kerseymere morning frock, cut in the novel fashion of the one I myself wore at the moment. This the faint light enabled me to perceive; but the features of his face I could not distinguish. Upon my entering he strode hurriedly up to me, and, seizing me by. the arm with a gesture of petulant impatience, whispered the words "William Wilson!" in my ear.

I grew perfectly sober in an instant. There was that in the manner of the stranger, and in the tremulous shake of his uplifted finger, as he held it between my eyes and the light, which filled me with unqualified amazement; but it was not this which had so violently moved me. It was the pregnancy of solemn admonition in the singular, low, hissing utterance; and, above all, it was the character, the tone, the key, of those few, simple, and familiar, yet whispered syllables, which came with a thousand thronging memories of by-gone days, and struck upon my soul with the shock of a galvanic battery. Ere I could recover the use of my senses he was gone.

Although this event failed not of a vivid effect upon my disordered imagination, yet was it evanescent as vivid. For some weeks, indeed, I busied myself in earnest inquiry, or was wrapped in a cloud of morbid speculation. I did not pretend to disguise from my perception the identity of the singular individual who thus perseveringly interfered with my affairs, and harassed me with his insinuated counsel. But who and what was this Wilson? — and whence came he? — and what were his purposes? Upon neither of these points could I be satisfied; merely ascertaining, in regard to him, that a sudden accident in his family had caused his removal from Dr. Bransby's academy on the afternoon of the day in which I myself had eloped. But in a brief period I ceased to think upon the subject; my attention being all absorbed in a contemplated departure for Oxford. Thither I soon went; the uncalculating vanity of my parents furnishing me with an outfit and annual establishment, which would enable me to indulge at will in the luxury already so dear to my heart, — to vie in profuseness of expenditure with the haughtiest heirs of the wealthiest earldoms in Great Britain.

Excited by such appliances to vice, my constitutional temperament broke forth with redoubled ardor, and I spurned even the common restraints of decency in the mad infatuation of my revels. But it were absurd to pause in the detail of my extravagance. Let it suffice, that among spendthrifts I out-Heroded Herod, and that, giving name to a multitude of novel follies, I added no brief appendix to the long catalogue of vices then usual in the most dissolute university of Europe.

It could hardly be credited, however, that I had, even here, so utterly fallen from the gentlemanly estate, as to seek acquaintance with the vilest arts of the gambler by profession, and, having become an adept in his despicable science, to practice it habitually as a means of increasing my already enormous income at the expense of the weak-minded among my fellow-collegians. Such, nevertheless, was the fact. And the very enormity of this offence against all manly and honorable sentiment proved, beyond doubt, the main if not the sole reason of the impunity with which it was committed. Who, indeed, among my most abandoned associates, would not rather have disputed the clearest evidence of his senses, than have suspected of such courses, the gay, the frank, the generous William Wilson — the noblest and most commoner at Oxford — him whose follies (said his parasites) were but the follies of youth and unbridled fancy — whose errors but inimitable whim — whose darkest vice but a careless and dashing extravagance?

I had been now two years successfully busied in this way, when there came to the university a young parvenu nobleman, Glendinning — rich, said report, as Herodes Atticus — his riches, too, as easily acquired. I soon found him of weak intellect, and, of course, marked him as a fitting subject for my skill. I frequently engaged him in play, and contrived, with the gambler's usual art, to let him win considerable sums, the more effectually to entangle him in my snares. At length, my schemes being ripe, I met him (with the full intention that this meeting should be final and decisive) at the chambers of a fellow-commoner, (Mr. Preston,) equally intimate with both, but who, to do him Justice, entertained not even a remote suspicion of my design. To give to this a better coloring, I had contrived to have assembled a party of some eight or ten, and was solicitously careful that the introduction of cards should appear accidental, and originate in the proposal of my contemplated dupe himself. To be brief upon a vile topic, none of the low finesse was omitted, so customary upon similar occasions that it is a just matter for wonder how any are still found so besotted as to fall its victim.

We had protracted our sitting far into the night, and I had at length effected the maneuver of getting Glendinning as my sole antagonist. The game, too, was my favorite *ecarte!* The rest of the company, interested in the extent of our play, had abandoned their own cards, and were standing around us as spectators. The parvenu, who had been induced by my artifices in the early part of the evening, to drink deeply, now shuffled, dealt, or played, with a wild nervousness of manner for which his intoxication, I thought, might partially, but could not altogether account. In a very short period he had become my debtor to a large amount, when, having taken a long draught of port, he did precisely what I had been coolly anticipating — he proposed to double our already extravagant stakes. With a well-feigned show of reluctance, and not until after my repeated refusal had seduced him into some angry words which gave a color of pique to my compliance, did I finally comply. The result, of course, did but prove how entirely the prey was in my toils; in less than an hour he had quadrupled his debt. For some time his countenance had been losing the florid tinge lent it by the wine; but now, to my astonishment, I perceived that it had grown to a pallor truly fearful. I say to my astonishment. Glendinning had been represented to my eager inquiries as immeasurably wealthy; and the sums which he had as yet lost, although in themselves vast, could not, I supposed, very seriously annoy, much less so violently affect him. That he was overcome by the wine just swallowed, was the idea which most readily presented itself; and, rather with a view to the preservation of my own character in the eyes of my associates, than from any less interested motive, I was about to insist, peremptorily, upon a discontinuance of the play, when some expressions at my elbow from among the company, and an ejaculation evincing utter despair on the part of Glendinning, gave me to understand that I had effected his total ruin under circumstances which, rendering him an object for the pity of all, should have protected him from the ill offices even of a fiend.

What now might have been my conduct it is difficult to say. The pitiable condition of my dupe had thrown an air of embarrassed gloom over all; and, for some moments, a profound silence was maintained, during which I could not help feeling my cheeks tingle with the many burning glances of scorn or reproach cast upon me by the less abandoned of the party. I will even own that an intolerable weight of anxiety was for a brief instant lifted from my bosom by the sudden and extraordinary interruption which ensued. The wide, heavy folding doors of the apartment were all at once thrown open, to their full extent, with a vigorous and rushing impetuosity that extinguished, as if by magic, every candle in the room. Their light, in dying, enabled us just to perceive that a stranger had entered, about my own height, and closely muffled in a cloak. The darkness, however, was now total; and we could only feel that he was standing in our midst. Before any one of us could recover from the extreme astonishment into which this rudeness had thrown all, we heard the voice of the intruder.

"Gentlemen," he said, in a low, distinct, and never-to-be-forgotten whisper which thrilled to the very marrow of my bones, "Gentlemen, I make no apology for this behavior, because in thus behaving, I am but fulfilling a duty. You are, beyond doubt, uninformed of the true character of the person who has tonight won at *ecarte* a large sum of money from Lord Glendinning. I will therefore put you upon an expeditious and decisive plan of obtaining this very necessary information. Please to examine, at your leisure, the inner linings of the cuff of his left sleeve, and the several little packages which may be found in the somewhat capacious pockets of his embroidered morning wrapper."

While he spoke, so profound was the stillness that one might have heard a pin drop upon the floor. In ceasing, he departed at once, and as abruptly as he had entered. Can I — shall I describe my sensations? — must I say that I felt all the horrors of the damned? Most assuredly I had little time given for reflection. Many hands roughly seized me upon the spot, and lights were immediately reprocured. A search ensued. In the lining of my sleeve were found all the court cards essential in *ecarte*, and, in the pockets of my wrapper, a number of packs, facsimiles of those used at our sittings, with the single exception that mine were of the species called, technically, arrondees; the honors being slightly convex at the ends, the lower cards slightly convex at the sides. In this disposition, the dupe who cuts, as customary, at the length of the pack, will invariably find that he cuts his antagonist an honor; while the gambler, cutting at the breadth, will, as certainly, cut nothing for his victim which may count in the records of the game.

Any burst of indignation upon this discovery would have affected me less than the silent contempt, or the sarcastic composure, with which it was received.

"Mr. Wilson," said our host, stooping to remove from beneath his feet an exceedingly luxurious cloak of rare furs, "Mr. Wilson, this is your property." (The weather was cold; and, upon quitting my own room, I had thrown a cloak over my dressing wrapper, putting it off upon reaching the scene of play.) "I presume it is supererogatory to seek here (eyeing the folds of the garment with a bitter smile) for any farther evidence of your skill. Indeed, we have had enough. You will see the necessity, I hope, of quitting Oxford — at all events, of quitting instantly my chambers."

Abased, humbled to the dust as I then was, it is probable that I should have resented this galling language by immediate personal violence, had not my whole attention been at the moment arrested by a fact of the most startling character. The cloak which I had worn was of a rare description of fur; how rare, how extravagantly costly, I shall not venture to say. Its fashion, too, was of my own fantastic invention; for I was fastidious to an absurd degree of coxcombry, in matters of this frivolous nature. When, therefore, Mr. Preston reached me that which he had picked up upon the floor, and near the folding doors of the apartment, it was with an astonishment nearly bordering upon terror, that I perceived my own already hanging on my arm, (where I had no doubt unwittingly placed it,) and that the one presented me was but its exact counterpart in every, in even the minutest possible particular. The singular being who had so disastrously exposed me, had been muffled, I remembered, in a cloak; and none had been worn at all by any of the members of our party with the exception of myself. Retaining some presence of mind, I took the one offered me by Preston; placed it, unnoticed, over my own; left the apartment with a resolute scowl of defiance; and, next morning ere dawn of day, commenced a hurried journey from Oxford to the continent, in a perfect agony of horror and of shame.

I fled in vain. My evil destiny pursued me as if in exultation, and proved, indeed, that the exercise of its mysterious dominion had as yet only begun. Scarcely had I set foot in Paris ere I had fresh evidence of the detestable interest taken by this Wilson in my concerns. Years flew, while I experienced no relief. Villain! — at Rome, with how untimely, yet with how spectral an officiousness, stepped he in between me and my ambition! At Vienna, too — at Berlin — and at Moscow! Where, in truth, had I not bitter cause to curse him within my heart? From his inscrutable tyranny did I at length flee, panic-stricken, as from a pestilence; and to the very ends of the earth I fled in vain.

And again, and again, in secret communion with my own spirit, would I demand the questions "Who is he? — whence came he? — and what are his objects?" But no answer was there found. And then I scrutinized, with a minute scrutiny, the forms, and the methods, and the leading traits of his impertinent supervision. But even here there was very little upon which to base a conjecture. It was notice-able, indeed, that, in no one of the multiplied instances in which he had of late crossed my path, had he so crossed it except to frustrate those schemes, or to disturb those actions, which, if fully carried out, might have resulted in bitter mischief. Poor justification this, in truth, for an authority so imperiously assumed! Poor indemnity for natural rights of self-agency so pertinaciously, so insultingly denied!

I had also been forced to notice that my tormentor, for a very long period of time, (while scrupulously and with miraculous dex-terity maintaining his whim of an identity of apparel with myself,) had so contrived it, in the execution of his varied interference with my will, that I saw not, at any moment, the features of his face. Be Wilson what he might, this, at least, was but the veriest of affectation, or of folly. Could he, for an instant, have supposed that, in my admonisher at Eton — in the destroyer of my honor at Oxford, — in him who thwarted my ambition at Rome, my revenge at Paris, my passionate love at Naples, or what he falsely termed my avarice in Egypt, — that in this, my arch-enemy and evil genius, could fall to recognize the William Wilson of my school boy days, — the namesake, the companion, the rival, — the hated and dreaded rival at Dr. Bransby's? Impossible! — But let me hasten to the last eventful scene of the drama.

Thus far I had succumbed supinely to this imperious domination. The sentiment of deep awe with which I habitually regarded the elevated character, the majestic wisdom, the apparent omnipresence and omnipotence of Wilson, added to a feeling of even terror, with which certain other traits in his nature and assumptions inspired me, had operated, hitherto, to impress me with an idea of my own utter weakness and helplessness, and to suggest an implicit, although bitterly reluctant submission to his arbitrary will. But, of late days, I had given myself up entirely to wine; and its maddening influence upon my hereditary temper rendered me more and more impatient of control. I began to murmur, — to hesitate, — to resist. And was it only fancy which induced me to believe that, with the increase of my own firmness, that of my tormentor underwent a proportional diminution? Be this as it may, I now began to feel the inspiration of a burning hope, and at length nurtured in my secret thoughts a stern and desperate resolution that I would submit no longer to be enslaved.

It was at Rome, during the Carnival of 18—, that I attended a masquerade in the palazzo of the Neapolitan Duke Di Broglio. I had indulged more freely than usual in the excesses of the wine-table; and now the suffocating atmosphere of the crowded rooms irritated me beyond endurance. The difficulty, too, of forcing my way through the mazes of the company contributed not a little to the ruffling of my temper; for I was anxiously seeking, (let me not say with what unworthy motive) the young, the gay, the beautiful wife of the aged and doting Di Broglio. With a too unscrupulous confidence she had previously communicated to me the secret of the costume in which she would be habited, and now, having caught a glimpse of her person, I was hurrying to make my way into her presence. — At this moment I felt a light hand placed upon my shoulder, and that ever-remembered, low, damnable whisper within my ear.

In an absolute frenzy of wrath, I turned at once upon him who had thus interrupted me, and seized him violently by tile collar. He was attired, as I had expected, in a costume altogether similar to my own; wearing a Spanish cloak of blue velvet, begirt about the waist with a crimson belt sustaining a rapier. A mask of black silk entirely covered his face.

"Scoundrel!" I said, in a voice husky with rage, while every syllable I uttered seemed as new fuel to my fury, "scoundrel! impostor! accursed villain! you shall not — you shall not dog me unto death! Follow me, or I stab you where you stand!" — and I broke my way from the ballroom into a small antechamber adjoining — dragging him unresistingly with me as I went.

Upon entering, I thrust him furiously from me. He staggered against the wall, while I closed the door with an oath, and commanded him to draw. He hesitated but for an instant; then, with a slight sigh, drew in silence, and put himself upon his defense.

The contest was brief indeed. I was frantic with every species of wild excitement, and felt within my single arm the energy and power of a multitude. In a few seconds I forced him by sheer strength against the wainscoting, and thus, getting him at mercy, plunged my sword, with brute ferocity, repeatedly through and through his bosom.

At that instant some person tried the latch of the door. I hastened to prevent an intrusion, and then immediately returned to my dying antagonist. But what human language can adequately portray that astonishment, that horror which possessed me at the spectacle then presented to view? The brief moment in which I averted my eyes had been sufficient to produce, apparently, a material change in the arrangements at the upper or farther end of the room. A large mirror, — so at first it seemed to me in my confusion — now stood where none had been perceptible before; and, as I stepped up to it in extremity of terror, mine own image, but with features all pale and dabbled in blood, advanced to meet me with a feeble and tottering gait.

Thus it appeared, I say, but was not. It was my antagonist — it was Wilson, who then stood before me in the agonies of his dissolution. His mask and cloak lay, where he had thrown them, upon the floor. Not a thread in all his raiment — not a line in all the marked and singular lineaments of his face which was not, even in the most absolute identity, mine own!

It was Wilson; but he spoke no longer in a whisper, and I could have fancied that I myself was speaking while he said:

"You have conquered, and I yield. Yet, henceforward art thou also dead — dead to the World, to Heaven and to Hope! In me didst thou exist — and, in my death, see by this image, which is thine own, how utterly thou hast murdered thyself."

LaVergne, TN USA
19 August 2009

155101LV00007B/146/A